DRAGONSTRIKE

HUMPHREY HAWKSLEY has been a BBC Correspondent in Asia for ten years. In the eighties he was in Sri Lanka, India and the Philippines. From 1990, he was based in Hong Kong as a regional correspondent. He has reported from more than twenty Asian countries during the most exciting time of their twentieth-century development. In 1994 he was appointed China Bureau Chief and became the BBC's first television correspondent based in Beijing. Since then he has travelled extensively through the country.

SIMON HOLBERTON has completed two tours of Asia. Most recently he was Hong Kong Bureau Chief for the *Financial Times* (1992–1996) where he reported on China's preparations for the takeover of the colony, and the modernization of its vast economy. In the mid-1980s he reported on Japan and Korea for the Melbourne *Age* (1984–1986). In 1996 he returned to the *Financial Times* in Britain where he writes about energy.

DRAGON STRIKE

THE MILLENNIUM WAR

**HUMPHREY HAWKSLEY
& SIMON HOLBERTON**

PAN BOOKS

First published 1997 by Sidgwick & Jackson

This edition published 1997 by Pan Books
an imprint of Macmillan Publishers Ltd
25 Eccleston Place, London SW1W 9NF
and Basingstoke

Associated companies throughout the world

ISBN 0 330 35036 6

A CIP catalogue record for this book is available from
the British Library.

Typeset by SetSystems Ltd, Saffron Walden, Essex
Printed and bound in Great Britain by
Mackays of Chatham plc, Chatham, Kent

For Jonie
and
for Kerryn

CONTENTS

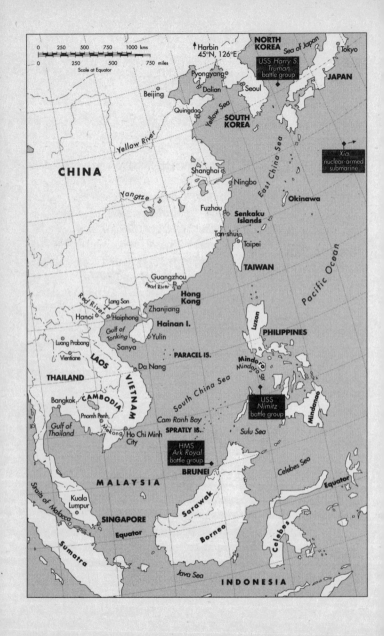

PREFACE

The events described in this book have not yet happened
... It is a future history, an exercise in military and political
prediction, about a country whose emergence as a world
power is one of the most important developments of the
late twentieth century. The arrival of China on the world
stage, however, poses problems not encountered by the
world's democracies for well over fifty years. Like Europe
challenged by an ambitious Germany in the first half of
this century, Asia is challenged by China, which has marked
out its own plans for expansion in its detailed claims to
Tibet, the South China Sea, and Taiwan. In the spring of
1996, along China's eastern coastline, the People's Liberation Army conducted extensive military exercises that were
little more than practice for an invasion of Taiwan. The
year before there were skirmishes in the South China Sea
as China sought to underline its disputed claim to that
territory.

At the same time, China claims America has plans to
contain its growth and begin a new Cold War. Those who
have spoken out on this range from moderate academics
to the present day leaders themselves such as President
Jiang Zemin and Prime Minister Li Peng. The 1996 best-
selling book by five young writers called *China Can Say No*
encapsulated a new wave of belligerent Chinese nationalism
which regards a confrontation with America as inevitable.

With *Dragonstrike* we have taken current trends, created
a scenario, and seen it through to the end. To illustrate the
threatening side of China's policy we have drawn on

already published material, especially from the army news-paper *Jiefangjun Bao*, with its detailed claims to the South China Sea and how the military plans to achieve them. Most of what we put in the mouth of Wang Feng, our fictitious Chinese President, has been said by Chinese officials or appeared in the official Communist media over the past few years. In a similar way we have used authentic Japanese voices for some of what Noburo Hyashi, our fictitious Prime Minister of Japan, has to say. His account of the Amber system on pages 173–4 and much of his speech to the nation on pages 255–8 is taken from *The Japan that can say 'No'*, by Akio Morita and Shintaro Ishihara. We have given references for our published sources throughout.

The political, military, and financial sections were dis-cussed and worked on at length by experts. David Tait, former Operations Officer of the attack submarine HMS *Opossum*, helped us design the submarine battles exploiting to the full Chinese diesel-electric technology. John Myers, a former Royal Navy submarine commander, and Richard Sharpe, a former nuclear submarine commander and Editor of *Jane's Fighting Ships*, read and helped authenticate it. Former Royal Marine raiding troop officer David Dunbar helped plan the amphibious and helicopter assaults of the first day of Dragonstrike. Thanks are also due Ian Strachan, former fighter test pilot with the Royal Air Force, for his advice on the conduct of air warfare, and John Downing, a former Royal Navy intelligence officer, who helped with some of the information-warfare sections of the book. Many other still serving European and American military and intelligence officers gave their time to ensure the accuracy of the air, sea, and land battles, but their identities must remain secret. Any mistakes, of course, are our own.

Patricia Lewis made helpful comments on the design of the Japanese nuclear bomb, while Steve Thomas commented upon the sections on Japan's nuclear weapons capability. Damon Moglen and Shaun Burnie supplied documents and advice on the same, while Nick Rowe helped with details of how civilian populations and their local officials might react in the event of a nuclear war. Our researchers included Sophie Gregg, Charlie Whipple and Gene Koprowski, Kurt Hanson, Keiko Bang, and others who prefer to remain anonymous.

Diplomats constructed the meetings within the Western governments and we drew on the advice of experts in Hong Kong and London to piece together the impact Dragonstrike would have on financial markets. Peter Gignoux, John Mulcahy and RoseMary Safranek suggested how the Chinese might structure their manipulation of the markets. We used published sources, together with oil company executives who prefer to remain anonymous, for broader views about the outlook for oil markets, and the level of future oil exploration in the South China Sea. Ian Harwood and John Sheppard advised on how the world economy and major stock markets might look in 2001, and Paul Chertkow and Adrian Powell helped on foreign exchange matters.

The real potential of China has only become apparent during the Clinton presidency. Yet at the time of writing, America has failed to draw up a comprehensive policy on how to deal with it. Ten years after the collapse of the Soviet Union, another power bloc is emerging. It is wealthy. It is expansionist. It has yawning cultural differences with the West. It is embittered about its past. China is a non-democratic one-party state, whose government has to prove itself to survive. This book has been written as a warning of what might happen if Western, and especially American, policy towards China is allowed to drift.

HH SH

PREFACE
TO THE PAPERBACK EDITION

There is always a risk in writing a book about the future that one will be proved wrong. However, since the publication of *Dragonstrike* in April 1997 events in East Asia have served to support our apprehension about China's rise as a world power. Indeed some events described in this book have now taken place.

China has encroached upon disputed territory in the South China Sea. Its forces have skirmished with the Philippine Navy. It has taken an oil exploration vessel into Vietnamese-claimed waters. As forecast in *Dragonstrike*, China has bought two Russian frigates in its continuing efforts to create a blue water navy. The government has announced a strategic alliance with Russia to take it into the 21st century. There have been demonstrations against the Japanese occupation of the disputed islands in the East China Sea.

One of China's first acts after taking back Hong Kong was to repeal human rights and democracy legislation. The government is continuing to ignore appeals about human rights abuses in China. The Communist Party has reaffirmed its commitment to indefinite one-party rule.

This paperback edition is going to print as President Jiang Zemin is due in Washington for a summit with President Clinton. This will help determine modern China's position on the world stage. The main debate however about whether China is a weak developing nation or a global threat will continue. We expect more elements of the *Dragonstrike's* future history to be proved correct. But we hope that ultimately enough attention is paid to China to ensure that our final predictions are wrong. As yet, we are unconvinced.

HH SH

CHRONOLOGY OF EVENTS

Dragonstrike describes a series of events that are global in scale. In the table that follows the clock times in six of the most important time zones in the world are shown as they are at the beginning of each chapter.

France and Germany are an hour ahead of GMT, Moscow two hours, and both the Spratly and the Paracel island groups are eight hours ahead, in the Chinese time zone. Because the tables show clock time the figures are different from those in a map of time zone differences which would show for example +8 as −8 because the sun passed across it at noon eight hours earlier.

Dragonstrike event	**Page**

Seattle -8	W'ton -5	GMT 0	Vietnam +7	China +8	Tokyo +9
Sat 17	Sat 17	Sat 17	Sun 18	Sun 18	Sun 18
1300	1600	2100	0400	0500	0600
1500	1800	2300	0600	0700	0800
1500	1800	2300	0600	0700	0800
1500	1800	2300	0600	0700	0800
1545	1845	2345	0645	0745	0845
		Sun 18			
1615	1915	0015	0715	0815	0915
1630	1930	0030	0730	0830	0930
1700	2000	0100	0800	0900	1000
1755	2055	0155	0855	0955	1055
1800	2100	0200	0900	1000	1100
1830	2130	0230	0930	1030	1130
1900	2200	0300	1000	1100	1200
1930	2230	0330	1030	1130	1230
Sun 18	Sun 18		Mon 19	Mon 19	Mon 19
1100	1400	1900	0200	0300	0400
1300	1600	2100	0400	0500	0600
1415	1715	2215	0515	0615	0715
1445	1745	2245	0545	0645	0745
1500	1800	2300	0600	0700	0800
1545	1845	2345	0645	0745	0845
1600	1900	2400	0700	0800	0900
		Mon 19			
1700	2000	0100	0800	0900	0800
Mon 19	Mon 19				
0200	0500	1000	1700	1800	1900
0300	0600	1100	1800	1900	2000

Seattle −8	W'ton −5	GMT 0	Vietnam +7	China +8	Tokyo +9
0530	0830	1330	2030	2130	2230
					Tue 20
0730	1030	1530	2230	2330	0030
0730	1030	1530	2230	2330	0030
0730	1030	1530	2230	2330	0030
0745	1045	1545	2245	2345	0045
				Tue 20	
0810	1110	1610	2310	0010	0110
			Tue 20		
0945	1245	1745	0045	0145	0245
1500	1800	2300	0600	0700	0800
1500	1800	2300	0600	0700	0800
		Tue 20			
1700	2000	0100	0800	0900	1000
		Monday 23 October 2000			
1830	2130	0230	0930	1030	1130
1900	2200	0300	1000	1100	1200
2100	2400	0500	1200	1300	1400
	Tue 20				
2200	0100	0600	1300	1400	1500
2300	0200	0700	1400	1500	1600
Tue 20					
0030	0330	0830	1530	1630	1730
0030	0330	0830	1530	1630	1730
0300	0600	1100	1800	1900	2000
0320	0620	1120	1820	1920	2020
0400	0700	1200	1900	2000	2100
0430	0730	1230	1930	2030	2130
0430	0730	1230	1930	2030	2130

Seattle −8	W'ton −5	GMT 0	Vietnam +7	China +8	Tokyo +9
0500	0800	1300	2000	2100	2200
0500	0800	1300	2000	2100	2200
0520	0820	1320	2020	2120	2220
0600	0900	1400	2100	2200	2300
0700	1000	1500	2200	2300	2400
					Wed 21
0715	1015	1515	2215	2315	0015
0730	1030	1530	2230	2330	0030
			Wed 21	Wed 21	
1100	1400	1900	0200	0300	0400
1130	1430	1930	0230	0330	0430
1230	1530	2030	0330	0430	0530
1245	1545	2045	0345	0445	0545
1300	1600	2100	0400	0500	0600
		Wed 21			
1800	2100	0200	0900	1000	1100
1830	2130	0230	0930	1030	1130
1900	2200	0300	1000	1100	1200
1930	2230	0330	1030	1130	1230
2000	2300	0400	1100	1200	1300
2045	2345	0445	1145	1245	1345
2050	2350	0450	1150	1250	1350
	Wed 21				
2200	0100	0600	1300	1400	1500
2230	0130	0630	1330	1430	1530
Wed 21					
0100	0400	0900	1600	1700	1800
0100	0400	0900	1600	1700	1800
0400	0700	1200	1900	2000	2100
0400	0700	1200	1900	2000	2100
0700	1000	1500	2200	2300	[0300]¹
0700	1000	1500	2200	2300	2400

¹ A position west of Wake Island, 12 hours later than (clock time before) Greenwich.

Seattle −8	W'ton −5	GMT 0	Vietnam +7	China +8	Tokyo +9
					Thu 22
0800	1100	1600	2300	2400	0100
				Thu 22	
0900	1200	1700	2400	0100	0200
			Thu 22		
1200	1500	2000	0300	0400	0500
1600	1900	2400	0700	0800	0900
		Thu 22			
1730	2030	0130	0830	0930	1030
1800	2100	0200	0900	1000	1100
1800	2100	0200	0900	1000	1100
1800	2100	0200	0900	1000	1100
1800	2100	0200	0900	1000	1100
1800	2100	0200	0900	1000	1100
1815	2115	0215	0915	1015	1115
1900	2200	0300	1000	1100	1200
1930	2230	0330	1030	1130	1230
[1645][2]	2245	0345	1045	1145	1245
[2100][3]	2300	0400	1100	1200	1300
2030	2330	0430	1130	1230	1330
2100	2400	0500	1200	1300	1400
	Thu 22				
2200	0100	0600	1300	1400	1500
Thu 22					
0100	0400	1000	1700	1800	1900
0200	0500	1100	1800	1900	2000
0400	0700	1300	2000	2100	2200
0530	0830	1330	2030	2130	2230
0545	0845	1345	2045	2145	2245
0600	0900	1400	2100	2200	2300

[2] On Aleutian (far western Alaskan) time, 11 hours earlier than (clock time after) Greenwich.

[3] Mountain time, 7 hours earlier than Greenwich.

Seattle −8	W'ton −5	GMT 0	Vietnam +7	China +8	Tokyo +9
0600	0900	1400	2100	2200	2300
0700	1000	1500	2200	2300	2400
0700	1000	1500	2200	2300	2400
				Fri 23	Fri 23
0900	1200	1700	2400	0100	0200
0900	1200	1700	2400	0100	0200
			Fri 23		
0930	1230	1730	0030	0130	0230
1000	1300	1800	0100	0200	0300
1000	1300	1800	0100	0200	0300
1200	1500	2000	0300	0400	0500
1300	1600	2100	0400	0500	0600
1330	1630	2130	0430	0530	0630
3 MAR	3 MAR	3 MAR	4 MAR	4 MAR	4 MAR
1530	1830	2330	0630	0730	0830
14 MAR	14 MAR	14 MAR	15 MAR	15 MAR	15 MAR
1515	1815	2315	0615	0715	0815
1530	1830	2330	0630	0730	0830
1530	1830	2330	0630	0730	0830
1800	2100	2400	0700	0800	0900
		15 MAR			
1800	2100	0200	0900	1000	1100
2100	2300	0500	1200	1300	1400
30 APR	30 APR	30 APR	30 APR	1 MAY	1 MAY
0830	1130	1630	2330	0030	0130
			1 MAY		
1600	1900	2400	0700	0800	0900

ONE

Beijing, China

A thin frost covered the paving stones around Tiananmen Square: the most haunting symbol of Chinese Communist power. The lights on its edges shone through the smog which hung around the city. The bored and cold figures of the young soldiers stood guard around the square, a monument to the Party's success in ruling the motherland. Apart from them it was empty. A furtive, eerie silence lingered across its hundred acres and its buildings.

To the south was the Mausoleum of Mao Zedong, the twentieth-century emperor, whose turbulent revolutions had laid the seeds of today's robust one-party state. Out of granite he had built the Monument to the Martyrs of the People, 30 metres tall with 170 life-sized figures and a plinth, inscribed in his own handwriting *Eternal Glory to the People's Heroes*. To the east were the gigantic Museum of the Chinese Revolution and the Museum of History. To the west, the pillars and steps of the Great Hall of the People stretched more than 300 metres from one end to the other. Its banquet hall held 5,000 guests and the Hong Kong, Macau, and Taiwan Rooms served as memories to China's once lost territories and the humiliating dismemberment of the motherland. To the north was Tiananmen Gate, where Mao Zedong proclaimed Communist Party victory in 1949 and where his enduring portrait still hung. Five bridges ran from there towards the gates of the Forbidden City. Tiananmen Gate was the link between the new and the old emperors. The Forbidden City was the Great Within. There were 9,000 rooms in over 250 acres once attended by 70,000 Imperial Eunuchs. Its doors opened onto the square, from which was drawn the power and patriotism for the whole of China. Tonight this was the reference point for the man who wanted to be emperor.

A few hundred metres to the west, next door to the Forbidden City, were the high, red-painted walls of Zhongnanhai. The sign inside the main gate proclaimed in large Chinese characters: *To serve the People*. Along the wall on the west side of the gate a slogan read: *Long live the great Chinese Communist Party*. On the east wall another paid tribute: *Long live the unbeatable thoughts of Chairman Mao*. The broad, uncluttered roads, the drooping willows, frozen lakes, reception rooms, and luxurious houses were more modern but no less mysterious, no less prohibited, than the Forbidden City was in Imperial times. The symbols of power in the modern state were everywhere – surveillance cameras, microwave dishes, and radio transmitters. The armed men in green uniforms at the gates belonged to the Central Guards Regiment, once known as the legendary unit 8341, which had protected China's leaders since the Revolution. Their success record was remarkable for such a turbulent country. The unit of more than 8,000 men secured the secrets of the Communist Party. For Western intelligence, this was one of the least penetrable centres of power in the world. Recruits to the Guards Regiment had to be illiterate or barely educated and were usually from peasant families in remote mountainous areas. Not one senior leader had been assassinated since 1949. The guards were told that the Chinese President would leave shortly before 0500 hours. When the motorcade of three stretched Mercedes 88-series limousines approached, the heavy wooden gates swung open. Four motorcycle outriders on turbocharged 1100cc BMWs flanked the convoy at the front and back.

They drove without flashing lights and sirens. It was a

black convoy. The moon barely cut its image through the pollution. The streets were deserted. The homeless warmed themselves around fires under flyovers. The latest figures reported to the Politburo said the number of unemployed had now reached 250,000,000. That was the population of America wandering the country, homeless, tired, penniless. They had yet to become violent, but poverty had severed their bond to the Communist Party. Only fear kept them quiet.

Chinese leaders usually preferred to travel by the network of underground roads and railways, but tonight President Wang wanted to savour the city he was about to change for ever. No one spoke in his car. The driver turned west onto the Avenue of Eternal Peace. To the left, they passed the Ministry of Foreign Trade and Cooperation, which had so skilfully coaxed in foreign investment. America's blue-chip companies, Boeing, Motorola, McDonald's, and others, were entrenched in billion-dollar investments and twenty-year finance plans. The landmarks above the Socialist buildings were the neon signs Kenwood, Digital, and Rémy Martin. All had ignored the pleading of human rights groups and continued their business with the world's biggest authoritarian government. All had made money and advocated constructive engagement with Communism which had allowed the economy to boom. On the right, they passed the Air China offices, the Minzu Hotel, and the Bank of China. They crossed the Second Ring Road and went by the Military Museum, which would soon have another glorious victory to add to its exhibits.

Further west, outside China Central Television, the regular guards had been replaced by a detachment from the Guards Regiment. They would also be outside the Xinhua (New China) News Agency building. Beijing's street lights became intermittent, the landmarks less important. In less than half an hour they passed the Summer Palace, the imperial retreat sacked by Western armies in the nineteenth century. The road wound round towards the Botanical Gardens, where they turned left into a country road flanked by peach orchards. Military aerials protruded from the ground. Antennas were on the hills in the distance. The Operations Command Centre of the People's Liberation Army was carved out of the mountain in the fifties when China believed it was under nuclear threat from the United States. The cavernous rooms were still used now.

This was the culmination of the President's career, which began when he was given a pistol by his father at the age of five. He was born in the early 1940s in the mountains of Yan'an where Mao was running the civil war against the Nationalists. Wang's father, Wang Fei, was a veteran of the Long March and a Marshal. As the Communist Party became entrenched in power, the young Wang made friends with the sons and daughters of the leaders. He attended the elite 101 secondary school, where he was a star of the soccer team. In the army, he served in Yunnan in the south-west and in Heilongjiang on the Russian border in the far north-east, but the turning point of his career was the command of a regiment in the war against Vietnam of 1979. The campaign was a military disaster. It was meant to teach Vietnam a lesson for overthrowing the Chinese-backed Khmer Rouge government in Cambodia: instead, the skilled Vietnamese fighters slaughtered Chinese troops as they charged across the border in human waves. China lost between 15,000 and 20,000 men. Wang managed to capture the main border town of Lang Son. He blew up the city centre before withdrawing, and was convinced then that China had to modernize its armed forces. It should never be humiliated again by a foreign army. He also harboured an ambition to avenge the deaths of so many Chinese soldiers. Now, almost a quarter of a century later,

Wang was about to launch his terrible riposte. Before the week was over, the strategic map of the Pacific would be redrawn. China's honour would be upheld and Wang's position as paramount leader established as unassailable.

The motorcade turned right off the road into a straight driveway and under an arch decorated with a lone red star in the middle. The cars were expected. Sentries saluted. The convoy drew up in front of an innocuous ferroconcrete building. The lift to the underground operations centre was waiting. President Wang stepped out onto a gallery overlooking the control room. Below him was a large, well-lit oblong room and opposite was a screen stretching almost the full length of the long wall. It displayed the southern half of China and South-East Asia to the coast of Australia in the south. From their consoles operations staff, using a computer mouse, could point and click on any highlighted object and bring up all current intelligence, including the whereabouts of political leaders. They could bring up other areas which might be involved in the theatre of war, such as troop deployments in northern India on the border with Tibet, Russian border activities, and Russian naval deployment in the northern Pacific. The disposition of the PLA Air Force and PLA Navy were shown. Red stars identified their position, next to which dialogue boxes identified the size, type, and disposition of the forces in question. The key enemy positions identified were Vietnamese, Philippine, Indonesian, Thai, Singaporean, and Malaysian air force units and warships. The state of alert of defence forces on Taiwan was being closely monitored. Agents would be updating regularly any civil disturbance in Taiwan, Hong Kong, or the more unruly provinces of southern China. A special unit of analysts was watching the military movements of the larger foreign powers: the USS *Nimitz* carrier group, on exercises in the Sulu Sea off the west coast of the Philippines, the joint British,

Australian, and New Zealand carrier group on a goodwill visit to Brunei, and American and Japanese air and naval forces in the East China Sea.

An aide to the President motioned him towards a flight of steps leading to the operations floor. As he began to climb down his presence in the room became known and a hush descended. When he reached the bottom he walked straight to a podium bedecked with the Chinese flag. An officer called the assembled officers and men to attention.

'For too long, Comrades,' the President began, 'China's enemies have exploited the oil riches contained in the waters around the Nansha [Spratly] and Xisha [Paracel] Islands. Our scientists estimate that there are 10 billion tonnes of oil beneath the surface of our great southern sea. This is Chinese oil and China's 1.3 billion people need it. China is a poor, developing country and we cannot continue to import oil at the present rate demanded by the growth in our economy.

'Vietnam has illegally occupied the Nansha and Xisha Islands. Vietnam has ignored the consistent stand of the Chinese government and hindered our legitimate activities. The Chinese people love peace and do not hope for war. But the Vietnamese authorities are wrong in thinking that we are weak and easy to bully simply because we desire peace. This mission you embark upon this morning is a warning to President Tai to abandon once and for all his ambitions of swallowing up China's sacred territory.

'Comrades, these are momentous times. In a short while units of our heroic air force and navy will set out on a mission no less important than any our mighty revolutionary army has faced in the past. Success in the battle will ensure a bright future for our Party, our motherland, and our people.'

Cam Ranh Bay Naval Base, Vietnam

Local time: 0600 Sunday 18 February 2001
GMT: 2300 Saturday 17 February 2001

The roar of the engines from twelve Chinese Su-27 Flanker air-defence fighters crackled through Vietnamese airspace and soon the aircraft were over the coast above the target of Cam Ranh Bay. The Flankers gave protection to twenty A-7 attack aircraft, the new generation of Chinese ground-attack aircraft developed from the Russian Su-24 Fencer. They came in low on terrain-following radar. The pilots used head-up cockpit displays which showed their instruments without the need to look down. Once over the target, the Chinese unleashed a deadly cocktail of weapons on the Vietnamese defences. The weapons of choice for this operation were cluster bombs which, on release, sowed a path with smaller bomblets that had warheads for cratering concrete, delayed-action mines, and fragmentation for damaging 'light structures' such as aircraft, vehicles, and personnel caught in the open. Most people woken by the noise had no time to escape before the bombs hit. Debris fell throughout Vietnam's main naval base. The mines did further damage later and delayed clearing-up operations.

As soon as the Fencers pulled up from the first attack, those with gun pods pulled round hard to strafe any undamaged elderly Vietnamese MiG-21 Fishbed fighter/ground-attack aircraft lined up along the airstrip of the naval base. Lack of warning had prevented the Vietnamese from dispersing their aircraft to make them more difficult to attack. In less than five minutes, part of Vietnam's air-defence system lay in twisted wreckage. Many buildings and radars were damaged, and the control tower was temporarily out of action. But a heavier attack would be needed to complete the destruction. The Chinese pilots pulled away, climbing fast at over 1,000 kilometres an hour, their aircraft now light and manoeuvrable. A single message from the Chinese attack leader crossed the airwaves: 'Dragon.' This told the next attack wave that the defences had been suppressed.

Immediately, there was a different kind of engine roar, the drone of twenty-four Chinese H-6 bombers – copies of the Soviet Tu-16 Badger. The 2,000 kilometre radius of action with a bomb load of 5,000 kilograms was enough for the flight from Haikou airbase on southern Hainan Island. From the ground, the bomber group might have appeared unmanoeuvrable and vulnerable. They may have been subsonic but they were well protected. Pilots from twelve Shenyang J-8II Chinese-designed delta-winged interceptors guarded them. Their Russian Zhuk radar system could simultaneously track ten enemy aircraft and guide anti-aircraft missiles. They had extended their range to that of the bombers with air refuelling and ferry tanks, now jettisoned ready for combat. The tankers orbited 500 kilometres away to enable them to reach home after the attack.

The first air-to-air combat of the Dragonstrike war lasted less than thirty seconds. A J-8 pilot locked on to two elderly Vietnamese MiG-21 Fishbed fighters returning from a routine dawn patrol, and launched two missiles. The missile warning systems on the Fishbeds were old. They probably never knew what was coming towards them when the first aircraft was hit. The second aircraft was lucky at first because its missile's homer was confused by the two aircraft in formation and it passed between them. Unfortunately the formation was too close and the first aircraft, out of control, crashed into his number two and both exploded. There was only a small fireball because they were very low on fuel.

It was 0610.

The bombers approached the naval base in formations of three. They were met in the first instance by light anti-aircraft fire from two positions which had escaped the Fencer strike. Two of the escort J-8s silenced them with gunfire in short bursts. Figures running across the base, lit up by the fires, half dressed and just woken, fought back ineffectively with small-arms fire which always passed behind the targets. They were engulfed in the inferno when the bomb struck seconds later. Most died. The Chinese pilots had been given precise orders. The first H-6s finished off the work of the Fencers by turning the aircraft and their parking areas into a flaming mass of churned-up concrete and contorted metal using more cluster bombs. Aircraft fuel tanks exploded. Flames caught in the undergrowth of the dry, flat grassland around the base. The second group destroyed the command centre using conventional single-warhead bombs with radar airburst fuses to increase the area of damage on structures such as buildings. The third hit the fuel and ammunition dump with a mixture of cluster and airburst weapons. The flames caught the poor quality housing, weakened by the shock waves from the airbursts. The domestic gas pipelines were not deeply buried and they burnt, adding to the inferno. It was a catastrophe which would never have happened in a NATO military base. Cam Ranh Bay had been built by the Americans, but taken over by the Soviet Union in 1979. Survivability for a determined surprise attack had not been an issue.

Even before the H-6 bombers had finished their task, another squadron of Fencers approached the base. Each carried four C-802 anti-ship missiles. Within minutes the waters in the harbour of Cam Ranh Bay were ablaze, although some missile homers were confused in the congested space and took their warheads to unexpected targets. If anything, this increased the chaos. Again, the message received from the air commander was simply 'Dragon'.

800 kilometres north, the Chinese pilots found success more elusive. Thick cloud hung over the main Vietnamese airbase at Da Nang. The twelve Su-27s, twelve Fencers, and twelve PLA Navy Jang Hong 7 fighter-bombers made their approach for the attack at 0620. There had been a crucial ten-minute delay. The slower JH-7s held up the group.

The PLA Air Force had never wanted the navy along. The air force had long ago rejected the JH-7's outdated airframe, avionics, and Rolls Royce Spey engines which left it underpowered by modern standards. But the Military Commission insisted on a joint operation. Politics won over practicality and the animosity continued into the cockpits. The weather was appalling. Visibility was bad and there was risk of flying into the ground. The JH-7 group commander misread his terrain-following radar and climbed too high. The aircraft were picked up minutes before the Su-27s electronically jammed the Vietnamese radar. It was enough time for fifteen Vietnamese aircraft to become airborne.

The Vietnamese MiGs should have been no match for the faster and more versatile Su-27s, whose avionics and attack capabilities were greatly superior. But the Vietnamese pilots were more familiar with their old aircraft, and better trained in realistic combat tactics. Vietnam gave its pilots at least 16 flying hours a month. It was less than half of America's C-1 (fully combat ready) 33 hours a month, but twice the training given to the Chinese. The first Chinese casualties were two of the less manoeuvrable JH-7s, and before the sleeker Su-27s became orientated one was hit by a Vietnamese air-to-air missile. Another JH-7 was downed by an SA-6 missile fired from the ground.

Then the Vietnamese pilots turned west. Over the next thirty minutes, the scramble alarm was sounded from north to south throughout the narrow strip of country which is Vietnam. Pilots took to the skies from their bases, and flew their aircraft out of Vietnam into the two countries they had used as traditional sanctuaries from combat – Laos and Cambodia. In wars against its more powerful twentieth-century enemies, the French, the Americans and the Chinese, Vietnam concealed its combat forces and saved them to fight at a place and time of its choosing. The enemy won some of the battles: Vietnam won the wars. The Chinese pilots badly damaged Da Nang airbase, but when the military successes were recounted in the *People's Daily*, the number of Vietnamese aircraft destroyed was not mentioned, nor were the Chinese losses. By the time the Vietnamese pilots had touched down in Cambodia and Laos, the first news of the attack had reached the White House.

It was 0645.

The Paracel Islands, South China Sea

Local time: 0700 Sunday 18 February 2001
GMT: 2300 Saturday 17 February 2001

From the Russian-built M-17 troop transport helicopter, Discovery Reef in the Paracel Island group looked like two large horseshoes placed end to end. In the shallow waters in the middle was Discovery 1, a 160 man oil well undergoing tests and due to begin production in April. The thirty men working there first heard the throb of the rotor blades, then watched the chopper's nose dip as it swooped down towards them. In the distance, in the medium swell of the South China Sea, six fibreglass raiding craft powered by twin 150 horsepower engines sped away from the *Yukan* class tank-landing ship 927. Each craft carried ten men towards the rugged terrain. The helicopter hovered menacingly. Warning shots were fired into the water. The boats slowed from 40 knots. The Chinese Marine commandos came ashore among the inhospitable rock faces and reefs and took up positions. With them was a unit from the PLA's special film unit, which had recorded Chinese military history since the Revolution. This morning China heralded its total control of the islands and rugged atolls which were an inseparable part of its sovereign rights.

The commandos were under orders to minimize bloodshed. Discovery 1 was an Anglo-Japanese joint venture involving a subsidiary of British Petroleum and Nippon Oil. Once the water-borne Marines had secured the ground, the helicopter landed on the rig's helipad with another twenty troops. A burst of small-arms fire into the air convinced the maintenance crew that spanners and wrenches were no match for automatic weapons. The communications officer had enough time to broadcast an alert before a Marine stopped him at gunpoint and changed the frequency. The chopper left. All but two of the raiding craft were returned to the supply ship. The PLA film unit covered the raising of the flag. The commandos sang the national anthem. Then both attackers and captives stayed silent as they were addressed by President Wang Feng through the PA system which the Marine signals corporal had rigged up through the radio.

'Like Hong Kong, Taiwan, Macau, and Tibet, the territory you have recovered today is an inalienable part of our motherland. In recent years there has been a situation of the islands and islets being occupied, sea areas being carved up, resources looted, and marine rights and interests being wantonly encroached upon. But we gave serious attention to the strengthening of our naval and air force construction. And today we proclaim victory. You should all be proud of what you have achieved, not only for your success today, but also for the direct bearing it will have on our country's thousand year cause, and on our descendants for all generations to come.'

That was the last action China had to take to secure the whole of the Paracel Island group and was the easiest task assigned to the Marine units. In the Spratly Island group, 800 kilometres to the south, the offensive would not go so well.

The Spratly Islands, South China Sea

Local time: 0700 Sunday 18 February 2001
GMT: 2300 Saturday 17 February 2001

China had never carried out an air and naval operation of this magnitude before. The area to be seized and held covered 340,000 square kilometres. The targets were twenty-one islands and atolls, fifty submerged land spits, and twenty-eight reefs, most of which were underwater. These rugged and inhospitable places were of use as strategic footholds and as a source of oil and mineral wealth. Only soldiers lived there, with their national flags. Most of the camps were erected on stilts, high enough to avoid the waves which swept over the rocky landfalls and the tides which immersed the bases in water. The Spratly Islands were nightmare postings.

The northern and easternmost reefs were claimed by the Philippines. The southernmost islands were occupied by Malaysian troops. One, Terumbi Layang-layang, had an airstrip and a naval base. To the west were Vietnamese forces.

China's only outpost of any substance was Fiery Cross Shoal. It was 26 kilometres long and 7.5 kilometres wide. In 1988, Chinese engineers blasted the coral with explosives to allow warships through the reef. They built a wharf, roads, a helicopter hangar and landing pad, and a two-storey barracks covering 1,000 square metres. The upkeep had been shoddy. The sanitation and water supplies were broken down. The Marines, who had been living there cheek by jowl, cheered when they heard their orders. They wanted to be anywhere but Fiery Shoal.

The first Chinese Z-8 Super Frelon helicopter took off

at 0620 with ten Marines on board. Soon eight were in the air heading towards a cluster of Vietnamese-held reefs 70 kilometres to the east. Seven Su-27 Flankers joined them for air support from their base at Lingshui on Hainan Island. They were refuelled 120 kilometres out from three Chinese Il-76 tankers, converted from transport aircraft. Each aircraft could run out three fuel pipes with refuelling drogues on the end, one from each wing and one from the under-fuselage.

The Su-27s were able to stay above the conflict area for at least thirty minutes, and complete the 1,500 kilometre round trip using tanker support. Months earlier, there had been fractious disagreement among the Communist Party leadership as to whether the PLA could launch Operation Dragonstrike without an aircraft carrier to project power throughout the South China Sea. One document leaked from the Central Military Commission argued that 40 aircraft on board a carrier could achieve the combat effectiveness of 200 to 800 land-based fighters. But to obtain, equip, and train crews for carrier operations takes years. Disagreements about the timing of carrier capability ranged from as late as 2015 to as soon as 2005, which would be a Harrier jump-jet operation. But the political leadership in the Communist Party said that even that might be too late. 'By then,' said the document, 'American hegemony would have taken over our coastal cities as the European powers did in the nineteenth century. The Americans would attempt to split China through whatever means and the motherland would be dismembered again.'

In the mid-nineties the Chinese air force carried out a number of in-flight refuelling tests. They negotiated with Israel for technology, but the deal never went ahead because of pressure on Israel from Washington. Western intelligence believed the Dragonstrike refuelling technology had been bought from the Pakistanis, and the refuelling drogue units made in China. The probes to take the fuel were simply bolted into the refuelling pipes of the fighters and helicopters and the valve nozzles copied from the standard NATO type. It worked, and gave potentially unlimited extra range and flexibility, although the unmanoeuvrable tankers were vulnerable unless well protected.

The seven Su-27s headed for Vanguard Bank, at the south of the Spratly group and occupied by Vietnamese forces. Because of thick cloud and poor visibility, the pilots at first failed to identify the correct islands. They flew over them once before realizing they had gone too far, giving the Vietnamese a first advantage. Three SA-6 missiles were fired from the ground, but the Chinese pilots dropped clouds of chaff-like metal strips and turned sharply at maximum G. The force generated by this manoeuvre pushed their bodies deep into their cockpits despite their anti-G suits, which squeezed their legs and abdomen in an attempt to prevent the blood pooling in the legs and draining the brain of life-giving oxygen. The SAMs missed. Then four Vietnamese MiG-21 Fishbed fighters entered the conflict from their base in Ho Chi Minh City, destroying two of the Su-27s with air-to-air missiles while they were distracted in trying to evade the SAMs. The surviving Chinese aircraft separated, and with their superior manoeuvrability found two of the Fishbeds. The two Vietnamese pilots dived to 120 metres and pulled up, each with an enemy plane locked on. One Fishbed exploded on the impact of a missile. The second started to lose a wing. The pilot ejected. The plane spiralled into the sea. Then an Su-27 pilot, distracted by the explosion of the Vietnamese plane, was killed in a direct hit on the cockpit by another SA-6.

Down at surface level, the twin 100mm gun on the bow of China's *Luhu* class destroyer *Haribing* opened up on the Vietnamese positions. The destroyer was also equipped with French surface-to-surface missiles, Italian torpedoes, and American engines. It was a example of the mixture of systems in China's armed forces, causing problems in training, resupply, and maintenance. For four minutes the 15 kilogram shells pounded the reef while the dogfight continued above it. Then a Vietnamese *Shershen* class fast attack craft joined the battle, heading towards the *Haribing* at 45 knots. The Principal Warfare Officer in the combat room first gave the command for a surface-to-air missile to be launched. It destroyed another Su-27. Five seconds later, he fired two 533mm torpedoes at the *Haribing*. One passed in front of the bow. The second hit. As the Vietnamese warship sped away, the *Haribing* fired a surface-to-surface missile. A Zhi-9a Haitun helicopter also managed to take off, and caught up with the Vietnamese. Then suddenly it was enveloped in a rain squall, lost visual contact, and had to concentrate on not ditching into the sea. The SSM veered off course, allowing the Vietnamese to escape.

The damage to the *Haribing* was not critical. The gun was still in action, although the mortar, used for anti-submarine warfare, was unworkable. Another seven Su-27s had now come in from Hainan. The dogfight was over. The eight transport helicopters from Fiery Cross Shoal were clear to land the troops. They came in under fire, but the Vietnamese had already taken heavy casualties. Their resistance had weakened. Chinese troops took only 23 prisoners. They found 106 bodies. The Chinese flag was placed on Vanguard Bank at 0645. Within the hour it had been raised on other Vietnamese outposts nearby.

There was fighting throughout the Spratly Islands that morning, while reef by reef and atoll by atoll China pushed through its territorial claim with military force. Philippine troops put up a lacklustre fight, then surrendered. Malaysia and Brunei had told their troops to hand over their positions without resistance. Apart from Vanguard Bank, the fiercest battle took place around the craggy coastlines of Itu Aba Island, Sand Cay, and Spratly Reef, where Vietnamese and Taiwanese troops joined forces to hold off an invasion force of Chinese Marines. At first, they set up a line of fire at two jetties. Then, keeping that covered, they waited as the Marines tried to land on the small beach on the other side of Sand Cay. They mortared the landing area and destroyed the boats with heavy machine-gun fire. They mortared the back of the beach where the Chinese Marines were running for cover. They turned the beach itself into a killing zone. Most of the Chinese were killed over the next fifteen minutes. The wounded were picked off by snipers, until two Chinese Zhi-9a helicopters came in with covering fire. The Taiwanese and Vietnamese made a controlled retreat, sacrificing a small vanguard group. They escaped in a Taiwanese PCL type offshore patrol craft and a Vietnamese *Poluchat* class coastal patrol craft. Despite her speed of 20 knots the helicopter crew were able to target the Vietnamese vessel. Those on board the Taiwanese warship survived.

The White House, Washington, DC

The secure telephone rang on the desk in the Oval Office of the White House. President James Bradlay had been elected only three months earlier in a landslide victory. Charismatic, good-looking, youthful, though not young, a family man who, unlike his immediate predecessor, felt no need to prove his manhood with every pretty stranger he met, Bradlay had seized the opportunity to preach the gospel of renewal after riots had turned many inner cities of America into no-go zones for most of the summer. He had galvanized the electorate when in Chicago he faced down an angry crowd on the Southside, quelling what the authorities feared would be the worst civil unrest in that city since the Democratic Convention of 1968. In his inaugural address, less than a month earlier, he was concerned almost solely with domestic issues, especially the need for a new covenant between black and white. He paid ritual homage to the United Nations, the need for Japan to open its domestic market to foreign trade, and to his administration's desire for a cooperative relationship with China.

He had stopped in at the Oval Office to look through papers on welfare reform before going on to a small dinner in the White House. The telephone interruption reminded him of the time. Only a handful of his closest colleagues had the number. Bradlay picked it up. The caller was Marty Weinstein, his National Security Adviser. 'Mr President, I'm sorry to disturb you,' he said.

Briefing

China's readiness for war

On the eve of Operation Dragonstrike China was an economically powerful one-party state, ruled behind the scenes by the People's Liberation Army, a military force of two million men under arms. At the leadership's disposal were strategic nuclear weapons, a blue-water navy and a modernized air force.

The economies of Russia, the United States, and Europe were inextricably linked with China. Boeing, Motorola, Mercedes, Siemens, GEC, and other multinationals had factories and investment locked up in the Chinese market. The Russian arms industry, the main survivor of the Yeltsin years, supplied much of the equipment and technical know-how to China's growing military-industrial complex, especially its air force and navy. Western democracies had become resigned to Chinese human rights violations. The hope that the country would fragment like the former Soviet Union had proved to be an illusion.

The Chinese economic miracle had astonished the world, but the Communist Party's leaders were themselves only too aware of the problems posed by sustaining such rapid growth. Corruption was widespread; food shortages returned to haunt the Party. It had to keep 1.3 billion people believing (or at least not resisting the thought) that only the Party held the Mandate of Heaven to rule China. To bolster its popularity, the Party developed an ideology of authoritarian nationalism which stressed the unique qualities of Chinese culture and civilization. It reminded the Chinese people that democracy was alien to their society. It invoked the great sage Confucius, who said the bonds that united the Chinese nation were like those which held the family together: respect for one's parents and for the institutions of government. Opponents of the regime argued that this selective mixture of nationalism, authoritarianism, xenophobia, and expediency was not much more than an Asian form of Fascism. They warned that China posed the greatest threat to world peace since the rise of Fascist Germany and Italy in the 1930s.

By the mid-nineties, the Party leadership was convinced that the United States planned to contain China's growth. Confirmation came in March 1996, when United States warships were deployed in the South China Sea to protect Taiwan during Chinese military exercises. The PLA vowed that it would never again be humiliated by America. Funds being used for civilian infrastructure development were diverted to accelerate the modernization of the military. The areas of concentration were the navy, air force, and missile research. A strategic partnership with Russia was forged.

There were also economic reasons to build up the nation's military capability. China's independence in energy supply was being eroded by its rapid development. To maintain the momentum China had become a huge net importer of oil. It felt vulnerable to the vagaries of the international oil markets. The government believed the only largely untapped reserves of oil were around two remote and uninhabited groups of reefs and shoals in the South China Sea known as the Spratly and Paracel Islands. They were 800 kilometres apart, and lay in one of the world's busiest waterways. Oil exploration had been limited because the territory was contested. China had a historic claim to the whole of the South China Sea, but its ownership was disputed by several countries in the region: Vietnam, which argued a history of occupation and development of the islands, and the Philippines, Malaysia and Indonesia, all of which could mount plausible claims to some of the islands and a lot of the South China Sea. These waters, which carried the shipping routes between the Indian and Pacific Oceans, were a vital waterway for all countries of the region, especially Japan, which had to import virtually all the energy it consumed. Nearly a quarter of world ocean-going trade crossed them each year.

By the end of the twentieth century, as the forces of national pride and economic vulnerability converged, East Asia became embroiled in an arms race. There was a sense that the serene days of living under the security umbrella of the United States would soon end. America was tired. Its carping about human rights had made it unpopular among nations whose Western-educated leaders preached the virtues of strong leadership and warned of the dangers to social cohesion of Western decadence. The region felt it was ready to look after itself; it was impatient to do so. Many of the South-East Asian countries prepared to defend themselves. Both Japan and China were jostling to inherit the mantle of regional leader. Yet Japan was unwelcome because of its record of colonization during the first half of the twentieth century; China because of its cultural chauvinism.

Defence spending in East Asia became the highest in the world. Between 1994 and 1996, budgets in some countries went up by more than 20 per cent as they commissioned new aircraft and fighting ships. Japan became the highest spender on defence of any country in the Pacific apart from America. Its security relationship with the United States, once rock solid, was cracking under the strain of yet more vociferous American demands for Japan to open its market, and a desire among a new generation of Japanese leaders to see the country stand on its own two feet.

China's plans remained veiled in secrecy. It designed fighter aircraft with Pakistan. It bought warplanes and fighting ships from Russia. It hired teams of Russian scientists to work on delivery systems for long-range missiles. It dispatched agents to Europe, America, and Australia to bring back technology which was denied to it by the international community on the open market. Within a few years, it had created the ability to project its power regionally through combined naval and air operations. What it lacked in technology it made up for in human ingenuity.

The overriding consideration for China's leaders had remained unchanged since Mao proclaimed the founding of the People's Republic in October 1949: preservation of Communist Party rule. Yet, by the dawning of the twenty-first century, the Party's grasp on power was uncertain. The leadership's fear of *luan* (chaos) was palpable. They needed a fresh mandate. A war to recover sovereign territory rapidly moved from being a plausible to a necessary way ahead. In pursuit of their aims, China's leaders were prepared temporarily to forfeit economic development for nationalism, and to take casualties in war. President Wang concluded that none of China's smaller Asian neighbours would risk conflict, nor were they united enough to confront China as a single military force. Only Vietnam would fight. Wang knew from personal experience how well the Vietnamese could fight. This time, however, the outcome would be different. Historically, the Chinese and Vietnamese were known as 'brother enemies'. The Vietnamese Communist Party had already held provincial-level elections and had hinted at full parliamentary and presidential elections within the next five years. It had signed a bilateral defence treaty with France, its former colonial power.

Dragonstrike, the Chinese military occupation of the South China Sea and the humbling of Vietnam, would receive widespread support throughout China. It would legitimize the Party's grip on power, secure energy supplies, challenge the military power of America, and declare China the regional leader in East Asia.

Downing Street, London

The interruption came at the end of an informal dinner with Michael Stephenson, the Prime Minister, Charles Wentworth, the Foreign Secretary, Peter Makinson, the Party Chairman, and their wives at No. 10 Downing Street, the Prime Minister's official residence in London. A light-hearted conversation about the party's bank overdraft was quickly forgotten when a duty officer handed the Prime Minister news of the Chinese attacks.

The Chairman and Secretary of the Joint Intelligence Committee, together with the Chief of Defence Staff and the Defence Secretary, were contacted and told to stand by. Staff monitored two television sets, tuned to the BBC and CNN. Downing Street opened lines to Permanent Joint Operations Headquarters in Northwood in North London, Britain's joint military command centre. Minutes before informing Downing Street, Northwood had itself been alerted by Government Communications Headquarters (GCHQ) in Cheltenham; GCHQ had been informed by Britain's Far East listening post in Darwin, northern Australia.

Wentworth was quickly told that the White House regarded the attack as a serious international crisis and was planning a response by 0045. It was not known exactly what line the Americans would take. The Prime Minister asked for a verbal report and draft statement by 0025. His Press Secretary, Private Secretary for Foreign Affairs, and a senior official from the Foreign and Commonwealth Office drew up Britain's reaction. The Foreign and Commonwealth

Office made sure the Press Association and Reuters were ready to put it out immediately.

On the other side of Downing Street, at the Foreign Office, officials collated the assessments of Britain's representatives in Hanoi, Beijing, and elsewhere in the region, in time for the Foreign Secretary to present them for the 0045 meeting. From Hanoi the Ambassador reported that there were 1,750 permanent British residents in Vietnam and possibly up to 5,000 tourists. Unconfirmed reports from the bombing were one British engineer dead and two slightly injured at Cam Ranh Bay. Russians, French, Germans, Americans, and other Westerners were believed to be hurt. The Consul-General in Hong Kong said that eighty-seven British nationals were listed as working on the rigs in the South China Sea. An unknown number of Hong Kong Chinese with British Dependency passports were also employed there. At least seven might have been on Discovery Reef at the time of the attack. It should be assumed that they were being held by Chinese troops. In a telephone conversation with the Resident Clerk (Duty Officer) at the Foreign Office, the Consul-General in Hong Kong said the situation in the territory was volatile: 'We must do everything to retain the confidence of the Chinese. They think we are trying to destabilize the situation here. This South China Sea adventure could not have come at a worse time.' The British Ambassador in Beijing spoke on the telephone from a secure room inside the embassy known as the Wendy House. He had not had official confirmation of the attacks. His information was coming from CNN and the BBC. He urged London to treat the Chinese leadership carefully. 'These are highly intelligent and highly motivated national leaders who are facing a domestic crisis. It may be a dictatorship, but it's fracturing. Corruption's rampant, food shortages abound, and there's a shortage of oil. My advice is to tread carefully and see what they say. China is a nuclear power with large ambitions.'

By 0050 Wentworth was nearing the end of his report. He noted that Britain had treaty obligations to Malaysia, one of the claimants to the South China Sea islands, under the Five Power Defence Agreement drawn up in the 1960s. If the Malaysians asked for Britain to honour it, Australia and New Zealand would also be involved.

The Prime Minister asked: 'What would they do?'

The Foreign Secretary replied: 'New Zealand, for what it's worth, would support us. Australia, which is more important, may well take a lead from Asia. It would have to consult its Asian neighbours. It doesn't have the European Union. It doesn't have the North America Free Trade Agreement. If it puts a foot wrong in East Asia, it loses the only operational trading bloc to which it aspires to be a member.'

Wentworth then told the meeting that the Ambassador in Paris reported that France's reaction to the attack on Vietnam would be volcanic. The Ambassador had recalled a conversation about Indochina with the French President, who said bluntly: 'We once owned the jewel of Asia. We lost it in 1954. We don't intend to lose it again.' He pointed out that after the Vietnamese provincial elections Paris and Hanoi had begun drafting a mutual security treaty. France might use this to take a military position in support of Hanoi.

A message from the Ambassador to the oil-rich sultanate of Brunei reminded the ministers that a British naval group led by the aircraft carrier HMS *Ark Royal* was paying a visit to Brunei on its way to Australia. Deliberately, this was not included in the Foreign Office statement which came out in time to lead the 0100 radio news bulletins:

'The British government is deeply concerned about the

violence and loss of life in Vietnam and the South China Sea. We are in contact with our European and American allies and urge China to withdraw from disputed territory to avoid further bloodshed. The government calls on China and Vietnam to uphold the pledges made over many years: that sovereignty disputes in the region should be resolved through peaceful means.

'The government is particularly concerned for the safety of British nationals in the war zone.'

As soon as the statement was broadcast, both BBC and CNN switched to the live press conference from the State Department in Washington.

The Presidential Palace, Hanoi, Vietnam

Nguyen Van Tai, President of Vietnam, had planned a visit to Hue, Vietnam's old imperial capital, that morning, but for the past forty-five minutes he and his staff had been poring over maps of Vietnam and the South China Sea. Tai, the man known as Vietnam's Gorbachev, an honour he did not fully accept, sat at the head of an ornate nineteenth-century French table, his generals and civilian advisers on either side. Two portraits hung on the wall opposite: Ho Chi Minh, the founder of Communist Vietnam, and General Giap Vo Nguyen, who delivered defeat to the French at the siege of Dien Bien Phu in 1954. As the faces of these two great Asian leaders looked down upon their successors, President Tai was concluding his summing up.

'So you are telling me, gentlemen, that our best course of action is inaction,' Tai said. 'I should order our air force to stay in Laos and Cambodia. Our navy, or what is left of it, I should keep at sea running away from China's attacks. So be it and so ordered. General Diem, see that the air force and navy are informed immediately. I am not, however, entirely happy with the idea of doing nothing other than protecting our military assets. I want the Chinese to pay for what they have done. We should unleash a reign of terror along our mutual border. Nothing big. Small units only. I want our best troops held back to defend Hanoi. What I have in mind are guerrilla operations. Surgical and clean, but designed to produce maximum impact. General Thu, please see to it. Finally, I think we should involve the international community, especially France and the United States. I will put in a call to President Dargaud and I will see the US Ambassador here.

'In the meantime, I want a full statement issued over Radio Vietnam condemning the Chinese unequivocally. I also want a clear exposition of the legitimacy of our claim to the islands. It should conclude with a call to the United Nations to intervene. That is all.'

Radio Hanoi broadcast:

'This morning at dawn the Chinese government launched an unprovoked attack on our air force and navy aimed at destroying our capacity to defend the nation. This is a dagger aimed at the heart of the Vietnamese people who in 10,000 years will never forget this perfidious act. At the same time the Chinese navy has laid siege to the oil-production facilities on the Hoang Sa (Paracel) and Truong Sa (Spratly) Islands in the Bien Dong Sea (South China Sea). The government of the Democratic Socialist Republic of Vietnam calls on China to withdraw immediately and renounce its rebel claim to Vietnamese territory or accept the consequences of protracted war.'

Briefing

Vietnam's claim to areas of the South China Sea

'In the face of the extremely serious situation in the Truong Sa archipelago area, since December last year Vietnam has three times proposed to the Chinese side to open talks for the settlement of differences concerning the Truong Sa archipelago and other disputes over the common border and the Hoang Sa archipelago. (Notes respectively dated 17th December and 23rd December.) At the same time it proposed that pending the settlement of disputes by means of negotiations "the two sides should refrain from the use of force to settle disputes and avoid any clashes that may aggravate the situation". (Note dated 26th December.)

'The Chinese authorities slanderously labelled the Vietnamese proposals "hypocritical" in order to reject negotiations with Vietnam and have not responded to Vietnam's proposal that the two sides undertake not to use force to settle disputes. All this shows that China continues implementing a policy of hostility against Vietnam, and continues its acts of usurpation in the Truong Sa archipelago. In the face of China's policy of reliance on the use of force, the Democratic Socialist Republic of Vietnam is determined to defend its sovereignty and territorial integrity. Chinese actions in the Hoang Sa archipelago previously, and in the Truong Sa archipelago at present, in fact are nothing more than part of China's expansionist and hegemonist policy towards Vietnam and South-East Asia.

'These two archipelagos lie 800 kilometres from each other. They consist of a large number of islands and coral reefs and shoals. The total emerging area of each archipelago is about 10 square kilometres. The value of both archipelagos lies in their strategic position in the Bien Dong Sea and their great riches of oil and natural gas. Vietnam's case is that it has maintained effective occupation of the two archipelagos at least since the seventeenth century, when they were not under the sovereignty of any country, and the Vietnamese state has exercised effectively, continuously, and peacefully its sovereignty over the two archipelagos until the time when they were invaded by the Chinese armed forces.

'Relations between Vietnam and China have not developed as well as the Vietnamese people hoped. Along with the escalation of provocative acts and land-grabbing operations along the land border, in January 1974 Peking used a military force to attack and occupy the remaining western group of islands of the Hoang Sa archipelago. With the war by proxy of the genocidal Pol Pot clique in south-western Vietnam, the war of 1979 involving 600,000 Chinese troops in the northern border regions of Vietnam, and now this disgraceful attack, Peking has brought Sino-Vietnamese relations to their worst. The realities of the last twenty years and more have clearly shown that China has turned the tables, switching friends and foes and brazenly carrying out an anti-Vietnam policy.

'Throughout the past thousands of years, China had never exercised sovereignty over these two archipelagos. What China did, though, was by the gradual use of military force between 1956 and 1999 occupy the Hoang Sa archipelago. And what she has been doing since the end of last year is to begin threatening the occupation a number of rocks and reefs in Vietnam's Truong Sa, again by use of military force. Thus, China is translating into action the 30th July 1997 declaration made by former Chinese Foreign Minister Geng Wuhua: "The Chinese territory spreads down to the James Shoals near Sarawak (Malaysia) ... You can carry out exploitation as you wish. When the time comes, however, we will retrieve those islands. There will be no need then to negotiate at all, these islands having since long ago belonged to China."

'Chinese claims to sovereignty over the islands are nonsense. Peking has cited the astronomical surveys by the Yuan Dynasty (thirteenth century) in Nanhai to conclude that the Xisha archipelago lay within Chinese territory under the Yuan. Nevertheless, it is written in the official history of the Yuan Dynasty itself that the Chinese domain under the Yuan Dynasty extended only to Hainan Island in the south and not beyond the Gobi Desert in the north, that is to say, it did not include the islands which China calls Xisha today. China has cited a patrol cruise by Vice-Admiral Wu Sheng in the years 1710 to 1712 or so during the Qing Dynasty alleging that Vice-Admiral Wu himself set out from Qiongya, proceeding to Tonggu, Qizhouyang, and Sigengsha, making a 5,000 kilometre tour of inspection. On this basis, China asserts that Qizhouyang is the present-day Xisha archipelago area which was then patrolled by naval units of Guangdong Province. Qiongya, Tonggu, and Sigengsha are names of localities on the coast of Hainan Island, while Qizhouyang is a maritime zone lying between the north-eastern coast of Hainan Island and the group of seven islets situated to the north-east of Hainan. So that was just an inspection tour around Hainan Island. Peking's conclusions are obviously contrary to historical and geographical facts.

'Besides, if maritime patrol and inspection tours are presented as an argument proving Chinese sovereignty over the two archipelagos, one may wonder whether China is going to claim sovereignty over such territories in relation to which Zheng He under the Ming Dynasty seven times (between 1405 and 1430) dispatched a large naval fleet with more than 60 gunships and 28,000 men to impose Chinese hegemony on territories within the Indian Ocean zone and undertake territorial exploration in the Red Sea zone and along the coast of eastern Africa.

'Comparing the respective cases of Vietnam and China, one can see that China has never administered the Hoang Sa and Truong Sa archipelagos and it is all the more impossible to say that China has exercised effectively, continuously, and peacefully her "sovereignty" over these islands. The claim of Chinese sovereignty is one that China has not up to now been able to prove. The state of Vietnam has effectively occupied the two archipelagos of Hoang Sa and Truong Sa since at least the seventeenth century and has effectively, continuously, and peacefully exercised its sovereignty ever since. From the seventeenth to the nineteenth century, Chinese dynasties had never protested but implicitly recognized Vietnamese jurisdiction over the archipelagos.

'Our jurisdiction over the islands is recognized by many leading countries, including France. One the basis of equality and mutual respect the government of Vietnam has asked France to send a detachment of troops to help with the assessment of damage that the Chinese have inflicted upon our military forces. We confidently expect a positive response from France.

'The developments up to the present day point to all the dangers inherent in China's policy of reliance on the use of force. A peaceful settlement of the dispute over the archipelagos of Truong Sa and Hoang Sa would respond to the desire for peace of the peoples of Vietnam and China, in conformity with the principles of international law and the UN Charter, with the interest of peace, stability, and cooperation in South-East Asia, the Asia-Pacific region, and the whole world. This is the most correct way. Public opinion in South-East Asia and in the whole world is looking forward to China's positive response. Being one of the five permanent members of the UN Security Council, China has a major obligation to abide by the UN Charter.'

The State Department, Washington, DC

Local time: 2000 Saturday 17 February 2001
GMT: 0100 Sunday 18 February 2001

The first statement from the United States came from the State Department spokesman, Donald Bryant, who called a news conference for correspondents accredited to the department.

BRYANT: As you know, we are still trying to ascertain exactly what is happening in Vietnam and the South China Sea. The President, the Secretary of State, the National Security Adviser, the Defense Secretary, and the Joint Chiefs have been briefed. The President has been meeting with the Secretary of State and the National Security Adviser at the White House for the past half an hour.

The President has issued the following statement: 'The American government is disturbed by the outbreak of violence in the South China Sea. Our first reports indicate that there have been substantial casualties, particularly among Vietnamese civilians. We are shocked by the bloodshed. This is a part of the world which had been an example to us all of how to make trade and the creation of wealth a priority above all else. We urge both Vietnam and China to stop their hostilities. America will do everything in its power to end this dispute. We are still trying to ascertain the casualties among American citizens. You will be kept informed of any developments.'

Any follow-ups?

QUESTION: Have you any more on American casualties?

BRYANT: We believe some Americans may have been

hurt in the bombing of Cam Ranh Bay. Civilian areas were hit hard there. There are several hundred Americans on the oil rigs in the South China Sea. We don't know what's going on there at the moment. The Chinese have claimed sovereignty over the Crescent Group in the Paracels. They've announced it on their state radio. That's all we've got so far. Sarah.

QUESTION: You say civilian areas were hit hard at Cam Ranh Bay. Do you mean Vietnamese civilian areas in the town, or the quarters for Western workers there? And if so, are they strictly civilian? Aren't they helping the Vietnamese military?

BRYANT: Correct. I'm referring to the foreign quarters. But when you get to bombing homes with children in them, I think we're talking civilian.

QUESTION: Would you consider American oil workers out there on territory captured by the Chinese as being hostages or prisoners?

BRYANT: They are in captivity. We want them freed.

QUESTION: What are our embassies saying in Beijing and Hanoi?

BRYANT: The Assistant Secretary, Bostock, has spoken personally to each of our Ambassadors there.

QUESTION: So what are you saying: they don't know anything?

BRYANT: Our Ambassador to Hanoi is expected to meet with President Tai in a few hours' time. Our Ambassador to Beijing has not been told whether he'll be able to meet with a senior Chinese leader.

QUESTION: Why don't you condemn this definitely as an act of Chinese aggression?

BRYANT: I don't want to get drawn down a road of inflammatory language. China carried out air strikes on Vietnam. As the President said, there have been casualties. He also emphasized that we are friends of both countries.

QUESTION: What actions do you see Vietnam contemplating which would add to the tension?

BRYANT: Well, Barry, I'm not going to speculate about, you know, what we may be anticipating the authorities in Vietnam to do. I mean, one can imagine quite easily all kinds of things which would provoke the Chinese.

QUESTION: I'm trying to understand why you've chosen to volunteer an admonition to both sides.

BRYANT: We've been – we've been—

QUESTION: The Chinese are the people who are on the move. The Vietnamese are standing there, shaken a bit and wondering if anybody will help them, and you're telling them: 'Don't be provocative.'

BRYANT: Just— John? You got a question?

QUESTION: Where do we go from here? Is this one for the UN or for the Marines?

BRYANT: I don't want to second guess what the President and his advisers are discussing. I'll be here most of the night. I'll let you know if we've anything else to say.

Downing Street, London

Prime Minister Stephenson read the latest reports from Northwood Permanent Joint Operations Headquarters while waiting for the end of the State Department briefing, then he spoke to the President. The two men agreed that Europe and the United States must show neutrality at this stage. President Bradlay pointed out that America had a security treaty with Japan dating back to 1960. It also had commitments to the Philippines. If China interfered with shipping, particularly oil supplies through the South China Sea, then America would have to send a military signal to Beijing. Carrier groups in the region were on standby.

Shortly after midnight, the British Ambassador to Paris reported that between twenty and thirty French technicians and their families had been killed in the bombing of Cam Ranh Bay. French children were among the dead. The first television pictures would be aired within the hour. France was preparing a statement condemning China. Wentworth, the Foreign Secretary, remarked that France had only taken over the presidency of the European Union in January. There was a danger of it going public against China without consulting its fellow members.

In a telephone conversation Stephenson asked the French President, M. Dargaud, if France could ensure the neutral leadership of the European Union.

The President replied in English: 'Prime Minister, French civilians have been killed by Chinese bombs. French people know this. Do you expect me to parrot the American President and say we are friendly with both countries?

No. No. No. My statement is for France, not for Europe. It is for the families of those who were bombed.'

Stephenson repeated his request: 'Could France stay neutral at least until there has been a vote in the UN?'

But Dargaud was emphatic: 'What can I do? As soon as those pictures are shown, Prime Minister, I have to support Vietnam. Anything else would be political suicide. And you would do the same.'

'In which case, Mr President, can you make it clear you are speaking for France and not the Union,' finished the Prime Minister.

Wentworth, on another line, was speaking directly to the Ambassador in Germany. The Chancellor was about to issue a statement urging restraint and caution. His tone was to highlight the trade which would be lost if the crisis escalated. 'Can Germany keep the French in line?' asked the Foreign Secretary.

'Germany will keep its mouth shut when it comes to French citizens being killed in an act of war,' replied the Ambassador.

The Prime Minister's residence, Tokyo

Local time: 1100 Sunday 18 February 2001
GMT: 0200 Sunday 18 February 2001

The meeting room in the Prime Minister's residence was Spartan in appearance. An oblong beech wood table surrounded by armchairs dominated the room. At the head of the table sat Noburo Hyashi, the Prime Minister. On his right sat Yoichi Kimura, the Foreign Minister, and on the Prime Minister's left sat Yasuhiro Ishihara, the Minister of Defence. The three, together with Takeshi Naito (Trade) and Shigeto Wada (Finance), comprised the Defence Committee of Japan's cabinet. Only one official was present and he was General Shigehiko Ogawa, Director, Defence Intelligence Headquarters.

Hyashi was a formal man. He opened the meeting by thanking the ministers for coming at such short notice, then asked General Ogawa to brief the committee on the latest developments in the South China Sea.

'As you all know, China has taken control of the South China Sea,' General Ogawa said. 'In the process it has also set out to destroy Vietnam's capacity to retaliate. Our estimates are that the Chinese first strike against Cam Ranh Bay has resulted in the destruction or disablement of 40 per cent of Vietnam's navy.'

'Isn't that the same ratio as what we achieved in the attack on Pearl Harbor?' Hyashi interjected.

'For the navy, yes,' the General replied. 'But attacks on the main air force bases were less successful. The Vietnamese saved their aircraft by flying them to Laos and Cambodia. However, the Chinese have the ability to deliver a second strike and we expect them to launch it against the navy within the next twenty-four hours. The Vietnamese do as well. Reliable sources in Vietnam report that the remaining seaworthy elements of the navy are at sea or are putting to sea.'

'General, what do you expect next of the Chinese?' asked Hyashi.

'We expect them to secure their hold over the oil-production facilities,' he replied. 'There is one new facility in the Paracel Islands that has not yet reached full commercial production and three fully operational facilities in the Spratly Islands. There is a possibility that they will blockade access to the South China Sea for a period to validate their claim to the sea.'

'Thank you, General, you may be excused,' the Prime Minister said. 'Naito-san, what is the assessment of the Ministry of International Trade and Industry?'

'Profound concern, Hyashi-san,' his Trade Minister said. 'My telephone has not stopped ringing all morning, the Chairman of the Keidanren said industry expects a firm response. I couldn't get Tanaka from Nippon Oil off the telephone. His company is a big investor in the Paracel oil production facility.

'As you know we import 99.6 per cent of our petroleum products. Nearly 80 per cent of our crude oil imports comes from the Middle East – all traverse the South China Sea. We import oil from Brunei, Indonesia, and Australia. It all passes through the South China Sea, although Australian crude (which is a light crude good for making only gasoline) can be diverted. I am informed that our strategic stockpile will meet all our needs – gasoline and petrochemical – for two to three months. A similar situation obtains for liquefied natural gas or LNG. We import all our considerable LNG needs – some 60,000,000,000 cubic metres – and 90 per cent of those imports traverse the South China Sea. I highlight energy because that goes to the heart of our national survival. But Japan is nothing if it cannot trade.'

'Wada-san, what does the Finance Ministry have to say?' the Prime Minister asked.

'We think there will be considerable instability in financial markets when they open for trading tomorrow morning,' Wada said. 'The Bank of Japan will be prepared to step into foreign exchange markets to stabilize the yen against the dollar. Officials will be in touch with the Bundesbank, the Bank of England, and the US Fed, if they are not already, to talk about a coordinated response to this conflict. In closing, my officials expect a quite large fall in the stock market. The oil market will be unsettled, but there is little we can do about that.'

'Thank you. Ishihara-san, what is the state of our military preparedness?'

'Hyashi-san, we have been monitoring this situation closely and especially since relations between China and Vietnam deteriorated at the end of last year,' Ishihara began. 'We currently have a battle group on manoeuvres in the waters around Okinawa. We also have two submarines in the area, but, for operational reasons, I would rather leave that vague. We are in constant contact with the Americans. They have a number of naval deployments in the region. The USS *Harry S. Truman* is currently in the Sea of Japan, and the USS *Nimitz* battle group is in the Sulu Sea. The British also have a Commonwealth naval group performing exercises with the *Ark Royal* off Brunei. Since the Chinese attack began we have had long-range AWACS in the air from our bases in Okinawa. From these we have a detailed picture of the deployment of Chinese forces.'

'Foreign Minister, what is your assessment? What will the Americans do?'

'We have all of us, I think, expected this,' Kimura said.

'It was only a matter of time. The UN Security Council will meet, although we have little hope that it can do much. China will exercise its veto. Our best hope lies in our security treaty with the United States. I am, at best, ambivalent about this. Their economic relations with China have gone deeper and are spread wider than even ours – which are considerable enough at total investment of $120 billion. Moreover, ever since the Americans withdrew from Okinawa and Yokosuka I have felt that their commitment to the security treaty was more one of form than substance.

'I will be seeing separately the US and Chinese Ambassadors after this meeting.'

The Prime Minister gathered his papers. 'Very good, Kimura-san. Keep me informed.' He cleared his throat. 'Gentlemen, I do not think our nation has faced so great a threat to its survival since the Pacific War. But adversity often presents opportunities. China is pushing us, and the Americans, to the limit. Maybe the time has come for Japan to stand up.

'Of one thing I am certain, it is high time we put our treaty with the US to the test. Tell the American Ambassador that we expect to see the treaty honoured in full. A threat to Japan's national interests used to be a threat to America's. Is that still so, and what do they plan to do about it? As for the Chinese Ambassador, I think we need to be more subtle. Explain to him our interests in China and the region and the need to minimize conflict. And if we are to have difficulties with the Americans, perhaps we should massage the European Union round to our way of thinking.

'Gentlemen, I suggest we be prepared to reconvene at a moment's notice. Thank you for your attendance.'

The White House, Washington, DC

Local time: 2130 Saturday 17 February 2001
GMT: 0230 Sunday 18 February 2001

President Bradlay said he would take no more calls unless in extreme emergency. Any Vietnamese or Chinese leader should be put through without delay. He then formally convened an extraordinary meeting of the National Security Council and asked the Secretary of State to begin his assessment.

Mr Newton Fischer, the Secretary of State, described China's attacks as having an element of military surprise, but not unexpected. The threat, and the stated claim to the South China Sea, had been made public for years. Since the end of Deng Xiaoping's leadership the shift had been irretrievably towards nationalism. With restructuring of the military and the purchasing of new weapons, it was inevitable that sooner or later the People's Liberation Army would do something to justify its role.

Fischer stressed that President Wang was not a mad dictator. He was a shrewd strategist determined to project China's power. For years, China had flexed its muscles. As far back as 1989, the *People's Daily* observed: 'For a country to shake off foreign enslavement and to become independent and self-reliant is the premiss for its development ... Once people lose their sense of country, of national defence, and of nation, total collapse of the spirit will inevitably follow.'

'What do they want?' interjected the President Bradlay.

'They want us out of Asia, sir,' was the reply. 'It's been a long time coming. We have to face the fact that America will be dealing with a quasi-military government during this crisis. I have their most authoritative statement on the South China Sea and the islands which they claim as theirs. You get a feeling for the regime by the language they use.

'"Since Vietnamese warships were dealt stunning blows after encroaching on China's territorial waters in March this year, an upsurge of war preparations has been whipped up in Vietnam.

"Vietnam will simply be seeking its own destruction if it really wants a major confrontation with the Chinese navy. A major factor in boosting the Chinese navy's combat capabilities in recent years is its combined blue-water training to protect our sovereignty against aggression.

"According to the provisions of the 'UN Convention on the Law of the Sea' adopted by the world conference on the Law of the Sea, China has several million square kilometres of territorial sea including its continental shelf and associated economic zones, plus our original territorial waters. This vast sea area is extremely abundant in biological, mineral, and energy resources. Protecting and cherishing China's territorial seas and defending the country's maritime interests is the people's navy's unshirkable task ... This strong concept of territorial seas is deeply imprinted in the mind of every cadre and fighter."'

Bradlay said he was alarmed at the element of surprise exacted by China after so much material was in the public domain. Secretary Fischer replied that the lobby of businessmen and the public relations machine of the Chinese government had been a far more persuasive force than defence analysts.

The meeting was interrupted by a flash telegram from the US Ambassador to Malaysia.

Five American oil workers escaped with Malaysian troops in the first few minutes of the attack on the Malaysian-claimed territory. They report that their naval patrol boat came under fire from the Chinese. There were Malaysian, but no (repeat no) American casualties. However, the Chinese opened fire when they stormed the atoll. The oil workers believe that some of their colleagues may have been hit. The Malaysians had been under standing orders to leave if confronted by overwhelming enemy forces. The oilmen will not (repeat not) be available to the press. Both they and the company believe they can go back to work once the conflict has ended.

Fischer responded that Malaysia would not be expected to react without consulting its neighbours from the Association of South-East Asian Nations (ASEAN). ASEAN itself would probably take a non-confrontational line. He did not expect a military response from these nations. Even collectively they were no match for China. The wealth in those countries was controlled by Chinese businessmen. They might live away from China, but they cultivated contact with the Communist leadership in order to win contracts. The Secretary of State reminded the President that one such Chinese/Malaysian family was a large investor in financial services in Maine, the President's own state, and that they had attended his inauguration only one month earlier.

The overriding threat of the Chinese adventure was to Japan. Its total European and South-East Asian trade traversed the South China Sea. Moreover, Japan was a big oil importer with no supply of its own. Three-quarters of its oil came from the Middle East, and the rest from Brunei, Indonesia, and Australia. The major issue, the Secretary said, was the security treaty with Tokyo. The consequences of any American equivocation on the issue would almost certainly end the treaty and unleash on Asia a more militarily assertive Japan.

'Mr President, it is my considered advice that we move very carefully in this area. We have had a military alliance with Japanese since 1960. One should not discard a relationship like that lightly. I know there are those who will say China matters more – indeed, some at this table – but the Japanese have been good friends to the United States.'

President Bradlay then turned to Martin Weinstein, the National Security Adviser, who confined his report to the intelligence-gathering activities of both governments.

'We put a network of satellites over the region when the military exercises began. We've had AWACS in the air and we've got Aegis cruisers with a carrier battle group off the Philippines. Not much moves there without us knowing it. I'm happy with our IMINT and SIGINT [imagery and signals intelligence]. The Chinese have their own satellites, but the technology is faulty and outdated. We can assume they don't watch everything. But we don't know what they're missing.

'The flaw in our operation is HUMINT [human-source intelligence]. We do not have any quality operatives on the ground in Beijing. We have no one inside Zhongnanhai. We don't know what Wang Feng is thinking. Are there divisions between him and the other powerful players in the government? How supportive is MOFTEC [Ministry of Foreign Trade and Economic Cooperation] towards the PLA action, which has extreme economic risks? In most countries, including the Soviet Union when it existed, we had scraps of the jigsaw thrown out to us. We ran agents. We had good networks. We don't have that anywhere important in China. Zhongnanhai is an impenetrable cita-del. The best we get is information mainly from the children of the officials who live there. A lot of them fly over here and our agents befriend them. But it's gossip. Occasionally, one will leak a document to the *New York Times* or somebody.'

'What do they have on us?' asked the President.

Weinstein referred to his notes: 'Their espionage operation is run through the Ministry of State Security or MSS. We believe in the United States itself the MSS draws upon the services of 1,500 Chinese diplomats and commercial representatives, 90 other Chinese establishments and offices, and 20,000 Chinese students arriving annually. They are either recruited to gather intelligence while here or debriefed back in China. If they don't comply their families are put under pressure; loss of job, home, medical care. That sort of thing. On top of that we have 15,000 representatives travelling through in about 3,000 delegations a year. The same happens to them. And there's an ethnic Chinese community of several million. In short, Mr President, if we enter into hostilities with the People's Republic of China they could have agents in every city.'

Bradlay turned to Peter Ray, the Director of the CIA. 'So far, can you tell me what they know that they shouldn't know?'

'I can tell you the type of material. Two years before Richard Nixon redrew our China policy, the Communists knew of his desire to open diplomatic relations with them. In 1970 one of our analysts, Larry Chin Wu-tai, gave them a classified document which outlined his plan. They were able to adjust their foreign policy accordingly. We thought we were surprising them. They were across us all the time. Larry Chin worked for the CIA for thirty-seven years. He was indicted in 1981.'

'Are you telling me they have agents in our government?'

'I'm telling you, Mr President, that we don't have anyone with them. We don't know if they have anyone with us. The MSS actively seeks to penetrate American intelligence and policy-making agencies. Just recently, we had to bring out a communications officer from the embassy in Beijing. They had tried to recruit him. If they had succeeded, they would have had access to all embassy communications. We can be damn sure they'll be turning on all the taps today. We're watching. But HUMINT in Chinese society is very difficult.

'The other thrust of their intelligence operation is for technology. The South China Sea air strikes today could have been made possible by American technology. And you have to admire their nerve. The China Aero-Technology Import & Export Company, CATIC, bought a Seattle company which made aircraft parts, called Mamco Manufacturing Inc., in the late 1980s. Mamco had technology which could provide the Chinese air force with in-flight refuelling capabilities. In February 1990 we closed the operation down. But you look at the number of American engineering and technology companies now owned by Chinese firms. All those companies are ultimately responsible to the Communist Party. This is the policy of trade, interdependence, and constructive engagement. But tonight it reads to me like one of enemy infiltration.

'One point which also comes under the Joint Chiefs,' he said, winding up. 'PLA intelligence activities have increased across the land border with Vietnam. In the past month, there have been low-level assassinations, the laying of mines, the killing of livestock. All no more than five miles across. A Vietnamese soldier was captured and tortured to try to get the Vietnamese order of battle. He escaped.'

'What are you saying?'

'We're watching that border, Mr President.'

Bradlay asked the Chairman of the Joint Chiefs to give his assessment.

'There's no doubt that the United States has the capability to regain control over the oil facilities in the Spratlys and the Paracels and to reopen the South China Sea to international navigation. Two carrier battle groups are close enough by to be there in a day.

'The Chinese have taken control of the oil-production facilities with Marine commandos. To retake them would not be easy. The best estimate is that at least several wells would be destroyed Iraqi-style, which could lead to an environmental disaster.

'The Chinese have stationed surface ships and submarines at the chokepoints to the South China Sea. These are the straits of Malacca, Sunda, and Lombok, through which, most crucially, Japan's oil supplies go. As of a few minutes ago, President Wang cited China's 1992 Territorial Waters Act, banning military and nuclear-powered ships. Commercial shipping is allowed.'

'What's it doing?' interrupted the President.

'Some tramp steamers are going through. The big shipping lines are telling their captains to hold back.'

'I think, then,' said the President, 'for the sake of tonight's assessment we should think of this blockade as not being on just Japanese or East Asian trade, but on American trade. We get a lot of stuff through those sea routes. With American national interest threatened, our thinking will be much clearer. My next question is a natural follow-on. What happens if we go in with the carrier battle groups?'

'Ultimately, they would be unable to defend themselves. But it will not be like the 1996 Taiwan stand-off. I understand that after that a policy was put in place by the PLA to fight and shed blood rather than be humiliated by a foreign hegemonistic power. So we would win, but we could take horrible casualties. Our Navy SEALS would be in hand-to-hand combat to take back the reefs. There is no reason to believe that the Chinese commandos would not fight to the death. In the sea battles, they have fifteen to twenty submarines out there. We might get nineteen of them. But two torpedoes could kill a lot of our servicepeople.

'As yet we are uncertain of support from our allies in the region. South-East Asia has become rich through pragmatism and neutrality. If they believe that China's going to win this, they're not going to let us use their ports and airports.

'Effectively, Mr President, they are daring us to go to war or give up our security role in Asia. What they lack in training and technology, they make up with balls and numbers. They also have location on their side.'

Ms Bernadette Lin, the Commerce Secretary, spoke with what had been the predominant voice in the Sino-American relationship, but she began on a personal note.

'We all heard the CIA assessment of Chinese intelligence-gathering operations here. I would like to stress one point. Please, no witch-hunts. No leaks to the press that every Chinese could be a spy. I am a Chinese-American. As a child, I fled from Shanghai in 1952. Our immigration policy doesn't come without risks. Let us accept the risks and not create a knee-jerk reaction which might effect the lives of hundreds of thousands of American citizens just because they look Chinese. It's not going to be an easy ride for any of us until this crisis winds down.'

'Your point is taken, Madam Secretary,' replied the President.

'Now, I'll be blunt,' Ms Lin continued. 'Corporate America does not want confrontation with China. The country has too much to lose. In the mid-nineties, China sold $30 billion worth of goods to us. We sold $9 billion to them – which meant that if there had been a trade war we would have won. Since then, that gap has closed. It's not equal yet, but China has diversified so that its exports now go in large quantities to South-East Asia, Europe, and Latin America.

'What would happen if we stopped buying Chinese goods? Sure, China would be hurt bad and people would be thrown out of work. But it would not be crippled. If China stopped buying American goods, Mr President, it would cost us maybe $15 billion this year. There are fifteen states whose economies are heavily reliant on trade with China. I'll list examples. In California, exports to China keep 216,000 people employed. In Seattle, Washington 112,000, many of them with Boeing. In Arizona, 16,000. New York, 100,000. Clearly, there would a domestic political impact with many families affected. That would be reflected by the electorate in the next elections. And to give you an idea, California has fifty-two Congressional seats going in the next election. Washington has nine; Arizona, six; New York, thirty-one. Florida, with 32,000 jobs at stake, has twenty-three seats. Throughout America there are 469 seats whose representatives will take China trade to their election platform.

'It's true that in China millions more will be thrown out of work. What are all those farmers going to do who gave up the rice paddies to set up a Barbie Doll factory? I can tell you what they're not going to do, Mr President. They are not going to protest. They are not going to vote out the government because they can't. Throughout America, there are one and a quarter million jobs which need China trade. Taking families and dependants into account, that means upwards of five million Americans would suffer severely if we let this crisis spiral.

'There are a number of blue-chip companies which consider China to be an integral part of their growth and survival. Boeing estimates that the total market for the sale of commercial jet aircraft to China through 2013 will be worth $66 billion. Other companies like Motorola and

AT&T make similar sales projections. But the investments today are huge: Motorola has invested $1.2 billion in China and now makes the latest computer chips there. Hewlett-Packard and IBM both have $100 million investments as well. Auto makers have a big exposure to China – led by Ford with $250 million invested in three factories making components, light trucks, and vans, and followed by General Motors with a $130 million investment in three auto parts facilities. In all our top ten investors in China have more than $4 billion invested in the country and it will grow.

'Mr President, I watched when President Jimmy Carter tried to stop selling wheat to the Russians and the business went to the Australians and the Canadians. I watched when Ronald Reagan tried to stop construction of a natural-gas pipeline in the Soviet Union, as it then was, and Caterpillar almost went out of business. And I watched as Clinton flailed about on the issue of Most Favoured Nation status for China. He learned the lesson. The simple truth is that more and more, money not war is the major point in foreign affairs. This incident in the South China Sea is regrettable but it's not going to change that.'

The Foreign Ministry, Tokyo

Local time: 1200 Sunday 18 February 2001
GMT: 0300 Sunday 18 February 2001

Foreign Minister Kimura's official car pulled out of the drive of the Prime Minister's residence and made for the Gaimusho (Foreign Ministry) in Kasumigaseki. The steel gates of the Ministry building parted as Kimura's Nissan President approached. A polite salute from the gate attendant and his limousine was pulling to a dignified halt in front of the main entrance.

Kimura waited patiently for the arrival of Mr Richard Monroe, the US Ambassador. Kimura did not like Monroe. He was too casual. He did not understand the virtues of silence. Yet he was a man to be taken seriously. Monroe was a close friend of the US President. Monroe had helped get out the Irish vote in Boston, where he was the owner of Boston Analytics Inc., a computer software design company. He was also a major party fund-raiser.

Monroe walked in to Kimura's office as if he had just walked off a tennis court. Apologizing profusely, he explained that the Gaimusho's request for his attendance at this meeting had reached him at a friend's house where he had been playing rackets. Kimura, with a half-smile on his face, inclined his head towards his guest and motioned him to sit down.

'Mr Ambassador, we seem to have a ... little local difficulty in the South China Sea,' the Foreign Minister observed. 'My government views the moves by the Chinese government with the utmost concern. We believe that the decision by China to seize the oil assets currently under development in the South China Sea, as well as its unwarranted attack on Vietnam, constitutes a threat to our own vital interests in the region and directly impinges upon the security of this nation. I have been instructed by my government, therefore, to invoke Article 6 of our mutual security treaty. We want a return to the *status quo ante*; we want China out of the South China Sea; we want you to send a carrier battle group to this region to back up those demands.'

'Well, I hear what you say, Mr Foreign Minister,' Ambassador Monroe said. 'I shall report this immediately to the President.'

Half an hour later, the Chinese Ambassador walked into the room. Mr Bo Enzhu was a more ascetic diplomat, or at least liked to be seen as such. In reality he was exceedingly irritating. He had the habit of getting physically close, in a manoeuvre that suggested he was about to divulge some great truth, and then just spouting what he had read in that day's *People's Daily*. His cables to Beijing were colourless but accurate as to what was said to him.

'Ambassador, how kind of you to come at such short notice,' said Kimura, trying his utmost to sound solicitous.

'Not at all, Foreign Minister. It is always a pleasure to visit the Gaimusho,' Bo replied.

'We are ... puzzled by your country's manoeuvres in the South China Sea. Do you have any explanation for us?' Kimura ventured.

'This need be nothing to concern your government, Foreign Minister,' Bo began. 'China's sovereignty over the South China Sea is inalienable and historic. We have sought simply to make *de jure* what has been *de facto* for the past two thousand years. This represents no threat to Japan. China believes in the free passage of shipping through internationally recognized sea lanes such as the South China Sea.'

'And property rights?' Kimura asked.

'The sea and all below it and all it contains is ours. That, of course, is a statement about the future. We are not unaware of the existing facilities. I am instructed that there will be no change in ownership.'

'Tell your government that our concern is with economic security,' Kimura replied. 'Virtually all our oil passes through the South China Sea. A threat to that would constitute a threat to Japan.'

On the way back to the Prime Minister's residence, Kimura noticed a queue of motorists at a service station.

Briefing

China's financial war aims

General Zhao Yi was a man in his late fifties, thin, and true to his southern Chinese origins quite short. He was the Senior General in charge of the General Staff Department (GSD) and he planned to finance Dragonstrike by manipulating the world's financial markets.

He had had a remarkable career in the PLA. In an institution noted for its conservatism, his rise to eminence, after entering the services at the unusually late age of thirty-three, marked him as a special man. Like many of his generation, including President Wang Feng, he was born in Yan'an, although following Chinese tradition his official native place, his ancestral home, was given as Shunde, in the Pearl River delta of Guangdong province. His father Zhao Ping had survived the Long March and worked closely with Mao Zedong. In Beijing after the Revolution the family prospered. He was made a Marshal of the PLA; the family lived in a villa in Zhongnanhai. Zhao grew up playing and going to school with the sons and daughters of Liu Shaoqi, Peng Zhen, and Deng Xiaoping. His life of privilege came to a sudden end in 1967 as the Great Proletarian Cultural Revolution turned the world upside-down for China's 800 million subjects. Red Guard publications denounced Zhao for living a privileged life. He learned horse riding and motorcycling – pastimes beyond the reach of average people. At the time of his denunciation he was studying at Beijing University. At the beginning of 1967 he lost touch with his father and mother and two younger brothers. He was not to see his mother until 1971, three years after his father's death. During these 'lost years' Zhao lived the life of a fugitive. He made his way to Guangdong and, under an assumed name, worked on a ship sailing the Pearl River. His family in Shunde lent him some protection, but he was eventually caught and confined in a youth detention centre. And there he might have languished for many years but for the efforts of Zhou Enlai, the Chinese Premier and Mao's Lord Chamberlain. Zhou sought out Zhao and lent him his protection. That was in 1973.

Zhao's General Staff Department oversaw the PLA's sprawling industrial and financial enterprises, located within the GSD's Equipment Department. Since ancient Imperial times the military in China had been required to feed and clothe itself. But the PLA under late Communism had taken this tradition to extraordinary lengths. The military was in every form of industrial and financial enterprise known to man – engineering, pharmaceuticals, ship building, aviation, satellite launches, vehicle manufacture, stockbroking, and banking. Profits from these companies were meant to supplement the budget of the PLA. And they did. They had proved vital in buying many of the military's most prized assets, such as the Russian *Sovremenny* class frigate *Vazhny*, and in funding the ongoing cooperation between China and Russia in military aviation. The General Staff Department was Zhao's home. He had spent all his career with it and had a reputation as being one of the cleverest financiers in the military – the result, his colleagues noted, of natural Cantonese cleverness with money, honed by having to live his early life on the run.

From the outset of inner circle discussions about Dragonstrike Zhao had determined that his role would be to make money for the PLA. He knew that knowing in advance when China would strike Vietnam and seize the South China Sea gave him an enormous advantage in global financial markets. It was an operation that would need clearance from the highest level because it was not without risk. It would also need meticulous planning which would have to be kept totally secret. General Zhao's first meeting with the President took place six weeks before Dragonstrike was launched. Then he had explained to the President how financial markets were driven by information and how investors were like herds of cattle on stampede – rushing this way then that, but always staying close together. Information was the key. A correct buy or sell order placed before news of Dragonstrike broke could net an investor many millions in overnight profits.

'Your idea is an excellent one, General,' the President said. 'How much do you need? $50 billion?'

'No, sir, that would be far too much. To make the money I think we are able to make we need to keep our counterparts solvent. $50 billion runs the risk of ruining too many securities companies. Remember Barings?'

'Barings?' The President frowned.

'Nearly ten years ago a pillar of the British financial establishment collapsed, after losing nearly £1 billion. There was someone else, or a group of institutions, on the other side of those transactions who made £1 billion. Financial markets are zero sum, Mr President. Someone wins, someone loses. When we win, someone will lose. But the global financial system could not survive the loss of thirty Barings. It is not part of our war aim to bring down the world's financial system. It would not be good for China. So, we have to be more modest in our aims. We also have to invest in markets where governments are most active – principally the foreign exchange market. The British government lost billions – and traders made it – in 1992 when it tried to keep sterling within the European Monetary System. The amount of profit we could make is still unclear, but I think we could finance a large portion of the cost of the war through some carefully planned deals.'

The President accepted the General's explanation and instructed him to proceed with detailed preparations. He also made sure that Zhao was kept informed of all developments relating to Dragonstrike. With approval obtained Zhao moved quickly. Foremost was a visit to Mr Damian Phillips, Chairman of First China Securities, a Hong Kong investment bank. First China had come to prominence at the fag end of Britain's rule. It was founded by the son of a City of London financier and the son of a rice farmer – the very model of Anglo-Chinese cooperation. Phillips had seen the likely shape of the future well before most. He cultivated the local Chinese tycoons; they liked the attentions of an upper-class Englishman. When it came time to found First China he had a supportive group of local and mainland Chinese businessmen willing to stump up the necessary capital to get the business going. That was in the late 1980s and First China had never looked back. Phillips moved deeper into the Chinese community on both sides of the border. It was on one of his many trips to Beijing before the formal 1997 handover of Hong Kong to China that he met Zhao. Phillips was making a pitch – he hated the term, preferring presentation – to Multitechnologies, the PLA's leading arms trader and emerging domestic conglomerate; Zhao was its president. Phillips was explaining how, with the judicious use of offshore business structures, efficient, and anonymous, trading of currencies could be executed. The General had been impressed enough to risk some of Multitechnologies' hard-earned money playing the markets. Phillips' stratagems proved in practice as good as they had sounded. A relationship germinated. In the ensuing years Phillips saw to it that the relationship blossomed. He paid regular calls on the General, gave lavish parties for him in Hong Kong, and was always careful to leave him with a sure-fire investment tip – for himself, or his company – whenever they met. Slowly business grew. When Multitechnologies decided it wanted to base its international activities in Hong Kong, First China found a Hong Kong Stock Exchange quoted company it could buy. When Multi-Tech (Hong Kong) Holdings wanted to raise capital it was First China that drew up the prospectus and introduced the company to the big pension funds, mutual funds, and unit trusts. And First China wrote research on the company for foreign investors. Soon Multi-Tech (Hong Kong) had a modest following among US and European investors.

General Zhao arrived in Hong Kong five and a half weeks before Dragonstrike was launched. He entered as a civilian. Phillips sent his car to meet him at the airport. Instead of a meeting at First China's downtown head-quarters in Central district on Hong Kong island, the General was driven to Phillips' house on the Peak. It was set well back from the road and was overlooked by no one. Phillips was there to welcome the General personally.

'I'm sorry I couldn't be at the airport to meet you,' Phillips said with ritualistic politeness, 'but you said in your fax that you did not want attention drawn to your visit. Anyway, welcome and how are things in Beijing?'

'Cold,' General Zhao said, somewhat stiffly. 'I don't have much time. As you know I'm returning to Beijing tonight. Shall we get down to business? We at Multitechnologies have decided to broaden our involvement in financial markets. We have decided that we want to trade currencies and oil and that we want you to be our agent. It is vital, Damian, that we and indeed China are in no way connected to the activities I am about to commission you to execute on our behalf. Do you understand . . . ?'

'Completely.'

'Good, well, let's move on, then,' he said.

General Zhao proceeded to outline to Phillips Multi-technologies' plan to play the foreign exchange and oil futures markets. He gave him a list of international banks – mostly second- and third-line institutions keen to increase their involvement in foreign exchange – with whom he would parcel out his currency trades. His purpose was to accumulate US dollars and sell the Japanese yen. To buy dollars he had to sell another currency, and he wanted First China to borrow yen and sell them for dollars. Phillips thought that although the yen had not been particularly strong lately it would have to fall a considerable amount: for an investor to make much money out of selling it he would have to expect the yen to fall sharply so that when the time came to pay back the loans in yen – either prematurely or at maturity – the price of yen would have fallen to well below the initial purchase price. This is precisely what the General appeared to believe. However, he could not be seen doing it. Therefore if on any given day he bought $100 million through one bank, he should sell $20 million through another. His net accumulation would be $80 million, but the market would see him as trader, as a buyer and seller. When Phillips questioned the investment strategy all the General said was that First China would be indemnified. In all he wanted First China to have accumulated by mid-February debts – known as 'yen-shorts' – between $1.5 billion and $2 billion in yen-short positions. With the yen trading around ¥120 to the dollar, these debts should amount to about ¥240bn.

Similarly, though on a smaller scale, First China was to build up a large position in the oil futures markets in London and New York. In the jargon of the financial markets, the General wanted First China to go 'long' of the dollar and oil and 'short' of the yen. The oil trade would, however, have to be for much smaller amounts. Though the markets were large they were purely private markets with little overt government interference. Zhao said he did not want to get involved in problems of counterpart risk. 'The whole operation would be blown apart if we try to collect on a deal and find we have bankrupted Morgan Stanley,' he said, adding with a rare note of levity, 'as pleasurable as such an outcome might be.'

Having explained the purpose of the transactions Zhao then told him how he wanted First China to account for the trades. This entailed parking the proceeds of all transactions in companies registered in the British Virgin Islands (BVI). There were seven banks he was authorized to deal with, but there were fourteen BVI companies for the currency trades. This was to enable the segregation of purchases and sales of foreign currency with each bank, and meant that transactions could be ring-fenced if the prying eyes of regulators should spot something unusual. If one of the banks asked First China who its client was First China could truthfully answer that it was acting for a private investor operating out of the BVI with a company called Bright Future, or the like. If a regulator got wind of something and wanted to freeze assets the fallout would be limited to one company. The oil futures trades would be held in one BVI company, although First China would trade in its own name on the International Petroleum Exchange in London.

As General Zhao sat down on the first morning of Dragonstrike he was in expansive mood. He explained to the President in meticulous detail his contacts with First China and the trades they had been making with the banks over the previous four weeks. He opened the satchel that was resting on his lap and produced a small stack of spreadsheets. These showed each British Virgin Islands company and the size of its position against the yen. Over the period First China had been able to build up for Multitechnologies a short position in the yen of some ¥248 billion. Multitechnologies would make big money if the yen weakened to around to ¥150–¥160 to the dollar. Phillips had accumulated yen at an average cost to Multitechnologies of ¥124. It was currently trading around ¥125 to the dollar.

'Did anyone detect us?' the President asked.

'No, we don't think so,' said Zhao. 'There was a speculative report over the Bloomberg financial wire about First China. Their activity in the foreign exchange market in London had been noted. But Phillips handled it well. The overall operation went without incident. Sir, it is worth remembering that average daily turnover of foreign exchange is $1.2 trillion. In Tokyo alone the dollar/yen and dollar/euro trades are nearly $20 billion. So our activity, especially as we're buyer and seller, largely went unnoticed.'

'Profits?' the President murmured.

'We think the yen could fall by 20 per cent or more during the course of this conflict,' Zhao said. 'That's a ¥45 billion profit when we close the short position. But it's a conservative estimate; the yen could go a lot further, given the Japanese hypersensitivity about oil. The beauty of the deal for us is that when the yen begins to fall we will be one of the only buyers of yen in the market. It won't be at all difficult for us to cover our positions.

'Similarly in the oil market. We have nearly 20 per cent of the April futures contract. When the oil price begins to rise – as I think it will – we stand to do very well indeed.'

The South China Sea

At 1130 the Xinhua (New China) News Agency released a curt statement. 'In regard to the situation in the South China Sea, President Wang Feng drew attention to the Territorial Waters Act promulgated in 1992. Non-military shipping has right of passage in our sovereign territory. Military shipping and nuclear-powered ships must receive Chinese permission to pass through our waters. The sovereign territory is being patrolled by the submarines of the PLA-N.'

The Chinese were not bluffing. They had deployed twenty *Romeo* and *Ming* class submarines. The *Romeo*s were functional but ageing Soviet vessels whose design dated back to the 1960s. The *Ming* was a Chinese-built version. The submarines were loosely positioned in packs of five, organized in semicircles to guard the shipping routes of the South China Sea. Other *Romeo* submarines were in the shallower waters around the Spratly Islands, which although more dangerous were ideal places for the quiet diesel-electric engines. They could only wreak enough destruction to sink a modern warship if the crews of the antiquated submarines could outwit their high-tech enemies. In many modern navies the old diesel-electric design was being wound down for nuclear-powered submarines. China aspired to having a modern military, but knew that for Dragonstrike to succeed the PLA would have to revert to the tactics of barefoot warfare with which it won the civil war in 1949. The men would be familiar with their equipment and know the area of battle. Then with a

World War Two wolf-pack style of operations the naval commanders believed they could safeguard China's sovereignty.

Elsewhere in the South China Sea, three of China's Russian-built *Kilo* (*Granay*) class SSK attack submarines took up positions between Singapore and the Indonesian state of Kalimantan in Borneo; in the Luzon Strait between the northern Philippines and southern Taiwan; and across the Gulf of Thailand between southern Vietnam and the area around the Thai-Malaysian border.

Ten minutes after the Xinhua announcement, two torpedoes were fired by a *Romeo* class submarine off to the west of the Paracel Islands near the Gulf of Tonking, an area which so far had not been drawn into the conflict. A Vietnamese 400-ton *Sonya* class minesweeper/hunter split in two. The impact ignited the fuel tanks. All but one of the sixty crew died in the explosion, which even in daylight could be seen for kilometres around. The survivor lived for three more minutes before being sucked down by the wreckage and drowning.

'We have proved our point,' said Wang Feng so quietly that only the trusted officer from the Central Guard Regiment heard him.

TWO

The South China Sea

Local time: 0300 Monday 19 February 2001
GMT: 1900 Sunday 18 February 2001

Well before dawn on the second day of Operation Dragon-strike China deployed the three Russian-built *Kilo* (*Granay*) class SSK attack submarines at the chokepoints of the South China Sea. Capable of travelling at 17 knots, they were the cream of China's modern diesel-electric submarine fleet, the most exported of all of Russia's submarines. Each vessel had hull-mounted medium-frequency Shark Teeth sonar for both passive and active searches and high-frequency Mouse Roar sonar for active attack. Once the enemy was identified, the hunter-killers of the Chinese navy would track and destroy. Those were the orders of engagement. Each submarine had thirteen officers; many had been trained in Russia in a special programme launched by the PLA-N to put its submariners onto a war footing. Only a few years earlier, Chinese submarines were unable to stay at sea for more than a week at a time because of inadequate training. That problem was now solved.

At 0300 the Xinhua (New China) News Agency released a statement:

> The Chinese government hereby gives notice that all international shipping is banned from the area commonly known as the South China Sea (longitude 110° to 120° east of Greenwich and 5° to 22° of north latitude) until further notice.
>
> The People's Navy and Air Force are patrolling the South (China) Sea and will prevent all ships from entering this exclusion zone. International airlines are

also warned not to overfly the area. Ships will be prevented from entering the sea through the Bashi Channel and the Luzon Strait, as well as through the Mindoro Strait and the Balabac Strait. Although the Straits of Malacca fall outside Chinese sovereign waters, international shipping companies are advised to avoid these straits as shipping leaving them will not be permitted to enter the South Sea.

The State Council said that China's armed forces would enforce the nation's sovereignty in the South Sea and called on all fair-minded and peace-loving nations in the region to recognize the justness of China's claim. The State Council said it was not the Chinese government's intention to restrict access to the South Sea indefinitely and that shipping lanes would be reopened in due course.

The South China Sea

The Philippine Navy *Whidbey Island* class dock-landing ship *Cagayan de Oro* and the supporting corvette *Cebu* stopped 5 nautical miles off Mischief Reef, far enough to be out of range of Chinese heavy machine-gun fire. The moon dipped in and out of cloud cover. Four fibreglass rigid raiding craft, carrying thirty-six Marines, left the safety of the ship and moved off quietly towards the reef. Their destination was a grey metal and wooden structure which had been built by occupying Chinese troops in 1995 claiming they were shelters for fishermen.

The Marines were the most highly trained and motivated men in the Philippine military. Their orders were to go in under darkness, establish a foothold on the island, and observe enemy movement before being reinforced. A heli-borne platoon and more amphibious troops would come in at dawn to reclaim the territory. The Marines landed quietly among the rocks. Using dead ground, where they couldn't be seen from the main building, they found their positions and reported no enemy movement. The windows of the building were without glass. Polythene flapped in the frames, some of it torn by the strong winds. The whole place looked battered and weather-beaten, apart from the Chinese flag which flew pristine from a turret at the top of the building. There were no lights, no sign of life at all. An hour later, in that hazy period when the tropical daylight arrived, a Sikorsky Sea Stallion troop-carrying helicopter took off from the *Cagayan de Oro*.

More raiding craft sped from the ship, this time with

engines at full throttle. Four American-built F5A fighter aircraft screamed overhead, coming in from their base on Palawan Island 130 kilometres away. The F5As descended low over the structure, then two broke away from the formation and climbed high to give cover to the approaching Marines.

The Sikorsky was directed in by the troops already there, who had set up three fields of interlocking fire to cover the Marines now arriving. Two at a time fast-roped down from the helicopter. Others from the raiding craft ran up to predetermined assault positions. They had expected to have secured the whole reef, torn down the enemy's colours, and replaced it with the Philippine national flag within ten minutes.

The Marine corporal led his men forward. There was enough light to see the hazards among the rocks. Soon they were crouched up against the walls. Using mirrors they covertly looked through the windows, satisfying themselves that the structure had been abandoned. But this was a dangerous mission. Even several of the most highly skilled men hadn't seen action of this kind before. They continued with caution according to their training. They threw hand grenades through the windows and waited for the deafening noise to settle before bursting through the main door, firing their M-16 automatic rifles. The room was empty. They hung Philippine ensigns from the two windows nearest the door to indicate to the covering troops outside that those rooms were cleared. The corporal reported back on the radio the signs of habitation. A Chinese magazine, exalting the leadership of President Wang; a PLA cookbook; a printed canvas board for playing Chinese chess, crumpled and torn on the floor. The Marine corporal moved towards the next room.

Suddenly, a huge explosion tore through the building. The victim-initiated booby trap killed the corporal and three of his men instantly. Seconds later, Chinese Marines set off remote-control explosions in the central area of dead ground where the Philippine troops had based themselves. Seven Filipinos died. Twelve were injured. The Sikorsky pilot, flying low with the sun just rising behind him, spotted the Chinese position and fired his 12.7mm machine-gun. The bullets tore apart the timber and hit drums of fuel. The Chinese flag disappeared in an inferno of fire. Flames leapt up the timbers, but were slowed by the dampness which hung over the whole reef. The helicopter's heavy machine-gun continued to rip through the building. Then as the Sikorsky turned to line up on another target it exploded in a shattering, roaring fireball.

The Chinese soldier who fired the ancient shoulder-launched SA-7 surface-to-air missile died before the first pieces of debris from the Sikorsky hit the water. A hail of gunfire from the Philippine Marines ripped him to shreds. The Chinese returned fire. But the Marine lieutenant had chosen their cover well. Bullets sparked off the rocks around them, but harmlessly shot off into the water. They had direct lines of fire to the two main entrances to the structures, where the enemy was now identified. Now reinforcements came, the reserve platoons from the *Cagayan de Oro*, heading at full speed towards the battle. The Philippine F5s gave cover with cannon fire. Then six Chinese Su-27s attacked out of the sun. Each fired air-to-air missiles and although some missed or failed to detonate, the Philippine aircraft fled or were destroyed. The Su-27s split into two formations. Three, armed with anti-ship missiles, climbed steeply and flew back over the reef. Their radar-homing missiles hit the troop carrier amidships near the centre of the radar, passing through bulkheads before their relatively small warheads detonated, causing fires deep inside the vessel, which lost propulsion. The second formation attacked the men in the raiding craft with short bursts of cannon fire. The *Cagayan de Oro* was listing. One of the Su-27s had conventional bombs with short delay fuses, and ran in along the length of the ship, which was stationary in the water and defenceless. Two bombs hit the damaged ship and the larger warheads broke her back and she sank quickly. The last message from the captain said: 'Mischief Reef and all vessels lost.'

The Philippine Marine lieutenant waved the white flag of surrender. As he stood up from behind his cover, the Chinese troops held their fire. For the next half-hour, both Chinese and Philippine troops helped the other Marines up the rock faces. The field medical packs could do little to help the wounded. The final count was 152 Philippine servicemen dead and 7 injured. The only Chinese to die was the man who downed the Sikorsky.

A Xinhua (New China) News Agency announcement said: 'Sixteen Philippine military personnel whose ship sank in heavy weather have been rescued by the People's Liberation Army on the Nansha Islands. They will be returned to their units as soon as possible. Because of the swift and courageous action of Chinese troops, there was no loss of life.'

Hanoi, Vietnam

Unusually for the season, low rain clouds hung over most of northern Vietnam. The Chinese pilots came in with their Israeli Harpy V radar sensors activated. They were to destroy Vietnamese air-defence installations around the northern port city of Haiphong. Even in the appalling weather the sensors picked them up easily. The aircraft fired 30 kilogram fragmentation warhead missiles, guided onto the active radar signal, until they hit and destroyed. Then the skies over Haiphong were free for the city to come under attack. But it was too late to stop the alert. The Vietnamese early warning system had picked up the movements as soon as the Chinese aircraft had taken off from their base on Hainan Island.

Yet as the Vietnamese cities were about to come under attack, President Nguyen Van Tai prepared for a television interview. His country couldn't match China for weight of numbers, but it could in the skills of international diplomacy. During his time as Chairman of the National People's Congress in the nineties he had invited international observers to witness village and municipal elections. The State Department described them as a significant step towards creating a democratic Vietnam. CNN spotted him as a president in waiting. He was flown to their head-quarters in Atlanta as part of a policy to gain access to aspiring future world leaders. He was given a day-long course on how to handle the media, and later remarked that it had been the most useful six hours of his life. He was taught to sit in a fixed, and not a swivel chair; to keep his eyes on the interviewer; never to say anything in the studio which was not on the record; to make only one, at the most two points and to say them in twelve seconds; to watch the clock if he wanted the last word; to be on first-name terms with his interviewer; never to lose his temper. They also told him to pick his audience and venue. That's why Nguyen Van Tai had turned down CNN tonight. His message was to the people of France.

Rain swept across the boulevards of Hanoi. It streaked down the façades of the magnificent colonial buildings, many of which even now served as government offices. But Nguyen Van Tai had chosen the French-owned Metropole Hotel for the interview. He did not want the cameras to show the still entrenched bric-a-brac of the Communist regime which lingered in the corridors of the Imperial Palace. His underemployed staff, asleep with cooling jars of tea at their desks, would not have cultivated the image of an economic tiger on the brink of democratic government. Vietnam was not, but images were all-important.

The Vietnamese government paid for the suite. Listening devices, installed at the time of renovation, were activated. Nguyen Van Tai had insisted in going live into a rolling news late-night current affairs programme. As the microphone was clipped to his lapel, the producer revealed that the Chinese Ambassador to Paris would also be part of the discussion. Tai nodded. Vietnamese agents in Paris had already told him.

Then suddenly, only minutes before airtime, Nguyen Van Tai unclipped his microphone and excused himself to an adjoining room where his military intelligence chief was on a scrambled line to a colonel at the military headquarters in Hanoi. The Chinese attacks were expected to begin within the next five minutes. The aircraft were heading towards the northern port of Haiphong and the commercial capital Ho Chi Minh City in the south.

Nguyen Van Tai returned to his chair and allowed the Chinese Ambassador to speak first. The diplomat's French was imperfect. He stuttered and appeared to be unaware of the details of the Chinese military operation. Nguyen's turn came just as the first Chinese H-6 fighter-bombers broke through the clouds over Haiphong.

'Mr President, China says you started this conflict,' said the presenter in Paris. 'What is your response to that?'

'We and our ASEAN allies (that's Singapore, Indonesia, Thailand, Brunei, Malaysia, Myanmar, Cambodia, Laos, and the Philippines) have known about the Chinese claim to the South China Sea for some time. The Ambassador, I'm afraid, is telling the world nothing new. What he has failed to mention is the 1994 pledge by the then Chinese Prime Minister, Li Peng, that all differences would be settled peacefully. More to the point, China completely ignores the diplomatic note that passed between us as late as 26th of December last year. May I remind you of what that note said? We took the unusual step of publishing it in full yesterday. That note said "the two sides should refrain from the use of force to settle disputes and avoid any clashes that may aggravate the situation".

'Now China has broken that pledge in a most horrible and bloody way. The Ambassador has said we have illegally occupied reefs. He accuses our troops of violating the border area. I'm not going to answer those accusations because if I do your viewers will be asked to judge who's telling the truth and who isn't. The key element, which we all know to be true, is that French citizens have been killed by Chinese pilots. Vietnamese and other nationalities are also victims. We are not discussing the occupation of reefs. We are discussing the mass murder of civilians by the Chinese government.'

The anchor broke in: 'You talk about your ASEAN allies.

Are you convinced that they will support you against China?'

'That is what ASEAN has been about ever since its inception. The 1972 proclamation of South-East Asia as a zone of peace stated just that. Written into the articles of ASEAN is the pledge that no state may stand by and watch the dismemberment of another by a foreign power. In Asia we have a problem with short-termism. We have always put money ahead of culture and civilization, which is why we were so easily colonized in the nineteenth century.'

'So you are saying that—'

'Please let me finish, because it is important,' interrupted the Vietnamese President. 'My fellow leaders in ASEAN are right now under great pressure from the overseas Chinese businessmen who have an extraordinary control over the economies of their countries. For example, 10 per cent of the population of Thailand is Chinese. Yet Chinese business accounts for 90 per cent of the wealthiest families. It is the same throughout South-East Asia. These are the families who can coax China into change, who can bring pressure for reform. If they were united they could cripple the Chinese economy by freezing their investment. I urge them to act as we in Vietnam did with France and America. We fought and won. We sacrificed and now we are friends with both countries on equal terms. Our pride is high. Never has Vietnam put profits before its independence and freedom.'

'Do you welcome the support from the French government?'

'We can't win a war with China. We welcome support from whoever offers.'

'And from the Americans with whom you fought so bitterly less than forty years ago?'

'Before that we fought France. And you are invited back.

Our founding father Ho Chi Minh offered Cam Ranh Bay to the Americans in 1945. If they had taken it then perhaps there would have been no war.'

'Is it still on offer?'

'We have now seen that if a responsible superpower weakens in East Asia an irresponsible one moves in. And I would say this to the Ambassador in your studio. We might have fought America and France, but our soldiers have never been used to murdering their fellow countrymen – unlike those in China.'

The anchor turned to the Chinese Ambassador for a response.

'The Chinese nation has a history of five thousand years and has a national characteristic of strong self-respect,' he said. 'Over the past hundred-odd years, the Chinese nation has had its fill of aggression and devastation by Western foreign powers. We therefore highly treasure our independence and sovereignty.'

While the Ambassador struggled with his rhetoric, the head of Vietnamese security came into the room and slipped Nguyen Van Tai a piece of paper. The President read it, and then interrupted the Ambassador. His voice was transmitting while the cameras remained for a few seconds on the Ambassador's face. 'I am not sure what point the Ambassador is making, but I have been given some devastating news.'

'Go on,' prompted the anchor.

'Right now, Chinese attack aircraft are in action over civilian areas in our northern port city of Haiphong and Ho Chi Minh City, better known to many of you as Saigon. One of the Chinese missiles landed on the roof of the Rex Hotel. There were guests having breakfast. Many are dead. Residential areas in Haiphong have been attacked, mainly near the port. An apartment block, where port workers and their families live, has collapsed. Again, it was early morning. Many people were at home. Merchant ships have been sunk in Haiphong, but that appears irrelevant against the huge loss of life.'

Kabuto-cho Financial District, Tokyo

Local time: 0745 Monday 19 February 2001
GMT: 2245 Sunday 18 February 2001

It was still dark when the driver picked Kobayashi up and
handed him copies of the *Nihon Keizai (Nikkei) Shimbun*,
the financial newspaper, and the *Yomiuri Shimbun*, a
general news broadsheet. Kobayashi was the head of strategy and trading at Nomura Securities – Japan's, and the
world's, biggest dealer in shares and bonds. He looked first
at the *Yomiuri Shimbun*. It was close to Prime Minister
Hyashi's faction in the Democratic Party and in Japan, after
all, politics was business. Hidei Kobayashi's driver took the
same route every morning, and this morning was no
exception. After turning into Aoyama-dori Kobayashi's car
made its way east, towards the Imperial Palace and beyond
that Kabuto-cho. But this morning something was different. Along the way Kobayashi could not help but notice
the queues forming at gas stations. The Chinese attack on
Cam Ranh Bay had dominated the television news bulletins
the night before and the broadcasts that morning were
already full of the naval blockade of the South China Sea
and the attack on Haiphong and Ho Chi Minh City. The
Japanese motorists, he reflected, were taking no chances.

The sky was lightening with the approaching dawn as
he reached the Imperial Palace and it was serene. The moat
surrounding it was like a mirror reflecting perfectly the
massive cedars and cypresses planted to keep prying eyes
from the Imperial family. At the corner of Hakumi-dori
and Hibiya-dori – still dominated by the Dai-ichi Mutual
Life Insurance Company building from where the American General Douglas MacArthur ruled Japan after World

War II – he turned north along Hibiya-dori. This is the Marunouchi district of town where 'old money' corporate Japan has its headquarters. The great houses of Mitsui, Mitsubishi, and Sumitomo are headquartered here, as are some of the leading banks such as the Industrial Bank of Japan. Since the seventeenth century, when the Shogun Ieasu Tokugawa made Edo his capital, the commercial and financial heart of Tokyo had been to the east of and beyond the Imperial Palace. In the aftermath of the firebombing of Tokyo more than sixty years before Tokyo's owners had rebuilt the city, or at least this part, in the image of its destroyers. Marunouchi was one of the most Western-looking areas of the city. The streets were wide and regular, the buildings square and squat. On the street in some parts of Marunouchi, like the fashionable Ginza area, it felt almost Parisian. Small, immaculately manicured and boxed trees lined streets full of high-priced boutiques and smart coffee shops.

It was a glorious winter's morning: cold and crisp. It was also clear and that meant the sun would shine today. As Kobayashi surveyed the newspapers the headlines were universally gloomy. The *Nikkei*'s splash said it all: *Minami umi shokku!* it trumpeted. 'South Sea shock', indeed. China's military action the day before was sure to send share prices lower on the Tokyo Stock Exchange. The yen would come under pressure and the prices of government bonds would fall, which meant that interest rates would rise. Other Asian stock markets would not be immune from this. Kobayashi's job was to profit from this mess or, at the very least, minimize the losses to his firm. A kilometre or so north his driver turned left into Eitai-dori. As they crossed Sotobori-dori Kobayashi looked up, noticing the pre-war façade of the Bank of Japan, one of the few surviving buildings of the American firebombing. The Bank would have its work cut out for it today, he thought. The car turned north into Chuo-dori and drove toward Nihon-bashi, the graceful old two-arched bridge from where all distances from Tokyo are measured, and the headquarters of Nomura nearby. An item in the *Yomiuri* caught his eye. It was a commentary by Professor Hiroshi Sato, a foreign policy adviser to Prime Minister Hyashi. Professor Sato said he thought Japan could build something new from the current adversity. 'For too long we have been prepared to hide behind others' skirts. We have legitimate national interests and we should assert them with whatever means we have at our disposal.'

Briefing

Oil (I)

At the morning meeting of Kobayashi's strategy and trading team the only topic of discussion was the Chinese seizure of the South China Sea. Few could see any good coming from it for Japan. The nation's dependency on foreign energy supplies had been well canvassed in the press. Only 14 per cent of Japan's total electricity supply was generated by facilities totally within the nation's control – nuclear and hydroelectric power. The remaining 86 per cent was from oil-, coal-, or gas-fired power stations whose raw-material inputs were imported. The vast majority of those imports – more than 90 per cent – had to transit the South China Sea. The discussion turned to the effect a possible interruption to supply or a prolonged oil-price rise would have on Japan. An interruption to supply was not seen as likely. If international shipping was barred from the South China Sea then the ships from the Persian Gulf and from Australia could travel up the east coast of the Philippine islands. This would add four to five days' extra sailing time which, while unsettling, was well within acceptable limits given the country's stockpiles of oil. It would, however, raise the price of oil on a c.i.f. (cost, insurance, and freight) basis. That would impact on domestic gasoline prices. The bigger price effect, however, was judged to come from the reaction of international oil markets to the incidents in the South China Sea.

Oil was not the only factor. Many Japanese companies were involved in the Chinese economy. In the early years of China's opening the Beijing authorities, suspicious of outside influences, had encouraged foreign investors to seek local partners and with them form joint venture companies. Latterly however China had allowed foreign companies to set up businesses on their own, without local partners. In general, the companies more knowledgeable about doing business in China preferred these 'stand-alone' arrangements. Going it alone was not cost-free but it was a risk many took because management control rested firmly in the hands of the investor and profits did not have to be shared with local investors. A good, and now vulnerable, example of this was Matsushita Electric Company, best known for its National range of consumer electronics. It had invested heavily in China, especially in the north-east which was once called Manchuria or, when the Japanese controlled it, Manchuko. It was the north-east port of Dalian where Matsushita made its biggest investment – $180 million to produce video recorders. For the Chinese, the Japanese investment was rich with a bitter-sweet significance. This was the trading region which Japan invaded and seized from the crippled Nationalist government in the 1930s. Earlier, however, the Japanese had defeated the Russian Pacific fleet, and showed the world that Asians could fight and win against a European superpower. But Matsushita's managers also knew that China was a country of regions where local priorities often overrode national aspirations. So it spread its largesse up and down the country. In Canton (now called Guangzhou) it had invested $35 million in a plant to manufacture electric shavers, and $28 million in electrical appliances like rice cookers; in Beijing, it invested $28 million in telephone exchange relays. The not wholly unsurprising view of the meeting was that Matsushita was sure to be hit. Kobayashi observed that Matsushita was a little like Boeing, the US aerospace company. Both had made large investments in China and both had hitched their fortunes to the success of China's modernization programme.

Even more vulnerable to selling pressure would be some large firms, like Nippon Oil, which had big investments in the South China Sea itself and was a 30 per cent shareholder of the Discovery 1 oilfield in the Paracels. This placed Nomura in a tricky position. As Nippon Oil's broker, it was honour bound not to sell the company's shares. Years ago it had floated Nippon Oil's shares on the Tokyo Stock Exchange and was the company's agent in all dealings. And the relationship, now spanning thirty years, went deeper. Whenever Nippon Oil wanted to raise fresh capital for expansion Nomura advised on the best form of financing. Indeed, Nomura arranged the ¥30 billion loan which Nippon Oil issued to fund its share of Discovery 1's development. Nomura was the biggest securities company in Japan, with a 40 per cent share of turnover on the Tokyo Stock Exchange. But only 25 per cent was executed in Nomura's name. The rest was handled by subsidiary firms which traded under different names. Despite the high-tech façade, Tokyo was not like London and Wall Street. Honour, loyalty, and stamina created the Shoguns of Kabuto-cho. This was capitalism, Japanese-style. It worked. It had created the undisputed economic leader of Asia in less than a generation. But there was no way Kobayashi could be seen to be selling Nippon Oil's shares. To do so would be to tear the soul out of Japan's banking tradition. He also had to act within the best interests of his own noble institution. Kobayashi instructed a Nomura subsidiary to handle the Nomura *sell* orders, while Nomura in its own name would execute any *buy* orders that might come the firm's way. This way Nomura would be seen to be supporting Nippon Oil.

And who might these sellers be? They fell into two groups: retail and professional. 'Retail' was market jargon for household investors. These were the same people Kobayashi had seen queuing for petrol on his way to work and they were invariably women and they were powerful. Retail investors were responsible for 23 per cent of the Tokyo market's turnover. The Japanese housewife was every bit as determined as her 'salariman' husband. She managed the household finances, as is customary in East Asia, and was an experienced stock market investor. Having filled up the family car with petrol the next thing the formidable Mrs Suzukis of Japan would do was call their broker with a view to selling. Bitter experience had taught Kobayashi that the firm could not stand in the way of these women. It was best to redirect their funds elsewhere. With the yen under pressure, the dollar was the place to be.

Then there were the professionals. These were the big Japanese trust and investment companies that managed pension funds. They were huge and powerful but paradoxically impotent. They were so big that changing investment direction was akin to the difficulties the captain of a supertanker faced in attempting a U-turn. It could be done, but it required time and a lot of sea to execute. The professionals were to a large extent locked in. They could adjust their holdings at the margin, but not overall. They were at the mercy of the 'hedge funds'. These were the money managers who moved hundreds of millions of dollars in an instant from one end of the world to the other and back again. They placed big bets on shares, commodities, bonds, and currencies, and often won, and lost, spectacularly. But Kobayashi's real concern was the US mutual funds. Their power had become awesome. During the 1990s they became the preferred means for US citizens to save. By the end of 1995 their total value was $1.25 trillion. Since then they had grown, on average, by 10 per cent a year, and on the eve of Dragonstrike US mutual-fund managers controlled some $2.6 trillion of assets. Their asset base was staggering and they had a portion of it invested in Asia. But this was mobile money. Mutual-fund managers were notorious for being driven by the requirement to make short-term gains. Here today, gone tomorrow, their presence in Asia's stock markets had added considerably to volatility in share prices. A telephone call and an investor in Kansas could sell Hong Kong and buy US Treasury bills; sell Europe and buy Australia. Individual transactions, however, did not count when compared to the decisions of investment managers. Kobayashi knew from the business Nomura had seen coming in overnight that the mutuals – for all their belief in the Pacific Century – were about to repatriate their funds. And the decision the managers had taken on the Sunday was to sell.

Malacangang Presidential Palace, Manila

The Private Secretary to the Philippine President, Miguel Luzong, opened the high teak double doors to the conference room without knocking. As he walked across the room the President's concentration was distracted towards the news he was about to receive. The conversation around the table faded, then quietened while the man who used to command the Philippine Armed Forces was told about Mischief Reef.

'This has just happened, sir,' said the Private Secretary.

Luzong addressed the meeting of ministers and businessmen. 'Gentlemen, our troops have met resistance in their attempt to recover Mischief Reef and we have lost contact. We are sending reinforcements.'

The powerful Mayor of Manila, Hernesto Lim, a Chinese-Filipino, replied quickly. 'Don't, Mr President. Speaking for the overseas Chinese community, we ask you to back off. If we send reinforcements, they'll send reinforcements. We cannot hold that territory, nor for any reason except national pride do we want to.'

'National pride is not an unimportant sentiment, Hernesto,' Luzong countered.

'It is a disease which is afflicting the Chinese government at the moment and might well destroy it. This country suffered from the disease of dictatorship for twenty years. It made us the sick man of Asia. While Korea, Taiwan, Malaysia, and Thailand became rich, the Philippines became a joke. Mr President, this South China Sea conflict is not one for us. It is for America, China, and Japan. If we take sides, like we did during the Cold War, our national morale will be destroyed again. We will be accused of being an American puppet. Let us take a lead from Malaysia. They have abandoned the Mariveles, Ardasier, and Swallow Reefs, even their airbase at Terumbi Layang-layang. Forget about Mischief Reef. We rid ourselves of the Americans in 1992. We restored democracy. We are building the foundations of a Philippine heritage of which we can be proud. Our economy, much of which is interlinked to the Chinese communities throughout the world, is growing strong. We fought the Cold War while our ASEAN neighbours kept a low profile and became rich. If another global conflict is approaching, let us not get involved. Let us concentrate on building hospitals, roads, airports, ports, power stations, schools, and houses for our people. That, sir, is where our duty as leaders of the country lies.'

'And we let China take over the South China Sea?' prompted Luzong.

'What does it matter? They will allow trade.'

'My generals are restless.'

'Then they should pick a battle that they can win. If they can't defeat the Muslim terrorists in the south, they shouldn't pick a fight with the People's Liberation Army.'

Without calling for a vote, the President looked at each man around the room, then nodded to his Private Secretary to call off the recovery of Mischief Reef.

The White House, Washington, DC

Twenty-four hours after their first meeting, James Bradlay, the American President, was alone with Martin Weinstein, his National Security Adviser. The first pictures of the bombing of Ho Chi Minh City were being broadcast on CNN. The correspondent speculated that it had been targeted because it was a favourite winter retreat for the Vietnamese cabinet.

'It's to prove their long-range attack capability,' Weinstein said quietly. 'Saigon is 500 kilometres from Yulin, their southernmost airbase. It's evidence of their in-flight refuelling capabilities, which gives them at least thirty minutes to attack, turn, and go back. We call it loiter time.'

The appeal by Nguyen Van Tai, dubbed and translated, was run over the scenes of devastation on the roof of the Rex Hotel. An American woman, with blood streaming down her side, carried a child wrapped in a tablecloth away from the debris.

'So what have you got for me, Marty?'

The NSA outlined America's immediate military capability.

The 100,000 tonne nuclear-powered aircraft carrier USS *Harry S. Truman* had been redirected from the Sea of Japan towards the Chinese blockade. No public announcement would be made yet. She could be on the edge of the South China Sea within twenty-four hours. She was carrying 20 F-14 Tomcat fighters, 36 F/A-18 Hornet fighter-bombers, 4 EA-6B Prowler electronics countermeasures aircraft,

4 E-2C Hawkeye early warning aircraft, 6 S-3A Viking submarine hunters, and 8 SH-3 Seahawk rescue helicopters.

She led a formidable battle group which once within the South China Sea could project power throughout. It comprised the brand-new 9,217 ton *Arleigh Burke* class guided-missile destroyer USS *Oscar Austin*, commissioned only a year earlier, carrying Harpoon anti-ship missiles, anti-submarine missile torpedoes (ASROC), and Mk50 torpedoes; the 4,100 ton *Oliver Hazard Perry* class guided-missile frigate USS *Ford*, with similar weaponry; the 8,040 ton *Spruance* class destroyer USS *Hayler*, whose armaments included Tomahawk long-range land-attack and anti-ship cruise missiles and Sea Sparrow anti-aircraft missiles; the *Kilauea* class ammunition ship USS *Shasta*; the Jumboized *Cimarron* class oiler USS *Willamette*; and the 9,466 ton *Ticonderoga* class guided-missile Aegis cruisers USS *Port Royal* and USS *Vella Gulf*. They carried Tomahawks, Harpoons, standard surface-to-air missiles, ASROC, and Mk32, Mk46, and Mk50 torpedoes. Three submarines accompanied the group, the *Los Angeles* class USS *Cheyenne*, *Columbia*, and *Boise*.

Another American battle group was led by the aircraft carrier USS *Nimitz*, which because of her age was confined to the East Asia region. Joining her was the *Tarawa* class amphibious assault ship USS *Peleliu*. With 1,600 Marines on board, she had been on joint training exercise for international disaster relief with Philippine Marines, and was heading back to Hawaii when ordered to stay with the *Nimitz*. The battle group was holding its position in the Sulu Sea near the Cagayan Islands between Negros and Palawan. It was only eight hours' sailing time from the South China Sea.

'Are you telling me, Marty, we could just go in there and take back the South China Sea and the islands?' asked Bradlay.

'Yes and no, Mr President,' Weinstein replied. 'The Chinese might have a lousy army, navy, and air force. But when it comes to missiles you could say they are getting close to us. You only need one missile to get through the net to reap destruction. The *Bunker Hill* is there to help our own IMINT operations. She can watch any missile from its launch up through the atmosphere and down again to target. So the Chinese could up the stakes and threaten to send a missile into Vietnam or something if we move against them.'

'And we couldn't shoot it down?'

'There would be no guarantee. And there's one other thing.'

'Go on.'

'We have the same problem as China. We could take the South China Sea, but we couldn't hold it. The best damn navy in the world is simply not powerful enough. Our armed forces are suffering from the Base Plan implemented in 1992 by the then Chairman of the Joint Chiefs of Staff General Colin Powell. Our navy ships have been cut from 443 to 340; our carrier battle groups from 14 to 12; our air force fighter wings from 16 to 13. The armed forces have been cut and cut, yet our commitments are increasing.'

'But we can still send four more carrier groups to the South China Sea.'

'Again, Mr President, yes and no. We maintain 35 operational deployments around the world. There's 160,000 American service personnel out there in jobs ranging from the 35,000 on the Korean Peninsula to 2,000 in Burundi. They're costing money. Burundi is $120 million. The processing of Caribbean refugees at the Guantanamo base in Cuba by 1,100 soldiers is costing $250 million a year. Unforeseen flare-ups with Iraq and Libya amounted to $550 million. It's little bits here and there which mount up and get noticed by Congress. We have to go cap in hand every time we want to set up another operation.

'The current configuration of our armed forces is precisely for these multilateral operations and has been since the 1990s, when we went into post-Cold War deployment. But the reduction has meant that we are incapable of fighting two regional conflicts at once. One example is the new C-17 transport plane. Our operations mean the airlifting of thousands of troops very quickly. In this crisis, they would probably go to Vietnam or we could persuade the Philippines to let us back in. Our C-17 airlift fleet is thirty aircraft short because they haven't come off the production line yet. America's ability to fight two major regional conflicts will remain sharply limited until 2006.'

'I'm hearing you, Marty, but we've only got one conflict right now, in the South China Sea.'

'That's this week, Mr President.'

The two men were silent for a moment, watching the pictures of the bombing in Haiphong. Fire and black smoke leapt out from an apartment block. Ships listed, ablaze, in the harbour.

'Who's on our side, then?' Bradlay asked.

'Western Europe. Most of them will pontificate. But we can rely on France and Britain. Japan's an ally. But do we want it to get militarily involved? Shades of World War II and all that. India will stay neutral and privately back us. India's wary of China and of Pakistan. They like us around. Don't count on Pakistan. They've been thick with China. Their Karakoram-8 jet trainer, Khalid tank, HJ-8 anti-tank missiles, and Anza-2 surface-to-air missile are all based on Chinese design and technology. Burma's military is kitted out and bankrolled by the PLA. The rest of South-East Asia wants to make money. If America looks like jeopardizing that, they won't support us. Africa doesn't matter.'

'What about the Russians?' asked the President.

'They have teams of engineers right now down on Hainan Island, working on the Su-27s at Yulin, the *Kilo*s at the Sanya submarine base next door, and whatever else they've sold to China at Zhanjiang, the headquarters of the South Sea Fleet. On top of that, their scientists are helping with Chinese missile programmes. Without Russian cooperation, sir, we should be a lot better placed to go to war with the Chinese.'

The Tokyo Stock Exchange

Local time: 0900 Monday 19 February
GMT: 2400 Sunday 18 February 2001

The morning trading session, which in Tokyo lasts from 9.00 until 11.00, was overactive, with 200 million shares trading. But what was worrying was the scale of the fall in share prices in the Nikkei index of 225 leading Japanese stocks led by Matsushita, Nippon Oil, and a raft of blue-chip Japanese companies. The index had only sailed through the 40,000 barrier at the end of January, and it ended the morning more than 400 points, or more than 1 per cent, lower, at 39,700. More worrying still was the behaviour of the yen. It had been trading in a narrow band of ¥120 to ¥125 to the US dollar, but in the Tokyo morning session it had fallen ¥6.2 to ¥143.6 – a 4 per cent depreciation. The Bank of Japan was frantically selling dollars for yen, but dollars were what the market wanted to buy . . . except First China. As investors dumped the yen it began to calculate the value of its short-yen position. First China, with General Zhao's backing, had borrowed ¥248 billion and immediately sold it forward. For the bet to pay off, the spot yen rate against the dollar – the rate at which people deal minute to minute during the day – would have to weaken from the ¥124 average rate at which First China borrowed. The collapse in the yen was just what Phillips and Zhao had predicted. Trading through the day in Tokyo it managed to achieve an overall profit for General Zhao of 10.8 per cent or the equivalent of $181.95 million. But Damian Phillips was only a keen spectator on Monday. He knew the yen had far further to fall.

Briefing

Hong Kong

In 2001 the countries of South-East Asia possessed sizeable minorities of ethnic Chinese. Tens of millions had fled their country's civil wars, tumults, and famines to far-flung corners of the Earth. They built the railways in Canada, America, and Australia and stayed on to pan for gold and set up restaurants and business, but most emigrated to the countries bordering the South China Sea. In these countries their business acumen enabled them to build formidable money empires which dwarfed those of the generally less entrepreneurial native populations. Small in number, these overseas Chinese possessed great financial power. In Indonesia just 3.5 per cent of the population were ethnic Chinese yet they controlled 80 per cent of the assets of the top 300 companies. This pattern of economic dominance was repeated throughout the region. In the Philippines the ethnic Chinese represented 2 per cent of the population and controlled up to 60 per cent of the stock market; in Thailand, about 10 per cent of the population and 80 per cent of the stock market. Hong Kong was the point at which the overseas Chinese met the mainlanders. While they loathed the Communist system which had compelled many of them to flee China, their adherence to the teachings of the ancient Chinese sage Confucius and their yearning for China had not diminished. Importantly, neither were their links to the ancestral villages of their ancestors' birth completely severed. Chinese businessmen from Indonesia, Malaysia, Singapore, and the Philippines had traditionally used Hong Kong as the base for the 'offshore' wealth. Now it had become the beachhead for their commercial thrust into China and the place where they felt most comfortable wining and dining their mainland business partners and contacts.

Since the mainland takeover of Hong Kong on 1 July 1997 little appeared to have changed. Hong Kong still retained its astonishingly modern skyline. Towers of glass and steel, designed by some of the world's leading monument builders to the rich, were set dramatically against the steeply rising north face of Victoria Peak. To the tourist who stopped over for three days on his way to Australia, or before or after visiting China, Hong Kong appeared to be business as usual. The Stanley market still offered value with its cheap T-shirts and fake Ming porcelain, the jade market in Kowloon still did a lively trade, and, to the amazement of many (especially given China's tough laws on the export of antiquities) it was still possible to buy a horse from the Tang Dynasty (AD 618–907) in the antique shops along Hollywood Road in Central. But below the surface, the new tougher sovereign exercised power in place of its benign and neglectful predecessor. China observed the outward forms of civic life bequeathed by the British. Beijing had no need to send down officials from the capital to rule Hong Kong; through inducement they saw to it that their chosen people found success in elections to the local parliament, or in appointments to the top jobs in government, academe, and the media. The worst time for the local administrators was the winter. Since the takeover Hong Kong had become a popular place for the more elderly military and Party leaders to spend the harshest months of the northern Chinese winter. A vast estate on the south-east of the island at Chum Hum Kok – which the British had used to spy on China – had been converted into a resort for the leadership. The local Cantonese referred to the place as the 'retirement village'. But it was a

whispered joke. A telephone call from any of the thirty or
so senior leaders ensconced at the resort and a livelihood,
though rarely a life, could be lost. Outside the random
interventions of the elderly, Beijing's control was exercised
at a weekly meeting between Hong Kong's Chief Executive,
as the post-colonial governor was styled, and Beijing's
senior representative in the 'Special Administrative Region',
as the colony was now known. A curl of the Beijing
representative's lip or a flicker of his eyebrow was sufficient
to indicate to the Chief Executive whether his choice for,
say, the chairman of the hospital authority or monetary
authority was likely to find favour in Beijing.

The media marched to the beat of the same drum. The
Communist Party had been assiduous in infiltrating trusted
agents into the main Chinese language and English-
language newspapers and broadcast organizations.
Together with the Party's stranglehold on the universities,
the takeover of the media was one of the most successful
of its operations in Hong Kong, all the more for being
largely unnoticed. The people who rose to the top in Hong
Kong's news media after 1997 were well-educated and
articulate presenters of China's point of view. They ensured
media gave full and positive coverage to the Chinese
government's plans for the country's economic development. That morning the newspapers carried in full China's
reasons for seizing the South China Sea. China was simply
making *de jure* what had always been its *de facto* sovereignty
over the South China Sea. Its pre-emptive strike against
Vietnam was prudent, though the consequent casualties on
both sides were regrettable. The newspapers recounted
how generous Hong Kong had been in giving refuge to the
Vietnamese boat people during the 1980s and 1990s. The
only section of the media which remained relatively
immune from interference was the financial pages. Yet even
there care was taken not to offend any of the 'Better Hong

Kongers' – a group of Chinese tycoons who joined forces towards the end of 1995 to promote the view that it would be 'business as usual' in Hong Kong after the China resumed sovereignty. This was an astute move as most of the tycoons who wanted an active public life were allowed one.

Hong Kong was a HK$500 billion, or about US$65 billion, stock market: the region's biggest after Tokyo. Such a concentration of wealth was like honey to the world's investment-banker bees. They swarmed there. But the problem for Hong Kong was that the US mutual funds owned nearly 40 per cent of the market.

Exchange Square, Hong Kong

Local time: 0900 Monday 19 February 2001
GMT: 0100 Monday 19 February 2001

On the first trading morning of the crisis the position of
the overseas Chinese was far from the minds of traders in
Hong Kong. Confidence had taken a serious knock. The
Hang Seng Index of the top 33 stocks opened 120 points,
or half a percentage point, lower. Then, as the pressure of
selling by the US mutual funds gathered pace and brokers,
in a process known as 'bottom fishing', continued to cut
prices to see if investors would be tempted to buy, the
index continued lower. Citic Pacific, China's flagship enterprise in Hong Kong, lost nearly 10 per cent of its value in
the morning session alone. The pattern was repeated for
other Hong Kong stocks, both blue-chip stocks and the
'red'-chip stocks of the mainland Chinese companies listed
there. Foreign companies listed in Hong Kong fared marginally better, with the notable exception of Boeing, the US
aerospace group. It had recently acceded to a Chinese
government request to list its shares on a Chinese bourse
and had chosen Hong Kong.

As share trading got into full swing the Hong Kong
market was less concerned with elegant justifications for
China's actions than it was with rumours that some of the
selling pressure was emanating from Beijing. This was not
as strange as it first seemed. The military and party leaders
in Beijing were some of the biggest speculators on the
Hong Kong exchange. Hong Kong was a perfect place for
them. It was China yet in some mysterious way it was also
not China, it was foreign. It was a place where the delights
of the West could be experienced in total safety but without

the trouble of actually having to deal with foreigners. The banks were still relatively confidential and knew how to be discreet about money transfers, but most senior officials preferred an alternative to the local banks. They put themselves beyond the prying eyes of the secret police by dealing through nominee companies registered in the British Virgin Islands. The association with an outpost of Britain colonialism was painful but far from terminal. These companies required no audited company accounts to be submitted to the authorities, and allowed incorporation with just one company director, rather than the usual two directors in most other 'offshore' financial centres. This was as close to total financial secrecy as one could get. The gossip around Exchange Square was about which senior official in Zhongnanhai was liquidating such large positions. It didn't say a lot about the leadership's belief in success in the South China Sea operation for one of them to be so conspicuously on the sell side of the market.

Damian Phillips, Chairman of First China Securities, dismissed the rumour as idle speculation when rung up by a reporter from the *South China Morning Post*. Lunching that afternoon with a partner of Li & Li, a respected firm of mainly Cantonese brokers, in the Red Room of the Hong Kong club, his guest was heard to say: 'Then again, Damian, they are probably just forcing the market lower so they buy back at a cheaper level. It would be amusing if he was a PLA man, wouldn't it?'

'Indeed it would, Peter,' he said, betraying no more than civility.

Bundeskanzlerant, Berlin

The German Chancellor waited for the last member of the cabinet to leave the room, then told his Private Secretary that he was not to be disturbed for at least fifteen minutes. There had been surprising agreement among his ministers about the need to show neutrality in the South China Sea dispute. He had expected some token objections.

For weeks the Chancellor had dismissed the opposition's prediction that Germany was foundering and would soon go into an inevitable decline. But even the 1815 quotation by Goethe framed above the wall behind his desk reminded him of the challenge ahead: 'Anything in the world can be endured except a succession of prosperous days.'

Unemployment was at 4,000,000. Unofficial estimates put it at 6,000,000. The last time so many Germans were destitute and humiliated was in 1945 after the fall of the Third Reich. Welfare costs were rising. The Mittelstand – the small and medium-sized private firms that were the foundation of German manufacturing might – were losing their edge.

The German economic model was disintegrating as a result of high wages, low morale, a cradle-to-grave attitude among workers, bickering politics, and a changing global market which the Grossmacht had been too proud to respect. There was a brain drain of the best and brightest to Harvard and Stanford. The German universities were not good enough: yet before the Second World War Germany had been the world centre for medicine, chemistry, and physics. Research and development, the foundations of a strong economy, had become a joke. A similar tale of woe could be told about Germany's position in computers, office technology, and lasers.

Then there was the bureaucracy. While Britain had cut through red tape and attracted foreign investment, Germany had not. Investors had to wait on average three months in Britain, six months in France, and twenty-two months in Germany to get their investment plans approved. 'The Americans invent, the Japanese produce, while the Germans dither.' The words from the Hanover Chamber of Commerce echoed silently around the room. How many billions of Deutschmarks had been lost in business which had gone to the cheaper labour markets in Poland, Hungary, and the Czech Republic? A German worker charged $25 an hour. A Czech worker cost just $2. There could be no competition.

There was no guarantee that the wealth of the Far East would solve the problems. But the opportunity was too great to risk by being drawn into a regional conflict. The consumer market was growing so fast that each Chinese province would soon represent the buying power of a European country.

But today a spectre of morality had been cast across trade with China and the Far East. France, without consultation, was moving its warships and fighting men to protect a former colony in Asia. The Chancellor had no doubt that the British navy would get involved in a day or two.

He flicked on his television set to see France announce the deployment of warships from its base in Tahiti. He hoped, in the spirit of economic competition, that when the crisis had blown over he could announce new joint-venture deals worth billions of Deutschmarks, with Daimler-Benz moving into Chinese provinces once earmarked for Citroën.

Palais d'Elysée, Paris

Local time: 1200 Monday 19 February 2001
GMT: 1100 Monday 19 February 2001

After the television broadcast, in the car back to his official residence, the French President flicked through the cue cards to which he had referred. He knew the statistics intimately, knowing that his policies would be applauded in the cafés and tabacs throughout France. There were two unquestionable assets in French political life: a mistress and overseas troop deployment.

The President suffered no less from economic problems than his friend the German Chancellor. France was undergoing painful reforms to wean it off subsidy and welfare. Clawing back benefits had caused the worst riots since the 1960s. But the President had no doubt that both rioters and government ministers would agree on the announcement he had just made. Over the years, the statistics had been unchanged.

50 per cent of the public thought more should be spent on defence, compared to between 20 and 35 per cent who thought spending should drop. 45 per cent believed France's national security was better preserved with the North Atlantic Treaty Organisation (NATO) than with either neutrality (16 per cent) or a European alliance (30 per cent).

90 per cent of French people believed troops should be sent to free French hostages. 84 per cent said they should go to protect French lives. Whatever other political night-mares he was facing, French military action against China would be the one which could be carried out without dispute. Vietnam belonged to France, not to the European Union.

Rebuilding Vietnam, its roads, ports, telecommunications, and armed forces, would more than compensate for the irritating and difficult business of getting contracts in China.

The Foreign Ministry, Moscow

Local time: 1530 Monday 19 February 2001
GMT: 1330 Monday 19 February 2001

Light was fading over Moscow when the American Ambassador was shown into the suite of offices at the Russian Foreign Ministry. Even during the few metres from the Ambassador's limousine to the majestic front doors, the chill wind of the Moscow winter cut through his overcoat and numbed the exposed skin on his face. The Foreign Minister was sitting in a comfortable chair in the corner of the vast room. His manner was informal. The two men had worked with and against each other for nearly twenty years as the Soviet Union and then Russia lurched through its changing political face. The Foreign Minister had always regarded the Ambassador as a democratic ideologue who was short on pragmatism. Today he was preparing to give America a sharp jolt of reality. But he let the Ambassador speak first.

'Yergor, I will begin as a humble man always does, by quoting the words of one of my predecessors, Charles Bohlen, a far greater Ambassador to your country than I will ever be. He said: "There are two ways you can tell when a man is lying. One is when he says he can drink champagne all night and not get drunk. The other is when he says he understands Russians." Well, I can do neither, so can you help me?'

'You want to know what we are doing with China,' responded the Foreign Minister, without acknowledging the humour of the opening gambit.

'Perhaps we could start at the beginning. Did you know about Dragonstrike?'

'Is that what they're calling it? No, I didn't, Andrew. Nor I think did the President. Our generals, as you know, are a rule to themselves. But as it is difficult for anyone to know what the Chinese are thinking I wouldn't be surprised if they had been kept in the dark with the rest of us.'

'What, then, are you supplying to them in the way of military equipment and personnel?'

'Only what we are obliged to do under our contractual arrangements. I'm sure the CIA has as many details as I have. But there are the Su-27 attack aircraft, *Kilo* class submarines. They even keep talking about buying an aircraft carrier from us. For years our air force is flying men and equipment to China on Beijing's request. It is obliged to under the deal we signed with the People's Liberation Army.'

'We want you to stop.'

'It is out of my hands,' said the Foreign Minister. 'Why don't you call Rosvoorouzhenie, the state corporation for export and import of armaments and military equipment? They're handling it.'

'Yergor, don't get involved in this one. The world's getting dangerous enough with China going crazy. If Russia goes in . . .'

There was a silence of thirty-three seconds. The Foreign Minister then replied.

'Andrew, if I wanted to stop those airlifts, I couldn't. The generals would put the phone down on me. They would do the same to the President. And, frankly, during our negotiations over the past couple of years, America has been too blind to see what's going on. The dangerous world has been created by your policies, not by flying some aircraft spare parts to China.'

'I cannot agree to . . .'

'Then stop thinking about agreeing and listen for once.' The Foreign Minister got up and walked around the room as he spoke. 'What were you fighting against during the years of the Cold War. Communism? Or an expansionist Russia whose Marxist banner provided the excuse to plot her containment? Tell me, what do your analysts conclude is the character of my country? Are the Russian roots stained only with Bolshevism? Or will they always be at odds with what you call the Free World and the West because the Russian Bear will for ever be a threat?

'If you were fighting Communism, then you saved the Russian people and are now helping them recover, creating lasting democratic and economic institutions, and joining the global community as an strong and equal partner. But perhaps not. If Communism was the enemy, then why has your government been so friendly towards China? You have given us no evidence that America's campaign of containment was not against Russia herself; that America does not intend to weaken her and divide her. Many people think that America believes the long-term security of Europe lies with a feeble Russia, surrounded by an isolating cordon through which we cannot expand – and this is the view fuelling the constituencies of your enemies, the Communists and the Nationalists.'

'Which do you adhere to, Yergor?'

'I am not entering an academic debate, Ambassador. I am giving you a message for your President.

'The policeman to this cordon is the North Atlantic Treaty Organisation. This is a military and not a political organization. And far from leaving it as it was, an effective weapon for Western Europe, you are now allying yourself with Poland, Hungary, and the Czech Republic. You are parking your tanks on our front lawn. Poland says it is willing to host NATO nuclear weapons. It is an act of hostility.'

'But all this is being negotiated. It has been for years. What is the point of bringing it up now?'

'Because, Andrew, this is the reason I cannot call off the military airlifts to China. This is the reason that the nationalists and Communists are winning support daily among our electorate. Your policy – and I quote from Clinton at the 1994 NATO summit, "It's not a question of whether NATO will take on new members, but when and how" – is creating a Russian monster again. If you expand, you will transform millions of allies of democracy into allies of radicals and madmen. Russians will realize that they had been wrong to trust you. An embittered, defeatist complex would be cast over the country, of the sort that once brought Hitler and Mussolini to power and pushed the world into war.

'We are too weak to expand west. So if you expand east we have no choice but to go east as well. There's only one place to end up there and that's in Beijing. If I am not making myself clear, I will spell it out. You are bankrolling our former East European satellite states. This is only to be expected with shared white faces and civilization. But you are not bankrolling our former eastern states, filled with slant-eyed, brown-skinned Muslims. The Presidents of Kazakhstan, Kyrgyzstan, and Tajikistan, Ambassador, have been bought by China. Why don't you take a plane there and walk through the hotel lobbies in Dushanbe and tell me who you think runs the place? The tectonic plates of global power are scraping together this month. They have been activated by Dragonstrike and only your government is powerful enough to control the dangers it has released.'

Briefing

Of all the American companies affected by China's strike against Vietnam and its blockade of the South China Sea, Boeing had the most to lose. The company had become deeply enmeshed in China and its rapidly growing aviation market. A Chinese engineer, Wang Tsu, helped design the new 314 Clipper seaplane, which made its first transpacific flight to Hong Kong in 1939. A Boeing 707 carried Richard Nixon to China in 1972 in a historic visit which rewrote global power alignments. Shortly after that the Civil Aviation Administration of China (CAAC) ordered ten Boeing 707s to establish itself as an international airline. Deng Xiaoping visited the Boeing headquarters in Seattle when he went to America in 1979. When Jiang Zemin, the President of China when Deng died, went to America in 1994 he met an 'average' American worker and his family. That was in Seattle. The worker was an employee of Boeing. So far China had bought or ordered 224 Boeing airliners in contracts worth $9 billion. The company had field representatives in sixteen cities throughout China. A thousand pilots and engineers were trained by Boeing every year. It had installed flight simulators free of charge at China's Civil Aviation Flying College. There were joint-venture factories in Xian making Boeing 737 vertical fins, horizontal stabilizers, forwards access doors, and 747 trailing edge ribs alongside the construction of the H-6 bombers for the Chinese air force, and in Shenyang making Boeing 757 Cargo doors; a plant in Chongqing made aluminium and titanium forgings.

This was why Reece Overhalt Jr., Chief Executive Officer and leading proponent within Boeing senior management of its 'China push', was in his office at the company's Seattle headquarters at 6.00 on Monday morning. His office was sparsely decorated. Someone who liked the style might call it spare. Aside from a large desk, a Reuters monitor, computer, and scale models of Boeing aircraft, the only decorative feature was an example of calligraphy hanging on the wall opposite his desk. It featured a single Chinese character, itself made up of two separate characters: the character for *knife* and the character for *heart*. The former was on top of the latter and in combination they meant *endurance*.

Overhalt had seen the rise of Asia coming at the beginning of the 1980s. As Executive Vice-President of Overseas Business Development he had forged links with Japanese engineering groups like Mitsubishi Heavy Industries, who would provide the 'local content' needed to secure aircraft orders from Japan's international carriers. But he hadn't taken his eye off China, which was destined to become the single biggest aviation market in the world. Overhalt had spent three years in China in the early 1980s and he knew the country and its people from the ground up.

It had not been an easy time for a Western executive who had grown soft on the creature comforts of suburban Seattle. Overhalt liked to remind people how he spent three years cooped up in an ageing hotel where eager hall attendants constantly found reasons to enter his room without ever managing to replenish the soap or toilet paper. And how he worked in an unheated office in winter, and tried to monitor the work of mechanics who refused to read the manuals that explained how to maintain and repair million-dollar aircraft. Such experiences would have turned off many, but not Overhalt. He knew he was observing the first, halting steps of a giant that had been kept in the dark for so long that it was afraid of the light.

He was not starry-eyed about China. Chinese managers were chronically poor at planning; they had no concept of preventative maintenance, which they regarded as a waste of money; they were appalling communicators; and they had a 'petty cash' mentality. Overhalt never tired of telling the story of how the authorities refused to fly a damaged $4 million engine to the US for repairs, preferring instead to send it by sea because it was cheaper. The repairs took thirty days but the engine was out of commission for thirteen months. Yet he admired their tenacity. His other favourite story told of how in Shanghai he saw a disassembled Boeing 707. The Chinese had bought it in the early 1970s and, by his reckoning, spent $300 million trying to copy the design and technology of the aircraft. They couldn't do it.

The years in China stood him in good stead. As an adviser to the Civil Aviation Authority of China (CAAC), which at that time operated *and* regulated all non-military airlines in China, Overhalt got to make friends with many officials who, like him, would rise to prominent positions in China's deregulated airline industry years later. His time in China allowed him to renew his friendship with the man who became the Chinese Foreign Minister. They had been at Harvard together. Song had responded cautiously at first to the relaxation of Communist Party rule in the early 1980s, but by the time Overhalt left in 1985 Song was the proud owner of one of the only seven Cadillacs in Beijing. Song had also cultivated powerful political connections deep within the Beijing bureaucracy. Overhalt remembered vividly the afternoon Song took him to Zhongnanhai to meet the Politburo member with responsibility for aviation. It was late winter and bitterly cold but after the meeting they had walked around the partially frozen lake – the dominant feature of Zhongnanhai – and talked about China and its future.

That all seemed so long ago. As Overhalt looked at his Reuters screen he saw that Boeing's share price was beginning to sag – the company's share price was $5 and three-eighths lower than Friday's close. The New York Stock Exchange had just opened and of all the high-profile US companies with business in China, Boeing was seen as a prime loser. This was mirrored in other markets by other companies in Boeing's position. In Frankfurt, Siemens' share price was off; in London, GEC was also performing worse than the market as a whole. Both companies had made strategic bets on China in the 1990s and profited: GEC sold turbines for power stations, high-speed telephone switches to local telecommunications companies, and defence communications systems. Indeed, outside the NATO countries, China was the single most important market bar none.

The impact of China's actions was most keenly felt in the oil market, and in the Lloyd's insurance market. Brent Crude, the bell-wether crude traded in London, rose $1.40 per barrel to $26.40. When New York opened West Texas Intermediate, which historically always traded around $1.50 higher than Brent, rose to nearly $28 in sympathy with European trading. The world oil market was delicately poised. The big companies had been trying to achieve a 'just in time' delivery of oil to their refineries. They had taken the idea from Toyota, the Japanese car manufacturer, which organized the production of a vehicle so that the components for its manufacture arrived at the factory gate just in time for assembly. This cut the cost to Toyota of holding stocks of parts. So to the oil majors. They were trying to manage their refineries so that stocks (and attendant costs) were held to the minimum. But the winter of 2000/2001 was one of the fiercest experienced in northern Europe and the US. Demand for oil – especially heating oil – was up sharply. This weather-induced tightness in the market was exacerbated by the change in business practice to just in time delivery added to upward price pressures. World oil stocks were at a five-year low; the South China Sea oilfields were viewed as some of the most promising of any in the world. Oil futures rose strongly. The April contract, which was the most actively traded near-term contract and the one which First China had bought most aggressively, rose sharply. It closed at $35, up $10.

Trading was hectic on the International Petroleum Exchange in London. This was the home of the Brent Crude futures contract. More than 70 per cent of the world's oil was priced off this contract (that is, the prices of all other sorts of oil traded could be related to this price, as a margin either above or below it). The IPE was the world's biggest international oil exchange. It was that size – on average the exchange traded oil with a value of $2.4 billion every day – that offered oil companies, investors, and traders unrivalled opportunities to protect themselves and make money. First China had a seat on the IPE. In the month before Dragonstrike it had built up a position in the futures market of $600 million. This position consisted of 200,000 futures contracts, which themselves represented 200,000,000 barrels of oil. If First China could unwind its position in the futures market instantly General Zhao and Multitechnologies would reap $1 billion in profit. But getting out of 200,000 futures contracts was harder than acquiring them. As the price of oil began to rise, Damian Phillips told his traders to unwind their positions slowly. By the end of London trading they had liquidated 40,000 April contracts at various prices, and pocketed for General Zhao a $400 million profit.

The strife in the South China Sea reverberated through-out London and New York. There was an immediate impact at Lloyd's – the centre of the world insurance market. That Monday morning the War Risks Rating Committee had met to assess the significance of the conflict and to decide whether extraordinary premiums should be set on ships and their cargoes, as well as commercial aircraft. It set a new schedule of rates that ranged up to 3.5 per cent for Vietnamese ports. Rates for Singapore and Hong Kong bound cargoes were set somewhat lower with a minimum level of 2.5 per cent. For ships themselves, the Lloyd's market applied a rate of 5 per cent – a rate not seen since the Gulf War and one which drew howls of protest from ship owners. The supertankers transiting the South China Sea had a capital cost of some $60 million and more; $3 million in premiums for a single voyage was crippling. Similarly with aviation. British Airways was quoted a war risk premium of $162,000 for each Airbus 320 flight into Hanoi and $60,000 for a Boeing 747 to Hong Kong. An airline spokesman said that a war risk surcharge of nearly $845 was imposed on each passenger to Vietnam and almost half that to Hong Kong. The airline said it would continue to offer services for as long as it was safe to do so; others stopped operating altogether.

The drama in the oil market unsettled all others. In Europe and America financial markets have a way of taking regional conflicts in their stride, but the massive wave of selling that hit East Asian stock exchanges could not have come at a worse time. European and US bourses, after five years of virtually uninterrupted gains, were looking vulnerable to a setback. Some of the older traders drew parallels with 1987: the proximate cause of the October stock market crash was the disagreement that September between the US and Germany over interest rates. The Americans wanted the Germans to lower interest rates; the Bundesbank refused. Analysts in the City and on Wall Street reasoned that the Gulf War of 1990–91 – the last big regional conflict – had had very little effect on the stock markets of Britain, Germany, and the United States because oil stocks were high, the world was coming out of recession, and Saddam did not have a chance against the military might of the US and its allies. The West's response to Kuwait had been relatively simple: Saddam was a tyrant who garnered no support in the West. But China's foray into the South China Sea was perceived as more than just an East Asian version of the Gulf War – a grab for territory by the regional bully who, in time, would be put back in his place. Distance diminished the impact of what the Chinese were up to: Asia was a long way away and few really cared about the Vietnamese, or about the stretch of water between them and the Philippines known as the South China Sea. But the markets cared. The world economy was differently placed now. Stocks of oil were low, world output, especially in Europe and the US, was growing strongly, indeed too strongly, and China was manifestly not Iraq. China might be a tyranny, but it was also a commercial opportunity in ways which Iraq never was and never could be.

The FT-SE 100 share index shed 136 points to 6,347 and Wall Street was faring no better. The Dow Jones Industrial Average had sailed through the 8,000 barrier in January but on Monday morning it opened 300 points lower at 7,838. The rise in the oil price and the prospect of higher inflation and interest rates unnerved an already uneasy Wall Street. In the executive suites of corporate America, anxiety was growing. Reece Overhalt for one knew that that China's actions presaged ill for Boeing. The company's move into China was deeply unpopular with sections of the Boeing workforce, and the International Association of Machinists, Boeing's main union, was bound to exploit it.

The House of Commons, London

Local time: 1530 Monday 19 February 2001

Mr Stephenson, the Prime Minister: . . . That, Mr Speaker, is the situation as it stands right now. As I said, the Chinese have continued to attack Vietnam. There are civilian casualties, including Europeans and Americans. We do not have specific information about British subjects. We are hoping therefore that British casualties are slight. I have talked personally to my American and European colleagues and we have decided that nationals being detained on oil rigs captured by Chinese troops should be regarded as hostages, although we do not believe they are in any danger. No demands have been made for their release. We believe the Chinese are facing a logistical problem in getting them to a place where they could be freed.

Mr Andrew Dixon, Leader of the Opposition: While thanking the Prime Minister for his statement, I remain confused about his government's policy. I have heard no condemnation of the Chinese action. I see no indication that we will support Vietnam, as the French have done. I see no moral stand upholding the democratic principles which once made this country great. So could the Prime Minister, before the House, tell us whose side he is on in this conflict, and will he condemn the violence of a non-democratic, one-party state against that of new Asian democracy?

Mr Stephenson, the Prime Minister: Clearly the right honourable gentleman is unused to the responsibility of government. I understand that and should he come and sit on this side of the House, he would realize that glib comments and cheap political point-scoring are more often than not against the national interest. Often ministers must put aside their personal views and consider the wider issues. Long gone are the days when Britain sent expeditionary forces all over the world. Could he tell us if his party would support risking the lives of British servicemen in an area of the world where we have no substantive national interest and no substantive treaty obligation to the nation coming under attack? Could he tell us if he advises taking action against China which could throw British people onto the dole queues with little prospect of finding new employment? Could he not agree for once, instead of chirping like an untrained parrot, that it is right for Britain to wait and assess the South China Sea crisis – and only then, after talking to our allies, to formulate a policy which could well dictate the global geopolitical structure for the next fifty years?

Mr Andrew Dixon, Leader of the Opposition: Then tell us, yes or no, whether you support the French action?

Mr Stephenson, the Prime Minister: France has treaty obligations towards Vietnam. I support governments who honour their treaty obligations.

Mr George Cranby: In order to silence the Opposition benches and bring some national consensus to bear with this problem, could my right honourable friend tell us with which countries in the Far East do we have treaty obligations and in what way do we plan to honour them?

Mr Stephenson, the Prime Minister: We have long-standing arrangements with Malaysia, Singapore, and Brunei. Through the 1984 joint declaration with Hong Kong we have responsibility to ensure that the Chinese military campaign does not interfere with the Special Administrative Region in any way whatsoever. We also have military contractual arrangements with Indonesia and Malaysia which are included in the sale of aircraft and other equipment. We plan to honour all our commitments when and if we are asked to do so. So far no requests have come across my desk.

Sir George Fallon: The government has known for many years the nature of the Chinese government. It is a ruthless and repressive dictatorship which is no different from Saddam Hussein's Iraq, Gaddaffi's Libya, or Hitler's Germany. Frankly, I am appalled when the Prime Minister tells us that British jobs are dependent on doing deals with such a disgusting regime. Would we have let the Nazis across the white cliffs of Dover because BMW owned Rover? We on this side of the House have warned against your policy of 'economic interdependence' with China and 'constructive engagement'. Could the Prime Minister now tell us that his policy has been shamefully and morally wrong and that no more secret deals will be done with the regime in Peking?

Mr Stephenson, the Prime Minister: No.

Mr Fred Clarke: Could my right honourable friend assure us that he is not simply waiting for the telephone to ring to receive instructions from either Germany or the United States as to what path to pursue and that he will continue to ensure that Britain will safeguard its own national interests with its own policies in this most crucial time in world affairs?

Mr Stephenson, the Prime Minister: Britain will and always has followed its own path in foreign policy – in consultation with our allies. Nothing has changed in the past twenty-four hours to change that.

Ms Clare Truman: Then could the Prime Minister explain this to the House: if we honour our contractual arrangements to the authoritarian governments of Indonesia and Malaysia, because of our weapons sales to them, how can we bring pressure to bear on the Russians who as we speak are supplying hundreds of military advisers and tons of equipment to ensure that the Chinese war effort continues to be a success? And with that problem unsolved, Mr Speaker, could the Prime Minister tell us whether he welcomes a Newer World Order with a nuclear, non-democratic, expansionist China as the rising military superpower?

Mr Stephenson, the Prime Minister: I refer the honourable lady to the answer I made a few moments ago.

The White House, Washington, DC

President Bradlay's Private Secretary alerted him to the incoming call from Japanese Prime Minister, Noburo Hyashi. The two were not close, in spite of Hyashi's more than passable command of English. They had crossed swords in the mid-1990s, when after the collapse of the Liberal Democratic Party Hyashi had made a push for prominence on a veiled nationalist ticket that was implicitly hostile to the US. Bradlay was an up and coming senator who had sought to project himself as someone with a deep understanding of international affairs.

'Mr President,' Hyashi intoned.

'Nobby, is that you?' Bradlay replied.

'Yes, Jim, it's me.'

'And how's Mitsuko? I trust she's well?'

'Yes, Jim, she is just fine. And the First Lady?'

'Fine, fine. You've got a bit of a problem in the South China Sea over there . . .'

'We have a problem, Jim, and that's the reason for this call. Have you learned of the catastrophe with the Philippine Marines on Mischief Reef? My cabinet colleagues and I feel that we must invoke our security treaty. We need a combined show of force here to demonstrate to the Chinese that they have gone far enough.'

'We certainly need to do something, Nobby, I agree with that. This morning in New York we will be calling upon the Security Council to censure China and demand that it withdraw from the Spratlys and Paracels and compensate Vietnam for the loss of life and equipment over the past two days.'

'As you Americans would say – fat chance. The Chinese will use their veto to quash any such resolution. I think we need something firmer than just mere words. The French have sent troops to Vietnam.'

'We have been down that route before, Nobby. The American people have little appetite these days for foreign wars, let alone wars in that particular part of Asia.'

Bradlay returned the receiver of his secure telephone to its cradle. Hyashi had a point, but so too did the *Washington Post*'s latest poll. Its polling agency had pulled out all the stops on Saturday night, with a telephone survey of opinions about the Chinese seizure of the South China Sea and what, if anything, the US should do about it. A thumping 79 per cent of Americans, or at least 79 per cent of the 1,036 randomly selected Americans, thought the US should have no part of it. Moreover, an analysis of past crises and their effects on presidential popularity underlined the mixed nature of such events, from a domestic political point of view.

The piece pointed out that international crises historically tended to improve presidential standing. In three-quarters of the cases studied from the 1940s to the 1980s, presidents received boosts in popularity in the month following international incidents. The President's approval ratings rose 5 points after the CIA-backed invasion of Cuba at the Bay of Pigs in 1961, even though the operation failed. Lyndon Johnson's popularity went up after the 1965 invasion of the Dominican Republic; Gerald Ford's improved 11 points after the 1975 Mayaguez incident in which a US merchant vessel was seized by Cambodia; Ronald Reagan's approval ratings went up 5 points after the 1983 US invasion of Grenada; and George Bush's increased 14 points after he announced the Persian Gulf military build-up in 1990 and another 18 points when he launched the war against Iraq in January 1991.

So far so good. But this poll showed people saw the fight in Asia as unwinnable. There was also a racial tinge. The main body of the poll showed a rising concern about Japan and dislike for the Japanese. Anti-Japanese feelings had increased sharply in the United States. A growing majority of Americans were saying they were trying to avoid buying Japanese products. The constituency in the American heartland for risking American lives to protect Japanese interests was as thin a gruel as anyone could make. Unhappily it was a Republican, Mr Joseph Borchert, Senator for Washington state, who caught the popular mood. 'The overwhelming majority of Americans do not want the United States, by itself or in concert with other nations, to interfere in Asia,' Borchert said. 'There is no national security threat, no public policy reason, no excuse at all.'

Borchert had read the national mood with uncanny accuracy. As events unfolded that Sunday it became plain that whatever constituency there might have been in favour of United States intervention was evaporating quickly. Congressional leaders would have none of it. Congressional feeling was carefully stoked by some astute media management by Bland, Michael & Judd, PR adviser and chief lobbyist for the Communist Party. With a couple of telephone calls to leading Washington and West Coast thinktanks Judd pointed out that the various institutions' China experts' continued access to China might be helped if they adopted a balanced approach to the South China Sea gambit. At the same time others at the firm were making sure that talk show hosts knew the right experts from whom to seek comment. Throughout the day the White House switchboard was inundated with telephone calls, mostly from citizens opposed to any intervention.

Messages via less public points of access also started arriving from the chairmen and chief executives of some of the nation's leading companies – Boeing and Microsoft in Seattle, General Motors in Detroit, Compaq in Houston, and others. By the time the President was readying himself for a public engagement that evening he had pretty well made up his mind that the US would try and stay out of the conflict and seek to play the role of 'honest broker'.

The presidential motorcade drew up outside the severely classical entrance to the National Gallery. It had been built by a banker to house his collection, which he had generously donated to the nation. I. M. Pei, the Chinese/American architect, had designed a dramatic glass and poured-concrete extension to the main gallery but even that had failed to soften the severity of the building. The party at the National Gallery was one of those Washington events. The diplomatic corps rubbed shoulders with the cream of the Senate, the House as well as the administration. When Makoto Katayama, the Japanese Ambassador, first sighted Bradlay he was deep in conversation with the senators from Kansas and Washington state, a Long Beach, California congressman, and the chief Washington representative for Bland, Michael & Judd. With such a coalition there could be only one topic of conversation: China. These states were so enmeshed with the Chinese economy – aerospace in California and Washington, wheat in Kansas – that their representatives were sometimes referred to as the Congress's China clique. Katayama circulated as diplomats do on such occasions awaiting his opportunity to engage Bradlay.

Just then Katayama noticed a third secretary from the Japanese embassy making his way through the crowd. At the same time a White House aide was working his way towards the President. Both officials met their objectives at the same time. Katayama listened as the embassy official told him about the UN Security Council vote. As expected the Chinese had exercised their veto. There would be no UN condemnation of China's actions in the South China Sea. What was worse, however, was how the other members of the Council had voted. A smattering of African and South Pacific nations who sat on the Council by rotation had abstained. They were beneficiaries of Chinese military aid. Britain and France were prepared to condemn the Chinese but Japan's permanent representative at the UN had observed a certain reluctance on the part of the US to embrace the toughest language put up by London and Paris. Russia had abstained. In the end, however, the US had sided with its Atlantic partners.

As Katayama considered what he was hearing, another of Bradlay's aides approached. The President, he said, would like to talk to him. An ante-room in the museum was being prepared. When the President was due to leave he would make as if he was doing so, but stop by the ante-room on his way out. Could the Ambassador be waiting for him there? Katayama was more than pleased. He had not relished the task Tokyo had set: sounding out Bradlay at a public function.

The meeting, having been arranged in such an ad hoc fashion, lacked the usual formality that attends a meeting between the President of the United States and the Japanese Ambassador. For a start it was held in English, a language Katayama knew frighteningly well, although he affected to be a poor student. The encounter got off to a good start with Bradlay warmly shaking Katayama by the hand, but soon deteriorated when the Ambassador pressed Bradlay on what the United States would do about China's behaviour in the South China Sea.

'Well, Mr Ambassador, it seems as though we are back to the bad old days of the Cold War at the UN. As I think you already know, the Chinese representative vetoed a resolution at about the time we both arrived at this reception. It was no surprise to us. Indeed, we were less keen than our allies that we should attempt such a manoeuvre. China was always going to veto it.'

'Quite,' said Katayama.

'I spoke with the Prime Minister this morning,' Bradlay said. 'I appreciate the concerns you must have.'

That was the opening Katayama wanted. 'Indeed, sir. I am asked by Tokyo to convey your assurance that the United States intends to live up to its treaty obligations.'

The President stopped. He replied: 'Well, Mr Ambassador, you know as well as I do that our mutual security treaty – which has served both parties well – was drawn up during the Cold War, when the threat posed by Russian and Chinese Communism was at its height. Russia has changed. China has changed. The world has changed. We must change with it. Tell your government that I give the highest priority to settling this crisis in the Pacific in a peaceful way.'

Xiatong village, Sino-Vietnamese border

The guerrillas looked for all the world as if they were wearing black pyjamas. On closer inspection they were armed with the deadly attributes of highly trained assassins – a sub-machine-gun with silencer, knives, a wire garrotte. There were eight in all and they clung to the shadows as the passed through the virtually empty streets of Xiatung, a village some 7 kilometres across into Chinese territory from the Vietnamese border. Between the jungle fringe on the outskirts of the village and their objective – the compound housing the Party Secretary and the Head of Public Security – they had encountered only two Chinese. One, an alcoholic vagrant, the other, a woman on her way home, were killed efficiently and cleanly, their bodies dragged deep into the shadows to hide them.

It was nearly midnight and the moon was obscured when they came upon the compound at Huaihai Avenue where the village leadership lived. The entrance to the compound, 200 metres ahead, was guarded by one dejected-looking guard in the sloppy green uniform of the People's Liberation Army. He didn't even have time to lift his weapon to firing position before three rounds of silenced automatic gunfire ripped into his chest. They placed him inside his sentry box and moved through the open gate. Not a soul stirred. On gaining entry to the compound they spilt into two groups: one would take care of the Party Secretary and the other the Head of Public Security. They knew where the officials lived and moved with speed and economy of action towards their objectives.

The *Xiatong Daily* reported that both men put up a stout fight against their assailants. The truth, however, was more prosaic. The Party Secretary, a Mr Zhou Hua, lay asleep when the guerrilla leader came into his bedroom. His wife woke first and lived long enough to see her husband die before she too was gunned down. The Head of Public Security, Mr Sun Ping, was reading when he heard a knock at his door. To his horror he admitted four Vietnamese guerrillas. The leader, speaking rough Chinese, told him to kneel. He begged for his life before it was taken.

The eight left as they came: unseen and – until the morning, when the full horror of their actions was discovered – unnoticed. However, throughout the towns and villages along the Sino–Vietnamese border – from Zhelang to the west and Xiatong to the east – bands of Vietnamese guerrillas unleashed a series of 'pinprick' operations that struck terror in the hearts of local populations and a desire for retribution in China's leaders 2,200 kilometres to the north.

The South China Sea

The *New World* was the pride of Shell's fleet. Its Liberian-registered owner, New World Transport, was a company jointly owned by Shell Transport Maritime and Consolidated Navigation. Built by Hyundai at its Ulan complex in Korea six years earlier, it had cost nearly $60 million. It was the second of two sisters incorporating the latest 'Double-Vee' (double hull) design for very large ships, developed by Hyundai Heavy Industries, Korea's biggest conglomerate in collaboration with Monaco-based Consolidated Navigation SA, which enabled a deeper than usual forward double bottom to better absorb a hull impact, and additional ballast tanks to reduce hogging and sagging in rough seas. It was a mammoth vessel some 334 metres long, with a breadth of 59 metres and a depth of 31.50 metres. It had been designed to enable three grades of oil to be transported simultaneously. In all, it was carrying 270,000 tonnes of oil, which its giant seven-cylinder diesel engine (capable of 34,650 b.h.p.) managed to move through the water at a stately 15 knots.

The *New World* was bound for the Shell refinery near Tokyo. It had taken on its cargo of oil at the Saudi Arabian Ras Tanura terminal in the Persian Gulf, and sailed straight across the Indian Ocean to the Andaman Sea and through the Malacca Straits. It had entered the South China Sea 70 hours earlier, and was sailing at 16° 49′ N, 117° 66′ E, about 200 nautical miles to the west of the island of Luzon.

The Master, an Englishman in his late forties, had just looked up at the ship's clock on the bridge. He was weary.

All day he and his crew had been noting the position of Chinese naval vessels in the South China Sea. They were used to the scream of the engines of high-performance military jets passing overhead. They had also spotted submarine periscopes. He was hoping for at least a couple of hours' sleep. He took a fix with the ship's Global Positioning System (GPS) and noted it in the log. The Master spoke to Shell in the Hague, to confirm his instructions to keep sailing. His Belgian first officer was being woken up. The Master would wait for the BBC World Service radio news at midnight and then hand over the watch until 0300. As the news headlines were being broadcast, the night sound was shattered by automatic weapons fire. Bullets smashed the reinforced glass in the wheelhouse.

THREE

The South China Sea

Local time: 0010 Tuesday 20 February 2001
GMT: 1610 Monday 19 February 2001

The Master slumped to the floor, bleeding.

In the pitch black of night a lookout on the starboard side of the *New World* had failed to notice the two dinghies speeding towards the tanker. They had been launched by the Chinese submarine moments before. By the time he was aware of the dinghies' presence they were about to come alongside. Each carried six commandos. He froze. The twelve men were dressed in Chinese military uniforms. They carried assault rifles, handguns, and stun grenades. All wore steel helmets which partially covered their faces.

The Master had regained his composure and was on his feet once again. The bullet had grazed his forehead. He had a minor flesh wound. Nothing more. He turned to the starboard side of the bridge and peered into the chartroom, where his First Officer had been examining charts a few moments before. But instead of a man bent over a chart table, the master saw his First Officer standing with his hands in the air. In front of him was a Chinese soldier who was pointing a pistol at his head. Before the master could react another Chinese soldier appeared and began pushing him back. With his free hand the soldier opened fire on the ship's communications systems. 'Officer? Officer?' he yelled, waving the pistol at the Master. 'Me!' screamed the Master. The intruder turned to bundle the Master, still bleeding, down the bridge stairway and past a group of frightened seamen, the last time any of them would see him alive. The soldiers, who had since been joined by others, herded the remaining crew-members at gunpoint into a cabin on C deck. From there, the crew of the *New World* could only hear what was going on. There was the distant sound of shouting. Then the sound of a scuffle followed by running. A gun shot. Silence. The Master had been murdered.

On the bridge, a man in the uniform of Communist China was at the helm.

The Foreign Ministry, Beijing

Local time: 0145 Tuesday 20 February 2001
GMT: 1745 Monday 19 February 2001

Jamie Song stood just outside the perimeter of real power, but to the world's television audience he was the face of modern China. He cut an impressive figure. His command of idiomatic American English reflected his years at Harvard, first as a student then as a visiting fellow in the late eighties. Before the Communist Party recognized the worth of his unflustered urbanity, he became a millionaire software tycoon. He counted among his friends the chief executives of many of America's blue-chip companies whom he had guided over the bumpy path of making money in China. He knew they would be watching his interviews. He had turned down the BBC, France's TF1, Germany's ARD, and the other American networks. The televisions in the Pentagon, the White House, the State Department, and in the executive offices of the men who ran corporate America would be tuned to only one channel – CNN. That's why he had allowed CNN to install a satellite dish in the Foreign Ministry compound.

Song was a spiritual child of Deng Xiaoping. One of the sayings that made Deng famous throughout the China of the late 1980s and early 1990s was his injunction to Communist Party officials to 'Be bold'. By this Deng meant they should be imaginative in solving the problems of economic development. If this entailed being entrepreneurial then so much the better. After all, it was he who had also said 'to get rich is glorious'. Independently wealthy, Song's boldness was displayed for all to see in his television appearances during the crisis. The American government was his enemy. Through CNN the American people could be his allies. Wires trailed through his office. The camera picked up his library in the background with volumes of Mao, Deng, Adam Smith, Thatcher, Churchill, and others. A carved glass model of a golfer was on the window sill. His desk was busy enough to look as if he had been working. And it was getting close to peak lunchtime viewing on the American east coast . . .

ANCHOR: On today's show live from Beijing we have the first, exclusive interview with a Chinese leader since the beginning of the South China Sea crisis. He's one of the masterminds of Operation Dragonstrike and he's here to tell why China's doing what none us can understand. Jamie Song, the Chinese Foreign Minister, is going to tell us why China is attacking Vietnam. Why its troops have occupied the atolls and reefs of the Spratly and Paracel Islands – places most of us had not heard of a couple of days ago. You can talk soon enough, Jamie. And with me in the studio is Chris Bronowski, a China expert from the Rand Corporation. Chris is a specialist in the Chinese military. He'll tell us if Americans should be afraid of China. It's certainly a lot richer than it used to be. Welcome, Chris.

COMMENTATOR: Thank you.

ANCHOR: The first quick question for you, Chris. Should we stock up for war with China. A Communist state, we know. But surely not?

COMMENTATOR: I'd say not this month, Mike.

ANCHOR: Jamie. War or not?

JAMIE SONG: I hope not, Mike. Who wants war when we're all making so much money?

ANCHOR: You're not saying no, though. So why? An unprovoked attack on Vietnam? What is the point?

JAMIE SONG: Mike, as you Americans say, let's cut the bull. Vietnam is exploring oil reserves in what it calls the Nam Con Son Basin, in a joint venture with an American company, Conoco. There is a long-standing agreement among governments in this region to develop the resources of the South China Sea jointly. We have repeatedly said that we will not tolerate Vietnam's breach of the agreement. President Tai has put a Washington law firm, Covington and Burling, on retainer to act for Vietnam . . .

ANCHOR: And they say Vietnam is within its rights.

JAMIE SONG: That's what they're paid to say. Vietnam was not within its rights to start work without regional agreement. So we stopped them.

ANCHOR: You bombed Haiphong, Ho Chi Minh City, Cam Ranh Bay, and Da Nang.

JAMIE SONG: As you know, in any military action a government has a responsibility to safeguard the lives of its troops. To take the area back, we had to neutralize Vietnamese air and sea power.

ANCHOR: Chris, isn't that over the top?

COMMENTATOR: The Foreign Minister is a skilled advocate for his government. Technically, he is right about the regional agreement. He's reiterating a policy which has been in place for many years. You know, Mike, I hear many times people talking about the unpredictability of China. But China is about the most predictable country in the world. If it's going to attack Vietnam, it'll tell us some time beforehand. And there has been a lot of sabre-rattling.

ANCHOR: But Jamie says, apart from Vietnam, no war for the moment. Our first caller is from Europe, the German capital, Berlin. Go ahead, Germany.

GERMANY: Good evening, Foreign Minister.

JAMIE SONG: Good evening.

GERMANY: The definition of Fascism is authoritarian nationalism. Given the almost absolute control by the Communist Party, would you describe China as a Fascist country?

ANCHOR: An apt question from Germany. Jamie Song, are you a Fascist?

JAMIE SONG: We prefer the words disciplined to authoritarian and patriotism to nationalism. But Mike would be unhappy if I became semantically technical. Fascism like Marxism was or is rooted in Europe. In Asia, there is a cultural tendency to respect our elders, our parents, and our government. We tend not to question so much. We don't have political shouting matches like in your elected parliaments.

ANCHOR: Fascist or not, Jamie?

JAMIE SONG: I am the wrong generation. I am a Socialist and a Confucianist.

ANCHOR: Chris. Is Jamie a Fascist?

COMMENTATOR: Jamie's right when he says that Fascism is too European to have that label tagged to him. But the main difference is that Hitler destroyed Germany by overambitious territorial expansion. China isn't an empire builder in that style.

ANCHOR: Hanoi, Vietnam. You're live with the Chinese Foreign Minister, Jamie Song.

HANOI: Foreign Minister, while your aircraft are bombing Vietnamese people will you admit honestly that the assault has nothing to do with Conoco but that China is frightened of a newly democratized Vietnam?

JAMIE SONG: Absolutely not.

ANCHOR: Then what's the problem?

JAMIE SONG: Your anger should be against President Tai, who has misled the Vietnamese people into thinking they have sovereign right over territory which is not theirs – and for making them believe that China would not respond.

ANCHOR: What does that mean, Chris?

COMMENTATOR: This has happened before. There have been small naval battles over the past twenty or thirty years between China and Vietnam and China and the Philippines.

ANCHOR: Texas, you have a question?

TEXAS: I'm in the oil business, Foreign Minister. Our own surveys show – and excuse me for being blunt – that your northern oilfields are garbage. Fifty barrels a day per well. Your offshore fields are OK. But soon your country will need to import eight million barrels a day just to keep up with development.

ANCHOR: And your question?

TEXAS: You've taken the Spratly and Paracels because you're facing an oil crisis. Yes or no?

ANCHOR: Jamie, are you short of oil as well as grain?

JAMIE SONG: We're not self-sufficient. But neither is the United States. Your caller is quite right about our need to import eight million barrels a day. And we'll do that by securing our supply bases and diversifying.

COMMENTATOR: If I could clarify, Mike. Foreign Minister, is that why you've now implemented your claim to the South China Sea?

JAMIE SONG: We still intend to develop jointly with our neighbours. However, the threat posed by Vietnam – which also has a shortage of oil – has forced us to clarify the position. But I can assure all your viewers, wherever they are in the world, the trade routes to and from the Pacific will remain open. This is an isolated regional dispute about which there is nothing to fear. China's business is trade and development. Nothing will deter us from that course.

Highway One, Vietnam

Local time: 0600 Tuesday 20 February 2001
GMT: 2300 Monday 19 February 2001

The unprotected convoy of twelve Toyota Hi-Ace vans moved slowly west through the potholes in the appallingly unmaintained surface of Vietnam's main highway. The passengers, a mixture of Europeans, Japanese, Koreans, Americans, Canadians, and Australians, were used to the uncomfortable five-hour journey between the port city of Haiphong and Hanoi. There were three teachers of English, a banker from the European Union sent to advise on the setting up of small businesses, a doctor and nurse from Médicins Sans Frontières, two representatives from the UN's World Food Programme and UN Development Programme, a diplomat from the Australian embassy, seven Scandinavian aid workers, a Korean delegation examining bridge-building contracts, and, ironically, a Japanese team from Toyota, which was expanding its distribution network in northern Vietnam. Many of the passengers had been attracted by the backwardness of Vietnam. Haiphong, with its dilapidated French Colonial buildings, ugly Communist apartment blocks, and archaic, Soviet-style shipyard, instilled an even greater affection for this brave and battered country than the tourist stopovers of Ho Chi Minh City and Hanoi.

Rain fell in sheets. The driver of one van had to lean out and clear the windscreen with a rag because the wiper had broken. Often the convoy stopped, one of the vehicles trapped in a huge crater, its back wheels spinning, spewing up waterlogged filth, while dozens of people pushed from behind to get it out. The discussion among the foreigners was mainly whether they would take the French evacuation flight out of Hanoi that evening. Civilian flights had been stopped. Air Vietnam had flown its own airliners to Bangkok.

The swelling of the tributaries of the Red River made the ferry journeys more hazardous. The convoy was given priority, but that meant shifting other vehicles out of the queue, which stretched bumper to bumper from the riverbank. Out of the twelve vans, only nine made it on to the first ferry and three were waiting behind at the crossing when the tragedy happened.

Some of the passengers were having tea at the little stalls set up on the muddy roadside. Tiny cassette players blared out Western pop music. Hawkers attracted attention to themselves by banging their wooden boxes and yelling. The ferry arrived at the riverside with the clanking of its sides and shouts from the ferry boys who caught and threw ropes. Drivers started their engines. They revved and screamed as the wheels battled with the mud. Horns blared. All this sound drowned the first warning sounds of fighter aircraft overhead and low. Visibility was poor. Clouds came and went. The wind blew heavy thick gusts of rain into the river settlement. It wasn't until the clouds moved away for a moment that those on the ground were able to see clearly the dogfight going on above between one Vietnamese and two Chinese fighter planes.

In a computer-simulated battle the Vietnamese MiG-21 Fishbeds would have been no match for the two Chinese Su-27s. But computers rarely take into account human initiative and training. The Vietnamese pilot was forcing his aircraft to the limit, trying to throw off his pursuers, while, it was thought, escaping to the safety of Laotian airspace 200 kilometres due west. The Vietnamese took his MiG straight up, above the clouds. He straightened out for less than three seconds, then took the aircraft down to the predicted enemy position. On breaking cloud cover, he scanned for and found his target, quickly manoeuvring into a firing position and hitting one of the Chinese aircraft in the tail, rendering it out of control. It crashed and the pilot had no chance of survival.

But in his enthusiasm the MiG pilot had continued too close and his wingtip was damaged by debris. His aircraft went into an uncontrollable roll, and as it did so, tracer bullets struck it. The young surviving Chinese pilot kept firing short bursts from his 25mm nose gun until the MiG exploded in a fireball on the western side of the riverbank. The flames reached a petrol tanker, then in an inferno roared skywards. Vehicles all around the ferry jetty caught light. Those foreigners who had made it across in the first journey were burnt alive within seconds.

Even then, the Chinese pilot brought his aircraft around again, and opened fire with his gun, strafing the ground in short bursts until his ammunition was exhausted, before turning and heading back across the border into China. Many more vehicles burned. Petrol ignited. His act of vengeance killed 378 people. Of the 87 foreign nationals being evacuated from Haiphong, only 9 survived. One, from UNDP, videotaped the whole catastrophe. Within hours his pictures were shown on television news channels throughout the world.

The Prime Minister's residence, Tokyo

The Japanese cabinet was reasonably comfortable with Japan's stockpiles of oil. The government maintained a stockpile equal to eighty days' consumption, and industry a stockpile equal to seventy-five days' consumption. With the storage facilities dotted around the coastline, Japan could hold out for quite a while. There was no immediate cause for concern. However, the hijack of the Shell *New World* had raised the stakes dramatically.

The cabinet's Defence Committee meeting had been in progress for ten minutes when there was a knock on the door and an army officer walked into the room carrying a large envelope, requesting to see General Ogawa. General Ogawa rose, excused himself, and motioned to a younger officer to leave the room. The Prime Minister spoke.

'While the General is out of the room, I think it is very important that all of us when meeting Chinese officials in the coming days underline to them in the strongest terms our concern about their action in the South China Sea.' Just then General Ogawa came back in. Hyashi looked up and said: 'General, what news?'

'Bad news, I'm afraid, Prime Minister,' General Ogawa said. 'I have just had it confirmed that the Shell *New World*, a 296,000 tonne oil tanker bound for Yokohama, was indeed commandeered by the Chinese navy, as we thought. It's not wholly clear yet but it appears to be making for Zhangjiang – the home port of China's southern fleet.'

'Are you sure of this, General?' the Prime Minister asked.

'Absolutely sure, Prime Minister. We have infra-red

photographic evidence of the seizure and the Shell *New World*'s subsequent course change. As you can see from the photographs I am passing to ministers – which for reasons of security are not allowed to leave this room – a group of twelve Chinese commandos boarded the ship; they fired what appear to be automatic weapons and took a crew-member prisoner. The fourth photograph, which is an enlargement using the latest enhancement techniques, we believe shows the uniform of a Chinese Marine commando unit. The second series of photographs was taken on a subsequent pass over the area. As you can see the *New World*, which had been on a north-north-east heading, has changed course and is now on a north-north-west heading.'

'Was this operation sanctioned by Beijing, or is it a freelance operation by the Chinese navy?' Hyashi asked.

'We are not sure. Piracy – under cover of PLA Navy operations – has been a fact of maritime life since China opened its doors fully to foreign trade during the Deng era. This operation bears some similarities with previous free-lance operations by the PLA Navy but given what happened in the South China Sea yesterday, I would doubt it.'

'Right. I think we treat it as part of the conflict. Kimura-san, I think you should have another talk to Ambassador Bo. Tell him that the government of Japan will not sit idly by and see its vital national interests violated in this way.'

'Prime Minister, may I suggest that Tanaka in Beijing also seek a meeting with Foreign Minister Song to reinforce the message I give Ambassador Bo?' the Foreign Minister said.

'Agreed. Ishihara-san, I would also like you to prepare some recommendations for us concerning the sort of action, or demonstration, our military forces might be able to manage. I'm thinking here, Ishihara-san, particularly of the project in Ogasawara. Gentlemen, I think we have to consider all our options at this stage. I suggest we recon-vene here at 2 p.m.'

The Foreign Ministry, Beijing

Local time: 0900 Tuesday 20 February 2001
GMT: 0100 Tuesday 20 February 2001

Jamie Song squinted as the American technician turned the lights up full. A make-up assistant dabbed sweat off his forehead as he watched the second hand of CNN's clock move towards the hour for the beginning of another live interview.

'We are not looking for confrontation, Foreign Minister,' said the television producer. 'We covered your invasion earlier. We are now looking for you to explain China to our viewers – to sell them your style of government. Thirty seconds to airtime.'

ANCHOR: On this evening's show live from Beijing we are talking exclusively for the second time running to the Chinese Foreign Minister, Jamie Song. You're going to get to ask your questions direct. You're all familiar now with the news developments in the South China Sea. Jamie has agreed to come on this show to tell us about China, its value system, and what it's hoping to achieve in the long term. And with me in the studio again is China affairs specialist, Chris Bronowski. Seattle, you're on.

SEATTLE: Could Mr Song confirm that parts for the Boeing 757 and 737 are being made in the same factory in Xian as makes the H-6 bombers which attacked Vietnam? And that many of the workers there are in fact prisoners serving long-term sentences in your gaols? And if so, is that ethical?

ANCHOR: Let's get the facts before we move on to morality. Prison labour to make American airliners?

JAMIE SONG: This is a question for my colleague who deals with trade.

ANCHOR: Since she's not here, let's put it another way. If prison or military labour was being used to make American aeroplanes would you condemn it?

JAMIE SONG: Why should I? Some of America's best denim jeans come from prison labour. Do you condemn it?

ANCHOR: Do we, Chris Bronowski?

COMMENTATOR: On military labour, I guess that's one for Boeing. They know what deals they have struck. The other wider prison issue is that thousands of people in Chinese gaols are not muggers and rapists, but political prisoners. Many of them are in labour camps only because they have tried to exercise the freedoms that you and I take for granted.

ANCHOR: Is he right, Foreign Minister?

JAMIE SONG: You have in American gaols black kids, many of whom were born into broken families. They grew up in an environment of crime and drugs. Your social and political system doesn't allow for them. If it did, they wouldn't be gaoled as outcasts, they would be helped.

ANCHOR: But isn't it the—

JAMIE SONG: No, Mike, let me finish. This is a very important point. We don't have that problem. We have a handful, and I stress a handful, of people who we believe are a threat to the stability of our country. They are advocating the collapse of the Communist Party and multi-party elections. We in the Chinese government believe that if they had their way our country would fragment into warlordism, separatism, and possibly civil war. That handful of people is being confined so that 1.3 billion people have a chance of the best life we can give them. And I'm not talking about the vote. They have that in Russia and India, and I'm not seeing great hospitals, schools, roads, housing. We are seeing dead bodies in provinces like Chechnya and Kashmir which the central government is failing to control. There is instability, violence, and economic quagmire. And one final point. We don't seek to interfere in the internal affairs of the United States. May I respectfully suggest that you butt out of ours?

ANCHOR: Chris Bronowski, civil war if there are elections?

COMMENTATOR: The Foreign Minister is expressing a view which is prevalent throughout China. And he has got some plausible evidence, say from Russia or even Yugoslavia in the nineties, to back him up.

ANCHOR: So you're arguing that the Chinese one-party system is the most suitable for that country.

COMMENTATOR: I don't advocate, Mike. I explain.

ANCHOR: Bombay, India, your turn for Foreign Minister Song.

BOMBAY: Mr Song, why are you afraid of democracy?

ANCHOR: Have you answered that, Jamie?

JAMIE SONG: I think I did.

BOMBAY: You're talking absolute rubbish if I might say so. Our stock market capitalization is far higher than yours in Shanghai and Shenzhen. The fund managers in Schroders and Merrill Lynch attract American pension money to India far more than to China. It takes an average of three months to sign a joint venture in my country. Two years in yours. Our courts are not beholden to the ruling party. They are impartial. Both our countries are corrupt and you talk about Kashmir and war. Yes, we have problems, but our people know about them. You keep secret the body bags coming out of Tibet and Xinjiang.

ANCHOR: And your question?

BOMBAY: What is the point? The man is a bloody liar.

ANCHOR: Foreign Minister?

JAMIE SONG: Rivalry between India and China is traditional. It will be a hundred years before anyone can say for certainty which system is right.

ANCHOR: Bangkok, Thailand. Do you have a question?

BANGKOK: Yes. We in South-East Asia are worried about the attacks in the South China Sea. I would like to ask Mr Song, why was it necessary? Why is China destabilizing our region?

ANCHOR: That's back to lunchtime's session, Jamie?

JAMIE SONG: I know there is concern. But China is a superpower. Our defence forces will have to reflect that. You have the word of my government that trade which is the business of the Pacific Rim countries will not suffer. But as we have stated many times, we are only reclaiming sovereign territory which is rightfully ours.

ANCHOR: Gansu, China. You want to talk to your Foreign Minister.

GANSU: [*Inaudible*]

ANCHOR: You're live with the Chinese Foreign Minister.

GANSU: Why can't my government feed its people? [*disconnect*]

ANCHOR: Did you get that, Jamie? Why can't you feed your own people?

JAMIE SONG: The agreement for me to speak on your show was that I did not take calls from Chinese citizens.

ANCHOR: It slipped through, Jamie. I'll ask it. Are people starving in China?

JAMIE SONG: No.

ANCHOR: Are there food shortages?

JAMIE SONG: Absolutely not.

ANCHOR: Iowa, you have a question for Jamie Song.

MADISON COUNTY: Foreign Minister, I'm a grain farmer. Eighty per cent of my crop is sold to your country. To be frank, I'm scared. If things get really bad, will you stop buying my grain?

ANCHOR: Are you going to honour your grain contracts?

JAMIE SONG: We have never initiated a threat of sanctions against the United States. We have only ever said that if America starts a trade war we will retaliate.

ANCHOR: Is that going to hit grain?

JAMIE SONG: How can I say? Why don't you ask the President what sanctions he has in mind?

ANCHOR: Can China survive without American grain?

JAMIE SONG: Absolutely.

ANCHOR: Iowa, if all your grain sales to China stop, what happens?

MADISON COUNTY: I go bankrupt. The banks will recall the loans. I reckon that would be for most of the farms around here. That's why we need things sorted . . .

ANCHOR: Foreign Minister, how much can you hurt America in a trade war?

JAMIE SONG: I haven't sat counting, Mike. But it's going to be bad.

ANCHOR: [*pausing and adjusting his glasses to read a report put in front of him*] Now we have some horrifying news just in. Jamie Song, please stay with us for your comment. All we know so far is that Chinese aircraft attacked a civilian convoy leaving Haiphong. Dozens of people have been killed, many of them Americans.

Briefing

Oil (II)

Hidei Kobayashi, Nomura Securities' Head of Strategy and Trading, hated public speaking. But on the morning of Tuesday 20 February he was asked to make a presentation to Nomura's board of directors about the crisis in the South China Sea.

He began by explaining that Dragonstrike was only partly about territory, and partly about teaching a lesson in realpolitik to the lesser powers that shared a border with or harboured a claim to the South China Sea. Always at the forefront of concerns of China's leaders was the need to secure the oil and gas below the sea. By the end of the twentieth century there had been a fundamental change in the world oil market and a redirection of the market towards East Asia and away from Europe and North America. First of all there had been an important change in the relative power of the Organization of Petroleum Exporting Countries (OPEC) to influence oil prices. The mid-1980s were the nadir of OPEC's power, and its share of the market for oil fell to just 30 per cent in 1985 – down from 50 per cent in the mid-1970s, when it was at its peak of power and influence. But during the 1990s it rebuilt its position. This was not because of anything it did in particular but because of the rapid growth in the East Asian economies. As former exporters of oil – like China and Indonesia – began to grow rapidly domestic consumption absorbed more and more of their oil production. Discoveries of fresh oilfields could not keep pace with the speed of their industrialization.

For China the problem was particularly acute: by the turn of the century, after years of an average growth of 7 per cent in demand, it was facing a shortfall in oil of 3,500,000 tonnes a year and this had to be met by imports. Its efforts to find oil in home waters had been to little avail: the East China Sea produced some modest gas finds but no oil to speak of. The best find was a huge gas reservoir off the south coast of Hainan Island at the northern end of the South China Sea, and an 800 kilometre submarine pipeline had been constructed to pipe 2,900,000 cubic metres of gas a day to fire a power station in Hong Kong. Onshore, the application of new drilling techniques succeeded in extracting more oil from the Daqing field in the north-east, China's most productive – indeed the north-eastern oilfields accounted for 70 per cent of onshore production. The Tarim basin in the far north-west proved prospective, but it was just about as far as you could get from where it was needed on the coast and transportation costs added $3 a barrel. Against that background, Kobayashi told Nomura's directors, it was not difficult to understand the attraction to the leadership of seizing the South China Sea, especially when briefing papers were telling them of the untold riches of the sea. 'According to estimates,' one official document opined, 'Nansha's oil reserves total over 10,000,000,000 tonnes. Geologists believe that the area of the Zengmu Reef belongs to a shallow continental shelf, with sedimentary rock thickness of around 15,000 metres, and is one of the zones with abundant oil and gas resources. It is very likely to become the second Persian Gulf.' By way of comparison, in its heyday Daqing produced 1,490,000,000 tonnes of oil during the thirty-five years to the end of 1995. With estimated reserves of 10,000,000,000 tonnes available for exploitation China would not need to import a drop of oil for the foreseeable future.

This was not lost on China's neighbours, least of all

Vietnam. Since 1987, when it pulled its door ajar and allowed in foreign investment, Vietnam made the development of its offshore oil and gas industry its top priority. Fully one quarter of all foreign investment was channelled into the industry. Hanoi had big plans. It set a target of annual production of 20,000,000 tonnes of oil by 2000 – a target which it met with ease. It now set its sights higher and was aiming to extract 25,000,000 tonnes a year by 2005. This was not to say that to find oil in the South China Sea all one had to do was sink a well and hook it up to a tanker. Environmentally, the South China Sea was a difficult area to work in. Typhoons made drilling hazardous while strong currents led to the loss of many unmanned underwater vehicles. Adding to oilmen's difficulties the geology of the terrain under the sea was also complex and difficult to assess. Indeed the reserves for an early find at Dai Hung, in waters adjacent to the Spratlys, had been downgraded to around 200,000,000 barrels from more than 500,000,000 barrels. However, the Vietnamese authorities had encouraged the world's leading oil explorers to try their luck in the region, and it had paid off. British Petroleum had made major gas discoveries some 360 kilometres off the south coast of Vietnam, sufficient to power Ho Chi Minh City for twenty-five years, at least. BP was also a partner with Nippon Oil in a major oil-production facility in the Paracel Islands.

The Japanese interest in the South China Sea was two-fold. There were companies like Nippon Oil, Mitsubishi, and Mitsui, which were exploring for oil. Their investments were sizeable. But the greater interest was in the South China Sea's role as a thoroughfare for trade with Europe and the Middle East. The South China Sea was arguably the most important stretch of water for Japan, bar none. It was the lifeline along which travelled more than 90 per cent of the oil and liquefied natural gas (LNG) together with at least 70 per cent of the coal it used. The trade in oil was a \$500 billion a year business. Asia accounted for more than a third of it and Japan in turn accounted for half of Asia's consumption. Virtually all of the trade passed through the South China Sea. The economic significance of the South China Sea was not just confined to the trade in energy, important as that was. There were other cargoes to consider – agriculture and manufactures – and when these were added to the equation it became apparent that more than a quarter of the world's seaborne trade passed through this waterway.

Kobayashi reported to the meeting that the price of oil had risen \$5 a barrel on Monday. With the South China Sea fields shut down and Brunei and Indonesia out of the supply chain, he said the price of oil in the short term was bound to rise further. Although Japan had ample stockpiles currently there was no telling what damage could be done to production facilities now under Chinese control. He reminded directors that Saddam's retreating armies had put every oil well in Kuwait to the torch. Against such an uncertain background he said he thought the yen and the Tokyo stock market had nowhere to go but down. It had opened down 1,267 points at 38,033. US funds were big sellers of the market, as were Japanese investors who were switching into the US dollar en masse. The yen had continued to come under speculative attack as well. It had fallen 10 per cent on Monday and had lost a further ¥6.8 (5 per cent) to ¥144.2 in early Tokyo trading.

Kobayashi concluded gloomily. The big expansion in markets was over. Inflation was on a rising trend before the Chinese took their action. If the price of oil stayed high for long enough it would feed through to prices throughout the world economy. Stock markets were at their most vulnerable since 1987. New York, London, and Tokyo had all set all-time highs in January. Interest rates would be sure to rise as central banks sought to dampen the inflationary impulse from oil with dearer money. Already the Bank of Japan was tightening money to try to support the yen, though to little avail. 'In times of such uncertainty, gentlemen, it is hard to escape the conclusion that "cash is king",' he said.

Briefing

The ravages within China of her war policy

Jamie Song had pleaded genuine ignorance of the attack on the Haiphong convoy during the CNN interview, but he noticed the red light on the studio camera go out as his voice was run over the graphic video of the cannon fire slamming into the vehicles by the river. It would not make his job at Zhongnanhai any easier. The Chinese President had little interest in the nuances of international relations unless they had a direct influence on his stature within the country. The issue he faced was the strength of the American–Japanese security treaty and whether China had the nerve and military strength to stand up to it. If Dragonstrike was to be a propaganda success, Song would have to persuade the generals to rein in their troops' excesses against civilians.

The new spending policy had been in place for enough years for its effects to be felt. The sudden switch of funding from development to the military had created a confident and more streamlined fighting machine. China's missile capability and submarine force gave her a power projection which would have been unimaginable ten years earlier. This was one of the most guarded secrets of China's long-term planning. After President Clinton sent two carrier groups to protect Taiwan in March 1996, the PLA high command insisted that they be allowed to defend China's sovereignty and dignity.

'If we continue to chase blindly the dollar ideology,' concluded the then President, Jiang Zemin, 'we will become no better than the corrupt governments of the nineteenth century. We will be beholden to foreign trading companies and bullied by imperialist powers. Never again will the motherland exchange her freedom for wealth.'

The ravaging effects of the policy were kept away from public scrutiny. The suffering, the starvation, the riots, the mutinies, the summary executions, the hoarding of grain, were confined as much as possible to the remote areas, where access was difficult and the Communist Party could use force without repercussions. Money which should have gone towards irrigation had been spent on submarine training. A road was forfeited for thermal-imagery research. A province was short of medical supplies because the money was needed for aviation fuel.

China may end up with nothing except the divisions of its own pride, shared between warlords, Jamie Song jotted in his diary. On the way to meet the Central Committee in Zhongnanhai, he read cuttings from the Western press to remind him of the fragmentation within modern China.

Monday 23 October 2000

For hundreds of kilometres, the arid brown wastelands stretched in an inhospitable vista of hills and sky. Occasionally, there were clusters of peasants. Their grubby but colourful red or blue scarves stood out against the backdrop of the barren environment. The fields had been carved out of the hillsides by hand and sloped down the hills in terraces. The earth crumbled under the plough. Sometimes when rain fell it was too much. The land was parched and unprepared for moisture and the crops were washed away. But on most days the sky was cloudless. The sun drew up all life and the crops slowly died. For years the peasants had kept ploughing. Their faith lay in the motherland, the Chinese Communist Party, and its founding father Mao Zedong. Mao had made them the heroes of his Chinese revolution, and here, 3,000 kilometres away from Beijing, they believed it.

That was until just outside the small town of Dingxi a wiry, ill-fed horse collapsed while ploughing and died. The farmer walked to the town and asked for help to remove the carcass. He also needed another horse. He walked back to his farm and waited. A week later, the carcass was rotting on his only field. The corn crop was being destroyed. No official from the government had visited. The farmer returned to Dingxi. Outside the city hall was a banner of bright red Chinese characters, praising Chinese Socialism and Spiritual Civilization. The official who met the farmer didn't even offer him tea. Instead, the farmer was told that he was out of touch with developments in

China. The official was from Beijing and in his late twenties. Although only a few years younger than the farmer, with his smooth features, fast way of speaking, and fashionable suit he was a generation apart. He explained to the farmer that there would be no new horse from the government. In modern China, everyone had to look after themselves. Only the fittest survived. Some people suffered, yes, but it was the only way to make China rich so that it could stand up to Western hegemony.

The farmer had heard of the changes. He could now sell his crop to whomever he wished. But he had never been told that the Party would not provide if he was in trouble. The farmer asked if the government would help him change his crop from corn to sorghum. He had heard that sorghum needed less water so he might be able to plough the field by hand. But he needed to be told how. He would even try soya beans to harvest as an oil crop, because that would need only three-quarters of the water he needed now. But the official didn't know what the farmer was talking about. 'You can do what you like, but we can no longer subsidize you.'

On leaving the city hall, the farmer did an extraordinary thing. He acted not because of the loss of his horse, or even the prospect of having a spoiled crop that year. All those things were acceptable. They had been the fate of the peasant for centuries in China. And the peasant had always overcome the challenge to make the country great. He acted because the teachings of Mao Zedong were being betrayed. As he walked down the steps, he saw three government officials, laughing, like powerful men do when they are together. They got into a large black car and drove away so fast that a woman, carrying a baby on her back, lost her balance and fell over. The car didn't stop, but many of the hawkers left their stalls to help the woman. The farmer, who became quite famous after that day, remembered a passage from Mao Zedong's writings. *Several hundred million peasants will rise like a mighty storm, like a hurricane, a force so swift and violent that no power, however great, will be able to hold it back. They will smash all the trammels that bind them and rush forward along the road to liberation. They will sweep all the imperialists, warlords, corrupt officials, local tyrants, and evil gentry to their graves.*

As the car sped away the woman was helped to her feet, and the farmer let out a furious cry. He tore down the banner which stretched across the entrance of the municipal compound. He spread it on the ground and spat on it. Taken aback by his own audacity, he stood bewildered. But soon more and more people were showing their support for him. Some spat. Others trod. Some emptied jars of tea they were carrying over the cloth. Then three young men arrived on motorbikes. They picked up the now soiled and grubby banner, doused one end with diesel, and set it alight. A crowd gathered and watched. It didn't cheer. As the embers broke off and were blown away in the wind, the young men handed out leaflets.

They were written by the New Communist Party of China. They asked people to tick which category they believed they belonged to: the bourgeoisie; the semi-proletariat of peasants, craftsmen, hawkers, and shop assistants; the proletariat of farmers and unskilled labourers; and the lumpenproletariat or *éléments déclassés*, the group which Mao Zedong had believed was one of the greatest problems faced by China: *peasants who have lost their land, handicraftsmen who have lost all opportunity of employment as a result of oppression and exploitation ... they lead the most precarious existence of any human being.*

In Mao's time there had been twenty million. Today there were two hundred million. The farmer had just become one of them. That night, he didn't walk back to his house. After the burning of the banner, he found new friends who took him to a café and bought him beer. He explained the problem about his horse. He listened to the problems of others. Clearly, great injustices were being carried out throughout China. Later, about a hundred people returned to the municipal compound. They hurled rocks and smashed the windows. Then they broke in and ransacked the offices. They were about to set it alight when the People's Armed Police opened fire. Ten people were injured. Five died. The farmer was arrested and sentenced to fifteen years' hard labour. The young men who had given out the leaflets had left Dingxi long ago. *They have secret organizations in many places*, wrote Mao.

Exchange Square, Hong Kong

Local time: 1030 Tuesday 20 February 2001
GMT: 0230 Tuesday 20 February 2001

Damian Phillips, Chairman of First China Securities, was preparing the first of what would become regular reports for General Zhao. The result of trading on the International Petroleum Exchange (IPE) in London had been beyond his wildest expectations. The beauty of the IPE was that unlike the New York Mercantile Exchange there were no limits. Also, unlike the Americans, London asked no questions about the nationality of the investor; in New York the authorities want to know the identity of anyone who buys more than 20,000 oil futures contracts on the New York exchange. So on the eve of the war the previous Friday, First China had cornered 20 per cent of the futures market. The IPE's only concern was that First China topped up its margin every so often, which it did courtesy of the bottomless pockets of General Zhao and Multitechnologies. In his report to Zhao, which would be flown to Beijing by special air force jet, Phillips gave a precise accounting of profits to date. The $400 million from the first day of oil trading had been placed on the New York money market. That market was big, liquid, and anonymous. With the 'flight to quality' that also happened it was an astute investment decision. None of the currency gains had yet been booked. The further the yen fell the better their position looked. Book profits on Monday of $181.95 million had grown to $261.6 million. He warned the General, however, of the need to act quickly if there was a major change in currency direction and requested approval to act at will if he saw an opportunity.

Zhongnanhai, Beijing

Jamie Song drove through the gates of Zhongnanhai. The driver was his own, but the bodyguard who had been assigned to him two weeks earlier was seconded from the Central Guards Regiment. His assignment was to protect the Foreign Minister's life and report back on his activities. Being spied upon was one of the burdens of high office in the Communist Party.

A soldier escorted the minister and bodyguard up the stairs past portraits of former Chinese leaders. The President of China was waiting for him in a suite of offices at the south end of the building, with him were the four other members of the Politburo Standing Committee. Song was not a member, but as the only Chinese minister who could talk like an American the leadership both needed him and mistrusted him. Song had been summoned to address the Standing Committee only on the issue of the United States. Clearly, the meeting had been going on for some time. After Song took his seat, President Wang made no immediate mention of Dragonstrike.

'Our northern comrades are short of food, water, and oil. There is malnutrition. There are diseases which have never afflicted our people so widely before. Peasants who come from the womb of our Party are disillusioned. They are rebelling against us. They are organized. They have created their own institutions and they call themselves the New Communists. Our duty is to repair the bond between people and party. But look at us. The barbarian winds of Central Asia are sweeping across our deserts where nothing grows. Our oilfields are barren. Our harvests inadequate. If the Communist Party fails to feed, house, and guide our 1.3 billion people the Party itself will be destroyed. And without the Party there will be no motherland. We will once again be invaded by Western traders. Our rulers will be Boeing, Motorola, Toyota.

'Comrades, in unity is strength; in division there is only defeat and chaos.'

President Wang paused, then addressed Jamie Song directly.

'Foreign Minister, earlier this morning you made another live broadcast. Our embassies report that your first one was a success while our Ambassador to Paris was made to look like a fool by Tai. We have concluded that it's better to fight this propaganda campaign here in Beijing while liaising with our consultants in Washington and Europe. We would like to know how you will focus the next interview.'

'On sanctions, Comrade President. I believe it is possible to use American sanctions to resolve the internal problems you have been describing. In order to do that, we must ensure that apart from Dragonstrike China receives only a minimum of bad international press, which is inevitable.

'I have been studying reports of dissent among our peasants and of the growing popularity of the New Communists, which even the Western media has picked. It is remarkable that they were able to smuggle a statement about the incident in Dingxi out of the Lanzhou Number One prison and get it published in the *Washington Post*. I suggest that the Ministry of State Security transfers surveillance resources currently used on foreign businessmen, who we should regard as allies, back to Western reporters, who are traditionally hostile. Any Westerner with a video or stills camera found in the provinces should be picked up for questioning, the film taken, and if they are under suspicion of acting for a foreign news organization they must be expelled. But under no circumstances must they be treated badly.'

'What about tourists, Comrade?'

'Watch them. Now. There has been very little problem in the transport of grain between provinces, but due to the southern floods last year we estimated a shortfall of more than 30,000,000 tonnes, which we will have to import. The provinces most affected are the southern coastal regions of Guangzhou, Fujian, Yunnan, and the Yangtze River Delta around Shanghai. These are the areas which are being most troublesome in ignoring directives from Beijing. History may come to regard them as the cause of the fragmentation of China. They are rich. They buy much of their grain directly from America.

'I suggest, comrades, that as soon as Washington announces sanctions we retaliate with the cancellation of our grain contracts. Shipments on their way should be turned back. The American sanctions will target our manufacturing exports, for which most factories are based in the same southern provinces. The jobs of tens of thousands of people will be at risk. There is bound to be social unrest, particularly in the Pearl River Delta around Guangdong, Hong Kong, Shenzhen, and Zhuhai.'

'What exactly are you proposing, Foreign Minister?' interrupted the President.

'The art of war is to turn the inevitable attack of our enemy to our advantage. By ending the grain contracts, the American farmer will suffer. And the troublesome south will need our help to bring in supplies from elsewhere in China. As workers in the Special Economic Zones protest we will send in troops from other provinces to take control. In a very short time, Comrades, we can restore the power of Beijing in governing China. Provincial China will realize it needs us in the power from the centre.'

'And the grain shortages?'

'At the most the stand-off will last a few months. Then it will be business as usual. The Americans will renegotiate. If they don't we'll expel their multinationals, give the business to the Europeans, and buy our grain from Australia and Latin America.'

The PLA Dragonstrike commander interjected with a question about American military plans. Jamie Song was deliberately deferential. In modern China, the soldier, not the academic, had the power. 'I believe, comrade, that the American alliance with Japan is being severely tested. American businessmen are insisting on a quick diplomatic settlement. The Pentagon is not convinced it can commit forces to a protracted conflict in the South China Sea. I believe retaliatory sanctions together with – in the worst case scenario – a small number of American casualties would see the end of American involvement.'

The Prime Minister's residence, Tokyo

Local time: 1400 Tuesday 20 February 2001
GMT: 0500 Tuesday 20 February 2001

Prime Minister Hyashi's moment of truth came in the afternoon meeting of the cabinet's Defence Committee. He had been preparing for this for many years. During his time as Defence Minister he had immersed himself in defence issues – the state of Japan's readiness, the likelihood of a war with China, missile development, and the greatest taboo of all, nuclear rearmament. In choosing his cabinet Hyashi had paid heed to the wishes of the political barons who led competing factions. But Hyashi – whose faction was small – believed in the art of balance, not dominance. He had spent nights drinking with up and coming members of other factions, not to try to win them over to his group but so that when the time came some of them might serve with him in cabinet. His patience and perseverance had paid off. In Ishihara and Kimura – his Defence and Foreign Ministers respectively – Hyashi had two stout allies, men who were apprised of Japan's military position and men who, like himself, were prepared to think the hitherto unthinkable. The Defence Committee reconvened at Hyashi's official residence.

'Gentlemen, I hope you have all had time to read the telegram from Ambassador Katayama in Washington,' Hyashi opened. 'I think you will agree with me that it makes sorry reading and requires of us to take decisions today of far-reaching importance to Japan and the Japanese people.

'I want to say at the outset that I expected, when pushed, the Americans would not honour their treaty with us.

When the Nye initiative failed some years ago and was followed eight years later by American withdrawal from Okinawa I knew it was only a matter of time before the 1960 Security Treaty would either lapse or fall at the first hurdle. Bradlay's equivocation with me and subsequently our Ambassador as well leaves me in no doubt that the time has come for us to act.

'We Japanese have always been alone. The security treaty was never much more than a fig leaf, at least since the end of the Cold War with the Soviet Union. And racial considerations, or more directly racial prejudice, have always been the cancer at the core of US–Japanese relations. It is my firm conviction that the roots of US–Japanese friction lie in the soil of racial prejudice. American racial prejudice is based upon the cultural belief that the modern era is the creation of the white race.

'When I was Defence Minister I had the opportunity to talk to the Secretary of the US Navy about the Amber System. Amber is supposed to be the colour of caution and this system is named for this concept. Under the Amber System, ordinary vessels such as tankers and container ships are equipped with sonar on their bows. The sonar can detect underwater objects. Some are rocks, et cetera, which navigational charts will show. What the system is looking for is nuclear submarines.

'The Amber System alone cannot detect the nationality of the submarine; it cannot tell if they are American, Russian, or whatever. It simply detects the presence of some foreign object and this information is relayed directly to the Pentagon, which knows what is on the navigational charts and also whether the particular sub is American or not.

'I suggested that the US Navy equip all Japanese commercial vessels with this system. Japanese seamen are reliable and the Japanese merchant marine travels all the oceans and seas of the world. Japanese ships, including our oil tankers, could gather information along vital cargo routes and the US could analyse the information received from the Japanese ships.

'To my surprise, the Americans said that it was none of Japan's business. I asked how, in light of the very limited number of US ships, they could deny the need for such assistance. The answer: "We cannot leave such a critical matter with Japan." I asked whether it was appropriate to involve the British and the Germans, and he said it would be.

'The fact of the matter is that the Americans do not trust Japan. Japan would have no expertise with which to analyse the information provided by the Amber System, yet they were still worried about Japanese reliability in collecting it. American racial prejudice towards Japan is fundamental and we should always keep it in mind when dealing with the Americans. During the Second World War, Americans bombed civilian targets in Germany, but only on Japan did they use the atomic bomb. While they refuse to admit it, the only reason why they could use the atomic bomb at all was because of their racial attitude towards Japan.

'We Japanese now face choices on whether we can boldly proceed, or stand back quietly. It may be possible that Japan can secure a new future for itself based upon a truly independent posture in our region and in the world. We must not restrain ourselves to what we have done up to this point.'

'What sort of action does the Prime Minister have in mind?' Mr Naito, the Trade Minister, asked.

'I will come to that later, but I would have thought at the very least we ought to make it plain to the US and the world that the security treaty no longer exists. I think we should also give consideration to a demonstration of our military power so that China, in particular, recognizes our legitimate rights and interests in the South China Sea. You more than most, Naito-san, recognize the importance to our economy of free and unfettered access to that particular waterway.'

'Indeed, as I am also aware of our investment in China that might be put at risk if we were to take precipitate action against Beijing in the South China Sea,' Naito said. 'A shipment of oil is by no means a trivial thing, but is it worth risking what we have in China? Of the top thirty joint ventures in China, we are the leader with seven. We are the biggest importers from China in a trade that profits us greatly. I'm concerned about expropriation. I know industry is as well. Some leaders have called to say they are worried by this talk of military action.'

'The inevitable cannot be put off simply by hoping so,' Foreign Minister Kimura said. 'Besides, we are all Asians. I am sure we can reach an accommodation with China. Businessmen should do what they do best and keep out of politics.'

'I would now like Ishihara-san to give us a briefing on the state of readiness of our forces and the project on Ogasarawa,' Hyashi said. 'Ishihara-san.'

'Japan's military forces are at a high state of readiness, Prime Minister. Our southern fleet, which occupies the former US facilities on Okinawa, is at sea. It consists of a small carrier, three guided-missile cruisers, and associated support ships. We also have a submarine in the vicinity. Given the state of our technology, it is unlikely that the Chinese could inflict much damage upon us. But, of course, it does not pay to be complacent. Admiral Yamashita is in command.

'The facility at Ogasawara is, as you know, spread over

a number of small islands. The smallest is a test facility and, 22 kilometres south, the largest houses Defence Research Facility 317 and the some 165 or so scientists and soldiers working there. It too is in a high state of readiness. Indeed, all is prepared and awaits only the authorization of the Prime Minister.'

'I am aware of this secret facility,' Finance Minister Wada said. 'Its budget is hidden in the Agriculture Ministry's annual budget for research into rice. But I've never been told what 317 does and I'm bound to say, Ishihara-san, you've not enlightened me at all.'

'317 is a nuclear weapons research facility,' Ishihara said. 'It exists to pool and develop the government's efforts in the nuclear field. It was decided by the government of the day and has been upheld by subsequent governments that Japan should acquire the ability to manufacture a small number of nuclear weapons. It has never been the government's intention to compete with the United States, Russia, or China in the quantity of nuclear weapons the nation possesses. Instead we have gone for quality and deliverability. Given our own tragic experience as the only nation on earth to receive a nuclear explosion at a time of war we set out with the aim of making the cleanest possible device. The warheads we have made if used in anger would cause considerable initial damage but very little of the ongoing health problems that come from bombs which create a lot of radioactivity.'

The silence in the cabinet room was deafening. The Prime Minister decided to bring the meeting to an end.

'Although I was an early sceptic I believe the developments so far this week fully justify the decision to establish the 317 project. The proposal I wish to put before you is this. We need to be seen to be doing something; to be a part of this crisis not just an impotent onlooker. To achieve this I plan to authorize a test of one of our smallest devices, a 50 kiloton bomb to be detonated underground. I believe this modest explosion would announce to the world our coming of age as a nuclear power and simultaneously put China on notice that we will not tolerate its actions in the South China Sea.'

The Foreign Ministry, Beijing

Local time: 1400 Tuesday 20 February 2001
GMT: 0600 Tuesday 20 February 2001

The Indian Ambassador's car drew up outside the new Foreign Ministry building in Beijing five minutes before the meeting with Jamie Song. He was shown straight in. The two men shook hands and spoke on first-name terms. Later the Ambassador told the Press Trust of India that the talks had been businesslike, but friendly.

'Hardeep, the Ministry of State Security tell me you are moving extra troops into the border area with Tibet,' began the Foreign Minister.

'If that is so, Jamie, it is a mystery to me. I enquired this very morning with Delhi and they tell me we are watching, but doing nothing.'

'Can you check again?'

'I can, but I was also going to mention that RAW [the Research and Analysis Wing of the Indian security forces] is reporting increased dissident activities in Lhasa and other cities. I mention this privately, of course.'

'Of course.'

'And it believes there is a possibility of the dissident groups taking advantage of your military concentration in the South China Sea.'

'I trust India will do nothing to encourage this.'

'We give sanctuary, as you know. Nothing else. But I have been instructed by my Prime Minister to mention the following points officially.'

'Go on, Hardeep.'

'We are considering taking up a long-standing offer to expand our military training programmes with the Americans. As you know they began in 1991. Among other things, the Americans enjoy the high-altitude Himalayan training. I've been instructed to tell you that India is concerned about Chinese military expansion and we are seeking assurances.'

'Such as?'

'A halt in your sale of nuclear technology to Pakistan. A slowdown of your weapons sales to Pakistan. A removal or sharing with us of your military base on Hangyi Island in Burma which, as you know, strategically flanks the Bay of Bengal. And the same for the monitoring station on Burma's Great Coco Island north of our Andaman Islands.'

'You are forthright, Ambassador.'

'It must be our British colonial training. It is better for you to share what is not yours and keep my government happy.'

'If we don't?'

'If the fears of my government are not allayed about Chinese territorial expansion, we will display our nuclear arsenal.'

'A dangerous move, Hardeep.'

'The world is becoming a more dangerous place.'

'And if we comply?'

'We won't interfere in Tibet.'

The Kremlin, Moscow

Local time: 0900 Tuesday 20 February 2001
GMT: 0700 Tuesday 20 February 2001

The Chinese Ambassador to Moscow was summoned to the Kremlin at less than an hour's notice. The time-span had acute diplomatic significance, as did the rank of his host, the Deputy Foreign Minister. The Foreign Minister was otherwise engaged.

'Ambassador, my government is concerned about the civilian casualties caused by your attacks on Vietnam. We don't want to see any more.'

'This is an internal matter between China and—'

The Deputy Foreign Minister cut in: 'Not when Russian aircraft are involved.'

'What are you suggesting, Deputy Foreign Minister?'

'I will be frank. We are under pressure from the Americans to withdraw our technical support. If you can keep your campaign free of civilian bloodshed, preferably all bloodshed, then we will have no reason to comply. But the spectre of Russian aircraft bombing residential areas in Vietnam is one my government will not tolerate.'

The Foreign Ministry, Beijing

Jamie Song arranged his afternoon meetings with the French, German, and British Ambassadors at half-hourly intervals. He didn't want them to bump into each other, but he intended them to have reported back to their capitals and to have a response by early the next day.

He deliberately kept the French Ambassador waiting for seven minutes and was standing as he was shown in. Neither man sat down during the meeting.

'Ambassador, my government is surprised and saddened at the open support you are showing at this time for an enemy of China. I understand that French military personnel have been used against the People's Liberation Army.'

'We have, as you know, treaty obligations towards Vietnam.'

'These do not interest my government. In good faith, China allowed France to open a diplomatic mission in Beijing a full ten years before the Americans. We had regarded you as an old and trusted friend. There have been difficult times, such as your sale of warships and aircraft to Taiwan in the nineties. But nothing to equal the level of betrayal you have exercised in the past two days.'

'I will pass the Foreign Minister's comments on to my government.'

'You will do more than that, Ambassador. You will tell them that unless we hear an immediate declaration of neutrality from France, we will strike all French companies from tendering for new Chinese contracts and as from next week we will close your Citroën plant in Wuhan. That is all.'

Jamie Song was more cordial with the British Ambassador. The two men sat in the comfortable leather chairs in a corner of his office. 'We appreciate Britain's neutrality in this difficult regional dispute,' he began. 'Your deep knowledge of the Chinese people and their culture has helped you understand that these problems are much better solved without outside interference. After all, us Asians have to stand on our own two feet at some time or another, without American aircraft carriers smacking us over the bottoms.'

'Yes it is difficult, Foreign Minister. I am only instructed to say at this time, that we are concerned about British nationals at risk both in Vietnam and on the Spratly Island oil rigs which have been seized. The House of Commons is restless. As you know, democracies like easy solutions and quick action. If the Prime Minister could report their safety to the House this afternoon, our neutrality would be much easier to maintain. At the same time, the television pictures of the attacks on Vietnam are doing nothing to help China's international image. For the same reason, these will need to stop if Britain is to continue to argue your case.'

'That is an internal affair between China and Vietnam. Frankly, Ambassador, it is none of your business.'

'I'm afraid the world being as small as it is it will become an internal affair of Great Britain. When we sacked the Summer Palace in 1860, there were no television cameras to record the behaviour of the British troops. If the British people are outraged by your actions in Vietnam, British politicians – albeit reluctantly – may have to reflect that outrage.'

Jamie Song stood up to signal that the meeting was

over. He extended his hand and held the grip of the Ambassador as he said: 'I wanted to talk to you over the next few days about the airport contracts. There is a chance that they could all go to British companies, if we all play our cards rights. None would be more pleased than I.'

Jamie Song walked the Ambassador down the long corridor to the waiting lift which even in modern Chinese culture was a sign of great respect. But not greater than the figure of Jamie Song waiting at the top of the steps as the car of the German Ambassador drew up, or clasping the diplomat's arm and guiding him the lift and then to his office. A waiter bought a ready mixed Smirnoff vodka with fresh orange, which Jamie Song knew was his favourite afternoon drink. They sat in the same comfortable chairs. Mahler's Fifth Symphony drifted through the large room as background music. They spoke on first name terms.

'We are trying to account for all foreign nationals, Helmut. I spoke to the President just a few minutes ago. He tells me the military operations against Vietnam will be halted by the end of the day. The shipping routes are reopening. By the end of the week everyone will have forgotten about it.'

'The Chancellor has urged the international community to be restrained.'

'The President asked me to pass on his appreciation of Germany's mature approach to this difficult regional problem. Believe me, Helmut, once this settles down, there'll be no more talk of Asian flashpoints any more.'

'And the sea-routes?'

'We have only been worried about shipping getting caught in the cross-fire. I think the routes are opening even as we speak.'

'I'll tell the Chancellor.'

'Yes, and you might mention that we are very interested

in the latest Siemens, Mercedes, and Volkswagen joint-venture applications. I understand there's been some delays in the negotiations, but I think you'll find they'll be cleared up in the next few days.'

Boeing Headquarters, Seattle

The picket line stretched for more than a kilometre and would stay there through the night. Reece Overhalt, Chief Executive Officer of Boeing, looked down on the demonstrators from his executive suite: he knew he had no alternative but to tough it out. The demonstrators' placards denounced China and denounced Boeing. 'Stop the export of US jobs to China!'; 'Boeing supports Chinese Killers!'; 'Overhalt, Overdone, Throw him OUT!'. At the head of the demonstration was an official from the International Association of Machinists (IAM). The IAM had led a bitter seven-week strike in 1995 against Boeing, where the export of jobs to China was a key issue. To win Chinese aircraft orders Boeing agreed to export part of the aircraft's manufacture to China. The union's magazine, *IAM Journal*, said these 'offsets' were 'a thuggish game of job blackmail ... US aerospace giants don't seem concerned about giving it all away. They feed the Asian tiger, and the competitor grows.' The Chinese attack on Vietnam and its blockage of the South China Sea acted as a lightning conductor for union grievances. The IAM accused Boeing of selling the American birthright by agreeing that as much as 20 per cent of the value of Boeing's new 777 wide-body jet could be manufactured in Japan. One union official noted that China was building Boeing 737 tail sections in a military-run plant that made the same bombers which were attacking Vietnam. 'It is unlawful and ludicrous to expect American business and labour to compete with Chinese labour under military discipline.'

Overhalt's more pressing concern was Boeing's share price. It had taken a battering, falling $3 to $67.50. It was also depreciating at a faster rate than the market as a whole. The Dow Jones Industrial average had fallen 2.76 per cent while Boeing's price was off 4.4 per cent. There had been large sales of the company's shares in Hong Kong. He called Boeing's financial advisers, Goldman Sachs, the Wall Street investment bank, and asked them to find out who or what was behind the selling in Hong Kong.

China Central Television, Beijing

Local time: 1900 Tuesday 20 February 2001
GMT: 1100 Tuesday 20 February 2001

The appeal from an American oil worker was picked up and rebroadcast by the BBC and CNN. Both networks broke into their scheduled programmes and ran a ticker wire under the picture to explain what was happening. It had been the second item of the national Chinese television news. The first had been President Wang Feng meeting the visiting Foreign Minister of Iran in a villa in Zhongnanhai. The newsreader's commentary over the pictures of the two men shaking hands, then gripping each other by the elbow, spoke of the warm friendship between the two governments: 'Comrade Wang Feng said the people of China and Iran had set an example for others in the developing world to follow. We can unite, and together stand up to the so-called Western powers who not only have no respect for Asian cultures but want to stop them from prospering.'

Then, against a backdrop of a map of the South China Sea, the newsreader reiterated Beijing's territorial claim. As she was speaking, the picture cut jerkily to a videotape of the oil worker, who identified himself as Jake Walker from Minnesota. His black T-shirt was torn on the right shoulder. His face was peeling from untreated sunburn. His hair was knotted and uncombed. He looked haggard and tired. He began by explaining his appearance, saying that they had had little to eat since Sunday when Chinese troops took over Discovery Reef. The food was needed for the soldiers involved in the liberation of territory.

It was that phrase – liberation of territory – which set alarm bells ringing in the operation rooms in Europe and

America. The background was evidence that the men were still being held on the reef. The tone of Jake Walker's message was one of humiliation for America. Here were shades of Tehran in 1979, the Beirut hostages in the 1980s, the Somalia debacle of the 1990s.

'We have made many friends among the Chinese soldiers,' Walker said. 'They have explained their position, which we understand and now support. This whole problem could be solved if America, the country I love, withdraws and allows China, a country I respect and am coming to love, to recover its historical right.'

The White House, Washington, DC

Local time: 0620 Tuesday 20 February 2001
GMT: 1120 Tuesday 20 February 2001

The President snapped down the volume of the television set. He called through to his Private Secretary: 'Get the Chinese Ambassador round here, right now. Then get the National Security Adviser, Secretary of State, Defense Secretary, and the Chairman of the Joint Chiefs.'

FOUR

Seoul, South Korea

The first American fatality in action on the Korean Peninsula during the Dragonstrike campaign was shot with a 45mm automatic pistol in the shopping area of Itaewon, one of Seoul's busiest market areas. He collapsed near a Kentucky Fried Chicken store among the bags and coats hanging on a stall and died immediately. He was identified as a Marine corporal attached to the Embassy in Seoul. His killer melted into the crowd. Onlookers who saw the gunman did nothing but watch in terror. Over the next three hours five more Americans died in similar shootings, all carried out in the open in crowded parts of the city. Twenty-three South Koreans were also shot dead and seventy were wounded. There were at least four random drive-by shootings with AK47 automatic rifles: customers in a coffee shop, pedestrians crossing a major intersection, outside Chong-gak station, and a crowd coming out of the Piccadilly Cinema in Central Seoul, together with four drivers who died from sniper fire along the main highway north towards the demilitarized zone separating the two Koreas, less than 40 kilometres away. The South Korean Defence Ministry estimated that at least five small coastal submarines had landed up to a hundred special forces commandos along the South Korean coastline. The submarines were originally designed in Yugoslavia, but since the early 1960s the North Koreans had been building their own. About fifty of these boats of several different designs were operational. Some were tasked with minelaying, others with infiltrating the special forces, with torpedo attacks, and with reconnaissance. American satellite photographs taken hours after the first killings in Seoul showed that the submarines were operating from two mother ships, the adapted cargo freighters *Dong Hae-ho* in the Sea of Japan and the *Song Rim-ho* in the Yellow Sea.

Almost certainly more commando units were on board waiting for a second wave of landings. These troops were the elite of the North Korean military and their skills at survival, covert operations, assassination, and explosives were considered equal to or even better than those of the best Western powers. Those specifically trained for submarine operations belonged to the 22nd Battle Group of the Reconnaissance Bureau, a highly specialized unit made up of eight battalions. The Bureau worked closely with the Special Purpose Forces Command which was an elite army of its own with 88,000 men trained in all aspects of covert operations and amphibious and airborne warfare. It was with this force of just over 100,000 men that North Korea had fought its war of nerves with the South for so long. The men were chosen for their loyalty, stamina, physical strength, and intelligence. They trained to such a high level that many units were hired out to protect Third World leaders – they operated in at least twelve African countries and the late Prince Norodom Sihanouk of Cambodia had rarely travelled without them because of his fear of assassination. North Korean special forces had been blamed for a number of terrorist operations, including the murder of members of the South Korean cabinet in a bomb attack in 1983 during a visit to Burma and the destruction of a South Korean airliner in 1987. Tonight, as the world was preoccupied with the Dragonstrike war, the same deadly troops were in the heart of South Korea on a mission to destabilize the government, wreck the economy, and terrorize the population.

A security guard at the Westin Chosun Hotel stopped a

North Korean agent during the late evening rush hour. For years, as South Korea had fortified itself against northern threats, the eighteen-storey, half moon-shaped Westin Chosun had been a home away from home for diplomats, journalists, and the military. It was set back from the road by a long, curved driveway. The general manager was reluctant to disrupt his guest with stringent checks and searches, so he decided to increase covert surveillance. Security staff, mingling with guests, spotted a North Korean agent entering the huge revolving door into the foyer. He wore a badly cut suit and walked awkwardly across the marble floor. He was ill at ease in the warm and elegant atmosphere created by the oak panelling and Victorian gas-lamp-style lighting. Several times he asked the way to O'Kim's bar in the basement, a favourite haunt for expatriates. He approached the reception desk on the left, then walked quickly across to the coffee shop. He was both arrogant and impatient, swearing in Korean as his route was blocked by tour-group suitcases roped together next to the concierge's desk. By the time he found the stairs down to the bar, security staff throughout the hotel had been alerted. The agent was challenged. Immediately, the North Korean took out a knife, but not to threaten people around him. He held it out only to keep the guard at bay for the few seconds it took for him to draw a small pistol from inside his jacket and shoot himself in the head.

The White House, Washington, DC

China's Ambassador to Washington, Jiang Hua, made no secret of his displeasure at being summoned so summarily. But he shielded his anger with diplomatic urbanity and then genuine surprise. The Americans had broken with protocol and escorted him straight through to the President of the United States.

Bradlay chose to talk to the Ambassador sitting on the comfortable chairs. The other senior cabinet officials sat flanking the Ambassador. They didn't speak. It was enough that they were all connected with the defence forces. Commerce and trade were not an issue for this meeting. The President waited until the coffee was served. Tea, which he knew the Ambassador preferred, wasn't offered, with the message that coffee in the morning was an entrenched part of American culture. The President later admitted he had toyed with the idea of ordering in doughnuts, but thought that might be taking it too far. He first made small talk about the winter chill which was gripping Washington. The Ambassador mentioned the below-freezing temperatures in Beijing. Then when the President moved on to the South China Sea his tone hardened, but his manner remained amiable. 'Ambassador, we've just had some polls done on the broadcast by Jake Walker, the oil worker, which ran on your evening news. You must have seen it on CNN. China was pretty unpopular, what with Vietnam and all that, before the broadcast. Now my voters want me to blow your country to hell.'

'I don't think that is a helpful way of looking at complex international—'

Bradlay interrupted: 'We know that. That's why we're looking for your help.'

'You want my help?'

'Your government's help. Yes,' continued the President. 'I need to separate the issue of the South China Sea, which as you say is complex, from that of Americans being held hostage...'

'Hostage is not correct.'

'They can't leave. They are being held by Chinese troops. You're broadcasting badly shot videos as if you're a bunch of Middle East terrorists. So listen, please.'

The Ambassador nodded.

'Voters in a democracy do not explore issues with the complexity which we might sometimes hope for, Ambassador. We would like to deal with your claim to the South China Sea, your war with Vietnam, and the security of trade routes to and from the Pacific without American voters breathing down our necks. In order to do that, we need to get those Americans off the Paracel Islands and back home. So I have ordered one of our amphibious assault ships, the USS *Peleliu*, with support vessels to sail to Discovery Reef and pick them up. They should be there in twenty-six hours. Could you tell President Wang Feng that we are not challenging your claims? We are carrying out a humanitarian mission. Only after that is successfully completed will we talk to you about the more complex issues.'

'I will have to refer back to the President. I can give no guarantees.'

'We're expecting you to guarantee the safety of this humanitarian mission, Ambassador.'

The Mindoro Straits, South China Sea

The 36,967 ton *Tarawa* class amphibious assault ship USS *Peleliu*, which had been with the *Nimitz* carrier group off the Cagayan Islands, had already been alerted to the possibility of a marine rescue of American citizens. Her support ships took up positions. The nuclear-powered *Los Angeles* class attack submarine USS *Olympia* from Pearl Harbor led the group. The *Oliver Hazard Perry* class guided-missile frigate USS *Ford* and the *Spruance* class destroyers USS *Oldendorf*, USS *O'Brien*, and USS *Hewitt* spread out like a crescent in front of the USS *Peleliu* with the oiler USS *Willamette* nestled in the middle. The *Ticonderoga* class guided-missile cruiser USS *Bunker Hill* took up the rear. The battle group had five anti-submarine-warfare helicopters. Two flew ahead of the warships.

The USS *Peleliu* was one of the American navy's most versatile instruments of war, and especially suited for the type of operation in which the United States had found itself embroiled after the end of the Cold War. She was 65 metres high, the equivalent of a twenty-storey building, 250 metres long, equal to three football fields, and her flight deck was 35 metres wide. She could deliver a balanced payload of combat-ready Marines, together with equipment and supplies, and get them ashore either by helicopter or amphibious craft. Aft was a huge wet-dock. The stern of the ship was lowered into the water and the vessels floated out. Today the USS *Peleliu* carried 15 CH53-E troop transportation helicopters, each with a capacity for 36 Marines, together with 4 AH-1 Sea Cobra helicopters.

These sleek and dangerous aircraft were armed with a multiple weapons system of Hell-Fire, Tose, Sidewinder, and Maverick missiles as well as a 25mm nose gun. Tied down aft were 5 AV8-B Harrier air support vertical-take-off jets, based on the British Aerospace Harrier design, with a weapons payload of cluster and free-fall bombs, rockets, cannon, and air-to-air missiles. Her fixed on-board armaments were defensive. On the port-side bow was the Rolling Airframe Missile (RAM) system which could fire salvoes of two high-explosive and fragmentation missiles up to 4 kilometres. On the starboard side were two Vulcan Phalanx Close-In Weapons Systems (CIWS) capable of firing 4,000 rounds a minute of depleted-uranium shells at any approaching hostile object. In the holds were hundreds of tonnes of medical supplies and foodstuffs which could be delivered to disaster or war victims. The engineering plant could provide enough electricity and fresh water for a population of 6,000 people. Her hospital was designed to take up to 300 patients. It had four operating rooms where the most complex and difficult surgery caused by war and catastrophe could be performed. All the oil workers rescued from the Paracels would undergo a medical check here as soon as they were brought safely on board. She sailed through the Mindoro Straits, 150 kilometres south of Manila, at 20 knots. Her destination, the Paracel Islands, was twenty-six hours away. The USS *Nimitz*, with her formidable power projection, held back in the Sulu Sea on the edge of China's zone of control. The Pentagon believed the Chinese would now hand over the oil workers without conflict.

The orders to the captain of the USS *Peleliu* were to do nothing except take back the hostages and leave the South China Sea. The USS *Peleliu* and her escorts continued west-north-west towards the Paracels. 300 of the 1,800 Marines on board were made ready. Only twelve were to travel in

eight aircraft. Their task was to bring back twenty-four oil
workers in each helicopter. The ship's captain was in
contact with the Pacific Fleet headquarters in Hawaii. No
one expected a fight.

British policy on Operation Dragonstrike was being moulded by the brightest men in the Civil Service. The Cabinet Office Chairman of the Overseas Policy and Defence Committee prepared to open a meeting which would make recommendations to the ministerial committee within the next hour. He was also a member of the Joint Intelligence Committee, making him one of Britain's most influential civil servants. Eight of his colleagues put their papers on a large square table which dated back to the eighteenth century. The high-ceilinged rooms of the Cabinet Office on the corner of Whitehall and Downing Street had been used in crises for centuries to discuss British national interests in far-flung parts of the world. Today each of the salient departments was represented: the Foreign Office, the Ministry of Defence, the Department of Trade, the Treasury, and the three key branches of the intelligence services, the Security Service, better known to the public as MI5, which deals with any threat against the United Kingdom, the Secret Intelligence Service, or MI6, which unlike the Central Intelligence Agency deals only with intelligence which is gathered secretly, and the SIGINT GCHQ listening posts. A CIA representative was also present, in marked contrast to Britain's European partners, none of whom had been asked. Meetings like this were evidence that despite the public posturing of governments towards European integration and a common foreign policy, in a crisis America and Great Britain worked as one.

The Chairman opened the discussion by summarizing

the situation as of 1230. The meeting's task was to set out the options and recommend a course of action for the Cabinet Committee on Defence and Overseas Policy, which would begin at 1400, chaired by the Prime Minister. The tone was sober and practical. But they had to imagine the unimaginable: with the USS *Peleliu* entering the South China Sea, in what way would Britain give practical and moral military support if called upon?

The Ministry of Defence said that a significant British naval presence, together with Australian and New Zealand warships, happened to be in the South China Sea on deployment through Asia to Australia. The task force had been taking part in exercises of the Five-Power Defence Agreement off the Malaysian coast. The ships were anchored off Bandar Seri Begawan, the capital of Brunei. The 20,600 ton *Invincible* class aircraft carrier HMS *Ark Royal*, with 9 Sea Harrier fighters and 12 Westland Sea King and Merlin helicopters, led the most complex mixed group in the Asian region since the British withdrawal from Hong Kong four years earlier. Accompanying her were the *Duke* class frigates HMS *Sutherland*, which had only been commissioned in 1997 and HMS *Montrose*, and the nineteen-year-old Type 42 class destroyer HMS *Liverpool*. The state of the art 16,000 ton assault ship HMS *Albion*, commissioned only the previous year, had 300 Marines on board. They were being made ready for any evacuation of foreign nationals. HMS *Ark Royal* also had with her the *Trafalgar* class nuclear attack submarine HMS *Triumph*. The Australians had the *Anzac* class frigate HMAS *Parramatta* and the *Adelaide* class frigate HMAS *Sydney*, together with a diesel-powered *Collins* class submarine, HMAS *Rankin*, commissioned in 1997. New Zealand had the *Leander* class frigate HMNZS *Canterbury*. British, Australian, and New Zealand special forces, who had been training near Invercargill, on New Zealand's South Island, were being flown to Bandar Seri Begawan to join the ships.

The Ministry of Defence then said that the Sultan of Brunei had, however, asked that the warships remain anchored so as not to inflame the crisis. The CIA representative asked whether Britain would be prepared to go against the Sultan's wishes. The Chairman was equivocal, replying that because Brunei deposited much of its money in British banks, it would be better to leave his territory with his assent.

The Foreign Office said that more than 200 Britons were caught up in the conflict. Some 50 were oil workers. The rest were mostly in northern Vietnam, including a group of four English language teachers in the city of Lang Son, on the Chinese border. They had reported the city filling up with Vietnamese troops. Local residents were certain there would be an attack across the border. The CIA and GCHQ representatives confirmed that their own COMINT (communications) and ELINT (electronic) intelligence supported that account. The CIA representative affirmed that the National Security Agency also held that view. He added that satellite IMINT (imagery intelligence) had picked up Chinese Su-27s on the runway of the captured Terumbi Layang-layang island, which was claimed by Malaysia.

The CIA representative asked if any other European military forces would be involved. The Chairman replied that if the United States wished for symbolic support several other governments could be invited to join. If, however, they were actually going into action against China, it was best to keep it tight: America, France, and Britain. The conclusions of the meeting, which were, remarkably, unanimous for so many different departments, were printed out for the ministers within forty-five minutes. The Prime

Minister's Committee on Defence and Overseas Policy decided to give full public support for the humanitarian mission of the USS *Peleliu*. It decided that the *Ark Royal* task force would sail from Brunei with or without the Sultan's blessing. British support would continue through to conflict if necessary. High Commissioners reported back from Canberra and Wellington that Australia's and New Zealand's warships would stay with the group under the operational control of the *Ark Royal*.

The Foreign Ministry, Beijing

Local time: 2100 Tuesday 20 February 2001
GMT: 1300 Tuesday 20 February 2001

Foreign correspondents were called to the Foreign Ministry briefing room at thirty minutes' notice for a news
conference by Jamie Song. Unlike the previous venue at the
tatty International Club in the Jiangguomenwei diplomatic
compound, the media room at the new Foreign Ministry
building was a gleaming example of Asian high-tech communications. A huge screen behind the stage carried a
coloured map of South-East Asia. Technicians flashed lights
on and off to test the equipment before Jamie Song arrived.
The CCTV cameras were allowed to the front. Several
international networks were taking live feeds. The Foreign
Minister arrived twenty minutes late, walked straight onto
the stage, and spoke in English without interpreters for the
benefit of the live transmissions.

'I'm sorry to have called you all here at such short
notice,' he began. 'And to have interrupted your evening.
Unfortunately, it is turning into a busy few days. I have just
come from Zhongnanhai. I won't keep you long. About an
hour ago, the Ambassadors of Singapore, Thailand, Malaysia, Myanmar, and the Philippines, under instructions from
their governments, signed a Memorandum of Understanding which reaffirmed previous policy on the South China
Sea. In a nutshell, it means they recognize Chinese sovereignty. All exploitation of oil, gas, and mineral reserves will
be done in agreement with each other. No foreign forces
will be allowed in the area. China is responsible for security.
Commercial trade routes will not be affected. Outside the
MOU, all the governments have agreed to help bring

Vietnam back into our regional community. My government believes that after a decent interval, China and Vietnam can live in peace with mutual cooperation. I have time to take a couple of questions. But keep them specific on the MOU. I'm not taking anything on the South China Sea in general.'

'Foreign Minister. The BBC. Why is Brunei not included?'

'We wanted to follow the aspirations of the 1970 Declaration on the Zone of Peace Freedom and Neutrality, as laid down in the 1972 ZOPFAN guidelines. Numbers five and ten refer to foreign military presence in the region. Brunei retains a British military base on its soil. There are British warships there at present. This is not a major issue and as soon as the British leave, we will welcome Brunei with open arms. The French presence in Vietnam, of course, constrains the membership of Hanoi. We hope that, too, is temporary. We are in discussions with Singapore and Malaysia to bring to an end the facilities they offer to Western military powers. Those of you familiar with the ZOPFAN document may want to quote back at me guideline eleven which prohibits the use, storage, passage, and testing of nuclear weapons. I can reveal that President Wang assured the Ambassadors that China's long-term plan was to abandon its nuclear programme. But as you know these things take time.'

'CNN, Foreign Minister. What about Laos and Cambodia?'

'When Vietnam returns, so will they. Two more questions.'

'*Straits Times*, Singapore. Why has Indonesia not signed?'

'Indonesia is the largest country by far in South-East Asia. It is generally in agreement, but we need more time to work out the details.'

'*New York Times*. Will commercial shipping now be able to travel unimpeded and if that is the case will you now be returning the Shell *New World* to its rightful owners and releasing the crew from captivity?'

Jamie Song looked at his watch, then answered: 'The Shell *New World* incident is being investigated. The People's Liberation Army was not involved. Now, there are press kits on the table on the side. The enlarged map behind me sets out the new Friendship and Cooperation Zone of East Asia.' As the Foreign Minister left the stage, red lights illuminated the countries which had signed the MOU, so that they were indistinguishable from China itself. Chris Bronowski, commenting live into the CNN coverage of the news conference, said: 'We are seeing the first map of China's twenty-first-century empire.'

'Can you be more specific?' prompted the anchor.

'Yes. There is a swath of areas which historically came under the control of the Chinese emperors – and which China still claims. Burma or Myanmar, Thailand, Cambodia, Vietnam, and Laos were dominated by the Manchus. China claimed suzerainty over Korea. It claims and controls Tibet. It also has claims on the tiny Himalayan kingdom of Bhutan, where it doesn't recognize Bhutanese sovereignty, and on the Indian state of Sikkim, whose annexation by the Indian government it also refuses to recognize. It may want to revive a claim on Mongolia which came under Moscow's control when the Manchus collapsed in 1911. My guess is that President Wang wants to reassemble China in its former glory under the more acceptable Friendship and Cooperation Zone of East Asia.'

The Presidential Palace, Hanoi

Local time: 2020 Tuesday 20 February 2001
GMT: 1320 Tuesday 20 February 2001

Colonel Etienne Gerbet was shown into the President Nguyen's office. The President was on the telephone and Colonel Gerbet surveyed the room cautiously. The presidential office was dignified, but not overly stuffy. Pictures of the President's family were displayed on a sideboard along with a multitude of other photographs of world leaders and regional politicians Nguyen had met during his rise to power.

'Welcome to Hanoi, Colonel. I trust your flight was uneventful,' Nguyen said.

'Quite uneventful, thank you, sir,' the Colonel replied.

'Well, shall we get down to business? I understand from the conversation I had with President Dargaud on Sunday that he would be sending me something special. Are you it?'

'In a manner of speaking, sir. If I may be permitted...' The President nodded his assent; Gerbet opened an attaché case and removed some papers and computer floppy disks. 'What I have here, sir, is a suggestion for how we might be able to help you ... level the battlefield, as it were. How familiar are you with the term "information warfare"?'

'Not at all. Go on.'

'Your forces have since Sunday been engaged in operations in southern China. Groups of up to ten men have penetrated deep into Chinese territory and sowed confusion among the local townspeople. The attack on Monday at Xiatong when the local Party Secretary and Head of Public Security were killed in their beds was particularly effective. We have reason to believe that the Chinese have had about as much as they are going to take of this sort of harassment of their border towns. They are, in fact, preparing a force, lightly armoured, and of about 50,000 troops, to stage a retaliatory strike across the border. We have reason to believe that they plan to raze Lang Son in revenge.'

'I am impressed with your knowledge not only of our operations but also of the intentions of the Chinese. But what has this to do with ... information warfare?' Nguyen asked.

'I was coming to that. President Dargaud has authorized me and my men to assist your army in defeating the Chinese attack. We expect it will come quite soon.'

'We have had experience in beating the Chinese before, Colonel. Why do we need your help?'

'I have the utmost respect for the Vietnamese soldiers, sir, and I have no doubt that they could, as in 1979, deliver a bloody nose to the Chinese. However, what we are offering you is a way of preserving your army and delivering a knock-out blow to the Chinese at the same time.'

'Go on.'

'We have the capability to see the battlefield in its entirety and assist your army with target selection. In real time we can pinpoint the position of Chinese tanks and troop deployments. With this information your heavy artillery, rockets, and mortars ought to be able to do the rest. How can we do this? I am not authorized to go into details but we, like the Americans, and the Chinese for that matter, have satellites in the sky. We've positioned one of our best over the Chinese-Vietnamese border since the war began on Sunday. It is able to communicate with our embassy here in Hanoi and from there by microwave link to Lang Son. We can do the rest. But I am also authorized to make one more offer of assistance. The Chinese army has bought many, though not all, of its battlefield information systems from us. Indeed, they widely use a Thomson-CSF Star Burst battlefield information manager. Although I cannot go into details we are able to ensure that the system fails at a time that would be helpful to your forces.'

Zhongnanhai, Beijing

President Wang remained an elusive figure. In keeping with Chinese political tradition he cultivated an image of omnipotence through his skilful behind-the-scenes manipulation of events. His people saw pictures of him on their television sets and in the newspapers meeting foreign dignitaries and chairing important meetings. But unlike his predecessors he rarely left the high red walls surrounding Zhongnanhai to venture outside the capital and only marginally more often travelled within it. Throughout the day Chinese Central Television and local radio stations had been broadcasting that he would address the nation at 10.15 p.m. in a special TV news bulletin. A studio in Zhongnanhai had been fitted out especially for the broadcast. The President was to sit at a table. Behind him would be a deep red screen supporting a crane in full flight. The crane is north Asia's most prized bird – revered in China, as well as Korea and Japan. At 10 p.m. he entered the studio, chatted with the young female make-up artist and the crew. He sat down and waited for the signal to begin recording his message to the nation.

'People of China,' he began, 'I speak to you tonight about a crisis facing our country. I have no doubt that with the help of the great Chinese people we will succeed. Since the Opium Wars of the nineteenth century Western capitalism has never stopped its aggression against China and its plundering of China. Today our heroic forces are fighting to regain our sovereignty over the Nanshas [Spratly Islands] and the great waters that surround them – to preserve for the motherland riches that rightly belong to the people of China.

'Let me explain why. There is a vast sea to the south of the motherland – the South China Sea – which covers an area of 3,200,000 square kilometres of our territorial waters. The beautiful and bountiful Nanshas are located in the southern part of this vast sea. The Nanshas have belonged to China since ancient times.

'Yet the capitalist powers have never stopped casting their greedy eyes on the big treasure house of these islands. In the short period of sixty years since the first illegal survey of the Nanshas by a British ship in 1867, other countries occupied and plundered the archipelago on more than ten occasions. Even today, there are over fifty petroleum consortia from more than ten countries and regions that have long prospected for oil in the Nansha waters. Moreover, some forces have even attempted to turn the Nanshas into so-called international high seas and occupy the precious wealth.

'This brings me to the interference in the internal affairs of China by third parties. Any discussion of this can proceed only from the accepted principle that China brooks no interference in its internal affairs. We will absolutely not permit any foreigners to interfere.

'Even though the United States has the greatest national strength, it cannot have its own way to the point where it has the final say on world affairs. To maintain its status as the only superpower, the United States has to make a desperate attempt to contain other countries' development. US relations with foreign countries, such as with the European Union and Japan, are relations of cooperation rather than containment, while its relations with Russia and China are relations of containment rather than cooperation.

'The Chinese people desire peace. Why else would we

have signed today in Beijing a Memorandum of Understanding with our South-East Asian neighbours? We do not want war. We want peace. Today's agreement was freely entered into by all parties. China's place in Asia is at the heart of Asia. Our friends in the region understand that. Like us they view with anger and dismay the resurgence of militarism in Japan. Japan is the biggest threat to regional stability we have. There are none more so than the Chinese who understand the true nature of the Japanese. Their despicable grab for territory in the 1930s, their slaughter of women and children in Nanjing and Shanghai, their use of opium to control our people in old Manchuria showed the Japanese to be the vilest of all the imperialists who gorged themselves while the Chinese people starved.

'Following the end of the Cold War, Japan changed its defence strategy from one concentrated on repelling potential Soviet attacks to one based on confrontation with China. But we warn Japan, as we warn the United States, whoever plays with fire will perish by fire. And I remind both countries of the words of Long March veteran Wang Zhen: "We have the experience of dealing with the Americans on the battlefield. They are nothing terrible. The war theatre may be selected by the Americans, in Korea or Taiwan. They have nuclear weapons; so have we."'

The South China Sea

The water along the two main shipping lanes through the Mindoro Straits was only 60 metres deep in places. The Apo West Pass ran along the northern coastline of the Calamian Group of islands, rugged, poor, Philippine fishing outposts whose boats were ignoring the Chinese warnings and were out working. To the north-east was the Apo East Pass, which ran along the coast of Mindoro Island, and it was through here that the commander of the USS *Peleliu* steered his amphibious group towards the South China Sea.

The shallow water and the noise thrown out by dozens of small fishing vessels made it an ideal arena of battle for the Chinese diesel-electric submarines, waiting at 50 metres below the surface. Some were even resting on the seabed, their main motors cut and so completely silent that they were undetectable by even the most modern submarine equipment.

Yet the commander of *Ming* 353 knew exactly what he was looking for. Six hours earlier, when the Dong Fang Hong 6 Chinese military satellite was passing, the submarine had raised a satellite communications (SATCOM) mast to receive a message which was constantly beamed down from space. In less than thirty seconds the submarine went deep again. The order was to attack the USS *Peleliu* as soon as she entered the South China Sea. In the following hours, every other Chinese submarine in the South China Sea received the same instructions.

The fifty-seven officers and men had been cramped on

board *Ming* 353 for more than three weeks now. They slept in narrow three-tiered bunks which were squeezed against the bulkhead, sharing sleeping bags and pillows. Only a filthy cloth curtain divided each bunk from the corridor. Even the patience of the Chinese ratings, recruited from the harsh mountain provinces, was being tested. They couldn't wash. They had no change of clothes. Everyone had sprouted thin beards. The whole vessel stank of cooking fat, diesel, and sweat. Equipment was suffering from the constant changes of humidity. Condensation flowed down everything.

The task of identifying the American warship would have been the envy of any submarine commander. He knew when she was coming through and the course she was sailing. He also had on file the complete acoustic signature of the USS *Peleliu*, meticulously copied on the several occasions she had called in at Hong Kong before the British left in 1997. Chinese military intelligence operating in the Pearl River Delta was able to record every sound the ship made. In an ideal military world, the propeller design, size, and speed of naval ships would remain a closely guarded secret. But the USS *Peleliu* had been operating in the Pacific for twenty years and China had her exact propeller characteristics. It had also pieced together details as intricate and unique as a human fingerprint. It had recorded the auxiliary power plants; the sewage plant; the hydraulic lifts which carried aircraft from deck to deck; the compressors which filled hospital bottles with oxygen and gas. All of these sounds made up the ship's acoustic signature, which had been copied onto CD-ROM with the signatures of dozens of other warships. The Chinese had equipped their antiquated submarines with Pentium-chip laptop computers. They were no more than off-the-shelf office equipment. But this was a world where civilian technology was outstripping the military. The sonar operators on the *Ming* 353 simply recognized the USS *Peleliu*'s signature from their laptop screen.

The commander ordered the *Ming* up to periscope depth to try to confirm the target with Electronic Surveillance Measures. Within thirty seconds, the ESM mast had absorbed the electromagnetic spectrum around it, taking in the USS *Peleliu*'s navigation radar, encrypted tactical communications, and satellite communications. The data made up the ESM fingerprint, which was analysed with the acoustic fingerprint in the *Ming*'s own Tactical Weapons System computer. The submarine commander now had a near certain classification of his target and could take the decision to close within firing range.

When he was 1,700 metres away he had a strong urge to carry out a more dangerous, but also more accurate, 'eyes only' attack using the periscope. He knew the American anti-submarine warfare detection equipment might find him before the torpedoes hit. But that was the risk of the job. He would use straight running torpedoes, of the old 1960s design, weapons which in naval jargon cannot be seduced by electronic countermeasures. Their rudimentary mechanical system would ignore the decoys thrown out by the USS *Peleliu* to change their course. The American commander would attempt to project a bogus acoustic signature of the USS *Peleliu* several thousand metres away from the real ship. Another countermeasure would simply be white noise, like the hissing of a fire extinguisher, which would appear louder than the ship itself.

The commander kept the periscope up for five seconds to obtain a firing solution. He was 30° on the bow of the target. He put the periscope down. With his acoustic, electronic, and optical information matched, he opened the torpedo doors. He took the periscope up. What he saw, however, made him take it down immediately, wait ten seconds, and raise it again. The Seahawk helicopter crew had identified the periscope of a second submarine. The vessel went deep, but the helicopter crew dropped two Mk46 torpedoes. The explosion of a *Romeo* submarine being destroyed ripped through the water. This was the moment the commander of *Ming* 353 asked for his firing solution. He was 850 metres from the target.

He released the first weapon at a bearing of 90° to the target course. This was the middle torpedo of his salvo of three. The swell swept around the periscope, cutting off his view of the target. But he had already worked out the firing pattern. The next was fired 5° ahead of the bearing, the third 5° behind. He completed what is known as the zero gyro-angle shot, creating a spread of weapons to counteract either the target speeding up or turning away.

The Americans had twenty-six seconds to react. In a scrambling panic, they threw out electronic countermeasures. But the low-tech torpedoes, made up of only an engine and warhead, kept their course. The American captain began to turn the USS *Peleliu* to port to evade the torpedoes, but it was a useless gesture with such a lumbering vessel.

The *Ming* commander had set the first weapon with a proximity fuse which went off 2 metres below the hull. The explosion blew a hole in the bottom and ruptured systems in a large area of the ship. The second torpedo, with an impact fuse, had a direct hit, stopping the ship's engines. The third weapon passed in front of her bow and detonated.

The crew of a second Seahawk scrambled and took off from the USS *Bunker Hill*. They dropped a pattern of sonobuoys in the area of the attack and over the next three hours they found and destroyed one other *Ming* and two more *Romeo* submarines with torpedoes and depth charges. But *Ming* 353 and one other escaped. When the crews returned to their base on Hainan Island, they were hailed as heroes. There had been six submarines waiting to strike the USS *Peleliu*. Military experts debated as to how much the Chinese commanders had been inspired by the German Second World War wolf-pack tactic of stretching up to fifty U-boats in a net across the paths of Allied convoys in the Atlantic. They would often be on the surface and only dive when attacking. Some German commanders actually attacked on the surface, driving their vessels between the lines of the convoy using guns and torpedoes. The key was surprise and daring, similar to the risks taken by the commander of *Ming* 353. As the Dragonstrike war continued, Allied naval officers referred to the clusters of Chinese submarines as wolf-packs.

Normally a submarine commander would head away from the attack datum or area of battle. But *Ming* 353 went deep to 45 metres. Adopting the tactics of outdated warfare, the submarine headed towards the area of turmoil where the USS *Peleliu* was on fire, listing, and beginning to sink. The American helicopter pilots knew that the attacker was hiding among the debris of the sinking ship. The *Ming* crew could hear detonations on board and the crushing of the bulkheads under pressure. But the captain judged that Americans would never fire into sea where their compatriots were dying.

Water burst into the main decks, which were designed as huge aircraft hangars with no bulkhead divisions to seal one area off from another. The water moved back and forth in what seamen know as the free-surface effect. It sloshed in a swell from one side to the other, making the vessel more and more unstable. Unwittingly, firefighting teams added to the problems by pouring high-pressure water on fires which had broken out below decks. Pilots of three CH53-Echo helicopters managed to get airborne, cramming fifty passengers into each aircraft. Five lifeboats and two of the larger landing craft were launched. The USS

Peleliu took twenty-five minutes to capsize and sink. In that short time, 585 people managed to get off the vessel. But the rest, 1,960 American servicemen, including the United States Navy captain in command and the Marine Expeditionary Unit colonel, died.

The Chinese orders were to sink only the USS *Peleliu*, after which the PLA believed America would pull out of South-East Asia. Ironically, the last previous major American warship to be destroyed in battle was the fleet ocean tug USS *Sarsi*, blown up by a mine in August 1952 during the Korean War. In that conflict, China was also the enemy.

The White House Press Room, Washington, DC

The President's press secretary mounted the podium.

'The President will be coming down here shortly to make a statement about the sinking of the USS *Peleliu*. I am going to tell you now so there's no misunderstanding about ground rules: the President will not be taking any questions, you hear? Good.'

Just as his press secretary was concluding his remarks Bradlay appeared. He was wearing a dark suit and a black tie. Lack of sleep showed in the dark circles under his eyes.

'At ten o'clock Washington time, the USS *Peleliu* on humanitarian service in the international waters of the South China Sea was attacked by a Chinese submarine and sunk. We do not have precise figures as yet but I am advised there are unlikely to be many survivors from the ship's nearly 2,000 strong complement of men and Marines. The actions of the Chinese in perpetrating this deed are contemptible. Our prayers and thoughts are with the families of the men and women who served on the *Peleliu*. Their sacrifice will not have been in vain. It will be avenged. I have instructed my staff to prepare a necessary response to this outrage. I will be talking with our allies in the hours ahead and I plan to address the nation tomorrow morning with a definitive statement of our plans. Thank you and God bless.'

As Bradlay collected his paper and began to walk towards the exit the assembled reporters began to call out questions in the hope that he would respond.

'Mr President, are we going to strike back?'

'Have you placed our nuclear forces on alert?'

'What can we do—'

At the last he wheeled around, to the astonishment of his aides, and said: 'I'll tell you what we're going to do. We're going right back to where they sank our ship. We are going to recover our dead. And we are not going to let anything stand in our way.' And with that he was off through the entrance preserved for administration officials.

London, England

Local time: 1530 Tuesday 20 February 2001

Markets react to news like a barometer to pressure. The fall of the Dow Jones was as swift as the news of the *Peleliu* was terrible. Within minutes the index was 235.14 lower at 7,602.86. The dollar shot up. An indication of just how stressed markets became that day is given by the behaviour of currencies. The dollar is quoted in terms of yen, say, with one bank offering to buy at 144.45 yen and sell at 145.55. In big currencies like the yen the spread is always tight. On that Tuesday afternoon, the spreads widened a whole yen.

This was of little consequence to Damian Phillips. He had been called by his London office as soon as the news of the *Peleliu*'s sinking hit the trading screens in London. He had the event he was looking for. Now was the time to cover the short yen positions his dealers had built up in the previous month. There was an avalanche of yen for sale. Japan was seen as the big loser out of war between the US and China – a war that looked to be imminent. The yen had fallen to 152.55 to the dollar and was finding little stability even at those levels. The Bank of England, on behalf of the Bank of Japan, was buying yen for dollars, but to little avail. The Japanese currency had depreciated more than 20 per cent in two days. First China, which had sold little yen in the previous two days, was sitting on paper profits of ¥300 billion. As the currency fell against the dollar First China's 'yen shorts' were reversed.

In the dealing room of the Bank of International Commerce in London it was pandemonium. Dealers were screaming down telephones, some three at once. Patiently, however, Mark Fuller, chief dealer dollar/yen, was contemplating the arrival of all his Christmases at once. Fuller, thirty-two, was the classic London foreign exchange dealer. He had started his life in the City as a delivery boy and graduated to the bank's settlements department. His talent for numbers had been spotted by National Westminster Bank, where he worked for eight years. He had never looked back. He drove a Morgan (green) and lived in Chelmsford in Essex. He had been a seller of the yen all week. No one wanted to hold it. No one, that is, until First China told him to buy all the yen he could up to ¥124 billion. Fuller had never had an order like it before. He knew First China. For the past month it had been active in the dollar/yen market, especially in the short positions it had accumulated. He watched the screen before him. It showed all the banks making prices in dollar/yen. And, in the jargon of the market, he 'hit' them. In three hours he had bought all the yen First China wanted. What he did not – in fact could not – know was that at an average of ¥156.80 General Zhao of Multitechnologies had just made the best part of $210 million.

Oil markets took fright as well. The spot price of Brent Crude – the bell-wether price for over 70 per cent of the world's trade in oil – lurched higher and broke through the $40 a barrel barrier. In the futures market, the 160,000 April contracts which First China owned rose higher. First China's oil trader sold into this rally as much of the position he could. By the end of trading he had managed to sell a further 80,000 contracts at a profit to his client of more than $600 million.

The Ogasawara Islands, Japan

Local time: 0400 Wednesday 21 February 2001
GMT: 1900 Tuesday 20 February 2001

The underground control centre of Defence Research
Facility 317 had the well-lit antiseptic look of a hospital
and the decor to match. A Fujitsu supercomputer was in a
room of its own, slightly over-pressurized so that when its
door was opened the flow of air was out of, rather than
into, the room. In the main control area there were four
banks of computers and screens all manned by technicians.
On the far wall was a large electronic map of the western
Pacific. In addition to the geography of the area, it also
identified the position of the Japanese navy, as well as the
navies of China, Vietnam, and the Philippines. A digital
display was counting the minutes and seconds backwards
towards zero.

Defence Research Facility 317 was located on Chichijima, the main island in the Ogasawara group. The islands'
original settlers were a polyglot bunch of Americans,
English, Welsh, and Polynesians led by Nathaniel Savory of
Massachusetts. They arrived on Chichijima in 1830. It was
not until 1873 that Japan claimed sovereignty over the
islands; the settlers wisely acknowledged their new status
immediately by swearing allegiance to the Empire of Japan.
Even in 2001 many of the 'old islanders' had distinctly
European and Polynesian features. It was during the Second
World War, however, that the islands' strategic significance
was exploited. Chichijima was a major staging area for
Japan's invasion of the Marianas, Solomons, Philippines,
and points south. Its huge radio facility atop Mount Yoake
gave orders to Japan's entire Pacific fleet. One of the islands

in the group, Iwo Jima, was the site of some of the most bloody combat the Americans encountered in the spring of 1945 as they edged towards the Japanese mainland. It was not until 1968 that the Ogasawaras were returned to Japan. They were much as Japan had left them. The mountains were honeycombed with tunnels that led to copper-lined suites of rooms. Although they were put under the titular administration of the Ministry of Finance, the Japanese navy – then called the Maritime Self-Defence Force – reoccupied the islands. In the 1990s the air force built an airport on Anijima, just across from Chichijima. It was capable of taking the latest fighters and military transport aircraft.

The Japanese are a thrifty race. They waste little. Painstakingly they restored the tunnels and rooms. The copper was removed and recycled and in its place was put steel, lead, and concrete. Accommodation for more than 150 permanent scientists (and up to 60 visitors) was fashioned inside the rock. Electric power and state-of-the-art satellite communications were installed. By 2000 the facility was fully operational and its purpose as a nuclear weapons research facility a closely held secret. The research station deep in the mountains of Chichijima was, however, the most important part of a much larger enterprise. 50 kilometres to the east a tiny, never before inhabited speck in the Pacific had been prepared to receive Japan's first nuclear test. A hole some 120 metres deep had been drilled and a 50 kiloton device lowered to its bottom. To create an explosion equal to 50,000 tons of TNT is quite easy, if you have the materials. The 'active' ingredients for Japan's first nuclear test weighed barely 5 kilograms. A 50 kiloton bomb required a few kilograms of weapons-grade plutonium. The bomb had been assembled on Okinawa a week before the Chinese attack on Vietnam and its seizure of the South China Sea. It had been flown in utmost secrecy to Chichijima on Monday. Engineers worked throughout the night to lower the bomb to the bottom of the well.

The digital display counted back towards zero.

FIVE

The Ogasawara Islands, Japan

Local time: 0430 Wednesday 21 February 2001
GMT: 1930 Tuesday 20 February 2001

There was an air of quiet control in the room. No movement was wasted. Everyone was concentrating on the task at hand: a successful detonation and a comprehensive monitoring of the result ... 6, 5, 4, 3, 2 ...

In an underground nuclear explosion, the force is initially contained within the surrounding rock. The energy, unable to spread out as it would in the atmosphere, soon vaporizes the rock, creating a large hole. The pressure within this cavity rises to millions of atmospheres. The vapours expand in all directions, pulverizing rock further and further away from the point of detonation. Within 80 nanoseconds (80 thousand millionths of a second) the temperature at the bottom of the Ogasawara well was 130,000,000 degrees centigrade and the pressure 100,000,000 atmospheres. The Japanese had detonated the device far enough underground for most of the shock wave created by the explosion to be contained within the Earth's crust. Part of the wave, however, always breaks through the surface, where a tell-tale subsidence crater is visible; as it travels upwards it creates a chimney, whose floor is the explosion cavity, littered with pulverized rock. The rest of the wave travels through the ground that contained the explosion, taking many forms: a series of alternating compressions, a 'shear wave' which oscillates up and down, and a series of waves through the earth that resemble the waves of the ocean. Whichever form they take, however, the waves travel a vast distance, carrying an echo of the explosive event all the way around the world. It was this shock wave that special seismographs at Lop Nor in China and observation stations in Australia, Russia, and America detected soon after detonation. It was the first test of a nuclear weapons since 1996, when an international ban was agreed by the nuclear powers. Without warning to any of its allies, Japan had entered the nuclear club.

Seoul, South Korea

Local time: 0530 Wednesday 21 February 2001
GMT: 2030 Tuesday 20 February 2001

Massive television screens mounted on the sides of buildings throughout the city played news programmes about the killings through the night, interspersed with the first breaking news about Japan's nuclear test, the sinking of the *Peleliu*, and the escalating fear of war in East Asia. In a carefully balanced diplomatic act, South Korea condemned the Japanese nuclear test, regretted the sinking of the *Peleliu*, but urged restraint on all sides. In a private exchange it called on China to condemn North Korea's terrorist campaign in the South. American and South Korean troops guarding the Demilitarized Zone were issued with new body armour. Troops at the heavily fortified Fort Boniface some way back from the DMZ were put on the highest alert.

Just before dawn tens of thousands of North Korean students and trade unionists, in a well-organized demonstration, were chanting across the dividing line of the row of huts on the Panmunjon truce village. Waving flags, they demanded immediate unification with the South. North Korean generals gathered on the balcony of a meeting house only metres from the demarcation line. Just over a kilometre away loudspeakers rigged to a 160 metre high flagpole, the tallest in the world, broadcast anti-American propaganda. The slogans hailed the ideals of the Juche philosophy created by the Communist dictator Kim Il-Sung, who was installed by Stalin after the Second World War and ruled until his death in 1994. In 1950 he invaded the South, and with Chinese help produced a military stalemate with the Americans and Allied forces which was still in place today. Juche meant self-reliance and this philosophy had cut North Koreans off from the rest of the world for more than fifty years. They were controlled as no other people had been before and were told they lived in a paradise. Kim became the Great Leader, a godlike figure, many of whose people were so ignorant that they were not aware that a man had landed on the moon. He bequeathed the mantle of leadership to his erratic and spoilt son, Kim Jong-Il, and it was his message which was now bloodying the streets of South Korea. As a microcosm of the façade of North Korea, the village around the flagpole was uninhabited, although lights in the empty apartment buildings automatically turned on and off in an attempt to trick South Korean peasants into believing in the crumbling regime across the line.

A North Korean armoured personnel carrier drove into the DMZ, blatantly breaking the truce agreement which banned all weapons from the area. American and South Korean troops held their fire. 500 kilometres to the south, outside the port of Pusan, a South Korean merchant ship hit a newly laid North Korean mine and sank. The crew were rescued. Police sealed off universities in the main South Korean cities and arrested students suspected of supporting reunification with the North. For years the security forces had claimed that North Korean agents were infiltrating the universities. Today, stunned by events, no one came forward to mount the usual protests.

In an announcement, the South Korean government claimed that China had condemned North Korea, but there was no confirmation of this from Beijing. The details of the exchanges between the two governments only emerged later, when the complex role that China had played became apparent. During the first two days of the conflict, Seoul's Ambassador to Beijing was told only that China considered chaos on the Korean peninsula an internal affair and that it was friends to both countries. Under no circumstances would it interfere.

Two South Korean *Tologorae* and four *Cosmos* class mini-submarines which had left their base on Cheju Island, 60 kilometres south of the peninsula, were now in position in three groups in waters off both the east and west North Korean coasts. Each group was escorted by a larger *Chang Bogo* Type 209/1200 general-purpose attack submarine. The vessels were built in the Daewoo shipyard based on a German design and several of the thirty-three crewmembers had gone to Germany for training. Like their counterparts in the North, the small submarines were used for coastal infiltration, except these had never been in real action before. Now their mission was to destroy the bases for the North Korean mini-submarines at Cha-ho, Ma Yangdo, and Song Jon Tando, on the east coast, and the smaller base of Sagon-ni on the west coast.

At the first crisis cabinet meeting since the attacks began the American-educated South Korean President Kim Hong-Koo asked bluntly whom his colleagues thought China supported: even the South Koreans, steeped in the shadow-puppetry and nuances of East Asian political life, could not read the signals from Beijing.

'Our policy has always been unification by peaceful means and when the time is right,' said the president. 'We have never wanted a German model. The humiliation and loss of face for the North is not suited to our East Asian style of politics. The cost would also be prohibitive. It would damage our economic expansion at a time when our manufacturing base is beginning to compete head-on with the Japanese in the global market. Yet it seems the North is intent on wrecking the status quo. I would like to assume that it has not been encouraged by Beijing. If I am right in thinking that Chinese troops and weapons would not be used against us, it would be impossible for them to win. I would also like to assume that whatever their nuclear capability, either the detonation or the delivery system will not work. I would lastly like to assume that there are people working with Kim Jong-Il who have a degree of common sense.'

'You are assuming a lot, Mr President,' interjected the Defence Minister.

'Yes, I am,' the President replied. 'But if I don't, the two Koreas will sink very quickly into an apocalyptic bloodbath of destruction far greater than loss of face and unification. The most immediate task, gentlemen, is to neutralize the special forces troops now operating here and ensure they cannot strike again. We have to believe that if we do the South will not be subject to nuclear attack.'

The White House, Washington, DC

The last time the President spoke to Makoto Katayama, the Japanese Ambassador, was on Monday evening, when the two had met at the National Gallery. The meeting had not gone well. Katayama wanted to press him for a decision on military intervention in the South China Sea and the President was not prepared to give it. Now Katayama had been summoned to explain why Japan had detonated a 50 kiloton nuclear warhead in the Ogasarawas.

Ambassador Katayama was shown in. He was tall for a Japanese, nearly 2 metres, and he looked older than his fifty-four years. His hair was thinning and he had a gentle stoop which lent a slightly scholarly air to his appearance. Katayama's posting in Washington was near its end. He would be returning to Tokyo in the late spring to take up the position of Administrative Vice-Minister for Foreign Affairs at the Gaimusho (Foreign Ministry). It was the most senior job a fast-track official in the Gaimusho like him could aspire to. It would place him at the head of foreign policy development in Japan and it crowned a glittering career which had begun more than thirty years before with a first-class honours degree from the law school of Tokyo University.

The President gestured to a settee to the right of his own armchair and enquired whether the Ambassador would prefer tea, coffee, or something stronger. Katayama declined, and sat there waiting for the silence to be broken. The President cleared his throat. 'Well, Mr Ambassador, what are we to make of events at Ogasawara? I can tell, just having read the *Washington Post*'s poll of American attitudes to Japan, you have opened a hornets' nest. What do you say?'

Katayama waited for what seemed like an eternity to reply. And then he spoke. 'First of all, Mr President, may I, on behalf of the Japanese government and people of Japan, extend our profound sympathies at the loss of the USS *Peleliu*? It was a shock to us all. Tokyo has instructed our Ambassador in Beijing to make the strongest possible representations to the Chinese government. Now I turn to answer your question. It is a matter greatly to be regretted that things have come to this. But they have, and we have to move forward, not back,' he said. 'The simple fact is, Mr President, that you and your country can no longer make good your security treaty with us. This has been amply demonstrated by the events of this week. We understand that and have understood it for some time. The days of Americans fighting wars in Asia are over. You have made your sacrifices, you have safeguarded this region while we have grown strong and rich. But there comes a time in the maturity of nations when we have to bid our foster parents farewell and stand on our own two feet. We've had our growing pains. Need I remind you of New Zealand's effective pull-out from the ANZUS treaty in the early 1980s, your ejection from the Philippines in the early 1990s, and the hostility you've found in Okinawa since the mid-1990s? That your military withdrawal from Asia should coincide with the rise of China as a superpower was, as your government well knows, a matter of grave concern for us. It was a concern that was made no easier to bear with our own people by the incessant attacks successive governments have made on us in the area of trade. And all along you have said, spend more on defence. You cannot have it both ways. You cannot on the one hand require us to pay ever increasing amounts for our own defence and on the other seek to determine how we then act. That I think is what is meant by the term "imperial overreach", is it not? Japan, Mr President, has not stood still during this period. A new post-war generation has come to power. It has no memory of the Pacific War, it only has questions as to why Japan cannot look after its own affairs.

'Why are you surprised by our modest nuclear test? As I am sure you know better than I, the US government has been providing Japan with the technical know-how to build a nuclear device for well over a decade. We did not take the decision to go down the nuclear route lightly. This did not just mean building some bombs, it meant also having the capability to deliver them. And we have the capability, within a regional context, to deliver a nuclear warhead with accuracy.

'What I think you want to know is our intentions. Prime Minister Hyashi will be making an address to the nation on that matter shortly. I cannot pre-empt it but I can assure you that it holds no genuine surprises, that we look forward to continued close cooperation with the United States. But let me say this. We are in Asia; you are not. We have to deal with China as a military threat and a commercial opportunity; you just have to manage a commercial relationship. Our position is more complex as well. We have the legacy of history to overcome. Even as we speak, we have to assess this new outbreak of violence on the Korean peninsula. Here is a dangerous and unpredictable flashpoint in which people will look to Japan for leadership. All this will be the challenge of Japanese diplomacy in the coming years. As for American public opinion, we look to you to give your people the lead. Racism, an ugly word, has always been part of our relationship. Through leadership, on both sides, it can be ameliorated if not completely eradicated. We cannot run our affairs on the basis of opinion polls in newspapers.'

The Korean Peninsula

Local time: 0600 Wednesday 21 February 2001
GMT: 2100 Tuesday 20 February 2001

American satellite photographs showed no abnormal activity on the heavily fortified front line between North and South. The hills and rice paddies, covered with snow, frost, and thick ice, appeared as they always had done at this time of year. North Korean peasants worked muffled up against the sub-zero temperatures and biting winds. The food and fuel shortages had gripped their country for more than six years now since the first devastating floods. Bad times had arrived shortly after the death of Kim Il-Sung and they were not so sure about his reclusive son. They called him 'the iron lord of all creatures' and 'the great military strategist'. But Kim Jong-Il rarely went out among the people, nor did he offer guidance on agriculture, industry, and the Juche philosophy, as his father had. In the elite circles of Pyongyang there were stories of Kim Jong-Il in wild parties with prostitutes from Scandinavia, France, and Britain; of his drinking; of his deep depressions and uncontrollable temper. No one was sure of the true character of this enigmatic leader. But for the peasants he had certainly not been able to safeguard Korea from natural disasters. They lived on barely subsistence diets and it had been more than a year since their homes had had electricity or any fuel for heating.

Yet just underneath their fields were enough supplies to sustain whole towns, a complex of military installations which this most secretive country built to unleash its offensive against the South when the time was right. Artillery, tanks, fighter aircraft, and helicopters were hidden in tunnels and huge caves hewn out of the mountains. North Korea believed it could launch an intensive surprise attack by delivering artillery support without exposing the weapons. Short-range firepower would come from tank and mechanized units. Hundreds of amphibious vehicles would cross the Imjin River to send in troops and equipment. More than 2,000 prefabricated floating bridges were ready to replace the existing bridges which would be blown by retreating allied forces. In the late Nineties, Pyongyang had tightened its own defences with more than 15,000 anti-aircraft guns, together with 500 surface-to-air missiles and a new early warning radar system to intercept intruding aircraft, while the North's 170mm cannon and 240mm rockets would pound the heart of Seoul. One of the first targets would be Seoul's 88 Freeway, which straddled the city but could be used as a runway for the South's fighter jets.

As South Korea's special forces commandos left their submarines and headed for the Northern coastline, defence officials in Seoul were drawing up plans to defend the city in the worst-case scenario of a full-frontal assault from the North.

Each of the commandos knew the base he was attacking as if it was his own. They had studied photographs and been trained in model layouts, although none had believed they would ever have to move in for real as they were now. At Ma Yangdo twenty-four men made landfall inside the base perimeter to avoid the mined terrain on the other side of the fence. Six broke away, killed the guards, and waved ten other men forward. The remainder stayed with the boats. Explosives were laid around the main buildings and the fuel and ammunition dumps. Frogmen attached mines to twelve North Korean mini-subs on delayed timers. Three *Soju* class fast-attack craft were also in the port: mines were attached to them as well. Within ten minutes, and without being detected, the raiding party had finished its task. The explosives were designed to terrify and destroy. They cut through the buildings, spraying out smaller devices which booby-trapped the whole area around. North Korean troops were wounded and killed by them hours after the attack. The base itself was rendered inoperative, and before pulling away from the combat area mines were laid at the entrance of the port. Two of the other attacks also went according to plan, but at Sagon-ni a North Korean guard spotted the raiding party as the men came ashore. He opened fire, killing two immediately and wounding three more. Spotlights lit up the whole base and alarms wailed as the North Koreans took up positions on rooftops with heavy machine-guns. Six commandos slipped into the water and escaped. Five others were gunned down and at least four were captured alive. A television broadcast from Pyongyang showed the bodies of the commandos, filmed as they lay on the ground in the base. The newscaster interviewed South Korean prisoners, their heads hanging and rolling from side to side in what was meant to be a guilt-racked confession. The South denied the report outright. It said the men were North Korean actors. No mention was made by either side of the successful operations against the three other naval bases.

The *Guardian* newspaper offices, London

The exclusive front-page story in the third edition of Britain's *Guardian* newspaper reached the desks of world leaders less than half an hour after the newspaper hit the streets of London. It was judged important enough by the aides of the American President and British Prime Minister to be read raw without abridgement in bullet points on a briefing paper.

The article was written by the paper's award-winning Tokyo correspondent, Martin Miller, whose contacts in the security and defence industries were legendary. The swiftness with which he had compiled his well-documented account led to accusations that Miller had known of the Japanese plans to conduct a nuclear test for some weeks. But Miller turned the finger of blame back to the American establishment. The headline read: *America gave them the bomb with no regrets.*

Briefing

How Japan acquired the bomb

America gave them the bomb with no regrets

Japan's explosion of a small nuclear warhead came as no surprise to many Washington officials who for some years had advocated a controlled end to the outdated American security pact with Japan. While America's public policy was one of nuclear non-proliferation, a group of powerful officials has for many years been coaxing Japan towards the hallowed nuclear fellowship. They began during the Reagan and Bush administrations when the Soviet Union was seen as the major threat in the Pacific. After that, they believed as an inevitability that at some stage America's security role in East Asia would have to end, probably because of a challenge from an unfriendly power with whom it didn't want to fight. They decided, therefore, to help Japan, a staunch ally, to obtain a nuclear arsenal, before either India or Pakistan declared their bombs or China attempted to test the military resolve of its smaller Asian neighbours.

The policy was blindly simple. America and Europe helped Japan acquire a large stockpile of separated plutonium which immediately gave it an ability to make nuclear weapons. Much of the help came from Savannah River Laboratory. Scientists there passed on technology and hardware for use in two Japanese fast-breeder reactors (FBRs), producing high-quality plutonium, and considered a major threat to nuclear proliferation. The principal behind the FBR is that more plutonium is produced than is consumed. The extra plutonium can be used for other FBRs and so on. However, the FBRs also create plutonium which is far purer than even the weapons-grade plutonium. The International Atomic Energy Agency categorizes Japan's type of plutonium as 'super-grade'.

Congress effectively terminated America's FBR programme in 1983, even before US construction began. But Japan operates two facilities. One is the Joyo FBR at the Oarai Research Centre north of Tokyo, which reached criticality in 1977. The second is the Monju FBR near Tsuruga on the coast of the East Sea, west of Tokyo. Monju went critical in 1994. Of critical importance to the development of the nuclear programme was the Rokkasho Mura facility in Amori prefecture. Covering a vast site, the Japanese spent $18 billion on a fuel reprocessing plant alone. It is here that the *Guardian* understands the government also built a facility to take plutonium oxide, turn it into metal, and machine the metal into shapes suitable for weapons manufacture.

The move to close collaboration between the United States and Japan was sealed when it became clear that Japan was proceeding with FBRs yet America was not. Documents obtained by the *Guardian* highlight American commitment to keeping abreast of the FBR developments – even though they were banned in the United States itself. In 1987, as the programme was being formulated, the *Oak Ridge National Laboratory Review* published the following: '... this collaboration will allow the United States to maintain a core of expertise; ... technical experts can

stay abreast of developments in the reprocessing field as they participate in a viable, long-term mission ...'
And a year later William Burch, director of the ORNL Fuel Recycle Division, said: '... the bilateral agreement will be mutually beneficial ... Japan will be able to speed up its development period of reprocessing technology through its collaboration with the US, while also probably saving some money ... For the US ... the deal keeps us in the ball game ...'

Both American and Japanese politicians have publicly denied Tokyo's intention of going nuclear. In November 1992, as part of its attempt to develop a self-sufficient nuclear fuel cycle, Japan began to import large quantities of separated plutonium. It now has as much as 50,000 kilograms and by 2010 it's expected to have 90,000. Japan has never been more than thirty days away from constructing a nuclear weapon. All it needed was the political decision, which has now been made.

The statistics are chilling. As little as 3 kilograms is needed for one nuclear warhead with an explosive equivalent to at least 20,000 tons of TNT. With its present stockpiles, it's thought Japan has enough super-grade plutonium for more than 200 warheads. They could be attached to advanced cruise missiles, which we may see in tests the Japanese are expected to begin in the next few days. They would weigh no more than 150 kilograms and have a range of about 2,500 kilometres. Defence experts say that at least two of the recently commissioned *Harushio* class submarines could now be nuclear armed. At the same time, Japan has developed its H-2 space launch vehicle, which the Pentagon says has recently been developed for military purposes. It includes an

Orbital Re-entry Experiment capsule, with a payload capacity of 4,000 kilograms.

Japan has always reserved the right to go nuclear. Even in 1957, the then Prime Minister, Nobusuke Kishi, declared it was not unconstitutional for Japan to possess nuclear weapons provided they were within the definition of self-defence.

Since then subtle changes made to the constitution, coupled with a sea change in political thinking, has made the nuclear option acceptable. In October 1993 Masashi Nishihara of the National Defence Academy said: 'We are scared of China. Either we can allow China to become dominant, or we can be more equal by confronting them.' Nishihara believed Japan should treat China as the United States had treated the Soviet Union: face them down, then negotiate arms reduction treaties. But to do that, Japan needed the bomb. China's takeover of the South China Sea was the catalyst. Since the early nineties, concern has been growing throughout Asia about China's increased military budget and its plans for territorial expansion. Unconfirmed but well-publicized reports say that since the 1996 stand-off with two American carrier groups off the Taiwan Straits billions of dollars have been redirected to modernize the Chinese army and navy. But it is still no match for either America or Japan. Today, those two countries share global superpower status. Japan, as the new kid on the block, is being warned that any repeat of its Second World War atrocities will not tolerated.

While Asia is both suspicious and resentful of Japan, the alternative is even more ominous – the secretive, non-accountable, non-democratic, unmodernized regime of China. Over the next few weeks, the United States will encourage Asians and Americans to bury their memories of more than fifty years ago, and welcome Japanese military power as the new regional security umbrella. Japanese missiles may be able reach American and Indian cities. But today you can be sure they are programmed only towards China.

The White House, Washington, DC

Local time: 2130 Tuesday 20 February 2001
GMT: 0230 Wednesday 21 February 2001

The task of explaining America's hidden policy lay with
Marty Weinstein, the National Security Adviser, whom the
President summoned as soon as he had finished reading
the article. He asked for an explicit memorandum address-
ing the points raised by the *Guardian*, and an opinion poll
among those who had read the article to gauge the public
level of support. Weinstein explained that while Martin
Miller was broadly correct, there had not been an administration policy to help Japan build a nuclear bomb.
American nuclear scientists simply wanted to keep abreast
of technological development in a field for which Congress
had cut off funds. No American laws had been broken.
Without the cooperation of the Oak Ridge National Laboratory, Japan would still have nuclear weapons today.

'Marty, explaining away secrets doesn't worry me. We
do that all the time. But before sending a task force to blast
the Chinese out of the South China Sea, I need to decide
whether we should now condemn or cooperate with Japan.
Which course would save American lives and protect our
national interests?'

'I believe we should opt for cooperation, Mr President.
At the end of the day Japan is an ally. We have no conflict
of interests.'

'All right. But spell it out, Marty. As I will have to spell
it out to the nation.'

'Let's promote it as burden sharing. American cannot
indefinitely police the world. So, let's look first at the threat
and then with whom we are best allied. In Europe, we can

absolutely rely on the British and usually on the French. They are the grown-ups of the security alliance. They're nuclear. The others waver. We have no major unbreakable alliances in South Asia or the Middle East. India would be a natural ally. But historically it's suspicious. It has its own superpower aspirations. Our friends in the Middle East such as Egypt and Saudi Arabia have domestic political considerations to take into account. In the long term the danger is similar to that of China. The Islamic political and cultural system does not blend with ours. The values and aspirations are different. There is only so far a relationship can go. In East Asia, the ASEAN nations will waver. They know they can't take on either China or Japan. They prefer us but sense our time is up. They are pragmatic people. Their focus is on trade and development. They will accept a new order in China or Japan as long as it doesn't jeopardize trade. And we have the wobble of Russia. No one knows what will happen there. Russia is nuclear.

'Over the next fifty years or so Russia, China, and India will jostle for superpower position. Fine, none is a rogue state.'

'Marty,' interrupted the President, 'China has attacked Vietnam, taken over sea lanes to the Pacific, and sunk one of our warships with a huge loss of life.'

'Mr President, I'm talking from the viewpoint of history. We can sanction and bomb Iraq, Libya, Panama. We know their leaders are despots. China is not in that category, and I believe we must approach this from that angle. Look what's happened at the UN Security Council. Beijing vetoes every proposal we put forward.'

'OK. Go on.'

'We might have a public policy to fight two major campaigns at once, but as I said, it's becoming impossible because of budget cuts to the military. If we commit to the South China Sea, we will leave another flank wide open.

For example, the Sixth Fleet has a long-term NATO commitment in the Mediterranean. Iran, Iraq, and the Gulf remain areas of tension where we cannot afford to withdraw our forces. If Iran watched us at a stand-off with China, if we began to pour supplies into Vietnam or the Philippines as we did for the Gulf War in the 1990s, and then if Iran decided to flex its muscle in the Gulf, we couldn't handle it, Mr President. By that I mean we wouldn't be defeated in battle, but the costs, the body bags, the Middle Eastern and Oriental enemies on the television screens would turn the American people against what we're trying to achieve.'

'Like in the Vietnam War.'

'Precisely. We win on the battlefield but lose in Congress.'

'Are you speculating or do you know something, Marty?'

'I'm speculating with fact. China makes serious money out of selling weapons. In the last five-year period it came to more than $10 billion. Ninety per cent of that comes from the Middle East. Its closest relationship right now is with Iran, which, incidentally, is how they financed the sudden purchase of two very nasty warships from Russia in the past two years. They've bought the *Sovremenny* class frigates *Vazhny* and *Vdumchivy*, which we believe cost them a quarter of a billion dollars. These ships are armed to the teeth and what they carry isn't pretty, it's brutal stuff, Mr President. They scared us to hell in the Cold War days and they've now come back again to haunt us sailing under another flag. China's got missiles and nuclear technology. Iran's got oil money. Russia's got the toys.

'The Chinese violated the Missile Technology Control Regime [MTCR] accord which they signed in 1987. It bans the sale of missiles or technology for missiles that can carry a payload of more than 500 kilograms a distance of more than 300 kilometres. A year later, China sold thirty-six intermediate-range CSS-2 missiles to Saudi Arabia, which paid more than $3 billion for them. It was also working on a deal to sell its newly developed M-9 missiles to Syria. It's been involved with Iran, Iraq, Pakistan, Syria, Saudi Arabia, Egypt, and a few others. The common factor uniting those countries, Mr President, is that they are Islamic.

'We first put pressure on China in 1987 when it sold Silkworm missiles to Iran. Then it got worse. In 1989 and 1991 Chinese and Iranian companies struck what in public looked like a commercial deal. But the product was nuclear – an electromagnetic separator for producing isotopes and a mini-type reactor. The Chinese said it was being used for peaceful purposes; for medical diagnosis and nuclear physics research.

'Atom bombs can be made using a concentrated uranium isotope. That particular deal was dropped, we think because the Russians came up with a better one. But let us assume that Iran is about where Iraq was in the early nineties. It's exploring the nuclear path, but isn't there yet. The next thing we know is that China's sent over what we call *calutron* equipment, which is needed to enrich uranium. Our intelligence also finds evidence of China supplying Iran with chemical weapons material, thiodiglycol and thionyl chloride, both of which are very nasty substances. The upshot is an aspiring nuclear enemy, possibly with an additional arsenal of mass-destruction chemical weapons. But so far Iran's delivery capability is limited.

'Then we spotted two convoys carrying twenty-six missiles as well as launchers and other accessories moving through the outskirts of Beijing over a three-day period. They went to the main northern port of Tianjin. We believe they were East Wind 31, an intercontinental ballistic missile with a range of 8,000 kilometres. They're propelled by solid-fuel rockets, can be moved around by trucks and fired quickly. We can't detect them easily and they're pretty accurate.'

'And Iran might have them in its arsenal?'

'We're pretty sure it has, Mr President. They're not the best China has. The East Wind 32 was tested in 2000. It was fired from Xinjiang in the far west and travelled 3,000 kilometres overland and into the South China Sea. Its range is 12,000 kilometres. Its payload can be a 700 kilogram nuclear warhead. If fired from Chinese soil, Mr President, the East Wind 32 could get to Alaska or Western Europe. We also believe they're working on a new submarine-launched ICBM. If they get one of those into the Pacific, they could attack Washington and New York.'

'Thank you, Marty,' said the President. 'What exactly are you saying?'

'China sells cheap weapons to the Middle East. A Russian MiG-29 fighter costs around $25 million. A Chinese F-7M is no more than $4.5 million. It secures a relationship with oil-producing countries to ensure supplies for the 8,000,000 barrels a day it will need to import by 2010. It calculates that the relationship with the Islamic countries will withstand international pressure for sanctions against it. In the UN it uses its veto, as we know. With those blocks in place it takes over the South China Sea. After the 1996 stand-off during the Taiwan election, the PLA realized that it could not defeat our navy in battle, and wouldn't even be able to even equal it until around 2020. But it knows we can't handle two conflicts at the same time. So it ensures that Iran has the capability to start a diversion if we try another 1996 battle group deployment.'

'Do you know this will happen?'

'As I said, Mr President, our HUMINT is not good. We don't know what the leadership is thinking. But they don't want to fight us. They want us to lose our nerve and get out of the Pacific. In a normal world, all our concentration would be on this mess on the Korean peninsula. As it is, our resources are deployed against China and we're mostly using Japanese intelligence on North Korean troop and naval movements. If we're going to stay there with any credibility we have to do it in an alliance with Japan as a military and nuclear power which can face down China and keep her at bay.'

The Sino-Vietnamese border

Local time: 1000 Wednesday 21 February 2001
GMT: 0300 Wednesday 21 February 2001

Major Lon stared gap-mouthed as Lieutenant Claude Joffe of the French Army Signals Division set up his laptop computer. A French corporal orientated what appeared to be a satellite dish, but instead of heavenwards he pointed it south to Hanoi and the French Embassy there. Soon the exact location of all Chinese units presently flooding across the border would appear on Lieutenant Joffe's screen. The clouds over the battlefield had parted, giving the French spy satellite ideal conditions for monitoring troop movements 100 kilometres below.

300 kilometres to the north-west, in Nanning, a Chinese battlefield manager, Qiao Xiaoming, was engaged in much the same task, at much the same time. He was using a Thomson-CSF Star Burst battlefield information manager which enabled him to communicate electronically and through radio with officers in the field who had mobile versions of his equipment. The graphic display was functioning perfectly. Each armoured division and infantry battalion was illuminated on the screen before him. The images were not photographs, they were more schematic, but with the aid of a computer mouse he could zoom in on any unit and know its strength and capability and exact location in the jungles and on the roads of Vietnam to within 1 metre.

The humble camera had come a long way: it was now digital and connected to a high-speed computer and transmitter: but the satellite the French had stationed above the battlefield did more than just take photographs, process them, and instantaneously send them to an earth receiver. It also possessed a powerful transmitter for other equally secret operations. Like the Americans and the British, French arms manufacturers of 'intelligent' weapons liked to stay in control of what they sold to foreign governments, so they wired into the hardware of each piece of military hardware a device that could be activated remotely to render it useless. It could be turned on and off at will, suggesting to the unwary that it was suffering a malfunction. It was insurance, taken out on the basis that today's client might be tomorrow's enemy, or the enemy of a friend. The beauty of it was that the interference could not be traced back to the manufacturer – the Trojan Horse was wired into the silicon chips that in this case animated the Star Burst system.

As Qiao Xiaoming watched 50,000 Chinese troops flow across the Vietnamese border, supported by 250 battle tanks and numerous trucks and lighter vehicles, he was not sure whether to marvel at the wonders of modern science or give in to a sentimental feeling of pride at the activities of his comrades. He did not have time to mull the decision. His screen flickered and then the images upon it dissolved before his eyes. He hit it but it did not respond. He pressed an emergency call button, and then he turned the Star Burst system off and then on again. It seemed to right itself for a moment and then went blank. By the time it did that, half a dozen senior PLA officers were standing around with a look of horror on their faces. To a man they knew that their ability to manage the attack on Lang Son had just slipped from their grasp.

The Prime Minister's residence, Tokyo

Local time: 1230 Wednesday 21 February 2001
GMT: 0330 Wednesday 21 February 2001

Noburo Hyashi had been waiting all his political life for this moment – the day when he would lead Japan into complete independence and freedom. The NHK television crew was busying itself in his office with lights and leads for microphones. Frank Lloyd Wright, the American architect, had designed the official residence of the Japanese Prime Minister, which was situated in Nagatacho, near the Diet (parliament) building. While Hyashi had no particular liking for Americans as such he had grown to like his official residence. Lloyd Wright's use of blond woods was particularly attractive. He also put big windows in the walls which let in light and enabled Hyashi to look out on one of the most perfectly maintained small Japanese gardens in Tokyo. From his office he looked straight into a plum tree in full blossom. Prime Ministerial addresses to the nation were rare in Japanese politics. The usual practice would be for the Prime Minister (flanked by his cabinet three steps behind) to stand at a lectern in an anonymous white-walled room, make a small speech, and then take overlong questions from reporters. His Private Secretary cleared most of the papers from his desk. A tilted plastic autocue was placed directly in front of the desk, below the line of sight of the camera but high enough so it looked as though Hyashi was looking at the camera when he spoke.

'My fellow Japanese,' he began. 'I have requested the opportunity to speak to you today to explain the current situation and the government's response to it. As you know the government of the People's Republic of China launched an unprovoked air attack on the Republic of Vietnam on Sunday. At the same time it instituted a blockade of the South China Sea, denying to Japan and other peace-loving peoples in Asia the use of a vital waterway, and this morning China launched an invasion across the Vietnamese border. We are also trying to assess the fresh outbreak of violence on the Korean peninsula and determine to what extent that also threatens long-term peace in the Pacific. Since 1960 Japan has enjoyed a military alliance with the United States. Part of the requirements that treaty places on its two signatories is for one to come to the aid of the other when its national interest is threatened. Your government decided that such a threat to Japan's survival was created by China's actions on Sunday and through diplomatic channels we sought to invoke our treaty with the United States. Sadly, we could not agree that such a threat existed.

'The government concluded that to all intents and purposes the military alliance which we had with the United States had ended. This left Japan little choice but to act independently. The first part of that independent action occurred this morning when our military forces tested a small nuclear device. I fully understand that given our own tragic experience of nuclear weapons, many of you will be saddened by news that we too possess such weapons. Some, indeed, may be even angry. To those who are I can do nothing more than offer my sincerest regrets.

'It is not the place of the Japanese Prime Minister to lecture the United States. But I cannot conclude this part of my address to you without one observation on racism. The Americans should admit that racial prejudice does not hold any solutions to the problems developing in the world today. It is important that they face the situation aware of the historical context, seeing that the reality is that the power in the world, including economic power, is shifting from West to East. It may not be as strong a shift as used to be expressed last century with talk about the "Pacific era", but at any rate it is in America's interest to rid itself of prejudice against Asia, including that against Japan, in order to maintain a position of leadership in the world.

'Our new position in the world will require us to make changes and sacrifices. Although your government seeks no more for Japan than that it should play a role commensurate with its economic position in the world, we will have to be sensitive to feelings of our neighbours as they adjust to the new realities. We cannot become overbearing, which will not be tolerated in the new era, but by the same token an inferiority complex is equally harmful. The Japanese must move out of their current mental stagnation. If you stay silent when you have a particular demand or an opposing position to express, the other party will take it for granted that you have no demand or opposition. When you close your mind to the outside, remaining in a uniquely Japanese mental framework, you will be isolated in this modern, interdependent world.

'Let me explain the new role for our nation which the government foresees. Japan should open its markets to the extent where there will be no room for complaints from foreign friends, and we should provide money to help developing countries where people are not being oppressed. Japan needs to become aware of its responsibilities. I realize there is a cost associated with this. Certainly the full opening of our markets, and the advancing of large sums of money to developing countries, will be very painful and costly. However, things will not get better in the world until the pain is shared more equitably. How much pain do you think was involved during the Meiji Restoration [1868] when the privileged class of samurai gave up their power, cut their special hairstyles, and tossed out their swords? It allowed a bloodless revolution to take place within Japan. We need such a peaceful revolution in Asia.

'In spite of the legacy of the past, Japan has the capability to take a lead in Asia. I offer two examples from opposite ends of the scale. Japanese popular songs are heard all over Asia today. Karaoke is the most popular form of home entertainment in our region. From Dalian to Sydney this quintessentially Japanese pastime is enjoyed. Then there are cultural treasures such as the Miroku Buddha, or the Horiyuji Temple. They attract interest and respect from all over the world, beyond national, racial, and cultural boundaries. These are products of refinement from the Japanese people. The original image of Buddha came from India, by way of China and the Korean peninsula. The image of Buddha in Japan is the product of the refinement of Japanese art. The process has been constantly refined and it becomes a product of Japanese intellectual processes; it is clearly Japanese. Everything stops at Japan; the Japanese people refine what has come their way; Japan is the last stop in cultural transition.

'These are noble aims for the future. Japan stands ready to offer assistance to our neighbours in Asia, near and far. At the moment, however, we face as serious a threat as we have ever faced. China's adventurism in the South China Sea cannot go unchecked. We have a responsibility to broker peace on the Korean peninsula. We have no desire for dominance in Asia. We seek only stability so that trade can flourish. Yet already one oil tanker bound for Japan has been hijacked. We have dispatched a naval group to the South China Sea. Initially it will conduct missile trials. It will also offer protection for Japanese and Japan-bound shipping.

'The Japanese government stands ready to discuss these matters with the Chinese government. A negotiated peaceful settlement to this crisis has always been and remains the top priority of the Japanese government.'

Kabuto-cho Financial District, Tokyo

Hidei Kobayashi, the head of trading and strategy at Nomura Securities, switched the television set off. A hundred and one things were running through his mind at once as he tried to digest what the Prime Minister had said – shock at the nuclear test, fear at being cut adrift from the Americans, pride at hearing a Japanese speak so well – and tried to get all of that out of his mind and assess the investment decision. He did not take much time. He decided to buy selectively, especially in the defence area – Mitsubishi Heavy Industries, Mitsui, Nippon Steel, and Sumitomo Steel – which he calculated would benefit from bigger orders in the future. After all, Hyashi had said a 'security system to meet Japan's needs can be built' – implying that it had not yet been completed. Even the might of the Nomura could not turn the market. Foreign selling had become overwhelming. The Nikkei index, which had plunged 1,678 on Tuesday, fell precipitously again. By the end of the morning session it was 2,063 lower at 35,559.

The yen was under enormous pressure. The Bank of Japan virtually stood in the market and bought all the yen the market wanted to throw at it. From its New York close of ¥163.75 it fell to ¥168.75 in the first hour of trading. It was precisely at this moment that Phillips executed his winning deal. He gave instructions for the remainder of the yen position First China had accumulated for General Zhao to be unwound. First China was sitting on a ¥124 billion position – the remainder of the position it had built up when the yen was trading around ¥120 to the dollar. In the

London market the previous day some ¥124 billion had been reversed, netting General Zhao profits in excess of $200 million. In the Tokyo market, First China locked in the remaining gains. With the Japanese currency having fallen 36 per cent weaker, First China moved to cover its position, pocketing the best part of $256 million in the process.

In Hong Kong the market had opened sharply down. Hyashi's television appearance was seen throughout Asia on Star TV, the regional satellite broadcaster. Old memories die hard and the behaviour of the Imperial Japanese Army during the Second World War had been kept alive, partly because its deeds were so appalling and partly to use as a stick to beat Tokyo with whenever its compliance was needed. The market continued to slide all morning as Hong Kong Chinese investors liquidated their holdings of local stocks and switched their funds into US dollars. The Hong Kong dollar, pegged to the US dollar at a rate of HK$7.8 to $1 since September 1983, began to feel the strain of capital outflow. The Hong Kong Monetary Authority, which regulated banks and money markets, moved to support the local dollar by forcing a rise in interest rates. The authority was required by law to preserve exchange rate stability, so with the currency weakening it had to raise interest rates. This could not, however, have come at a worse time. The 0.5 per cent rise in short term interest rates to 11 per cent only served to weaken confidence in the stock market further.

The CNN Asia newsroom, Singapore

Local time: 1245 Wednesday 21 February 2001
GMT: 0445 Wednesday 21 February 2001

With the subtitle 'Breaking News' running at the bottom of the screen, CNN announced India's condemnation of Japan's nuclear threat. It was a 'disgrace and an abomination for the future development of the world'. India also blamed China for initiating its attack on Vietnam. 'That irresponsible act has been the catalyst for the creation of a new and unwelcome superpower. Just as the world was balanced, it has become tipped into a perilous adventure.'

Russia said the inevitable had happened: 'Nothing on this Earth can stand still. Japan has now barged its way into our exclusive club. Whether or not she will become a welcome member will depend on the level of maturity with which she uses her newly declared power.' The Russian government made no criticism of Operation Dragonstrike.

South Africa described the test as a disappointing trend. 'While South Africa and other nations voluntarily abandoned their programmes to go nuclear, Japan was secretly pursuing the path to creating the most destructive weapons available to man. We are waiting to hear what she hopes to achieve and more importantly what level of protection she will offer in treaty to non-nuclear governments and whether she will guarantee a no-strike policy against those of us without such weapons.'

The European Union said the test was a 'regrettable and unnecessary change to Japanese policy'. Spain called for an immediate international conference to determine new rules for the nuclear powers. Britain spoke of 'having to come to terms with the grim realism of international affairs. At the

end of the day Japan is an ally of the democratic West.'
Nothing should be done in the present 'climate of unpredictability in the Pacific' to damage that alliance. France
even came close to subtly contradicting the European
Union statement. 'It is regrettable that one Pacific rim
country has committed an act of such unpalatable
aggression to cause another to declare its nuclear arsenal.
If it comes to conflict between China and Japan, the
government of France will support the Japanese.'

The Korean Peninsula

Japanese early warning aircraft monitoring the theatre detected the launch of the Taepo-Dong ballistic missile from a site north of Pyongyang and within seconds South Korea fired Mark IV American-made Patriot missiles to intercept it. The Taepo-Dong had last been tested in 1998 and with a range of nearly 2,000 kilometres it could strike most places in North-East Asia. But the missile was destroyed well before it reached its intended target of Pusan, on the southern tip of the Peninsula. Then the Japanese spotted the mobile launchers for two shorter-range No-Dong missiles, both in the far north of the country near the Chinese border, where North Korea had built up its road and power infrastructure under the guise of creating a free-trade zone. Defence analysts believed the missiles were being moved out of hiding to launch places. While the defence network of Patriot missiles and early warning detection provided a formidable cover against attack, it was not watertight. The failure of Patriots against Iraqi Scud missiles during the Gulf War was a grim reminder of South Korea's vulnerability. Killings were continuing in Seoul itself and North Korean saboteurs had begun a second wave of terror in Pusan and Mokpo in the far south.

In Pyongyang itself there was a diplomatic silence. From Beijing Jamie Song, momentarily diverted from Dragon-strike, put a call through to the North Korean capital in an attempt to talk to Kim Jong-Il. But the Foreign Minister's secretary said that as soon as she spoke the line went dead.

All other numbers were either disconnected or rang without being answered. The Chinese Ambassador in Pyongyang said he had been trying to talk to the leadership for the past two days. The German Ambassador, one of the few Western diplomats accredited to the city, reported no unusual activity. There had been air-raid practices but this was routine. The city was blacked out after dark. Blinds were drawn down the windows of the Koryo Hotel, the only hotel open. Spotlights which usually lit up the Arch of Triumph, the statues of the Great Leader, the Juche Tower, and other symbols of North Korean greatness were turned off. But no extra troops were being openly deployed in this graceful totalitarian city, with wide boulevards for military displays, drab apartment blocks for the people, and imaginative monuments showing off the godlike qualities of Kim Il-Sung. The only sign of an impending war was the increased level of vitriol against America and South Korea on television and radio. 'Our dear leader Kim Jong-Il is a genius at military strategy and a genius at military leadership,' was one radio message. 'We have nothing to fear from the imperialist American invaders and their South Korean puppet army.' Meanwhile a television announcer chastized the selfishness of Western society: 'To pursue the right of the individual is to be no better than a worm,' he said. 'We have nothing to fear from the guns and missile of worms, for when they face the courageous and unselfish soldiers of the Juche idea, the worms will wriggle and crawl back into the ground.'

A squadron of South Korean F-16 aircraft crossed the Demilitarized Zone low enough to be underneath the enemy radar. They split into three groups to attack North Korean radar and air-defence positions with precision-guided bombs. The operation took a matter of minutes, but not without cost. The North Korean anti-aircraft defences, tested for the first time ever, were on a high alert and responded with enough accuracy to destroy two South Korean aircraft. As the South Korean pilots headed for home, the North scrambled its own aircraft, many of them from concealed hangars inside mountain bases. Over the next thirty minutes, South Korean air defences shot down five MiG-21 fighter aircraft, attacking them with surface-to-air missiles and F-16 fighters on both sides of the DMZ. One North Korean slipped through the first defences and crossed into South Korea, only to point his aircraft towards the sea and eject. He was picked up by American troops and taken straight in for interrogation. A second squadron of South Korean F-16s flew high above Pyongyang and further north to the suspected missile launch sites. They used both free-fall and guided bombs at points in the mountainous area specified on satellite photographs. As they headed back, one F-16 was shot down by a surface-to-air missile. The pilot died. The aircraft flew past a third squadron attacking radar and air-defence positions around Pyongyang, and a fourth which pounded the Yongbyon nuclear power facility, the focus of the North's nuclear weapons programme. For the next few hours, wave after wave of South Korean aircraft hit military installations in North Korea. Casualties were high. At the end of the day, South Korea had lost thirty-three aircraft. Only three pilots, who managed to nurse their planes back across the frontier, survived.

President Kim Hong-Koo spoke for less than ten minutes to Jamie Song in Beijing, after which he called a full meeting of the South Korean cabinet. 'The Chinese government says it will support any action we take to neutralize North Korea. The view from Beijing is that the present regime in Pyongyang could destabilize the whole of the East Asian region.'

'But China itself is destabilizing the region,' interjected the Foreign Minister.

'China may well win in the end. North Korea is bound to lose,' answered the President. 'Gentlemen, the way the Chinese Foreign Minister explained it to me was that we in Seoul had a duty to the region to bring stability back to the peninsula. China would play its part by offering diplomatic support and giving asylum to Kim Jong-Il and a select number of his cronies.'

'What will the Americans say?' asked the Foreign Minister.

'I can't see why they would disagree with China. A neutralized North Korea would be one less rogue state to deal with.'

The Sino-Vietnamese border

The Chinese met little resistance when they crossed the border. The Vietnamese forces, on orders, simply melted into the jungle. The Chinese commander took this as a sign of cowardice. His motorized units pushed on and were at the outskirts of Lang Son within three hours. There they halted, and fatally there they waited for the column behind to catch up.

Lieutenant Joffe motioned to Major Lon to commence firing. For the past ten minutes Joffe had been relaying detailed coordinates to Lon who, in turn, instructed his artillery officers as to elevation and type of ammunition to use. Lon commanded twenty-five 105mm howitzers. They could lob a shell 10 kilometres that would make a crater 3 metres in diameter on impact. In addition to the guns he had three batteries of multiple rocket launchers of a similar capacity. One after the other the big guns fired, interspersed with the woosh of the rockets. Together they hurled a deadly mix of high-explosive charges for the 'hard' Chinese targets, such as the tanks and trucks and armoured personnel carriers, and an assortment of projectiles with variable time-fused munitions that exploded in the air, unleashing wave after wave of shrapnel upon the advancing Chinese infantry. In near real time – with seconds' delay – the French satellites monitored the fall of shot and allowed for target corrections to be passed via Lieutenant Joffe to Major Lon. Many hundreds of Chinese fell where they stood. The pinpoint accuracy of the French 'firing solutions' enabled the Vietnamese to take out some of China's prized armour – armour developed after the Gulf War to perform better than the tin cans Beijing had sold Saddam to fight his war against Kuwait. The Chinese commanders did not know which way to turn. With their battlefield management systems inoperable they resorted to voice communications. But again the Vietnamese were ready. They homed in on the Chinese radio traffic, recording it and replaying back on the same frequency but with a half-second delay. The result was that all the Chinese commanders could hear was gibberish; likewise their commanders in Nanning and posts closer to the border. Faced with no means of communication the commanders on their own initiative began to retreat, but as those who survived the initial barrages of shells and rockets tried to go back the way they had come they met fresh troops coming towards them. It was chaos. Unfortunately for the Chinese the concentration of men and machinery this confusion produced simply provided larger targets for the Vietnamese.

In the first battle for Lang Son – the one President Wang participated in – the Chinese captured the town for the cost of 20,000 lives before they retreated across the border. This time the invading army didn't even make it to the town gates. Without even seeing a Vietnamese soldier, let alone killing one, the Chinese, in the space of five hours of concentrated and constant artillery barrage, lost 25,000 men – either killed outright, injured, or missing. Of the 250 battle tanks that entered Vietnam that day only 85 returned. 25,000 men made it across the border, harried and badgered by the Vietnamese Army all the way home.

The Foreign Ministry, Beijing

Local time: 1430 Wednesday 21 February 2001
GMT: 0630 Wednesday 21 February 2001

The Japanese Ambassador's Nissan President drew up in front of the Foreign Ministry ten minutes before his meeting with Jamie Song. Hiro Tanaka was a stocky man in his early fifties. He was a fluent Mandarin speaker who came from a long line of Japanese sinologists: his grandfather was a senior official with Japan's South Manchurian Railway Company, which was the colonizing power in north-east China during the 1930s and 1940s; his father was an army intelligence officer based in Shanghai. Tanaka, and a First Secretary from the embassy who would take notes, climbed the stairs to the Foreign Ministry and entered its somewhat musty interior. Inside another flight of steps greeted the visitors. These were covered with a light brown carpet and led to a suite of rooms, each more magnificent than the other, where Foreign Ministry officials met visiting diplomats and journalists. Tanaka and his official were shown into a medium-sized rectangular room. Along its walls were upholstered armchairs and in between them were tables with ashtrays and space for the ubiquitous blue and white mugs in which Chinese officialdom served green tea. The room was sparsely decorated although one wall was dominated by a painting of blossom – not badly executed but typical of the somewhat flaccid style favoured by China's post-Revolution leaders. Typical also of the room was its appalling overhead lighting. Light globes in Chinese official buildings are unique for their ability to shine but illuminate little. The room was unremittingly gloomy, though well heated.

The door opened. Jamie Song and his retinue swept into the room. Curt bows preceded handshakes and a gesture to take a seat. An assistant to Song handed the Foreign Minister a piece of paper. Song studied it for a while, looked up, and then began to speak.

'Ambassador, you have been summoned here to receive my government's formal protest at your government's nuclear test earlier today. It is a measure of China's horror at Japan's action that I, rather than the Vice Foreign Minister for East Asia, am delivering this note.

'The government of the People's Republic deplores in the strongest possible terms the decision by Japan to explode a nuclear device. The Chinese government has always stood for nuclear disarmament and has strenuously opposed the proliferation of weapons of mass destruction. The decision by Japan to detonate a 50 kiloton device at a facility in the Ogasawara Islands is a retrograde step and can only increase tensions in the Asia–Pacific region. At a time when China is defending its sovereignty in the South China Sea such a test can only be treated as a hostile act.

'The Chinese government calls upon Japan to renounce the use of nuclear weapons, to uphold the Japanese constitution and renounce war as a sovereign right, and to explain to the international community its reasons for this criminal act.'

Song look up. His face was expressionless. Tanaka, who knew a thing or two about looking impassive, returned his gaze, and held it.

'I shall report your views to my superiors in Tokyo,' he began. 'But I am also instructed by Foreign Minister Kimura personally to deliver a note myself. The government of Japan deplores the warlike actions of China in the South China Sea – actions in contravention of accepted international behaviour and in violation of international law. In particular my government views with the utmost seriousness the sinking of the USS *Peleliu*, a ship belonging to a friend and ally of Japan, engaged on a humanitarian mission. There can be no justification for this act of international terrorism. My government will render any and all assistance the United States requests.

'The government of China must pull back from this adventurism in the South China Sea, to seek a compromise with interested parties, and to return to the path of peace which the world has the right to expect. The government of Japan stands ready to defend its vital interest.'

Seoul International Airport, South Korea

Local time: 1800 Wednesday 21 February 2001
GMT: 0900 Wednesday 21 February 2001

The two bombs that tore through the international transit lounge at Seoul airport killed 87 people and injured more than 200. They exploded six minutes apart with such horrific force that part of the building collapsed, crushing many of the victims. Another 150 people died when aircraft were wrenched away from their boarding bridges. The fuel tanks of one exploded, sending searing hot metal and fireballs across the runway. Everyone on board that Boeing 737 died. A Boeing 757 was engulfed in flames, although many passengers were able to escape because the aircraft doors at the side were still open. Throughout the terminal, panic led to stampedes and further death, with people being crushed on staircases and in doorways as thousands headed for the freezing open air where they believed there would be safety. But out there the North Korean commandos had set up a suicide killing squad. The crowds were raked with machine-gun fire. Hand grenades exploded, the shrapnel tearing into the bodies of innocent women and children. As South Korean troops moved in, the gunmen became more and more determined. One ran from his hiding place, spraying bullets from two sub-machine-guns before being cut down. Another fired grenade after grenade. A third shot dead 4 South Koreans before being killed himself. It was never known how many North Koreans were involved in the attack, nor if any escaped. 11 were eventually killed. None was captured alive. 403 people died during the attack. Another 23 died from their injuries over the next day. The airport, which had opened less than two years earlier, was shut down. North Korea had achieved its goal to terrorize the people and strike at the heart of its enemy's economy.

The Foreign and Commonwealth Office, London

Local time: 0900 Wednesday 21 February 2001

The blue Rolls-Royce Silver Spur II, with the number plate CHN1, pulled out into Portland Place in the West End of London from the compound of the Chinese Embassy. At this time of day, with rush-hour traffic still thick in Regent Street, the Haymarket, and Piccadilly, the journey to the Foreign Office in King Charles Street could take anything up to twenty minutes. It was unusual for the Permanent Under Secretary to summon an Ambassador at such short notice and at such an early hour. But the Ambassador to the People's Republic of China did not regard it as an insult. Dragonstrike was one of those rare watersheds which determine global history. His only problem was that he had received no instructions from Beijing since the operation began. He welcomed the meeting with the PUS, if only to determine what was going on. He had memorized the speeches by President Wang and had committed to memory the more salient phrases in Jamie Song's television interviews. And as his chauffeur snaked his way around Piccadilly Circus and down towards Whitehall, and his Private Secretary read the morning newspapers, the Ambassador became curious as to how London was able to retain its history so beautifully, while in Beijing the past was relegated to museums and usually falsified.

The car drove under Admiralty Arch into the Mall. The royal standard was flying over Buckingham Palace, indicating that the monarch was in residence. The chauffeur turned left into Horse Guards Parade and left again across the gravel of the parade ground, down the side of the garden wall of No. 10 Downing Street to park in the little-known Ambassador's Entrance at the back of the Foreign and Commonwealth Office. Security was efficient, formal, and fast because the car was expected. The Ambassador was shown up the Grand Staircase, with its marble banisters and deep red carpet, and shown to a familiar, special waiting room on the first floor. He sat for four minutes on a green and cream sofa. Opposite him was a gilded mirror set against gold-painted wallpaper. The most dominant feature was a large picture of St Cecilia, the patron saint of music, playing the organ. The Ambassador had been here several time before, but found this visit brought home to him the irreconcilable differences between the Chinese and European cultures. One preserved its history, with all the flaws and follies. The other, his own, destroyed it and told fairy tales about the past so no one ever knew what happened.

The Permanent Under Secretary, the Head of Britain's Diplomatic Service, made a point of being both cold and official. His job was to convey Her Majesty's Government's displeasure in such a way that the Ambassador would relay the full message back to Beijing. The PUS's Private Secretary took notes.

'The British government deplores your action in the South China Sea. There can be no justification for China's actions. The sinking of the USS *Peleliu* is contrary to everything we have been trying to achieve in the arena of world peace and the invasion of Vietnam is without question unacceptable. We will not tolerate the continued detention of British citizens caught up in this conflict. All Chinese forces must be withdrawn from all arenas of conflict and hostilities halted immediately.'

'I will report your comments to my government,' replied the Ambassador.

'We will be making public today our intention to

support the United States in whatever way is necessary to free the foreign hostages and to secure the shipping routes through the South China Sea.'

'Does that mean you will make a military contribution?'

'It means what it says, Ambassador. You must draw your own conclusions.'

'There are as you a know a number of trade contracts under consideration, and the President of the Board of Trade is due to visit Beijing in May.'

The PUS's response was swift: 'We have been down this road several times before, I'm afraid. The trade delegation has been postponed. British companies will be withdrawing their tenders until such a time as things get back to normal. The airport radar, the metro construction, the aerospace joint ventures are all on hold, Ambassador.'

'You are imposing sanctions?'

'Not at all, Ambassador. Our company executives simply believe it is too risky to embark upon business ventures in a country with which we might soon be at war. Your fellow Ambassadors in Europe, America, Canada, Australia, and Japan are being given a similar message. We will no longer assist in the building of a modern China.'

'There are others who will help us,' replied the Ambassador.

'I'm sure the Russians and Indians will oblige,' said the PUS, ending the exchange. 'But you could hardly describe their infrastructure and technology as modern.'

The Chinese Ambassador was shown out as he arrived, with cold civility.

The White House, Washington, DC

Local time: 0700 Wednesday 21 February 2001
GMT: 1200 Wednesday 21 February 2001

With the autocue rolling, the President of the United States looked straight into the camera. He waited for the recording light above the lens to go red. Then he began his address to the nation. Every network broke into its programming schedule. Most had been running rolling news about the sinking of the USS *Peleliu* the day before. Although it was nearly twenty-four hours since the tragedy there were no pictures, and that was how the President wanted it. The first section of the address recounted the developments of the past four days, beginning with what the President described as an 'unprovoked attack' on Vietnam and 'unauthorized closure of vital trading routes in the South China Sea'. The President spoke about the tragic loss of life. He then paused before moving on to the sinking of the USS *Peleliu*. He noted that the last American ship to be sunk in conflict was in 1952 during the Korean War. 'China was also our enemy then,' he said. He reminded the American people that the USS *Peleliu* was not sailing to war, but to rescue American citizens, civilians, who had become stranded on one of the disputed reefs in the conflict area. It had been the President's intention to ensure civilian safety before embarking upon complex and dangerous negotiations with China. He described the attack as an act of terrorism.

'Yet our response has been far more measured than that of our allies, the Japanese. Yesterday they declared themselves to be a nuclear power in the Pacific by exploding an underground nuclear device. I have expressed my regrets personally to Prime Minister Hyashi, but we agreed that neither of our great nations should lose focus about what we needed to achieve. That is to secure the trading routes of our oil and other supplies from the Middle East and South and East Asia; and to safeguard the lives of American citizens in the area of conflict. This is also the view of our European allies who have their own security arrangement with governments of the region.

'Therefore, Prime Minister Hyashi, the Prime Ministers of Great Britain, Australia, and New Zealand, and the President of France have joined me in committing their air and naval forces to free the South China Sea from Chinese control. Our military action has just begun.'

The South China Sea

Local time: 2000 Wednesday 21 February 2001
GMT: 1200 Wednesday 21 February 2001

The first Japanese military aircraft to fly across the 25° latitude line which cuts across the northern tip of Taiwan was a new Boeing 767–200 AWACS early warning spy plane, which had begun operations in 1999. It was vulnerable to attack and was kept well back from possible offensive aircraft. 8 kilometres below, Japan's navy was putting its stamp on the new balance of power in the Pacific. The *Kongou* class destroyers *Myoko* and *Kirishima* and the *Asagiri* class destroyers *Umigiri* and *Sawagiri* sailed through the Luzon Straits into the South China Sea to go to war with China. The amphibious troop and tank carrier *Yokohama*, with 550 Marines on board, was deployed to take over from the USS *Peleliu*, but this time both to rescue civilian hostages and recover Discovery Reef and the control of the BP–Nippon Oil drilling rig there. Three *Harushio* class SSK submarines, the *Fuyushio*, *Wakashio*, and *Arashio*, were on patrol ahead. The *Yuushio* class SSKs *Yukishio* and *Akishio* followed. The crews of Sea King and Sea Stallion helicopters dropped patterns of sonobuoys to detect enemy submarines.

100 kilometres ahead of the Japanese task force was the USS *Harry S. Truman* carrier group. Already her F-14 Tomcat fighters with air-to-air missiles and F/A-18 Hornets with laser-guided bombs and anti-radar missiles had penetrated deep into China's self-declared airspace. Their target was the Woody Island military base on the Paracel Islands. With the Tomcats giving air cover, the Hornets flew in to attack it.

Seven Su-27s scrambled from their base on Hainan Island, and within minutes had engaged the Tomcats in the first ever combat test of strength between the two aircraft. The Su-27 had been designed by Soviet aerospace engineers to beat the American F-14, F-15, F-16, and F-18. They drew from the American design with the advantage that the competing aircraft had already been built and were operational. The Russian aircraft was one of the first to be fitted with air-to-air missiles with their own active seeking device, which allowed the pilot to 'fire and forget', or turn away from his target as soon as he had released the weapons. Each aircraft carried ten missiles, six on the wings, two beneath the engine intakes, and two under the fuselage. For ground attack, it had five-round packs of 130mm rockets and could also carry the much-feared Moskit anti-ship missile. A few days earlier, in their missions against Vietnam, this technological edge in performance was incidental. But now, as the Tomcats were in a forward role of air defence to protect an American carrier group, the stark truth had finally travelled all the way from the Pentagon to the White House: Soviet Cold War technology had been transferred to another, more durable Communist power and Americans were facing the consequences.

The fight began when the aircraft were far apart. A Tomcat observer spotted on his warning receiver a signal which he identified as radar guidance for a missile fired from more than 110 kilometres away. The American rules of engagement then allowed the Tomcats to fire. Two had eight long-range Phoenix air-to-air missiles guided to different targets by the track-while-scan AWG-9 radar. Although this was old equipment dating from the 1970s, it had been upgraded and was still a lethal combination. The air was soon full of fourteen Phoenix missiles speeding to their targets, one having misfired on its pylon, and one having failed to guide after launch, falling into the sea. The aircraft with the misfire jettisoned the now-useless missile. But what the Americans did not know before the war began was that the enemy had developed jammers which would confuse the homing heads of the Phoenix that were needed for terminal accuracy. Only two of the seven Su-27s succumbed to the Phoenix attack, and the remaining five closed for the dogfight with their guns and infra-red missiles, which homed on to their targets by fixing on heat generated by their engines. Manoeuvrability and training is the key to the dogfight, and although the Su-27s were more manoeuvrable than the Tomcats the pilots were not as well trained as the Americans with their Red Flag and Top Gun training systems.

The American pilots eluded and attacked the enemy with manoeuvres they called in their jargon yo-yos, max-G turns, offensive barrel rolls, rolling scissors, and diving for the deck. One pilot, who died, was hit not by air-to-air missiles, but by enemy cannon fire when he inadvertently turned his aircraft across the nose of one of the Su-27s, which he had not spotted. One Tomcat observer saw a missile-launch warning from a tail direction. He guessed that from that quarter it would be an infra-red missile. His pilot waited a fraction of a second, broke sharply towards the sun, and the observer fired off flares which exploded into sources of intense heat designed to seduce away the missile. It worked. While up-sun of his attacker, the pilot reversed his turn and in the short time it took his opponent to realize what he had done he was in a firing position with an AIM-7 Sparrow radar-guided missile, albeit at the edge of its capability. The Su-27 pilot heard in his radar warning receiver the Tomcat radar lock on and he released chaff clouds. This decoyed the first Sparrow but not a second which followed in salvo. The Su-27 was hit and spiralled into the sea. Another Su-27 had used its afterburner too much and became stuck in reheat; it ran low on fuel, and one engine failed. It lost combat energy and was soon picked off by a Tomcat, the pilot ejecting as soon as he realized that he was being attacked.

As the dogfight raged overhead, the Hornets kept to their ground-attack mission on the Paracels. Their air-to-air defence capability was limited because their AIM-7 Sparrow and AIM-9 Sidewinder anti-aircraft missiles had been removed so the aircraft could carry laser-guided conventional and cluster bombs together with some AGM-65F Maverick and HARM anti-radar missiles. The formation leader flew a two-seater with a weapon system operator in the back who was able to concentrate on electronic warfare. The Hornets' jammers first sent out a wave of high-intensity microwaves which filled the skies with radar energy across a wide frequency band. This was called noise-jamming. Then the jammers confused the enemy radar further with more sophisticated methods involving cunningly synchronized pulses and Doppler shifts which pretended to be non-existent targets. Sometimes enemy radar screens were almost obscured by massive jamming which produce a series of spikes emanating from the centre of the radar displays – completely confusing the radar operators.

The Chinese fired at least four surface-to-air missiles, but these were easily seduced away by the countermeasures, and seconds later the radar and anti-aircraft defences were being destroyed. Fire-and-forget radar-homing HARM missiles took out two radar-guided anti-aircraft positions. The other radars took the hint and switched off. A third SAM site was spotted when it fired a SAM without preliminary radar lock. The aircraft of the pilot who had seen it was equipped with large laser-guided bombs. He released one but unlike the HARM, he had to keep the laser beam on the target until the bomb hit. Although the laser target designator was stabilized and did not need manual aiming, it limited his manoeuvre. He failed to detect a missile fired from high above by an Su-27. By the time his missile warner alarm sounded, it was too late to escape. However, the missile warhead failed to detonate and the missile streaked close by without doing any damage. The Hornet pilot thought he had escaped but the Su-27 had fired a salvo of two – the second one worked and it destroyed the aircraft. The bomb, unguided without being able to home to the laser marker on the ground, did not even detonate, having lost laser-lock, a device introduced to avoid civilian damage in earlier wars. The ground attack continued. Once the defences were taken out, cluster fragmentation bomblets with a wide area of effect were used on the runway and aircraft storage areas. Any aircraft on the ground was a soft target and was either destroyed or damaged by the bomblets and ricochet debris. The runway was pitted with small craters and small mines were also dispensed from the clusters.

Within twenty minutes, all Su-27s had either been shot down or had retreated. Two Su-27s ditched before they could reach friendly land. The Chinese had provided no tanker in-flight refuelling support. The Americans lost two Tomcats and the Hornet which attacked the SAM site. Several Tomcats had to be air-refuelled on the way home. Another Tomcat was damaged so that it could not land on the aircraft carrier; the crew ejected and the aircraft ditched alongside. They were picked up unharmed by the duty rescue helicopter. The Tomcat squadron leader, who himself had shot down an enemy plane and shared another kill, said caustically: 'I guess it shows it don't matter how good your aircraft is if you are not trained to fly it properly and don't have the back-up.'

1,200 kilometres to the south, the *Nimitz* carrier group entered the conflict area through the Balabac Straits. With the same combination of Tomcats and Hornets, the

American aircraft first sank the *Luhu* class destroyer *Haribing*, already hit at the beginning of the conflict by Vietnamese torpedoes. After returning to the carrier, another squadron took off to destroy the Chinese positions on Mischief Reef. There was no resistance.

French Dassault Rafale multi-role fighters headed for the Spratly Islands, flying from Ho Chi Minh City where they had arrived from Europe only hours earlier. They shot down three unmanoeuvrable Chinese air-refuelling aircraft and picked off four Su-27s which were still heavy as they were on their way to give air support to the Chinese navy. For the second time in the Dragonstrike war, Vietnamese aircraft took off from Cambodia and Laos. From Vientiane, refuelling at Vinh on the north-east Vietnamese coast, they struck the Chinese naval base on Hainan Island 800 kilometres away. From the Laotian royal capital of Luang Prabang, they attacked PLA land troops positioned in the northern border area.

HMS *Ark Royal* carrier group left Bruneian waters to lay claim to the most dangerous waters in the South China Sea. The British warships sailed due north to the heart of the Spratly Island group, where the sea was shallow and the Chinese *Ming* and *Romeo* submarines were known to be lying in wait. During the Cold War anti-submarine warfare had become a British speciality, so in Asia as it joined forces again with the Americans, Britain took on the same task. But before reaching the area, news came of a failed American attack on the air and naval base at Terumbi Layang-layang. Since its capture from Malaysia, the Chinese had flown in their most sophisticated radar and anti-aircraft systems, together with more than twenty Su-27 fighters and Fencer ground-attack aircraft. Western intelligence had failed to detect the extent of the defences there. In a first wave, three Tomcats and four Hornets were shot down. The Americans were unable to put up a second attack immediately because of the rescheduling of other commitments and the repair of battle damage on some aircraft. Also the rescheduling of aircraft maintenance programmes from peacetime to wartime was still underway. Nevertheless plans began for a massive airstrike when they were ready. The airbase gave China a formidable power projection throughout the South China Sea, equivalent to having its own aircraft carrier, which could cause enormous Allied casualties. Meanwhile, Britain was asked if commandos from the Special Boat Squadron on board HMS *Albion* could help disable the Chinese defences there.

The Pacific Ocean

5,000 kilometres to the east in the Western Pacific, the Chinese *Xia class* type 092 nuclear-powered submarine was being tracked by the *Seawolf* class USS *Connecticut*. The *Xia* was travelling at 6 knots, 20 metres below the surface. It was more than a month since she had left China. She had only received three instructions and each time she was to maintain her course towards the Eastern Pacific. When the USS *Peleliu* was attacked, the *Xia* was more than 2,000 kilometres east of the Marianas Islands and 1,000 kilometres north of the Marshall Islands. Although both island groups were technically independent, they were regarded by the Pentagon as American soil. The closest landfall was Wake Island, an American airbase in the middle of nowhere. This part of the Pacific was an empty and lonely piece of ocean, so remote that the environmental outcry caused by what the commander of the USS *Connecticut* was about to do soon subsided.

He was 360 metres deep and undetected by the *Xia*. He released two Mk48 ADCAP torpedoes. After the initiation phase at 55 knots, they increased speed to 70 knots. They took one minute and eighteen seconds to hit the *Xia*. Almost instantaneously, the hull collapsed from the explosions and as it sank below 300 metres, it was crushed by the pressure, killing all 104 men on board.

The Pentagon statement explained that the nuclear reactor, sealed in its own pressure chamber, was built to withstand the destruction of the submarine. The twelve nuclear warheads could travel hundreds of thousands of metres out of the atmosphere and back again. They were sturdy enough to remain intact on the seabed of the Pacific Ocean without leaking. The Chinese submarine was already within striking distance of American territory. With another four days' sailing, she could have targeted Pearl Harbor, Hawaii, with a nuclear missile.

Boeing Headquarters, Seattle

The telephone rang twice before Reece Overhalt, Chairman and Chief Executive Officer of Boeing, picked it up. His PA told him it was Jamie Song on the line from Beijing. Song and Overhalt had been at Harvard together thirty years ago. Both had lived at Elliot House, where their rooms were across the hall from one another. Overhalt had been watching Boeing's share price sag all morning. A big selling order out of Hong Kong had spooked investors in Europe and now the US as well. Overhalt had ordered an immediate inquiry into who had been behind the selling, but he knew the search would probably end with a $2 nominee company in the British Virgin Islands and no one would be any the wiser. He waited as Song's secretary put the call through to the Chinese Foreign Minister.

There was warmth, tempered with a certain wariness, as the two went through the pleasantries.

'How's Betty?' said Song.

'Fine, fine ... and Helen? Is she well?' enquired Overhalt, wondering quite what Song was aiming at.

'I'll get straight to the point, Reece,' Song said. 'We think it might be helpful in the current circumstances if you paid a visit to Beijing. You are an old friend of China and we think you might be able to help us work through our current problems. You can tell by the way I am talking, openly like that, that this is a serious request. We can guarantee confidentiality; I assure you we would not seek to make propaganda out of you being here.'

Overhalt was nonplussed. At his level in corporate

America he was used to meeting Presidents and Prime Ministers, but he was a cautious man; above all he was a company man. As he ruminated Song cut in. 'Reece, I know what you must be thinking. Don't answer now. Think about it. Call me, say, in three hours?'

The White House, Washington, DC

The President was briefing a delegation of state governors when the call from Overhalt's office came in. The President and Overhalt had known each other since they were undergraduates at Harvard. It was at Harvard where they met Jamie Song, who was there attending a post-graduate fellowship in international affairs.

'I see that our old friend has been in contact,' the President said. 'I've just been watching a recording of that son-of-a-bitch on the television. He hasn't changed a bit. Smooth and slippery as eel and with a bite to match.'

'Jamie was on the phone to me an hour ago. He came on with the "old friend of China" line and wants me to fly over and see him. In very non-specific terms he hinted at a solution. I can tell you I need this like a hole in the head. Someone is screwing around with my stock price and my investors do not like it. Anyway, what do you think? Can I be of service?'

'Reece, I think it would be a very good idea for you to go to Beijing. Events, I can tell you, are moving very quickly. Between us, I'm not quite sure where they are going to end. But we may need someone like you – trusted by both sides, but in the employ of neither. I want you to go to Beijing. Our Embassy there will extend to you all the help you need.'

The South China Sea

During the night, French pilots shot down two more IL-76 refuelling tankers. Ten Su-27s were destroyed in a Vietnamese attack on Hainan Island. A joint force of British, Australian, and New Zealand special units paralysed the defence systems on Terumbi Layang-layang. They infiltrated the inadequate perimeter fence and destroyed the radar equipment before they were discovered making their escape along the runway. Chinese troops engaged them in a firefight, but explosive experts managed to lay charges on seven aircraft. The blasts threw the Chinese troops into confusion, allowing the Allied forces to slip away. The British suffered two wounded and one dead. There were no casualties among the Australian and New Zealanders. The casualties among the Chinese were unknown. The bulk of the Su-27 advanced fighter squadron was destroyed. As the commandos made their escape, the Chinese base was rendered useless by American Hornets with air cover from Tomcats and British Sea Harriers from the *Ark Royal*. A second raid sank the *Luda* III class destroyer *Zhuhai* and two escort vessels which had been patrolling around the base. In all China lost twelve of the more than forty surface vessels which made up its South China Sea task force, as wave after wave of aircraft from three carriers continued their attacks. By dawn, the Chinese military command had ordered all ships to head north to areas where they would have more air cover. The exception was the new Russian-built *Sovremenny* class frigate, the *Vazhny*, renamed the *Liu Huaqing*, which slipped out of the headquarters of the southern fleet. There was thick cloud overhead and it entered the South China Sea undetected by military satellites and spy aircraft.

SIX

The Korean Peninsula

President Kim telephoned James Bradlay, who said immediately that he was happy for South Korea to commit its own military forces to the war with the North. Bradlay had a far larger crisis on his hands and was thankful that South Korea would handle its own problems. The United States, however, would provide the technology and advisers and it was they who primed and guided the first launch of the McDonnell Douglas Sea Slam surface-to-surface missiles from the three South Korean *Ulsan* class frigates *Chung-ju*, *Che-ju*, and *Masan*. All the South Korean naval officers had done extensive training and exercises with the American navy for such an operation. The missiles had never before been used with such pinpoint accuracy, skimming over the sea then the rugged terrain around the Demilitarized Zone and finally cutting in to fly straight into the underground bunkers which hid the military machine threatening Seoul.

American and South Korean troops abandoned the DMZ, drawing back from their unprotected positions in Panmunjon and right along the demarcation line. The watchtowers and the truce village were unmanned. The huts where demarcation disputes had been negotiated over the years were empty. The most heavily fortified front line in the world went on the highest alert. A skeleton defence force of men and women from the US Second Infantry Division was deployed at Camp Greaves, the closest position to the DMZ. Each wore the motto of their unit on the uniform, saying "in front of them all".

The first South Korean missile smashed into a rockface just metres from a tunnel entrance. Another flew straight over the hilltop and skidded into a field without exploding. The third, however, was successful and slammed into a row of concealed tanks. The explosion, made more powerful in the confined space, ignited both fuel and ammunition supplies. The tanks closest to the entrance were crippled. The mangled armour blocked the exit so those behind were rendered useless. Over the next forty-five minutes computer-guided missiles negotiated their paths inside many of the hidden places. Others missed and exploded harmlessly in the countryside around, but the attack had the desired result of forcing the North Koreans to show their hand: as their equipment was threatened, they moved it out into the open so it could be used more effectively. The roads around the border suddenly filled with armour, artillery, and supply vehicles. More vehicles appeared on the Kim Il-Sung highway, which ran all the way from Pyongyang to Panmunjon and was built to take both fighter aircraft and tanks. As the data was processed through the South Korean surveillance system squadron after squadron of F-16s, F-5s, and F-4s screamed across runways throughout the south, became airborne, and headed north to the Demilitarized Zone. The pilots' orders were to destroy everything they saw above ground.

President Kim knew he had taken one of the riskiest decisions in modern military history. In the face of almost certain destruction, the North would have no choice but to launch a land and missile offensive on Seoul, and that attack had to be stopped. Yet if his defence planners had misjudged, it could be only a matter of hours before a North Korean tank was on the streets of Seoul. Already, enemy aircraft had penetrated the airspace. A mixture of advanced tactical warplanes, MiG-23s and MiG-29s, together with the mainstay fighter wing of MiG-19s and

MiG-21s, flew towards the Southern capital. Most were engaged by South Korean aircraft and it quickly became clear that with its bad maintenance and poor training schedules the North Korean Air Force would soon be beaten. Plane after plane was shot down by surface-to-air missiles and the air-to-air missiles carried by the South Korean interceptors, but among such a wave of thirty or forty aircraft several made it to Seoul. They had no specific targets and they unleashed their bombs and rockets into civilian areas. Then some turned their aircraft towards the ground in suicide dives, each one careening into a high-rise building and exploding into a devastating fireball. Thousands died. In the 63 Building, built like two hands in prayer, more than 500 people died, many trapped in stairwells and lifts which had shut down as the air raid began. Sirens wailed and millions sought refuge in the subways and basements of their buildings. The hospitals overflowed with victims. The rescue services, which for decades had been prepared for this moment, were immediately overstretched, with hundreds being left to die in the streets and buildings abandoned to burn unchecked.

Tiananmen Square, Beijing

Local time: 0800 Thursday 22 February
GMT: 2400 Wednesday 21 February 2001

Icy winds of the past week had swept away the layers of pollution which hung over Beijing for most of the winter. The sun broke through the cold and cast a glitter over Tiananmen Square. The roads around it were closed off to the public and bedecked with bright red bunting. School-children, packed ten deep, lined the pavements, each holding the national flag and raising it high above their head on the command from their cheerleader. Loudspeakers, attached to lamp-posts, broadcast the national anthem and Chinese songs of liberation from its past of foreign control. Communist Party officials had been summoned to Beijing from every province. They watched events from the steps of the Great Hall of the People to the west and from outside the Museums of Chinese Revolution and History to the east. Camera crews from China Central Television roamed freely around the square. Throughout the morning, the national network showed films about China's suffering during the occupation by foreign forces. The British were criticized for the nineteenth-century Opium Wars and for seizing Hong Kong. The Americans stood condemned for their support for the Nationalist leader Chiang Kai-shek in the 1940s and his rebel armies which had taken Taiwan. Film of the Korean War in the 1950s told how Chinese troops defeated British, American, and other imperialist forces. Speckled black and white footage showed slaughtered troops and survivors, emaciated, cold, and dejected. The Japanese were described as guilty people for all millennia. They had treated their fellow Asians with more humiliation and suffering than any Western power. Japanese soldiers were shown massacring Chinese civilians in summary executions, beheadings, and beatings. One Chinese peasant was tied to a lamp-post, his head hanging down. Japanese soldiers skinned him until he died from shock and loss of blood.

During the horrific scene, the CCTV commentator said: 'Never again will the Chinese people become slaves to foreign forces. Even if they have to eat the roots of trees and live in caves, because of the hatred of China by the world, they will remain free and proud. Long live President and Party Secretary Wang Feng.'

Military vehicles rolled slowly in from the west. A line of main battle tanks led them. Then came towed artillery, multiple-rocket launchers, self-propelled guns, mortars, surface-to-surface and surface-to-air missiles, anti-tank guided weapons, and air-defence weapons. A ceremonial procession followed, during which pictures of submarines, aircraft, and naval warships were shown on huge screens mounted all over the square. A display of missiles ended the parade. The CSS-4 or East Wind 5 was the first to rumble into the Square. It had been unveiled in 1981, with its range of 15,000 kilometres and single re-entry vehicle 5 megaton warhead. The smaller submarine-launched CSS-N-3 or JL1 with its range of up to 3,000 kilometres and 2 megaton warhead moved in behind it. There were several others, well known to defence attachés. But the last weapon in the parade was the pride of Chinese military power. It took its place just south of the flag podium. Shown live throughout the world, the missile was immediately recognized as the weapon which could hit the continental United States and anywhere in Europe. This was the solid-fuel-powered East Wind 32. Its range was 12,000 kilometres. Its accuracy had been honed with a new technical guidance system provided by a team of Russian scientists. It carried a lighter warhead, and, most dangerously, it was fired, not from a silo, but from a mobile launch vehicle. The East Wind 32 would be almost impossible to find through satellite reconnaissance until it was fired. During the day it could hide. During the night it could be deployed to its firing position. Mobile missiles with nuclear warheads had haunted the Pentagon during the nineties, because of the failure to track down and destroy Iraq's Scud missiles during the Gulf War. They had been concealed under bridges, in shelters, or parked in heavily populated civilian areas which the enemy could not bomb without international condemnation. Today, China wasn't keeping secret its missile capability. It was taunting the world's most powerful nation. China calculated that just one explosion on American soil would be enough to deter the United States from getting involved in a nuclear war with China. America had never before experienced conflict at home.

The warhead of the East Wind 32, its colours of red and silver sparkling in the winter sun, pointed directly north towards the Gate of Heavenly Peace where President Wang Feng, flanked by generals, had climbed to the rostrum to address the Chinese people. Wang had chosen a moment and place embedded with historical significance. This is where Chinese emperors had handed down edicts over the centuries and where Mao Zedong had declared the founding of Communist China in 1949. The view over the exhibits of Chinese military power was richly symbolic, the architecture of Chinese Communism, the Great Hall of the People, the Monument to the People's Heroes right through to Chairman Mao's Memorial Hall, where the body still lay embalmed. When Wang spoke, he chose not his own words, but those delivered by Mao Zedong in 1949.

'Our work will go down in the history of mankind,

demonstrating that the Chinese people, comprising one quarter of humanity, have now stood up. The Chinese have always been a great, courageous, and industrious nation; it is only in modern times that they have fallen behind. From now on our nation will belong to the community of the peace-loving and the freedom-loving nations of the world and work courageously and industriously to foster its own civilization and well-being and at the same time to promote world peace and freedom.

'Ours will no longer be a nation subject to insult and humiliation. We have stood up. Our revolution has won the sympathy and acclaim of the peoples of all countries. We have friends all over the world. The era in which the Chinese people were regarded as uncivilized is now ended. We shall emerge in the world as a nation with an advanced culture. We shall be strong and feared. The Chinese people are no longer slaves.'

The Party controlled the cheers and waving of flags. But that made the response even more awesome. China had been down this road before. And each time it had ended in death, bloodshed, chaos, and the fragmentation of the ruling dynasty.

New China News Agency, Beijing

The **Xinhua** (**New China**) News Agency statement on China's changing military policy was characteristically vague. It said the State Council had reassessed the communiqué of 16 October 1964, the day China carried out its first nuclear test. It then listed seven principles, the first and most important being that at no time would China be the first to use nuclear weapons. The statement said: 'The reassessment has become necessary because of recent moves by foreign forces to invade the motherland.

'In a Western imperialist conspiracy, the brave officers and men of the People's Liberation Army are being slaughtered by foreign powers intent on the containment of China. This happened in the nineteenth century. In the twentieth century many Chinese lived as the slaves to Japanese, American, British, and French colonial powers. We will never be slaves again. It is the duty of the Chinese people to protect the motherland with any weapons they might have. China is a poor nation. But it can and will defend itself. As Mao Zedong said: "No matter what country, no matter what missiles, atomic bombs, hydrogen bombs . . . we must surpass them."'

Kabuto-cho, Tokyo

When the Xinhua statement flashed across the screens of dealers in Tokyo their immediate, reflex response was to sell the yen. The prospect of a nuclear exchange between China and the US and the likelihood that Japan would also be a target was more than the Japanese currency could endure. It dropped ¥10 to ¥178.60 and stabilized. But soon it dawned on financial market operatives that the threat of nuclear annihilation altered the calculus of financial markets. Foreign exchange turnover in Tokyo on a good day exceeded $20 billion. But as the morning wore on activity in the market became sporadic. Huge bursts of activity punctured long periods of virtually no trading. The client of Damian Phillips was sitting on nearly $260 million. Ahead of Xinhua's announcement he had risked interception by foreign intelligence agencies and telephoned Phillips in Hong Kong. He spoke two words and hung up: 'Buy Japan.' The Nikkei Index was in free fall when First China began selective buying of blue-chip Japanese stocks. The index had fallen 5.5 per cent the previous day. It had opened another 5 per cent lower at 34,056 and fell further as the morning progressed. Phillips had had his orders. First China, acting through Nomura, bought selectively but in size. It picked up 3 per cent of Nippon Oil, 1 per cent of Toyota, a 4 per cent stake in Matsushita, and a smaller, undisclosed, stake in Sony. Phillips had taken General Zhao at his word and did not feel constrained to use just the trading profits for the currency dealings to buy Japanese equities; he also dipped into the $1 billion and more profits First China had made on oil trading.

The South China Sea

209 American servicemen died when the Chinese navy penetrated the defences of the USS *Harry S. Truman* carrier group and sank the guided-missile destroyer USS *Oscar Austin*. The ship was first hit by three surface-to-surface Sunburn missiles fired from the *Liu Huaqing*, which was 100 kilometres north-east of the Paracel Islands. She was less than twelve hours out of base. Then two of her 533mm torpedoes ripped through the crippled ship's hull, causing explosions and fires. Attack aircraft scrambled from the USS *Harry S. Truman*, and within minutes their air-to-surface missiles and laser-guided bombs were unleashed upon the Chinese frigate. But like over Woody Island the day before, the Americans were up against Soviet Cold War technology. The first wave of missiles and bombs was seduced away from the ship by decoy chaff launchers. Three Hornets were shot down by surface-to-air missiles. The crew failed to eject. Two Tomcats were also hit. One returned safely to the carrier. The other crashed into the sea and the pilot was picked up. As the escort vessels moved in towards the *Oscar Austin* to rescue survivors, an undetected *Romeo* submarine fired two straight-running torpedoes at the oiler USS *Willamette*. Only one torpedo hit and the damage was contained. Ten of the 135 crew died. Twenty were injured. Like the *Ming* which attacked the USS *Peleliu*, the *Romeo* headed into the rescue area, where the commander knew he would be safe from attack. Three hours later the attack submarine the USS *Cheyenne*, trailing the *Liu Huaqing* from behind and remaining undetected, fired three wire-guided Mk48 torpedoes. All hit the frigate, sinking her. The *Romeo* which attacked the USS *Willamette* escaped.

The White House, Washington, DC

Local time: 2100 Wednesday 21 February 2001
GMT: 0200 Thursday 22 February 2001

The President's light supper, which had been arranged to brief senators, broke up early when the Xinhua dispatch came through. Bradlay called in Weinstein, the National Security Adviser, Collins, the Defense Secretary, Kuhnert, the Chairman of the Joint Chiefs, and Gillchrest, the Secretary of State. The problem put forward by the President was whether the Allies should now attack mainland Chinese military bases, particularly those known to hold nuclear weapons. Kuhnert quoted the time-honoured nuclear adage: 'Use them, or lose them.' He said if the Chinese were now only bluffing they would be motivated to open up their nuclear arsenal if it were under threat. He believed that within the next twelve hours the Allied forces would have secured the South China Sea and China would have lost any aspirations of power projection. To bomb the mainland would rub their noses in it and make them a more dangerous animal to deal with in the future. The Secretary of State noted the political problems facing Britain in deciding whether or not to attack the Argentine mainland during the Falklands War in 1982.

'We would lose the support of the ethnic Chinese community around the world,' he said. 'The South-East Asian nations which are now neutral might turn against us. It would be more an act of symbolism than of military practicality. We might hit a handful of warheads, but there are others they could launch. And there's bound to be allegations accompanied by television pictures of civilian casualties. Indeed, there would be civilian casualties.' He said that America's policy objective was to safeguard the trade routes between the Indian and Pacific Oceans and to protect the lives of American citizens. That was being done. Vietnam's objective was to protect its territory from further air and naval strikes, which gave it justification for air strikes on mainland bases. They were already being helped by Western intelligence. Perhaps, if military planners believed further mainland attacks were necessary, they should be carried out by the Japanese in their new role as a military regional power.

NSA Weinstein said that the main Chinese nuclear threat came from mobile launchers which could be transported by road or rail. They could be moved at night and hidden during the day. He had brought a folder containing two sets of 8 × 10 colour photographs taken along the rail track between Shenyang and Harbin in northern China. The ability of America's eyes in the sky to spy on the world below was nothing short of astonishing, and it astounded the President every time such photographs were placed before him. They had been gathered by Big Bird satellites orbiting only about 180 to 290 kilometres above the Earth. Because of their miniaturized rocketry they were highly manoeuvrable. The satellites were fitted with image-forming systems with multiple arrays of tiny electro-optical detectors. Each detector produced an electrical signal proportional to the amount of light falling on it. When put together, the information collected by the thousands of detectors mounted on the satellite produced an image of the terrain below. The resolution was extraordinary. It was so good that individuals could be identified. Moreover the satellites were programmed to transmit only pictures that they had been instructed to notice, such as missile silos, submarines, military aircraft. If the analyst who was viewing the pictures on his computer screen wanted to take a closer look at some unusual terrestrial phenomenon, the satellite responded. After Big Bird's onboard computer digitized the photographic data it was transmitted to a relay satellite in geosynchronous orbit and in constant view of its ground-receiving station at the National Security Agency, outside Washington.

The first set of photographs the President viewed that evening had been taken at 0848 Beijing standard time, the second fifteen minutes later at 0903, and the others at further fifteen-minute intervals. They showed a series of railway cars, carrying container-like boxes, except far longer and clearly not made of metal, because on one the front end looked torn with a missile head pointing out.

'These are mobile launchers, Mr President,' said Marty Weinstein. 'They are being moved outside of their usual exercise pattern. Liaoning is the base for unit 80301 of the Second Artillery, the regiment which handles China's ballistic missile programme. We believe the train is heading towards Harbin. But we lost it after dark. The weather didn't help.'

'Can they launch from this?' asked Bradlay.

'If they fired enough, one would work. But there's something else. In May 1995 the Second Artillery finished building a network of modern missile-launching positions which now covers the whole country. It took them fifteen years to do it and they call it the Great Wall Project because of its role in defending Chinese territory.' The NSA opened another folder. 'These are truck-launched missiles being moved out of the Second Artillery's base in Huangshan in Anhui Province. Unit 80302.' He shuffled through to another set of photographs. 'Here's more truck-launched missiles coming from Unit 80303 in Kunming in Yunnan. They are almost certainly being targeted on Vietnam. And look at this. Unit 80306 at Xining in the north-west desert area where it's more difficult to hide. No forests or built-up areas. This launch site is in the open and look at the elevation. These could go any minute and they're aimed at Western Europe. The ones in Anhui could hit Japan. In Liaoning they could hit Japan or continental America.'

'We can't afford a nuclear attack,' said the President.

'That is why they've raised the stakes,' said Secretary of State Gillchrest. 'They know our thinking.'

Weinstein continued: 'The Chinese also have a sea-launch capability. But we have sunk the *Xia* which was heading towards the Eastern Pacific. The Russian-built *Kilo* class submarine has sea-launched cruise missile capability. That would be good up to 2,500 kilometres. Tests have been carried out on the updated *Xia* class submarine with a JL2 ICBM with a range of 8,000 kilometres. We have no intelligence that the submarine is anywhere but in port. Tests have been inconclusive. We believe it's not even ready for use.'

'Do they know we know?' the President asked.

'The first question we ask in intelligence, sir, is why are we discovering this. In Xining, definitely, they have ensured we know what they are doing. Or they wouldn't have brought them out in daylight. The Chinese always announce their intentions, Mr President. They're telling us they might nuke us any time.'

The President turned to Kuhnert: 'Arnold, if you were going to hit their nuclear arsenal, how would you do it?'

'The main targets would be the Second Artillery units in the north at Shenyang, Harbin, and Yanbian. Simply because of range, that is where the launch would probably take place. I would like to also target the Nanjing, Guang-zhou, and Chengdu military regions. To do it effectively would need a lot of firepower. The attacks would have to be simultaneous and even then it would impossible to guarantee the destruction of China's military arsenal. The only possible way to deter them from using nuclear weapons, Mr President, would be to carry out a nuclear strike on China first. But frankly, knowing a bit about Chinese military thinking, I don't think it would work. I believe the military mindset right now is that they would see their whole country wiped out before being defeated by the United States.'

The President's Office, Seoul, Korea

Seoul was engulfed in smoke and raging fires. President Kim took a call on his direct line from Jamie Song.

'We have put an end to it,' said the Chinese Foreign Minister, speaking in English. 'Xinhua will be putting out a statement within the hour, saying that Kim Jong-Il and his close associates are on an official visit to China. We sent our own special forces units into Pyongyang to bring him out. There was fighting at the airport and our first aircraft was destroyed. But several army units have now come over to our side. Troops around the Presidential Palace have been neutralized. Kim Jong-Il is in the city of Yanji, across the border, under close guard. There'll be a statement from Pyongyang announcing the formation of a new government, but that might not be for some hours.'

'What about the current offensive?' interjected the President.

'I have no idea if the guys taking up the reins in Pyongyang have the power to call off the attack. On that one, you're on your own. And one other thing: once the truce is secured, we want the Americans out within a month.'

The first North Korean T-62 tank circled through the Demilitarized Zone as if the driver was in a manic frenzy, before crashing through one of the truce huts and heading straight for the South Korean military positions. Allied troops stopped it with an anti-tank missile. Then the North Korean artillery opened up with a ferocious barrage. Four Americans died from one shell explosion in Camp Greaves. Six were wounded. Five American helicopters, two giving covering fire with rockets and heavy machine-guns, came in to take out the dead, wounded, and survivors. Camp Greaves was empty when four North Korean T-62s broke down the perimeter fence. North Korean artillery was being destroyed by guided bombs and missiles fired from aircraft, warships, and land positions. The highway running north to Pyongyang was littered with the burnt-out wrecks of armoured vehicles. Fires raged below ground in the tunnels and caverns. But, unlike Saddam Hussein's Republican Guard in the Gulf War ten years earlier, it took far more to cripple the North Korean military machine.

Tens of thousand of troops poured south. Some emerged running across fields. At first, as they crossed the line, they were mown down with machine-guns or blown up by mines. Others came out in company strength through dozens of tunnels which had been dug over the years but not used. Hovercrafts with platoon-size units sped down at 40 knots landing men wherever they could find suitable landfall. Antonov troop-carrying planes dropped paratroopers. Hundreds were shot as they came down. Planes filled with men were blown out of the skies. By early afternoon, when the North Korean land offensive was at its height, it appeared that Fort Boniface would have to be abandoned. One North Korean commando unit penetrated the outer bunkers and there was hand-to-hand fighting on the sand-bagged defences. But the Americans put up a protective cordon of helicopter firepower around the base and soon the sheer devastating force of the South Korean and American counterattack put a stop to the first wave of enemy advance.

Skirmishes were continuing when Radio Pyongyang announced a change of government in the North. It broadcast a command for a ceasefire and within an hour of the news being known a Chinese military Boeing 737, met by escorting South Korean F-16 fighters on the

Northern border, headed for Pyongyang. The troops advancing on the South fell into disarray. Soon it became clear they were without commanders and over the following hours many of those caught in forward positions changed from being the enemy to peasant refugees seeking sanctuary under UN protection.

At a military airbase near Pyongyang, Chinese and South Korean officials stepped off the aircraft to be met by their North Korean military hosts. A temporary treaty, brokered by China, was signed in a run-down and unheated building which later became as famous as the buildings around Panmunjon. Photographs showed the participants muffled up in military greatcoats as they put their signatures to the document.

It stated that the Korean Peninsula would be reunited under a formula of one country, two systems. The demarcation line along the 38th Parallel would remain in place to ensure that South Korea was not flooded with refugees. There would be two separate currencies. But the border would be open for trade and investment and in a gradual process the two societies and governments would be completely integrated. Monuments to the Great Leader Kim Il-Sung would remain intact, as would his Juche philosophy. The few monuments to Kim Jong-Il would be removed. Kim Jong-Il himself would remain under indefinite house arrest in Yanji. Once the Dragonstrike crisis was over, joint military celebrations of the unification would be held in both Pyongyang and Seoul. The last clause of the treaty specified that all foreign troops would be asked to leave the peninsula once a genuine peace had been restored.

Capital Airport, Beijing

As soon as the American military Boeing 707 entered Chinese airspace, it was intercepted by four Shenyang J-6C Farmer air-combat fighter aircraft. These ageing warplanes were copied from the Soviet MiG-19s with a design which dated back to the 1960s. They would be no match for the American Tomcats in action over the South China Sea. As American, British, and Chinese lives were being lost at war, the Chinese fighter pilots followed the Boeing in and stayed with it for the safe landing at Beijing's Capital international airport. This was the only foreign airliner there. All civilian aircraft had left China within the past forty-eight hours. China's own civilian air fleet was either grounded or being used for troop transport. Even during the flight, first from Seattle to Tokyo and then on to Beijing, Reece Overhalt had never imagined that the passenger terminal in Beijing could so quickly be transformed into a military installation. Camouflage had been taken off anti-aircraft positions in the dusty fields around the runway. Rows of Sukhoi Su-24 Fencer-C all-weather ground-attack and interdiction aircraft together with the Shenyang J-6Cs were parked where just a week ago United Airlines and British Airways Boeing 747s would have been. Two Air China Boeing 747s were at air bridges at one of the main terminal buildings where Overhalt's plane came to a stop. As he disembarked, hundreds of Chinese troops were milling around, waiting to board for their deployment on the Vietnamese border.

United States Embassy officials met Overhalt near the circular central information desk. On the way down the wide corridor to the Arrivals Hall, he saw the officers in meetings in the First-class Lounge. There was an echoing sound of army boots and weapons, of a country going to war. The Immigration and Customs desks were unmanned. Crews of armoured personnel carriers stood vigil where hotel cars and taxis had been only a week earlier. There were military checkpoints on both sides of the airport expressway into Beijing. The Embassy's Lincoln Continental slowed at each one and was let through. A squadron of Chinese fighter aircraft took off and screamed overhead to go to war against Japan in the Yellow and East China Seas.

The South China Sea

The British and Commonwealth task force led by HMS *Ark Royal* was having to defend itself, mainly from China's guerrilla-style submarine warfare. The *Ark Royal* and her escort vessels were caught in a network of *Romeo* and *Ming* submarines patrolling the Spratly Islands in boxed-off areas. Each submarine commander was under orders to attack any vessel which came into his zone of control. The diesel-electric submarines waited very quietly for the targets to approach them. The *Ark Royal*'s captain wrote in his diary that it was like being on a jungle patrol where the enemy was hidden in the undergrowth and a sniper could attack at any time.

'I was reminded of films about guerrilla jungle warfare. The only difference is that we were in the open sea, with blue skies and a clear horizon. It was frighteningly empty, but we knew the enemy was in the waters beneath us. We were aware it wouldn't mind losing three or ten vessels to our one. Our opponents were Mao's barefoot submariners. We were NATO's digital navy. We found some of them. But mostly they hid like snipers, mocking our technology. It was only when we detected the streak of the torpedo that we knew we were under attack. And by then, it was often too late. When it was over I felt obliged, as a naval officer, to salute their courage and daring.'

The first ship to be attacked was HMS *Liverpool*. A torpedo exploded 3 metres under the hull. The blast destroyed the engine room, killing twenty-three men. Then there was a direct hit astern. Another five men died with the initial impact. Seventeen more were dead by the time the ship sank. Half an hour later the crew of the attack submarine HMS *Triumph* avoided a salvo of three Chinese torpedoes. The commander at first speeded up, then turned away and slowed down. His decisions were partly based on guesswork that the Chinese torpedoes would be of the same type that had sunk the USS *Peleliu* and would not change course with countermeasures. Minutes later he was given a firing solution for the *Romeo* which was destroyed with one Spearfish wire-guided torpedo. Merlin helicopters from the *Ark Royal* hit another submarine using sonobuoys and a Stingray torpedo. HMAS *Rankin*, the Australian *Collins* class submarine, was the only vessel able to play the Chinese submarines at their own game. By adopting the Chinese tactics and waiting silently, sometimes on the bottom, the *Collins* commander was able to pick off two more of the enemy, giving him the highest hit rate of any submariner since the Second World War. He returned to the Darwin Naval Base a hero.

Hollywood, Los Angeles, California

There was no official announcement from the White House, Pentagon, or State Department, but within an hour of the satellite photographs arriving on the President's desk, CNN broke the story of an imminent nuclear strike. The network, which had been running rolling news, abandoned even the existing schedules. Rival networks followed and soon every channel was a mix of analysts' comment and live contributions from correspondents across America. The impact was chilling. Discussions swiftly moved from the threat of China, to the threat within the United States itself. Speculation began on the ability of the security forces to keep control, and then shifted to the impact on the medical system, communications, transport, and banking.

'Are you telling us that if a nuclear bomb hits America, the government infrastructure will be unable to handle it?' asked one anchor.

'I am telling you,' replied the commentator, 'that people had better make sure they have money, enough food in the cupboard, a full tank of gas, an up-to-date first-aid kit and the view that no one will look after their families except themselves.'

No one was sure what sparked the riots, but that was the most likely broadcast. The first looting officially linked to Operation Dragonstrike was on a delicatessen in Hollywood. One witness said she thought it was a drive-by shooting and took cover in an alleyway two blocks from the shop. The attackers shot down the ground-to-ceiling window with automatic weapons and a pump-action rifle. Then they backed a station wagon onto the pavement and loaded the food into the back. They sped off, firing their weapons into the air. Police logged the time as 1917. By midnight, hospitals, gas stations, and supermarkets throughout the country were being ransacked.

The White House, Washington, DC

Local time: 2230 Wednesday 21 February 2001
GMT: 0330 Thursday 22 February 2001

Mr Jiang Hua, the Chinese Ambassador, was a man of great dignity and never tired of reminding people of it. He swept into the Oval Office, apologized for being held up in traffic, and mentioned nothing about being called to the White House at such a late hour. His composure remained unruffled even when the President, abandoning diplomatic courtesy, confronted him. 'What in God's name does your government think it is doing?' he began. He threw the folder containing the photographic intelligence on the coffee table before the Ambassador.

Everyone in the room was standing. The Ambassador remained silent for almost half a minute, then replied: 'I have no idea what you are talking about, Mr President.'

The President gave a blunt response. 'Don't play dumb, Ambassador. These photographs show Chinese missiles being prepared for a strike on the United States.'

The Ambassador shuffled his feet. 'I have been instructed to inform you that the government of China is prepared for every eventuality. May I point out that the United States has brazenly supported the splittist activities of rebellious groups acting against the Chinese people? You have sold sophisticated weapons to our enemies and given sanctuary to those trying to overthrow our government. Therefore it is necessary, resolutely and forcefully necessary, to hit back at these rude acts of interference, subversion, and extortion by the American hegemonists. The officers and men of all ground, naval, and air units are ready to take orders from Comrade

Wang Feng and the Chinese Communist Party Central Committee.'

'Mr Ambassador, I suggest you go back to your Embassy and tell President Wang to stand those missiles down. On the first sign of a launch, we will obliterate China.'

The commander of the *Vanguard* class strategic missile submarine HMS *Vengeance* received his orders to prepare for a nuclear launch from an extra-low-frequency radio message which penetrated the ice cap under which he was patrolling. Any target in the northern hemisphere was in range from these waters around the North Pole, where Soviet and NATO submarines used to gather in a crowded cat and mouse game during the Cold War. HMS *Vengeance* operated with the luxury of knowing that no Chinese submarine was there now. They had no ability to go under the ice and the submariners had no substantive cold-water training. HMS *Vengeance* was being guarded by the *Trafalgar* class attack submarine HMS *Trenchant*, whose sonar operators had been keeping watch on a Russian *Typhoon* class strategic missile submarine and an *Akula* class attack submarine. The *Akula* followed HMS *Vengeance* as it moved to prepare for the launch. In the control room, the computer automatically still listed Russian vessels as hostile.

Within an hour the commander had found the *polynya* or clear water surrounded by ice through which he could launch the Trident 11 (D5) missiles. Every action he took was verified with his Weapons Engineer: they held separate keys which would initiate the launch. Each missile had a three-stage solid-fuel rocket and carried eight MIRVs with 100 kiloton warheads. The launch could be detected by Chinese satellites fifteen seconds before it happened, with an increased swell and generation of white water around the submerged submarine as the torpedo chamber doors opened. At four seconds to launch the sea would begin heaving violently. Then a rumbling sound would begin as if there was a huge thunderclap. All around, the sea would turn into a turbulent pitch and roll, and in a mixture of spray, fire, and froth the missile would rise out of the sea and turn towards its target 5,000 kilometres away.

The first missile was programmed to hit Desired Ground Zero One in Beijing. During the Cold War, DGZ-1, the precise spot where the first nuclear warhead would explode, was Lenin's mausoleum in Red Square. In China, DGZ-1 was the mausoleum of Mao Zedong in Tiananmen Square at the coordinates of 116° 23′ 35″ East (longitude) and 39° 53′ 58″ North (latitude). In the same salvo the south section of Zhongnanhai would be destroyed at 116° 22′ 40″ North (longitude), and 39° 54′ 25″ East (latitude); and the Party's secret grain supply on Tiancun Lu, west Beijing, 116° 14′ 50″ North (longitude) and 39° 55′ 45″ East (latitude).

The target coordinates had been programmed into the missile computers in code. Not even the men who pressed the launch buttons knew where they were heading.

To keep the Russian submarine at a safe distance, the commander of HMS *Trenchant* made clear the British presence by cycling his main vents and blowing out his sewage tanks. The *Akula* commander replied by sending out a ripple transmission through his Shark Gill sonar. Russia was watching but not interfering. Close to the surface, HMS *Vengeance* trailed a very-low-frequency wire. The crew waited for orders to fire.

US Space Command Center,
Peterson Air Force Base, Colorado

Signals from every available strategic recce and intelligence satellite were drawn into the US Space Command Center. Sensors were monitored in the NAVSTAR nuclear detonation detection system satellites. Data from ballistic-missile early-warning systems at Thule in Greenland and Fylingdales Moor in the United Kingdom was watched second by second. Radar crews were put on high alert in stations in Turkey, Italy, Diego Garcia, and across the United States. The special Pave Paws phased-array radar in Massachusetts, Georgia, Texas, and California tracked objects more than 5,000 kilometres away. Other detection and tracking radars were in operation on Kwajalein Atoll in the Pacific, British Ascension Island in the Atlantic, Antigua in the Caribbean, and at the Lincoln Laboratory at the Massachusetts Institute of Technology.

Like HMS *Vengeance*, commanders of the American strategic missile submarines of the *Ohio* class USS *Nebraska* and USS *Louisiana* in the northern and southern Pacific and the USS *Rhode Island* under the polar ice cap were given orders to prepare for a Trident launch. In Turkey, Italy, Guam, and Japan, American B2 Stealth bombers were being fitted with guided nuclear bombs. In the two American carrier groups, Tomahawk cruise missiles, mostly with 200 kiloton warheads, were being prepared for firing. In the deserts of central America, technicians made ready the Peacekeeper and Minuteman III intercontinental missiles in their 25 metre deep concrete and steel silos, capped with retractable steel covers. The silos were at least 6 kilometres apart to minimize the damage of a direct hit. The regional control centre was 18 kilometres away and the crew of the National Emergency Air-Borne Command Post patrolled the skies in case it had to take over. Both the Minutemen and Peacekeepers carried 331 kiloton W-78 nuclear warheads and could hit targets nearly 12,000 kilometres away. The Peacekeeper, with ten individual warheads and a computer system which could make two million simultaneous calculations a second, had taken over from the Minuteman as the ICBM programme's first-line defence. As America and Europe braced for a nuclear war with China, missiles were programmed to hit the cities of Beijing, Shanghai, Dalian, Chengdu, Harbin, and Shenyang. Guangdong was not targeted because of possible fallout onto Hong Kong. Xiamen and Fuzhou escaped because of their proximity to Taiwan. The North Sea Fleet headquarters at Qingdao, the East Sea Fleet at Ningbo, and the South Sea Fleet at Zhanjiang were to be destroyed together with the air and submarine bases on Hainan Island. Other specific targets were the naval academies at Dalian and Qingdao, the Engineering College at Wuhan, and the Nanjing Naval Staff College.

The aim of the strike was to destroy the People's Liberation Army and the Chinese Communist Party.

Tokyo

Japanese television channels illustrated the tests with colourful graphics. Clusters of people gathered around the windows of television shops on their way back from work. The huge screens in the airport and bus and underground stations showed the firing of four medium-range ballistic missiles from Okinawa and four Chinese made Tomahawk-style terrain-following cruise missiles from the *Kongou* class destroyers *Myoko* and *Kirishima* which were 1,000 kilometres further south in the South China Sea. Two cruise and two ballistic missiles landed 3 kilometres off the Chinese coast at Tianjin, the port city only 120 kilometres from Beijing. Another ballistic missile hit the sea just outside the southern naval base of Zhanjiang and the fourth fell at the mouth of the Yangtse River near Shanghai. A cruise missile landed off the coast near the Yulin airbase on Hainan Island and the final one was targeted on waters around Xiamen, the thriving port city across the straits from Taiwan. None carried warheads. Television commentators aided by more graphics explained how the missile tests coupled with the nuclear explosion confirmed that Japan was now a global military power. The sheer numbers of warheads Japan was able to fire against the enemy meant that some would get through and there would be no protection. People all over Japan celebrated through the day. There was no criticism of the tests by Western powers.

United States Embassy, Beijing

Local time: 1300 Thursday 22 February 2001
GMT: 0500 Thursday 22 February 2001

The engine of the Ambassador's Lincoln Continental was running, with the heater warming the interior for Reece Overhalt on his journey to the Foreign Ministry. But the driver walked to the wrought-iron gate to confirm that the noise he was hearing from the narrow tree-lined Xiu Shui Street in Beijing's diplomatic district was a demonstration of students. He had seen nothing like this in China since the Cultural Revolution thirty years earlier. For many of the locally employed Embassy staff, who came out to the Embassy compound to watch, the chanting revived horrific memories of the Maoist-controlled violence which killed so many of their friends and relatives. The compound of lawns and tall green maple and fir trees began to fill up with people, both Americans and Chinese standing side by side in silence as the marchers came closer. The building itself was protected by concrete anti-missile and grenade barricades. The Marine Sergeant posted extra men inside the gate. A small queue of people lining up to get into the Embassy dispersed. Foreign shoppers from the nearby markets hurried away.

The leaders of the demonstration were from Beijing People's University, the spiritual home of the Chinese Communist Party. They had spread out throughout the Jianguomennei area, sealing off roads leading to many of the main embassies. Many wore red bandannas. Others were dressed in blue Maoist suits. Some kept their Western-style jeans. They laid bicycles down as blockades. Students began running, many shaking their fists and screaming as if in a frenzy. Shoulder high, they carried effigies of the Western and Japanese leaders, some made of plaster, some of cardboard and plywood. Outside the American Embassy they doused the plaster effigy of James Bradlay with petrol and set it alight. They stretched the American flag between stepladders until it was taut, then slashed it with knives before lighting it. One student, dressed like Uncle Sam in Stars and Stripes, was pulled forward. They hung a sign around his neck which read: 'I am a traitor to the people.' They put a cylindrical dunce's cap on his head, then knelt him down just feet away from the Marine guard on the gate. They pushed his head forward, pulled his arms up behind his back, then pretended to kick, slap, and taunt him. The Embassy compound was now surrounded. One by one students stepped out in front of the crowd to denounce America. There were similar displays of Chinese wrath outside the other embassies which had opposed Operation Dragonstrike. Just a few hundred metres away, the British Embassy and Ambassador's residence were sealed off. Firecrackers were thrown over the gates. On the fringes of the diplomatic area, which adjoined the main tourist district of Beijing, armed and uniformed troops from the Central Guard Regiment were on patrol, ensuring that no one interfered. The Xinhua (New China) News Agency called it a 'spontaneous outpouring of anger'.

Reece Overhalt was already half an hour late for his meeting with Jamie Song when he got through on the telephone. The Foreign Minister was careful in his explanation. The only hint that the demonstration was out of his control came when he said: 'The timing is unfortunate for our business discussions.'

Overhalt was familiar with Chinese nuances. But he had already decided to play the part of the Western cultural idiot. He believed bluntness was the most effective way to send a message via the Ministry of State Security's telephone tapping agents. 'Jamie, we've got submarines with firing solutions ready to go. If we so much as see a tweak of launch preparation from your missiles, you, I, and those students are going to get fried.'

'They won't do it with you here, Reece.'

'Like hell they won't, Jamie. And there are a lot of people in the Pentagon who think we should have done it a damn sight earlier.'

Briefing

The effect of a nuclear explosion on a Japanese city

Japanese houses and low-rise apartment buildings were made to fall over. A history of constant earthquakes conditioned the Japanese people to view their housing as essentially temporary structures. It was a mindset reinforced by Imperial ritual. To the south of Tokyo, on the Ise Peninsula, were the Great Shrines at Ise. These commemorated the founding of the Imperial line in the mists of time, and were maintained by Shinto priests. Since AD 478 they had torn down and rebuilt the shrines every twenty years. Sometimes a massive earthquake destroyed everything – as in 1923, or the Kobe earthquake of 1995 which devastated that port city – but most of the time people's houses and apartments were buffeted and jolted by an almost continuous series of small and large tremors. Their buildings were therefore lightweight – wooden frames and a ferroconcrete surround – and made to flex with the movement of the earth. If the earthquake was strong and they fell over they were comparatively cheap to replace. Light, flexible structures were well suited to surviving low-level earthquakes but were about the worst shelters to use in the aftermath of a nuclear attack. This was not so much because they collapsed in the face of the huge pressures and winds generated by a nuclear explosion: those near the epicentre and for many kilometres beyond were flattened. The lightweight construction of Tokyo's houses and apartments meant that the ones which survived a nuclear attack – the ones at the periphery of the explosion – provided so little protection from the effects of radioactive fallout as to be virtually useless. Gamma radiation passed unimpeded through the roofs and walls of the houses.

The best piece of advice the authorities had given the people was to own a fire extinguisher. Given the materials used in the construction of the Tokyo housing stock, fires were likely in the event of an attack. For survivors of an attack the first two or three days after are a critical time. During this period it is best to stay indoors, because radioactive fallout is at its most lethal immediately after a nuclear explosion. Food, water, and bedding supplies were centralized. A ward could feed up to 300,000 for a day or two; it had 51,000 blankets, 51,000 straw mats, 2,300 portable toilets, and, in underground emergency reservoirs, it had 52,700 metric tons of fresh water. But the surviving population was meant to make its way to designated safety areas where the local government would distribute food and medical aid.

The street that ran past the entrance to Monzennaka-cho on the Tozai line of the Tokyo underground was like any in Tokyo. Next door to Chozushi sushi shop, just four doors from the entrance to the station, is a Japanese sweetshop; next to it a cheap coffee shop, and then Mr Donuts, a popular chain outlet catering to commuters, schoolgirls, and local mums and their children. With a dozen tables and a counter that seats a dozen, Mr Donuts is crowded with as many as a hundred patrons at a time. In the front, two girls bag takeout doughnuts for customers as fast as they can. The store is a virtual madhouse at most hours of the day. The west entrance-exit to the subway is just outside Mr Donuts' door, bounded on the far side by an eat-as-you-stand *soba* and *tempura* shop. A woman sits in a tiny news-stand located between the two doors at each end of the *soba-tempura* shop. Around the corner is the local police *koban*, sandwiched next to a shoe shop. Then comes Kentucky Fried Chicken, another *soba* shop, a barber's, a pub, and McDonald's.

It was cold and grey but the *teikiya*, or outdoor market, was in full swing. Twice a month, the street vendors converge on Mon-naka, setting up their booths on the broad footpath that stretches from the Mitsubishi Bank east for several blocks past the Tomioka Hachiman shrine. The first booth usually sells Brother sewing machines, with a hawker proclaiming the wonders of home sewing. Down the line there are booths selling hard rock sweets, dumplings with octopus in them (*takoyaki*), round *monaka* full of sweet bean paste, fried noodles, underwear apparently targeted at women over sixty, plastic toys and masks, wind chimes, barbecued chicken (*yakitori*), pottery, pirated tapes and CDs, potted plants, and cut flowers. These vendors turn up on the 22nd of each month, and when they do, the elderly residents come out to browse. Bent backs and canes are the mode of the day, and it can be a nerve-racking task to walk that side of the street. The confusion and congestion is compounded by store owners putting their own pavement booths out, competing with the *teikiya*.

The broadcasts started soon after 3 p.m. There were 111 public address loudspeakers in Koto ward, and three of them ran the length of the *teikiya*. Simultaneously the loudspeakers switched from the somewhat irritating low-level muzak that they usually emitted to the calm voice of a woman telling everyone to go home. That was all. Over and over again in a very calm voice she said everyone must go home and all businesses should close: there was an emergency. People stopped and just looked at each other. An old woman began to weep. In the *sushi-ya* the owner switched the television channel to NHK, the national broadcaster. A grave young woman said that China was threatening Japan with a nuclear strike. People should listen to their local officials and do what they were told.

Just before the public broadcasts began, the chief of Koto's Ward Disaster Preparation Committee had sent a message to local volunteers via the ward's additional network of 533 PA speakers situated in the homes of volunteers. He called them up to take the initiative in helping their neighbours. 'If they ask why, tell them that China has threatened to bomb us.' The emergency always talked about and prepared for was an earthquake. 1 September, the day of the Great Kanto earthquake of 1923 that devastated Tokyo, was set aside for the good citizens of Koto, indeed Japan, to practise what to do after a big earthquake. On 6 August 1945 the Americans dropped the atomic bomb on Hiroshima; three days later it was Nagasaki's turn. But there was not a 6 August day set aside to practise what to do in the event of a nuclear attack. The Japanese government did not have a plan as such for dealing with the bomb. The only disaster Koto was even partially equipped to deal with was an earthquake: local officials had to harness earthquake emergency procedures using the ward-wide PA system.

Koto had a problem with the emergency that gripped it that Thursday afternoon and it did not know quite what to do.

Briefing

Planning for a nuclear attack on Kent

The County Emergency Centre for Kent (pop. 1,500,000) is located in the basement under the canteen for the county offices on Sandling Road in central Maidstone. It is an unprepossessing accumulation of rooms that was adapted during the Cold War. But given the crisis that was to unfold many had cause to give thanks for that. The centre was designed primarily to protect its inhabitants from the worst effects of radioactive fallout from a nuclear explosion. Only 1 per cent of the radiation at street level could penetrate the bunker, or so its designers hoped. Structurally, however, the facility itself could only withstand the excessive atmospheric pressures created by a nuclear explosion of 1 lb per square inch (p.s.i.). A 1 megaton Chinese bomb would create an overpressure of 126 p.s.i. 0.5 nautical miles from the point of detonation. Implicitly, the designers of the bunker had therefore assumed that if Maidstone itself were a target then to preserve a local government presence was pointless when all the population was destroyed. Indeed, at just over a mile from point of detonation, a 1 megaton bomb produces an overpressure of 10 p.s.i. – an overpressure powerful enough to uproot all trees, destroy all houses, and shred most high-rise buildings. It was just such a bomb that a Xinhua report had said would be launched at the south-east of England.

The emergency centre had been designed to support forty-eight people for a month. It had an oil-fired generator to provide electricity, a tank of fresh water, food stores, accommodation for sixteen to sleep at any one time, and a warren of rooms crammed full of telephones – their cords hanging from points in the ceiling – arranged on long tables. The telephone was part of a network maintained by the government and was quite separate from the civilian telephone network owned and operated by British Telecom. In one room of the bunker was a green box, about the size of a refrigerator. Manufactured by Rainford Secure Systems of St Helens, near Liverpool, this was the telephone switching gear and it was meant to be impervious to the electromagnetic pulse, or EMP. The equipment would have to be sturdy because a 1 megaton nuclear weapon exploding at ground level generated 100,000,000,000 joules of energy. A fraction of a joule was enough to damage most modern electronic equipment; 1 joule was enough to render a telephone, or hospital life-support system, useless. Such widespread and indiscriminate damage to all electrical and electronic equipment could be expected within a radius of 10 to 20 kilometres from the point of impact of the Chinese bomb. The Kent local government's ability to communicate with the Cabinet Office Emergency Committee in London would depend crucially on just how good Rainford Secure Systems' shielding of the telephone switch gear really was.

By the time senior officials from the county council and the emergency services had been summoned to the emergency centre – just after 9 a.m. – they all knew why they were there. Since 7 a.m. the BBC and its commercial competitors had been broadcasting news of the Chinese threat. Although it would not be until 10 a.m. that the BBC began broadcasting its 'What to do in the event of a nuclear attack' television and radio programmes, many Kent citizens had decided the threat was all too real and had begun to flee the south-east. The roads had become congested, especially main motorways – the M20 to Folkestone and Dover, and the M2 to Ramsgate and Dover – and the faster

A roads leading north to the M25 orbital motorway that circled London and provided access to Gatwick and Heathrow airports. Chokepoints, such as the entrance to the Channel Tunnel at Folkestone, and the entrances to cross-Channel ferries at Ramsgate, Dover, and Folkestone were also very crowded with people fleeing. One of the first decisions the Emergency Committee had to take was whether to permit large-scale self-evacuation (and the attendant chaos on the roads that might bring) or attempt to keep the civilian population in their homes. One of the advantages of the timing of the warning was that most bread winners had not gone to work, so families were not dispersed. But to an extent the actions of people had pre-empted the discussion: self-evacuation was already taking place, and there was a spirited discussion between the police and the county council. The representative of the Chief Constable for Kent said he was sure his officers could control the situation and keep the roads clear for emergency use. The County Emergency Planning Officer disagreed. As the county was unable to guarantee personal safety the police should not hinder anyone's attempt to leave, rather they should ensure the roads were kept open. In addition, in the absence of emergency powers being enacted, while the police might close roads and maintain public order the legality of their restricting movement was judged extremely dubious. The county should, however, use local radio to send the message that people were likely to be safer in a properly constructed shelter in their houses than in a car if a bomb was detonated. The County Chief Executive came down on the side of his County Emergency Planning Officer and it was decided that the Chief Executive and the County Emergency Planning Officer would make themselves available for radio interviews after the meeting to explain the benefits of staying put.

Although many thousands had taken to their cars and

were driving north to the M25 motorway or to the coast in the hope of getting to France, many more people had either made the decision to stay or did not possess the means to leave. In the latter category were the homeless and elderly. Here it was decided that social services should immediately set out to determine who were at risk; to identify their whereabouts; and, in the case of the homeless, remove them to an appropriate residential establishment.

The subject no one really wanted to discuss but every one knew had to be discussed came towards the end of the meeting: health. Governments did not plan expenditure on the basis of the sort of medical facilities a country of sixty million people would need to survive a nuclear attack. Kent would have to make do with what it had. One of the consequences of civilian nuclear disasters is a rise in thyroid cancer. This occurs because radioactive iodine produced by a nuclear accident lodges in the thyroid glands of affected workers. One way of preventing thyroid cancer is to administer potassium iodate. This lodges in the thyroid and crowds out the radioactive isotopes which then pass through the body. Stocks of potassium iodate were at the Dungeness nuclear power plant on Kent's south coast, beyond the Romney Marshes, but they were hardly adequate for a county-wide emergency. Hospitals had been alerted and were instituting their own emergency procedures. But only one, the Royal Marsden Hospital at Sutton in Surrey, was geared up for nuclear accidents. It offered a procedure known as 'pulmonary lavage', whereby a patient who had breathed in radioactive particles was put on an alternative oxygenated blood supply while he had his lungs irrigated. Pulmonary lavage was, however, a complicated and time-consuming process, and Royal Marsden could accommodate only a fraction of the expected casualties from the Chinese bomb.

Royal Tunbridge Wells, Kent

Local time: 1000 Thursday 22 February 2001

Eric Wallace, father of two, looked out of his sitting room window on to St John's Road. It was usually a busy road – to the north it offered access to Tonbridge and Sevenoaks, to the south Lewes and East Grinstead – but on that Thursday morning it was bumper-to-bumper both ways. Wallace had talked things over with his wife, Cathy, and they had decided to stay put. 'If it's going to hit us direct then it doesn't matter where we are,' he said. He also thought that of all the places in the south-east Tunbridge Wells was about as unlikely a target as you could get … and London by far the more likely. In any event he was taking no chances.

The television had been turned on and tuned to BBC 1 since Wallace heard on his clock radio that south-east England might be the target for a Chinese nuclear attack. The calm voice of the announcer explained that the greatest threat to life was from gamma radiation. Some houses impede the progress of gamma radiation better than others. Caravans are next to useless as they stop virtually no radiation at all. A lot of modern houses are not much better. The best dwelling to be holed up in during a nuclear attack is in the basement of a three-storey block of flats. The announcer said that a Home Office study pointed out that the occupants of such a cellar or basement would receive one three-hundredth of the external gamma radiation. In general, cellars or basements are the best place to hide because they are furthest away from the roof, which lets in a lot of radiation, and because the ground is a good shield against radiation. Eric Wallace and his family, however, lived in a two storey mock-Tudor house without a cellar. On the ground, with only the windows blocked, more than 80 per cent of gamma radiation would pass through the house, without some protection.

Soon after he and his wife had decided to remain in their house Cathy set out for the shops in Tunbridge Wells. She was in charge of getting the family's survival kit together. She set off down St John's Road towards the town centre. The roads were packed with cars. The cars were packed with people and possessions. She passed car after car. None overtook her. She got to Grosvenor Road but Tesco's was closed. A crowd milled around its entrance. She continued on. She always shopped at Tesco's; it was the closest and they knew her.

Grosvenor Road became Mount Pleasant Road just at the point where Calverley Road met both. Calverley Road was a pedestrian mall and a short way down was Marks & Spencer. It was open, but an angry crowd was milling around the entrance like a swarm of agitated bees. Five policemen were attempting to restrain one group of people who had claimed that another had jumped the queue. Cathy spoke to one of the policemen who told her that Safeway's, down by the mainline railway station, was open, so she made for that. As she passed the Town Hall, a thirties structure of studied ugliness that dominated Mount Pleasant Road, she saw a Transit van full of vagrants being unloaded and taken into the town hall. Safeway's was as crowded and rowdy as the other supermarkets. Cathy queued and said little. All she knew was that she had a list to get, and then get back home although the prospect of a twenty-minute walk carrying what she had to carry scared the living daylights out of her. Eric had told her that they needed enough food for four for fourteen days. Since 10 a.m. the BBC had been broadcasting advice about what to buy. The government's advice was to stock up on sugar, jams, and other sweet foods, cereals, biscuits, meats, vegetables, fruit, and fruit juices. She also had to get batteries for the portable radio, pain killers, adhesive dressings, bandages, disinfectant, three buckets (with lids), and bin liners.

When she got home it looked as though a bomb had hit. Eric had removed doors and filled rubbish-bin liners with soil from the garden. He'd also painted the glass in the windows white and moved pieces of furniture in front of them.

The main ground floor room in the Wallaces' house ran the full depth of the house. The room was divided in two by sliding doors and they used the front half as their sitting room and the back half for dining. Behind the dining area was a kitchen and behind that a garden. Mr Wallace made his family's internal shelter in the dining room. Along the wall the room shared with the kitchen he propped four doors which he had removed from rooms upstairs. These were arranged in a 'lean-to' and secured on the floor by a batten running its length. According to the film which had been running continuously on the BBC since 10 a.m., the next thing to do was insulate the lean-to. This was most effectively done by filling rubbish sacks full of earth and placing them over it. He also stacked sacks of earth on the kitchen side of the wall the lean-to was using. In all, he managed to fill and stack more than fifty sacks of earth by lunchtime. The entrance to the lean-to posed a problem until he uncovered two old tea chests. He filled each with earth. He put planks of wood over the top of the chests and on the planks stacked more bags of earth. There wasn't much left of the garden after he finished.

With the shelter built Mr Wallace set about securing the room housing it. He closed the double doors, both of which were solid timber. The dining room had only one window. He painted its panes white – this might deflect the flash, although they would likely break if the bomb went off in Kent itself – and then set about bagging the window. After he'd done that he moved a cupboard to cover the bags. The last thing he did, before the period of waiting began, was to construct a makeshift lavatory. The BBC advice was to remove the seat from a dining chair and place a bucket, lined with a rubbish bin liner, underneath it. The three buckets with lids that Cathy had bought now had a use.

The Wallaces then began their wait. They sat outside their shelter, watching the BBC. They figured that once the TV went off they'd have time to get in the shelter.

SEVEN

The South China Sea

Local time: 1900 Thursday 22 February 2001
GMT: 1100 Thursday 22 February 2001

Throughout the day, Sea Harriers and Merlins had continued to strafe and destroy any Chinese ship they found on patrols. They were loaded with a mixture of Sidewinder missiles, American-made air-to-ground AS-16 Kickback missiles, specially designed for attacks on ships, together with anti-submarine Stingray torpedoes and depth charges. They destroyed a *Ming* submarine and sank a *Yukan* class LST which was reported to be carrying up to 200 troops. Most drowned.

Shortly before dark another *Romeo* struck, this time hitting the Australian frigate HMAS *Parramatta* near the bow. Five servicemen died, including an officer. Although the damage was contained, the frigate had been put out of action. The captain took her out of the battle area. The task force commander agreed to let HMAS *Rankin* escort her. Five hours later HMS *Triumph* destroyed the submarine believed to have carried out the attack.

'We expected more attacks at night,' wrote the captain of the *Ark Royal*. 'Strangely there was nothing. We sailed at half speed because the *Montrose* was under repair. There was very little moonlight. We scanned for periscopes like they would have done in the Second World War. I thought of them lying in wait, perhaps choosing not to fire in order to test our nerve. Our speed and our course were irrelevant. Our task lay in maintaining our presence in these contested waters, although in truth it was hard to see why British and Chinese servicemen were dying over such barren and remote landfalls. I must discipline my mind not to retreat down such a perilous path. What of those oft-quoted remarks after British campaigns in places long ago abandoned by us only to return to poverty and tribal killings: that such and such a battle was a good one to have on the CV? Perhaps 22 February 2001, the naval battle for the Spratly Islands, will also be good for our careers.'

The Vietnamese mission was to destroy China's ability to launch an attack. To complete the objective, Vietnam's own air force would be shredded. Casualties would be high. The international press would call it suicide. But it wasn't; this was how Vietnam had fought all its modern wars and won. The targets were the Chinese troops, artillery, and armour positions gathered along a 300 kilometre stretch of border; the Su-27 fighter base at Yulin on Hainan Island; the nearby submarine base at Sanya; and a return sortie to the headquarters of the Chinese South Sea Fleet, the Zhanjiang Naval Base. This forward command post for Dragonstrike was located on the east side of the Luichow Peninsula, which formed the dividing line between the South China Sea and the Gulf of Tonking.

The attackers did not expect to find any significant Chinese naval assets in port – they were either at the bottom of the South China Sea or patrolling parts of that great waterway beyond the control of the American, Japanese, and British navies. No. Their objective was the fuel dumps to the north of the dock and what had become known as the 'Russian quarter'. This was a group of low-rise buildings on the east side of the dock which housed Russian technical advisers (and families) and equipment.

Overnight, aircraft had been flown back from their refuges in Cambodia and Laos to military airstrips near Hanoi. The task of attacking Zhanjiang went to the pilots of a single squadron of twelve MiG-21 fighters. They headed due east, flying at 45 metres, too low to show up on Chinese radar. They would not be identified until they managed to make Chinese landfall: but the Chinese were expected to deploy their Su-27s and the MiGs would need to use all their countermeasures. The cover of night would help. Vietnamese pilots were more experienced fliers than their Chinese counterparts, who spent most of their training practising daytime missions.

The Vietnamese battle plan called for the squadron to divide into two parts. The first, consisting of five aircraft, would take out the oil installation. The resultant fire, it was calculated, would be helpful for the second part of the mission – the attack on the Russian quarter. The MiG-21s made landfall at 2114 and were immediately subjected to anti-aircraft fire in a continuous curtain from fixed installations along the coast to the naval base. But it was not aimed fire and the aircraft got through. Within minutes a squadron of Su-27s intercepted them before they began their bombing run on the oil installation. But this was where the Vietnamese showed their mettle. Also they were wearing night-vision intensification goggles and the Chinese were not. Flying at night can be a nerve-racking business at the best of times, but when you're making sharp turns while at the same time diving or climbing or rolling figuring out which way is up is often difficult. Two Chinese pilots lost their lives that night as they slammed their aircraft into hills after becoming disoriented and losing ground reference. The MiGs also hit three other Su-27s, but not before one of the MiGs was also hit.

They began the bomb run, seeing at night through the intensification goggles. The oil bunkers were close to the waterfront and extended over a large area. A direct hit on any one of the ten massive tanks might ignite the rest. The first MiG-21 to attempt an attack just exploded under a hail of well-aimed radar-directed ground fire. The second was hit badly, but at least the pilot had time to eject. The third aircraft scored a direct hit on an oil tank. The fireball that resulted shot 150 metres into the air, and adjacent tanks started to catch fire. All around, massive explosion followed massive explosion. The silhouette of the Shell *New World* could be seen against a wall of flame. The four remaining MiGs turned to complete their mission.

The attack on the oil bunker had lasted not quite five minutes, but that was enough time for the Russian technicians and scientists to look for cover. Except there was none. The MiGs – each equipped with a high-explosive bomb set to burst in the air, as well as air-to-ground missiles, and cannon – turned to begin their run. An Su-27, flying straight towards them, launched two air-to-air missiles. The pilot of the lead MiG did not even have time to press his ejector seat button before he was hit. His comrades kept to their course. The three of them managed to drop their bombs. These were not laser-guided smart bombs, but they did their work. The Russian quarter was reduced to rubble as the buildings collapsed. Eighty-five Russians lost their lives – mostly women and children. The mission was a success – both targets had been hit and the Vietnamese air force had five MiGs left.

The airbase at Yulin was deserted. All available Chinese aircraft were deployed over the South China Sea or in defence of Zhanjiang. Vietnam sent its own small Su-27 squadron into the main Chinese forward base for Dragonstrike. They flew fast and low through anti-aircraft fire, cratering the runway, and destroying the control tower, three IL-76 refuelling aircraft, and radar installations. Returning Chinese aircraft had to be diverted to the civilian airfield at Haikou, where there were no engineers or ordnance to turn them round for another attack. The Vietnamese attack on Yulin crippled the Chinese fighter force for long enough to give them clear skies for their two remaining targets. Climbing straight up from the attack on

Yulin, the Vietnamese pilots hit the Sanya submarine base. With rockets and cannon fire they cut communications and started a series of small fires. One *Romeo* class submarine was destroyed and sunk. Another was hit. Just as swiftly, the squadron, still without casualties, pulled away and headed back across the border to Hanoi. At the same time thirty-four Vietnamese fighters, bombers, and attack aircraft struck at Chinese positions on the border. Amid scenes reminiscent of American carpet bombing during the Vietnam War, the whole stretch of border lit up as airbursts and cluster bomblets combed the jungle where the Chinese artillery and troops were hidden. It was only on the second run that the Chinese guns jumped to defend the tens of thousands of troops massed there. The Vietnamese aircraft took casualties, losing twelve in the second run before the anti-aircraft artillery had been damaged, and another five in the third when fewer guns were firing. But as they pulled up and flew away the Chinese positions were in chaos, and command and discipline had broken down. The full extent of the casualties was never known. China said 600 men had been killed or wounded. Military satellite photographs suggested that the figure could have been as high as 4,000. There was no real cover.

All the attention had been on a ground assault into Vietnam and the Military Committee had decreed that the enemy air force had been eliminated. They were taken by surprise by the weight and accuracy of the attack. The airbursts and cluster bomblets killed any exposed personnel and damaged everything but heavily armoured vehicles. President Wang himself ordered the attack on Vietnam halted.

'Certainly nobody in this country has taken civil defence seriously for God knows how long, for twenty-five years, at least. It was recognized by most people that civil defence was kind of a silly idea, given the kind of thing it was supposed to protect against.' The broadcast was live from the University of Michigan in Chicago. The deep baritone voice was that of Edward Stone, the sixty-one-year-old veteran editor of *The Bulletin of the Atomic Scientists*. In the past day the hands of the magazine's fabled Atomic Clock had moved from nineteen minutes to just one minute to midnight, exactly the same spot it had been during the Cuban missile crisis with the Soviet Union in the sixties. Midnight signified the hour of the holocaust.

'It seemed possible to protect people in cities to some degree in fallout shelters,' Stone continued, 'by taking simple measures like ducking under tables or desks if you saw a flash, or ducking behind a tree or into a ditch if you were outside. But it was only when the possibility became dozens of nuclear weapons used against the US that things changed drastically. An all-out nuclear war as then planned by Moscow and Washington involved the exchange of thousands of nuclear weapons. It became pretty clear to most sensible people that civil defence against that kind of an onslaught would do no good. If you're in a city, and you're hit by a nuclear weapon, you're either going to be suffocated or burnt up or killed by the blast. Firestorms use up all the oxygen – you can't breathe. And the fallout itself doesn't go away after two weeks. You can't just magically get up out of your shelter and everything is fine and you go to the store and get some milk and resume your normal life. It just doesn't work that way.'

The anchor turned to Colonel David Blakeny of the Illinois National Guard. He had 10,000 troops under his command and spoke in clipped military sentences. 'As far as nuclear attack goes, any military unit, through their normal training procedures, would have only a limited capability of reacting to that threat,' he said. 'We can provide security, help with evacuation or rebuilding. We maintain a very low level of readiness. But through our day-to-day activities, and training, we could respond to that.'

'Respond, fine, Colonel,' pressed the presenter. 'But how effective would that response be? Have your men been trained for a nuclear attack?'

'Negative. No drills for nuclear war preparedness have been performed by the Guard for years. There are three reasons. We did not want to scare the populace. Acting out a simulated attack would be expensive. And thirdly, during the Cold War, preparation of a nuclear strike was considered a hostile act by the enemy.'

The anchor interrupted: 'You're telling me America is totally, I mean totally unprepared for this. Edward Stone, is this right?'

'We would respond in the same way as we do to any disaster. In the 1950s and 1960s the arms race ran out of control. We tried to stabilize it with the SALT 1 and ABM treaties in the seventies. The idea was to accept the concept of nuclear parity. Instead of one side always trying to get ahead of the other we would accept a situation, and they would accept a situation, where both sides had roughly equal forces. Each side could effectively destroy the other side, even if the other side struck first. In order to make Mutually Assured Destruction, or MAD, work, you had to make sure that neither side could protect its people or its forces. So from that perspective truly aggressive civil defence programmes would be seen as provocative. If the other side really began digging big, deep shelters and really equipping them, and acting like they were seriously beginning to protect their people, that would be seen as a provocation. It would be taken as evidence that they were planning something.'

The programme shifted to a live insert showing a street lined with palm trees in the Californian capital, Sacramento. Delia Murphy from the Department of Emergency Operations was waiting to go on air. The anchor explained how her department had responded to earthquakes, mud slides, floods, waste spills, race riots, and other disasters in recent years, but not nuclear attack.

'Until today, this hadn't weighed heavily on our minds,' said Murphy. 'We did have air-raid shelters in the fifties and sixties, but they've been abandoned. None of the county shelters have been stocked. If we are hit by a nuclear missile, a lot of people will die from the first hit. There's no preparation for that kind of situation. Through the sixties the shelters were stocked with crackers, candies, and sanitation kits. But in 1984 we sold all that stuff off to the Third World countries. The last time people got worried was during the Gulf War in 1991. They would ask where the nearest shelter was. I had to joke with them. I recommended that they go to a McDonald's, because they store food in the basement.'

'What are the signs of panic where you are, Delia?' asked the anchor.

'There's been some looting. But pretty much, I think people are staying calm, listening to announcements, and looking after their families.'

'We have a response now from the Federal Emergency Management Agency, FEMA,' said the anchor. 'They are very busy today preparing for something which we all hope will never happen. They are just confirming what we've all discovered in the past few minutes. Their federal initiatives and training programmes to assist American people during a nuclear holocaust were cut because of lack of funding. No one thought it would happen. Edward Stone, let me turn to you. I have a declassified intelligence document issued by Richard N. Cooper, Chairman of the National Intelligence Council. He says, and I quote: "China plans to update its ICBM force with new missiles and, unlike the Russians, to increase the number of missiles deployed. A possible future improvement is to include a mobile ICBM" – and he says: "Many of China's long-range systems are probably aimed at the United States."

'Edward Stone, if we knew this was happening why didn't we do something about it?'

'Clearly we misjudged China's intentions and resolve. Until two days ago, I didn't know anybody outside of the wacko hard right who really believed that the Chinese would launch a missile attack against CONUS.'

'Excuse me, CONUS?'

'Continental United States. Sure we know China has the capability of hitting one or two west coast cities. They couldn't hit Chicago or Washington. But they could do some real damage in California. That makes us conscious about the Chinese. We would never go to war with them. What President wants to lose San Francisco or Los Angeles? So that makes us a little cautious. That's the way deterrence works. Our policy toward China seems to be pretty fragmented. But it is some sort of constructive engagement. China has a very small nuclear arsenal, of 400 to 500 missiles. Meantime, the US has more than 20,000 such weapons. But if you're asking me to point out the flaws in our intelligence policy, I would have to say that we concentrated too much on the rogue states, Iran, Iraq,

Libya, Korea, and always hoped that China would remain at least militarily neutral. Not so.'

'I would just like to add,' said Colonel Blakeny, 'there would be millions injured in a nuclear attack. They won't be able to receive proper medical treatment immediately. There are only a few hundred intensive care hospital beds in the entire country, not enough to handle the horrendous influx of burn and radiation victims after a nuclear blast. I tell you now, if the leaders of China and America are unable to unwind this confrontation, there is nothing the National Guard of Illinois can do. We are heading towards a situation where the survivors would envy the dead.'

Wall Street, New York

Like the City of London a few hours before, Wall Street was pervaded by an eerie emptiness. Few employees had bothered to turn up for work. New York's subway system had ground to a halt, as had the train service from Grand Central Station that connected Manhattan to the dormitory suburbs in New Jersey and Connecticut. Those traders who had managed to get to work found financial markets in paralysis. Earlier the Bank of England, in conjunction with the main London based commercial banks, had announced a cessation of currency trading in the City. Special arrangements would be made, the Bank said, for the settlement of transactions due for Thursday and Friday. Without explanation it added that it was 'hopeful' that the crisis gripping the world would be resolved to such an extent that normal operations could resume the following Monday. Nothing like this had ever confronted the world's monetary authorities. The modern currency market had no way of preparing, or coping, for it. Since the 1980s a group of US, Japanese, and European banks had dominated currency market trading and had developed systems to enable them to trade around the clock. An electronic record of all the trades executed – known as the 'book' – was passed from Tokyo to London and from London to New York and from New York back again to Tokyo, where the whole process started again. No one had ever expected the clock to stop. So when the handful of dealers who managed to get to work in London arrived at their offices they found they were holding a book of deals which they could not trade with any confidence. Soon afterwards the Bank of England had issued a statement.

> Due to the unprecedented events in East Asia, the Bank, in consultation with the major banks, bullion dealers, and discount houses, announces that until further notice all screen-based currency market dealing in the London market will be suspended. The Bank will offer assistance to any London bank which is placed in difficulty by this decision. The Bank is hopeful that the current crisis will be resolved in the next day or so and is cooperating with monetary authorities elsewhere to stabilize financial markets.

The Federal Reserve Bank of New York – the arm of America's federal central bank which conducted market operations – issued a similar statement at the opening of trading in New York. Although there was little legal underpinning for the Bank's statement, there was none for the New York Fed. But that was as maybe. As with London, the Fed could not stop two parties agreeing a price between themselves, if they wanted to take that risk. But as there was no professional market to speak of – the 'book' had stopped in London – the Fed's calling a halt to trading was merely academic.

Zhongnanhai, Beijing

Jamie Song's Mercedes turned off Fuyou Street into the east gate of Zhongnanhai. Either side of the double gates was a PLA soldier and as Song's car slowed down they drew to attention. The road beyond the gate narrowed appreciably and the Mercedes proceeded at a snail's crawl. Low-rise concrete-block buildings jostled with formal highly decorated pavilions where the leadership gathered for important meetings. And it was at the steps to such a pavilion, built at the turn of the nineteenth century, that his driver deposited him. He got out. The air was cold and dry. The moon was trying to break through clouds that had lent a grim, grey aspect to the whole day. He got out and stretched his legs. Beyond the pavilion was a clump of trees and beyond them the Zhong Hai Lake. The entrance to the pavilion, at the side, was unprepossessing, just a sliding glass door in a wooden frame. The space immediately beyond it was equally unimpressive. More wood and glass, but the glass covered this time with an olive-green curtain. Song was led past this and into the room proper. A set of sixteen or so armchairs had been arranged in a U around a large conference table.

President Wang and the senior PLA and intelligence staff were waiting for him. The Foreign Minister took his seat at the end of the table, facing the President, who was flanked by the commanders of the navy and air force. Wang Feng opened the meeting by quoting from China's long-standing nuclear policy: 'Our aim since 1964 has been to have a limited but strategic nuclear arsenal as a shield to keep the more aggressive superpowers from attempting global hegemony. Today, our policy is being put to the test. Unfortunately, the United States has chosen to show that it can defeat us in a conventional naval battle. If we do not resort to our nuclear strength, we will lose our territories in the South China Sea. I am sure all the comrades here agree that that is an unacceptable prospect.' Wang paused and then asked for a military assessment.

The senior PLA General said that China had more than 500 nuclear warheads. About 120 missiles were ground based. Some were hidden in caves and could be transported to launch sites under the cover of darkness. There were 120 aircraft, capable of delivering another 250 warheads, but these would only be effective against Vietnam and Taiwan. They might reach Japan without being shot down. The main Chinese strength was its submarines. There were now two submarines within nuclear striking distance of the American mainland, with no signs yet that they had been detected. The new version of the *Kilo* class diesel-electric attack submarine was now off the coast of California. Before the 1996 Taiwan incident she was due only to be commissioned in 2001, but the timetable had been revised and the Russian Rubin Design Bureau had agreed to help. The submarine was carrying Russian-made sea-launched cruise missiles with 200 kiloton nuclear warheads, which could travel almost 3,000 kilometres into America. The cities at its furthest range were Minneapolis, Kansas City, Little Rock, and Houston. Those due for targeting were Denver, Salt Lake City, and Phoenix.

President Wang asked why military installations were not to be hit. The General replied that due to the limited number of nuclear warheads it would be far more effective to destroy population centres and instil panic throughout America. 'The American military machine cannot be defeated, but the nation can be defeated by its own people. Already they are frightened and have begun looting.'

'Then why not Los Angeles or San Francisco? They are more symbolic cities,' continued Wang.

'We want to retain the sympathy of the large Chinese populations there and of the other Asian immigrants. They are a significant economic force of investment into our country and they may become a powerful political force in America itself.'

Wang nodded. The General continued: 'But also 3,000 kilometres off the coast in the eastern Pacific is our updated version of the *Xia* strategic missile submarine. The *Xia* we sacrificed carried the JL1 ICBM with a range of only 2,700 kilometres. The new version is armed with the JL2, which can travel 8,000 kilometres. It means, comrade, that the destruction of Washington is in our reach. The Americans have no idea the submarine is so close. She left the North Sea Fleet headquarters at Qingdao some weeks ago, sailing in the wake of a freighter, which made her almost impossible to detect.'

'Are we going to declare the submarines?' asked Jamie Song.

'The Americans describe us as a deterred state,' said Wang. 'They believe that by threatening us with nuclear attack we will surrender. We have been set apart from Iran, Iraq, and Libya, which they regard as uncontrollable and undeterred. If we can convince President Bradlay that China, too, will not be cowed and that unlike in the nineteenth and twentieth centuries we will risk our own destruction to protect our sovereignty, then we will win the war. So by declaring one submarine we can avoid the mutual destruction of two great countries. And we will keep one secret to ensure that if the Americans are stubborn China will not be the only victim. I am quite prepared to destroy a city, although I can't see how it benefits either side. That, Comrade Song, will be your message to Mr Overhalt.'

Crescent City, California

Local time: 0600 Thursday 22 February 2001
GMT: 1400 Thursday 22 February 2001

The wireless transmission mast of the Chinese *Kilo* class submarine was spotted by the captain of an American fishing trawler 25 kilometres off the coast of Crescent City, California. The two vessels nearly collided as the submarine came to periscope depth to receive a radio message. The skipper alerted the Coastguard, which sent a boat from Crescent City and a helicopter from Humboldt Bay, 125 kilometres away. Before it reached the area, the *Kilo* had gone deep and sonar operators monitoring microphones anchored to the sea bottom along the coastline had failed to pick up her acoustic signature. The *Los Angeles* class attack submarines USS *Asheville* and USS *Jefferson City* were diverted from their northern coastal patrols to find the vessel. But it seemed the Chinese vessel was quieter than the background noises of the ocean herself. The American commanders increased their own exposure to enemy attack by using active sonar transmissions which might reveal an echo of the *Kilo*'s position. They found nothing. Helicopters dropped patterns of sonobuoys. Surveillance ships deployed towed arrays and a long string of hydrophones in the hope of finding the Chinese submarine.

This was the unseen enemy, moving through the darkness of the sea. In modern warfare there is nothing so deadly. As far back as the eighties, the Pentagon was faced with the harsh evidence that America's high-technology national defence system could be defeated by a single submarine. During American–Japanese war manoeuvres in the Pacific seven submarines tracked down three aircraft carriers. With anti-submarine warfare surveillance constantly operational, and cruisers, destroyers, and frigates hunting for the submarines, two of the carriers and eight other warships were sunk at the cost of four enemy submarines. The debate on how to proceed with naval defence was never settled. Futuristic schemes were put forward on how to tackle the threat of quieter and quieter submarines. Questions were asked as to whether so much emphasis should be put on carrier groups, the centrepiece of American defence, when they had proved to be so vulnerable. There was disagreement over funding priority, particularly for the Star Wars space defence system, which few scientists believed would ever work. Efforts were made to move submarine detection away from its reliance on acoustics. Special radar was tested on satellites to recognize anomalies on the sea's surface and compare them, like a signature, to computer-generated images. Submarines would create tiny variations in height and roughness of surface waves. The surrounding sea water would change temperature. Marine organisms would be disturbed. The vessel would leave behind tiny particles. All this would show up on satellite pictures to reveal the wake, which was far longer but far more difficult to see than the wake of a surface ship.

There had been a fierce argument within the Chinese navy over whether to send a diesel or nuclear-powered submarine. The argument was won by those who favoured the low-technology *Romeo* and *Ming* tactics in the South China Sea battle. They believed the American navy, with its emphasis on NATO defence, was not trained to handle the sort of threat presented by the *Kilo*.

CNN Studios, Atlanta

From all over America reports were coming in of looting, murders, fires, and mob violence. Correspondents in Los Angeles, New Orleans, Washington, New York, Chicago, Dallas, and the farmlands of Middle America told similar dark and bloody stories of a people in a selfish panic to survive. Thousands of properties were broken in to. In the early stages the police blamed gang warfare, but it soon emerged that respectable middle-class families were also loading up their cars with stolen food. They armed themselves and killed to get their supplies. By midmorning supermarket chains were closing down. The staff and their families were allowed to stay inside until the crisis was over. In Memphis, looters backed a pick-up truck into a restaurant. When the forty-two-year-old proprietor tried to stop them, his chest was blown away with both barrels of a shotgun. In Albuquerque, hundreds of people besieged a supermarket just before the steel rollers were pulled down for it to close. Two cars smashed into the front glass to wedge the rollers up. The crowd poured into the store, taking all the fresh and canned food and jamming it into sacks, boxes, trolleys, and anything they could find. The staff locked themselves into the store room. As the looting spread, more vicious methods were adopted; arson, petrol bombs, even grenades and flame-throwers. In New Orleans, fifteen people died when they were trapped in a basement bar and petrol bombs were thrown down the stairs. In Los Angeles, parts of the city were taken over by organized looting teams which engaged the police in firefights. An armed motorcycle gang devastated Rodeo Drive in Beverly Hills before moving into the wealthy suburban areas where the National Guard set up a cordon of water cannon, backed up by armoured cars and military helicopters. In most American cities conditions deteriorated. The air was filled with wailing sirens of ambulances and fire engines and gunfire. Some of the worst-hit areas were the China-towns, which were attacked by mobs simply trying to vent their anger. The police and National Guard, already over-stretched, and with their own families threatened in the war, saw no reason to protect these ethnic communities. In Chicago, the husband and wife owners of the East Lake Restaurant hung a sign on the door in English saying: 'Please come in and help yourself.' They left through the back door with a suitcase just as their grandparents had done in Shanghai fifty years before. Most of the Chinese in Chicago and many other cities chose not to protect their properties, or to argue their innocence. They had learned about racism in America. They also knew how determined Chinese rulers were from time to time to destroy their country. With remarkable patience, thousands abandoned their life's work that day. Most ended up in queues outside European and Latin American consulates claiming to be refugees from political repression. In San Francisco seven were killed in a drive-by shooting while queuing up at the Brazilian Consulate.

Within a seven-block radius of the East Lake in Chicago were at least twenty other Asian restaurants and stores. Graffiti was sprayed on buildings all around them with the insignia of black street gangs which held territory just a few blocks south. The Vietnamese and Korean communities were less restrained than the Chinese. As the gangs moved in, they defended themselves with a ferocity which reminded Americans why they had failed to beat these nationals in two separate wars. The Asians lured the badly commanded black youths into ambushes. They engaged them in hand-to-hand fighting, killing with lethal kicks and chops. After a bloody firefight in which the bodies of gang members as young as twelve were left on the streets, the Vietnamese advanced south into the territory of a gang which had attacked their supermarket. They besieged a bar. Under covering fire, the Vietnamese exploded two barrels of fuel outside the windows, threw in hand grenades, shot the survivors as they stumbled out, and then escaped. One television commentator began speculating that tens of thousands of Chinese patriots were rising up on American streets at the command of the Communist Party.

In the countryside, where food was more plentiful, people organized themselves into self-defensive communes. There was a run on gun and ammunition shops. Farms were turned into self-sufficient stockades. As one sheriff in Wyoming said: 'No one seems to be breaking the law much. But there's a lot more guns around than there were twelve hours ago.' Car dealers also reported the buying up of four-wheel-drive vehicles, trucks, and station wagons. 'Some people are coming in with their money in sacks and buckets, taking a car, and driving off with it,' said a dealer in Kansas City. 'They don't take no papers and don't wait for me to count it. They're paying all right. Sometimes too much. Nuclear war sure is good for business as long as it never happens.'

State governors and finally the President went on network television to appeal for calm, but their appearances only seemed to increase the panic.

China World Hotel, Beijing

The driver of the Lincoln Continental navigated through the back streets of the diplomatic district to get to the China World Hotel, where the Embassy had booked a suite on the Horizon Floor. Half-burnt effigies lay in the roads. The military newspaper *Liberation Army Daily*, which many of the students had been carrying, blew around in the streets. Posters had been pasted up on embassy walls proclaiming the glory of President Wang. They only saw three cars on the short journey; taxis with foreign fares. The bicycle lanes were empty. These roads had been commandeered by the Party. They were off limits to the Chinese people. No one would dare venture in. A quiet hung over this part of Beijing, a sanitized section of China where the battle against Imperialism had been played out for a few hours and then just as quickly abandoned. Soon the car was in the China World Trade Complex, lit up and busy. The doorman, rugged up in a red coat, showed Overhalt in.

Music from a chamber orchestra on his right wafted across the lobby. He heard the beat of a Filipino rock and roll band from a darkened bar on his left. The staff kept an elevator waiting for him. The carpet inside said: 'Have a nice Thursday.' On the twenty-first floor Jamie Song's guards met him and took him straight to the suite at the end of the corridor. The Foreign Minister was already there and had mixed himself a vodka and tonic from the mini-bar.

'Reece, how good to see you,' he said in English.

'You too, Jamie,' replied Overhalt. Song told his aides to leave the room, but Overhalt spoke knowing that every word was being taped, translated at the Ministry of State Security technical surveillance post just behind the hotel, and fed straight to the Central Committee in Zhongnanhai. Overhalt believed all this would be an advantage. 'After you called me on Wednesday,' he continued, 'I spoke to the President. It was on his urging that I am here tonight. Your demonstrators, I fear, may have cost us time and raised the risk of a nuclear exchange.'

The Foreign Minister looked directly at Overhalt with a passive expression. 'There is nothing the Party can do against the people who wish to express spontaneous anti-imperialistic feelings.'

Overhalt ignored the remark and swiftly brought the conversation round to Dragonstrike. 'Anyway I am here now. This crisis, a crisis of your making, has got out of hand. So I will be quick and blunt. I told you earlier today we had missiles with firing solutions ready to go. I am now authorized by the President to tell you this: if China fires a missile we will launch a retaliatory strike. There are no ifs, no buts. We don't just mean Beijing. We mean Dalian, Qingdao, Shanghai, Wuhan, Chengdu. Your cities will become radioactive rubble. Your infrastructure will be broken concrete and twisted metal. Your country will no longer work.'

Jamie Song interrupted: 'Reece, hold back, hold back. Who's talking nuclear war?'

Overhalt was not sure whether his friend was genuinely unaware of how much the PLA had increased the stakes of the war. 'You have primed your land-based ICBMs for launch. You have abandoned your no-first-strike policy. Yet your naval forces are being slaughtered. If we wish we will destroy what's left of your air force. If that happens the PLA will be publicly humiliated. The Party will crumble.

Your dream of the economic superpower within the authoritarian state will never happen. Is that what you want, Jamie? For China to lose, like the Soviet Union? Is that your aim?'

'China will never again be humiliated into slavery,' said Song after a pause. 'We are a very old civilization. You may bomb our whole country, but we will recover, even if it takes a thousand years. Yet if we turn just one suburb of one city into what you call radioactive rubble, what will happen to America?'

'We can handle it.'

'Can you? Look at the television. Look how America panics as soon as its own country is threatened like ours has been so many times.'

Overhalt didn't answer.

'Why don't you compare us to an African-American gang in Los Angeles?' said Song. 'They're tearing around in their trucks shooting everything and getting shot back. Kids aged eleven, twelve, thirteen are being torn apart by automatic weapons. But they're still doing it. They expect to die. It's part of the gang life. If American citizens go out and destroy themselves, why is it so impossible for you to comprehend that China won't?'

'This whole conversation is putting a bitter taste in my mouth, Jamie,' said Overhalt. 'We've put a lot of time, money, and loyalty into your country, believing that you really did want to modernize and reform. But I'll tell you this, and make no mistake, America and Boeing would survive. India is already giving you guys a run for your money; Latin America is growing rapidly. Russia and Eastern Europe are queuing up for our technology and building skills. The days are gone when developing countries cry victim and get away with it. There are big markets out there that are much easier to get into than here. There are democratic leaders who have real plans to let their countries develop. China isn't special any more, and if you don't have us you won't have the European Union either. If Boeing goes, Airbus goes. You throw out Ford and Chrysler, Citroën and Mercedes pack their bags as well. You ban AT&T and Motorola, you won't get Nokia and Siemens. We'll all cut our losses and go. The people you are threatening with nuclear attack are the best builders of infrastructure in the world.'

At this stage, Jamie Song stood up and walked to the window. 'I've been authorized to tell you that our *Xia* nuclear missile submarine is in the Pacific with the new JL2 intercontinental ballistic missile. From where it is now, it can hit Washington.'

'We sank it,' snapped Overhalt.

'You sank the older *Xia* carrying the JL1. The commander of the *Xia* 407 is awaiting orders to launch. I have to return to Zhongnanhai and report our meeting. Why don't you talk to President Bradlay on the secure line from the Embassy, and we can meet back here in say two hours? You can tell Bradlay we won't launch until after our next meeting. You have my word on that.'

The two men travelled down together in the lift. It was approaching midnight. As they stood on the hotel forecourt the activity of night-time Beijing glittered in front of them as if nothing was untoward at all. Limousines drew up. They heard the horns of traffic along the Avenue of Eternal Peace. The smoke from fires warming the homeless under the flyovers was lit up by the street lights. Overhalt realized with irony that the band was singing a very bad version of 'Rocket Man', by Elton John. 'See, Reece,' said Jamie Song. 'While America burns, China is tranquil. We are in control of our people and our culture. Why don't you ask Bradlay whether he is in control of the American dream?'

The White House, Washington, DC

Local time: 1200 Thursday 22 February 2001
GMT: 1700 Thursday 22 February 2001

After speaking directly to Reece Overhalt from the
Embassy, President Bradlay ordered a unilateral ceasefire
among Allied forces in the South China Sea. All aircraft
except surveillance aircraft were to be grounded. There
would be no firing of weapons unless fired upon. National
Security Adviser Martin Weinstein said that the Chinese
might well be bluffing, but it was a risk America could not
afford to take: 'Gentlemen, we must assume we are two
hours away from a nuclear strike,' he said.

For some minutes there was confusion over the number
of Chinese submarines deployed in the Pacific. Military
intelligence had a near certain identification of a *Kilo* class
attack submarine off the Californian coast near Crescent
City. Its present position was unknown, although there was
a good chance that either the USS *Asheville* or the USS
Jefferson City would be tracking it within the next few
hours. At the time it was sighted, Jamie Song was with
Reece Overhalt in the China World Hotel. It was probable
that Song was unaware of its detection. He had declared a
totally different type of submarine, the strategic missile *Xia*
class, as still being several thousand kilometres out in the
Pacific.

'Let us get all this absolutely clear,' said the President.
'We are threatened by two submarines. The Chinese have
declared one. We know about the other. Right now, either
of them could launch an attack on the American people.
Are there any more submarines?'

'We don't think so, sir. But we don't know.'

'They could take out an American city and there's not a damn thing we can do about it.'

'We could pick a missile up on launch, but that would be only minutes before it hit the target,' said Arnold Kuhnert. 'The chances of us stopping it are not good.'

'And to stop it happening we have to surrender our right to the South China Sea.'

'That's about it, sir.'

'Or we could wipe out China, and lose Washington and a few other cities. How many dead – one or two million, maybe? The question in front of us, gentlemen, is whether it is worth sacrificing those lives in order to retain our leadership in global affairs.'

Beijing University

Throughout the previous evening events were being chronicled by students linked into the Internet. While the official state-run media continued to lambast American and Japanese aggression, there was no mention of the imminent nuclear threat. Since the beginning of Dragonstrike students had been holding informal salons to discuss the implications. The highly secret group of twelve young men and women of the New Communist Movement were now deciding at what stage the crisis should be exploited to force a change of government. A short-wave radio, tuned to the BBC World Service, was perched on a window sill with an aerial hanging outside because of the bad reception. The leader of the group, a twenty-one-year-old economics student, believed the movement had two duties. Reeling off a list of names including Mao Zedong, Mahatma Gandhi, and Nelson Mandela, he argued that to win victory for China they must be prepared to sacrifice their freedom and possibly their lives. But in reality the time was not right for demonstration. With the United States about to launch a nuclear attack it was the duty of the New Communists to give warnings to people to protect themselves. Over the past hours messages had gone out over the Internet to the movement's cells in Shanghai, Guangzhou, Hong Kong, Taipei, Lanzhou, and other major cities. Secret radio stations in Hong Kong and Taiwan were ready to begin broadcasts. There was another in Lhasa and the cell in Shanghai said it too was setting up transmission equipment. Every cell had made posters advising nuclear survivors what action to take.

The students had downloaded whole nuclear Web pages from the Internet and photocopied them. The leader of the Beijing cell said that in half an hour New Communists all over China would begin their announcements. Cars were waiting outside the university campus and the posters would be distributed around tenement blocks. After that, people would be warned through loud hailers. The leader made it clear that this was not a political action of any sort. The purpose was to save lives. Therefore, no posters would be put up in and around Tiananmen Square and other sensitive areas, nor would there be any announcements there.

As the meeting broke up, the Public Security Bureau moved into their dormitory, arrested the students, and confiscated the radio and computer equipment. The leader wriggled free and ran down the corridor attempting to escape. He was shot dead, in the back. PSB officials closed in on three cars parked on opposite sides of the streets 300 metres away from the university main gate. Two drivers were picked up. The third drove off at speed, but was met at the first junction by a hail of automatic weapons fire. The Volkswagen Santana turned over and smashed into a lamp-post. The driver died. The few witnesses who saw the killing were taken into custody. It became clear that China's massive security apparatus had been monitoring the activities of the New Communists for months and as the students were about to show their hand, they chose now to close in. At least eighteen others were shot dead, one in Xiamen, two in Wuhan, three in Lanzhou, one in Guangdong, three in Chengdu, five in Lhasa, and three in Shanghai, where police opened fire as soon as they burst into the room where radio transmissions were being made. The machine-gun fire was heard by the few listeners before the signal ended. The New Communist radio station in Hong Kong was on the air for twelve minutes before police found it. Signals from Taipei were jammed.

California Coast, Pacific Ocean

Local time: 0930 Thursday 22 February 2001
GMT: 1730 Thursday 22 February 2001

The commander of the attack submarine USS *Asheville* reported that he had a near certain acoustic identification of the Chinese *Kilo* class 10 kilometres south of where it was first sighted. His orders were to keep with the vessel, but not to destroy it yet because there was a temporary ceasefire. Trailing a VLF wire, he placed his submarine behind the Chinese and waited. The sea microphones were now picking up the same signature. An AWACS surveillance aircraft was dedicated to tracking it. Satellite photographs came back of the trail it was leaving. The commander of the USS *Asheville* waited. His sonar operators, picking up the mechanical sounds emitted by the Chinese submarine, reported that the launch procedures for the cruise missiles on board had not yet begun. They had not yet detected the torpedo tube doors being opened in preparation for firing.

Briefing

How America planned to survive a nuclear strike

While efforts to shield the civilian population had ended decades before, plans to rescue the nation's leaders, its heirlooms, and national documents remained in place, and key government personnel, together with the President and Congress, had nuclear shelters to go to. *Time* magazine, in a special four-sheet edition, claimed that the government was resurrecting a plan first drawn up in the 1950s to take the President out of danger of a nuclear blast. In Outpost Mission, as it was called, a helicopter was on standby. The pilots carried dark visors to shield their eyes from the atomic flash and wore 9 kilograms of protective clothing to block out radiation. It was supplied with decontamination kits and radiation suits for the President and the First Family, and even carried equipment to dig White House staff out of the rubble, if the bomb hit first. It would fly to the heavily reinforced communications ship the USS *Northampton*, off the Atlantic Coast, or to one of several hollowed-out mountain sites, although *Time*, which had written extensively about nuclear protection in the 1990s, speculated that the only facility still operational was Mount Weather, a bunker 80 kilometres from the capital.

Time was accurate. The underground shelter hewn out of Mount Weather was a forty-three-year-old complex. Officially it had never existed and was referred to only as the Special Facility, operated by the Federal Emergency Management Agency. The complex was tucked into a heavily wooded mountain ridge, and surrounded by a 3 metre high chain-link fence with six strands of barbed wire on top. Inside there were manicured lawns and buildings with antennas and microwave relay systems. The hard rock face was reinforced with 2.5 to 3 metre iron bolts. Underneath there was a giant disaster co-ordination complex, covering 18,500 square metres, with a blastproof steel door at the tunnel entrance. Offices were reinforced with steel and concrete. Drinking water was kept in an underground pond. There was a massive computer network and a television and radio studio from which to address the nation, together with a hospital, a cafeteria supplied with enough food for several weeks, a power plant, and dormitories. The most senior administration officials carried special cards, ranking them in order of importance for evacuation. They included Cabinet Secretaries and the heads or seconds-in-command of government departments and agencies. Private quarters were set aside for the President, Cabinet Secretaries, and Supreme Court Justices. Officials would be checked for radiation and those exposed would be decontaminated with showers and medicated soap. Their clothes would be burnt. They would be issued with military overalls. Electric golf carts would ferry the injured to hospital.

At the same time, Congress could seek refuge at the West Virginian resort of Greenbriar in White Sulphur Springs. The bunker was codenamed Project Greek Island, built under the hotel complex and equipped like Mount Weather, but with less luxury, to enable Congress to function for sixty days after a nuclear attack. The aim was to ensure that democracy did not collapse and give way to a military dictatorship. There were 1,000 bunk beds in eighteen dormitories, with communal toilets and all the character of a penal institution.

'What they envisioned during the Cold War, and are probably envisioning today,' wrote *Time*, 'is an America darkened not only by nuclear war but also by the imposition of martial law, food rationing, censorship, and the suspension of many civil liberties. It would be the end of society as we know it.'

While the government continued its no comment policy, previous plans on how American would salvage its heritage from nuclear holocaust were discussed. The original documents of the Declaration of Independence, the Constitution, and the Bill of Rights were to be flown from the National Archives, seven blocks from the White House, to Mount Weather. If there was time other documents such as a Gutenberg Bible, the Gettysburg Address, and the papers of James Madison, Thomas Jefferson, and George Mason would be taken there by truck. The National Gallery chose the works to save not by painting but by the size of the canvas. They included Leonardo da Vinci's *Ginevra de' Benci*, Raphael's *Alba Madonna*, and Rogier van der Weyden's *St George and the Dragon*, which was just the size of a post card. They were packed in lightweight metal containers where the humidity in the air was stabilized by bags of chemicals.

The Federal Reserve Board would make its own arrangements. It maintained a 13,000 square metre bunker with enough cash inside to bankroll a nuclear-blasted America. Wads of bills were stacked in polythene packets against a wall on wooden pallets which would be moved out by a fork-lift truck. Standard Oil's senior management was withdrawing to an emergency operating centre 100 metres underground, near Hudson, New York. Their job was to ensure a continuation of energy supplies. The Department of Agriculture had published a food-rationing programme, allowing survivors between 2,000 and 2,500 calories a day, including seven pints of milk and six eggs a week.

Government officials spoke the single code word FLASH to notify others that the operation had begun.

Washington, DC

National Guard units had been called out in all American cities. The President had declared a national emergency. Some of the worst rioting was now breaking out in Washington itself as rumours spread after the television networks began to speculate whether the President, his Cabinet, and senior officials would be airlifted to the Mount Weather bunker. 'We never discuss security arrangements for the President,' said a White House spokesman. The Marine Corps threw up a cordon around Capitol Hill and the White House. Like the enemy in Zhongnanhai, American leaders were travelling back and forth through a warren of underground tunnels and railways, too afraid to show their faces to their constituents. Members of Congress were reportedly preparing to go to the Greenbriar shelter, 400 kilometres away, built under a luxury hotel complex. 'We can neither confirm nor deny whether this facility is still in use,' said a spokesman. One Marine was shot dead in the neck by a sniper in the crowd. A rocket-propelled grenade was fired over the head of the Marines into a window of a Congress building. Helicopters dispersed the crowd with tear gas. Troops moved in with water cannon and rubber bullets.

The spectre of a nuclear holocaust could not be kept from the public, fear of an imminent nuclear strike had swept through the United States, and ignorance about what to do was shared between officials and members of the public. All had families to protect, children to be accounted for, supplies to be bought. The National Guard, army, and

Marines had taken over most city centres. Looting gangs controlled many other parts. Many people saw the country-side as a safer place to be and headed out in their cars: the roads became clogged and fights broke out. The public transport systems halted. Airlines abandoned their sched-ules and flew their aircraft south to Latin America or north to Canada. Newspapers put out extra editions with instruc-tions on how to handle a nuclear holocaust. Television news stations, which were now devoting all their program-ming to the Dragonstrike crisis, speculated on the Chinese nuclear threat while their commercial breaks concentrated on packed foods and survival kits. A *New York Times* opinion poll found that 64 per cent of Americans believed the government did have defences against missile strikes. The *Washington Post* estimated that two million Americans could die and two hundred thousand could be injured from just two Chinese missiles. It drew comparisons with data compiled during the Soviet threat, when twenty million people would have been killed and five million injured. Each 550 kiloton bomb would destroy all people and buildings within a 5.6 kilometre radius. Fires would damage areas almost twice that size, where about half the population would be killed and half would be injured.

The CNN Beijing bureau, quoting Foreign Ministry sources, was the first to report that a Chinese *Xia* class submarine had been declared in the Pacific. The announce-ment interrupted a discussion about Mount Weather to point out that the helicopter flight time from Washington to the shelter was about twenty minutes. The submarine's missiles could strike ten to fifteen minutes after launch.

A retired helicopter pilot, once assigned to rescuing the First Family, was interviewed on *ABC News*. 'Through the years, we always reacted like we could handle an all-out nuclear attack. I don't think people – even our top people in government – have any idea of what a multimegaton nuclear weapon attack on the US would do. We'd be back in the Stone Age. It's unthinkable.'

In the White House, President Bradlay told his inner cabinet: 'The American people are scared. They may become hysterical. After an attack we are going to have to be prepared to operate with people who are uncontrollably mad and frightened.'

There was a silence and the remarks of a relief worker being interviewed on television dominated the meeting for a moment. 'It is sham for me to tell people I can help them. We've gone beyond that. I cannot give people confidence that there is a system in place that will work, when in my heart of hearts, in the dark of night, I doubt it will work.'

Those remarks were followed by those of a former director of the Mount Weather complex: 'I would be breaking the law if I told you whether that facility is ready to receive President Bradlay and his administration. I will say only that our policy after the collapse of the Soviet Union was we shouldn't shut the damn doors yet. Remember what Plato said: "Only the dead have seen the end of war."'

China World Hotel, Beijing

'**President Bradlay has** asked whether China can meet the international conditions laid down to end the conflict,' began Reece Overhalt as the two men settled back into the suite at the China World Hotel. 'He also wants you to note the unilateral ceasefire in the South China Sea by Allied forces while we try to get this mess untangled. At the same time, British and American Trident submarines are ready to launch at any time. We have B2 stealth bombers in Okinawa and on Guam and the Peacekeeper and Minuteman missile silos have been prepared. The twin keys have been taken out of their boxes. Each officer at each launch station is on readiness to use them once the President makes his command.'

Jamie Song took a sheet of paper from his briefcase and laid it on the coffee table. He said, reading from it: 'President Wang will stand down our nuclear weapons on guarantees that the United States will withdraw its military forces from the South China Sea. If you do that, we will guarantee free passage of all non-military shipping, and we will allow limited Japanese naval patrols. After a decent interval of cooling off, American and Allied warships will be allowed in on a case by case basis, if for example you want to visit Hong Kong or Shanghai, or the British want to go to Brunei again. You will recognize there is a legitimate regional dispute over the Spratly and Paracel Islands and leave it up to the region to sort it out.' At this stage, he looked up. 'What we're saying, Reece, is leave Asia to solve Asia's problems. Draw back from where you're not needed any more and don't get involved in another war here which will kill thousands of Americans. Your Ambassador and I will sign a Memorandum of Understanding tonight. It will be followed up by a more detailed document to be negotiated by officials over the next few months. After that there should be an exchange of presidential visits and everything will get back to normal. President Wang also wanted to give his personal guarantee that trade will not be affected. We understand that we need your technology and investment to develop. He hopes that our trade privileges will also continue.'

Reece Overhalt returned to the Embassy to talk to President Bradlay. China gave America three further hours to reach a decision.

The White House, Washington, DC

Local time: 1500 Thursday 22 February 2001
GMT: 2000 Thursday 22 February 2001

A SIGINT report from Hawaii had picked up a frequency hopping encrypted exchange of signals, which analysts said could have been between the Qingdao naval base and the *Xia* submarine. Aircraft had been put up to try and find it. The nearest American submarine was 250 nautical miles away from the very rough position where the submarine could be. The President was told it was still like looking for a needle in a haystack. The British Prime Minister telephoned to offer continuing military support. He offered sympathy for the breakdown of civil society in the United States. Luckily Britain, having experienced the bombing of its cities before, remained more under control. He was also concerned about the closure of newspapers and radio and television stations in Hong Kong. The editor of the *South China Morning Post* had been gaoled. Both the BBC and CNN had been reporting mass arrests of suspected subversives. The Legislative Council had been suspended and the Chief Executive had announced emergency measures. The Japanese Prime Minister called on President Bradlay to pull back from a larger battle which neither America nor China would win. He said that Japan could live with Chinese sovereignty over the South China Sea as long as it remained an international trade route. But this was not an issue over which to launch thermonuclear war. The German Chancellor said he saw no good that could come of it. The French President said he was standing his forces down for the time being: he had no intention of getting into a nuclear exchange with China. Defense Secretary Matt Collins said confirmed reports were coming in of further mass troop movements on the Vietnamese border. The Guangzhou and Kunming military districts were still declared war zones. Satellite pictures showed artillery being moved back from its forward border positions. But there was no certainty that Vietnam was safe from Chinese attack. Some of the most powerful guns were in the Pingxiang area only 150 kilometres from Hanoi. Analysts were still working on photographs indicating imminent launches of the M11 missile, which could hit the outskirts of Hanoi. On Hainan Island there were signs that the M9 was being prepared. With a 600 kilometre range, the missiles could hit Da Nang and Hue. The Indian Prime Minister telephoned to say that he was getting reports of uprisings throughout Tibet. Troops had opened fire in Lhasa, Xigaze, and Gyangze. Hundreds had died. India was setting up refugee camps for Tibetans who tried to escape. Troops were being flown in to reinforce the border. The White House press office urged the President to confirm he would not be leaving the building. Both the National Guard and the Marine Corps anticipated even more dangerous riots if there was an evacuation. Mexican border police opened fire on Americans trying to flee into Tijuana and Nogales south of Tucson. There had also been trouble at other border posts. Canada had simply opened the border and let people drive in, urging them to keep going north to ease congestion.

As Reece Overhalt spoke to the President, the first reports came in of China's invasion of the Taiwanese island of Peikan, just off the coast of Fujian. Twenty minutes later the better defended settlement of Matsu had fallen. Within five minutes of that confirmation, President Bradlay ordered the USS *Asheville* to destroy the *Kilo* class submarine off the Californian coast. Reece Overhalt was still on the secure line. The Defense Secretary, the National Security Adviser, the Chairman of the Joint Chiefs of Staff, and the Secretary of State were included in the conference call. Reece Overhalt explained the Chinese policy of forcing America out of Asian affairs.

'Well, gentlemen, what do you suggest?' said the President.

'Mr President,' said the Defense Secretary, 'why are we even thinking about condemning millions of our country-men to death by nuclear weapons? I think the Chinese have offered us the makings of a deal, and I think we should grab it with both hands. Our decision to escalate to naval conflict was taken not in response to China's seizure of the South China Sea, but to their sinking of the *Peleliu*. The *Peleliu*'s mission was to rescue oil workers being held hostage. I have been told in the last hour that those men have now been freed by Japanese naval forces and are safely on board a Japanese naval vessel. I would like you to join with me in offering our thanks to the Japanese government. Japan, which is our ally, has emerged as a global power, to which we can hand over confidently the mantle of leader-ship in Asia. If the trade routes are guaranteed, what is the point of risking nuclear war? Apart from the loss of life, the global economy could be set back decades. There will be a shift of alliances and power which will take years to settle. America itself will undergo an internal psychological upheaval from which it will not recover in generations. Just listen to the television. As a nation we are still licking our wounds from the defeat in Vietnam nearly thirty years ago. Yet not one shell in that war landed on our soil. How long will it take us to be cured of the trauma of nuclear attack? Even without firing a missile, the Chinese have turned this country into a mayhem of rioting and looting. I urge us to sign the Memorandum of Understanding, get the missiles stood down and Wall Street reopened, and let America return to normal life. Properly presented, this will not look as if we are being forced out of Asia, which we aren't. We will emerge as the saviours of Asia and of Europe.'

A call from the press office interrupted the discussion. The President instructed a statement to be issued saying that he and his advisers would not be evacuating the White House. However, no details were to be given of the nuclear bunker facilities being prepared. On Capitol Hill, members of Congress were only leaving their offices for their homes. Without revealing the security details, several told interviewers that there was no way they would go without taking their families with them. And there was no facility for that. Both the White House and the Congressional Buildings were, in effect, under siege from demonstrators. The security staff had given a warning of the danger of helicopter flight. Agents in the crowd had reported people with firearms, including high-powered automatic weapons which could shoot down aircraft.

The Secretary of State, Larry Gillchrest, took up the argument on the other side. 'I don't think this is a time to take the easy option and cave in to China at the point of a gun,' he said. 'Other non-democratic governments around the world would regard the United States as a paper tiger. If China succeeded in facing us down there would be no democratic government with both the will and ability to police global affairs. A China unchecked will invade Taiwan – it's already begun to. It will seek to control Korea and Indochina. The ethnic Chinese business communities of Asia will support it and undermine our own influence. The end result will be international chaos, Mr President, not only in the balance of power, but also in the economies and in the dozens if not hundreds of smaller wars which will be ignited. Inevitably, they will lead to wider conflict, probably beginning in the Middle East or Europe, into which we will be drawn, as we were drawn in the First and

Second World War, into Korea, Vietnam, the Gulf, and Bosnia. If this discussion is about an option to escape conflict, then, gentlemen, we are living in dreamland. Men will die. Cities will be destroyed. The best option open to us is to retain control of the conflict throughout and emerge as the winners. If we do that, we will probably secure peace and the security of America for generations. If we don't, other men, or perhaps even we will be in this room in five years' time, threatened maybe by a nuclear alliance of China and Iran, or India and Russia, with better missiles and bigger warships which we would have difficulty defeating even in a conventional conflict. Is it that we can't win, Mr President? Or is it that the American soul is too vulnerable for the fight?'

'Marty,' said the President talking directly to his National Security Adviser. 'Do we have any evidence at all that China will settle if we back off and that after a time the policy of constructive engagement will see in a group of more reform-minded leaders with whom we can deal?'

'I believe that is possible. But we don't know how much more turmoil we have to go through to get there. Constructive engagement, a policy of the nineties, led to the situation we are in now. If we strike a deal with them and continue that policy, then it could go either way. China launched Dragonstrike for three reasons. One was to lay claim to the oil and gas reserves of the South China Sea and prevent it from being so reliant on international markets. The second was to consolidate the power of the Communist Party within China. The third was to proceed along what the Chinese see as an inevitable course of history, a return to their role as the greatest and oldest civilization in the world.'

'Do they want to be it, Marty? Or be recognized for it?'

'I think they would be happy with the latter, Mr President. If we want to stop a nuclear conflict today, we back down. If we want to try to mould the future for the next hundred years, we can go either way. If we want to keep China in line for say twenty or thirty years we launch a nuclear strike. My gut feeling, Mr President, is to keep on with the civilizing power of trade and support the younger, more international leaders who will become the leaders of China.'

At this stage another intelligence message came in via both the SIGINT station on Maui and the Ocean Surveillance satellite system. There had been a positive identification of the *Xia* class submarine and she was being tracked by the *Los Angeles* class attack submarine USS *Chicago* on patrol out of San Diego. Sonar operators had detected movements in her launch mechanism, with near certain evidence that preparations were being made for the launch of a ballistic missile. Pentagon analysts had also just discovered a mobile missile in place at a launch site near Harbin in the northeast. A large road vehicle, thought to be carrying a DF-32 missile, had arrived there with signs that it, too, was being prepared for launch. The White House press office called again to urge the President to do something to disperse crowds which were now crammed in around federal buildings throughout the country. It was only a matter of time before the government lost control with devastating loss of life and property.

Within half an hour, all radio and television channels told people to stand by for an announcement from President Bradlay. Helicopters flew over crowds broadcasting the message by loudspeaker: 'Go home. Go home. The President is about to address the nation. Go home and wait for his message.' A few did. But most stayed, although the crowds quietened. In Washington and New York, braving near-freezing temperatures, groups huddled around portable television sets. But they kept their people's cordon around the White House. In California, the crowds spread out. People sat on grass and parkland around the public buildings. In smaller towns, which had seen less upheaval, the authorities rigged up a public address system or erected large screens in the parks. In the Minuteman missile silos the officers were ordered to prepare for an imminent launch. On board the Allied Trident missile submarines the captains and executive officers authenticated their orders and the twin keys which each carried.

EIGHT

The White House, Washington, DC

Bradlay paced the Oval Office. He stopped and turned to
the assembled advisers and told them that he would
announce his decision to the nation during his address,
scheduled for 1730. Overhalt was instructed to tell the
Chinese Foreign Minister to await his statement. He then
thanked his advisers for their support and help during the
crisis. 'The nation is in your debt,' he said. An unusual
calm descended on the office. The President displayed an
otherworldly, almost mystical detachment. It was then that
he made up his mind and asked them to leave so that he
could collect his thoughts. Weinstein was the last, and the
President pulled him to one side and told him that five
minutes before airtime he wanted the latest intelligence on
the Chinese submarines. The technicians arrived to set up
their cameras in the Oval Office.

'My fellow Americans. I wish that I could appear before
you in happier circumstances. But events far from our
borders have conspired otherwise. As all of you know the
Government of China launched an unprovoked attack on
Vietnam last Saturday, at the same time seizing the South
China Sea. This illegal action was followed three days later
with the sinking of the USS *Peleliu*, a United States naval
vessel engaged on a humanitarian mission to save oil
workers manning oil rigs in the South China Sea. Since
then we have come to the brink of nuclear war. Indeed,
over the past days, Chinese submarines have been preparing to attack America. One reached the Californian
coast. I do not wish to sound melodramatic but I am told

these submarines are at a high state of readiness. Should the Chinese President so order, our nation's capital could be reduced to rubble within minutes. I have told President Wang that if he does so order we in retaliation would have no option but to destroy every Chinese city of consequence.

'So what does the moment require of us? I have to tell you, friends, that my advisers are divided.

'Some say we should fight at all costs. To give in now to the Chinese state would be a mistake. It would send a signal to every tinpot dictator that all they have to do is kill some Americans and the United States will fold. This is a powerful argument. It goes to the heart of what sort of world we, and our allies, have been trying to shape since our historic victory over Fascism in 1945 and Communism in 1989. The lessons of those two great wars was that it is the bullies who fold if you have the courage to stand firm. Democracy, freedom, free markets have triumphed. Evil empires have crumbled.

'Yet there is an alternative view. This holds that the conflict in which we became embroiled is only of regional significance. Our interests in China are greater than the concerns of a frightened and paranoid leadership hanging on to power well after its "sell by" date. Our great corporations have put down roots in China and are agents of significant political change. Our regional role is best suited when we adopt the posture of honest broker, rather than global policeman enforcing our will wherever we might find it questioned. As the events of the last few days graphically demonstrate, we have a lot to do.

'But my job is not to arbitrate between two contending schools of thought. It is, with the guidance of God, to govern wisely. That's what you elected me to do last November. That's what I pledged to the nation in my inaugural address last month. Then I warned of the uncertainties facing our nation and of the need for clarity of vision and single-mindedness of purpose. To govern is to choose. The choice I have made is for peace. I am tonight issuing orders for the immediate recall of all US forces west of Japan. We are not, however, walking away from the battlefield. That is not the American way. We have not come to the brink of nuclear war simply to capitulate.

'I have told President Wang that withdrawal of US forces is conditional upon the cessation of all hostilities by China, and by that I mean *all* hostilities. During these past days China has not only launched attacks on Vietnam but has also occupied islands in the Taiwan Straits formerly held by the Taiwanese government. I call upon China to restore those islands to their lawful and legitimate government. And I have also told President Wang to submit China's claim to sovereignty over that area to international arbitration. Provided certain guarantees are made concerning free access of international shipping to the South China Sea I can see little reason for the United States to raise any objections. We are confident that these guarantees will be forthcoming. The Chinese government has agreed to allow Japanese naval vessels to escort merchant shipping.

'If China agrees to our terms, the very real threat of nuclear war will have been averted. For that we should give thanks to God. For this is not a time for false triumphalism. As Nikita Khrushchev observed at the end of an earlier international crisis: they talk about who won and who lost. Human reason won. Mankind won.'

Zhongnanhai, Beijing

Wang Feng called the meeting at short notice. Present were Jamie Song, General Zhao – the wheeler-dealing soldier who commanded the People's Liberation Army's vast financial and industrial assets known simply as Multitechnologies – and Zhang Zhi, Politburo member responsible for security. Wang was agitated. He kept on referring to 'some people' who were questioning the course upon which he had set the country but a week before. He was not a man to show emotion and this uncharacteristic outburst underlined to those present the pressure he was under and the extent to which others in the leadership – the 'some people' he obliquely referred to – were ready to pick up the baton should he drop it. He had finished his telephone conversation with Bradlay only hours before. It was a conversation – mediated by interpreters at either end – that prevented a nuclear exchange and effectively brought Dragonstrike to a conclusion. Yet far from feeling elated, he was moody and dejected.

'So what have we achieved?' he asked rhetorically.

'A financial success beyond our expectations,' General Zhao said. 'We ought to be able to rebuild our navy with the proceeds of oil and currency market trading.'

'Really!' he retorted.

'Yes, Comrade,' General Zhao said. 'May I be permitted to explain?' He met no resistance and proceeded. 'I would ask that what I am about to say does not leave this room. This operation has been known to only three people. Briefly, Multitechnologies exploited its foreknowledge of Dragonstrike to make money for the PLA. We always knew our attack against Vietnam and the sequestration of the South China Sea would come at a price – the loss of important capital assets – and the President thought it prudent to provide for that contingency by some judicious investments. Excluding fees, Multitechnologies has done very well out of oil. Profits taken so far amounted to some $1.6 billion; this has been parked, temporarily, in the US Treasury bond market in short-dated T-bills. The biggest single trade we conducted was on Wednesday in Singapore, for $600 million. It was a special trade booked through the SIMEX exchange: our agent unloaded 30,000 oil futures contracts at $45 a barrel. We sold 80,000 of the original 160,000 IPE April contracts in the London futures market on Tuesday at a profit of more than $600 million, and still hold 50,000. Since the entry price into the market was $25 a barrel these 50,000 contracts mean we have $1 billion of paper profits to cash in. We plan to do so at the earliest opportunity. We also did quite well out of the yen. Deals in London and Tokyo netted $466 million. In short, Multitechnologies has made $2 billion in cash and has another $1 billion of profits still locked up in the London oil futures market. The bottom line, sir, is that Multitechnologies has doubled its money. We could buy a fully fitted-out aircraft carrier for that and still have change for a couple of submarines.'

There was a gasp from Song and Zhang. Wang brightened. Although he had been kept informed throughout the week of Zhao's progress he had no idea he had been so successful. Song, a former businessman, gave Zhao a slight bow in recognition of his skilful trading. Zhang, who was bowled over by what he had heard, soon recovered his composure and indicated that he too had some good news.

'Comrade,' Zhang began, 'we have extinguished the antirevolutionary so-called New Communists. These people have been like thorns in our side. Yet in our coordinated police action we were able to arrest more than 500. We have released some, but they remain under close observation, and 203 were officially charged and they will be given gaol terms ranging from seven to twenty years. Our interrogation so far has led us to estimate that eight of the ringleaders have managed to elude us. We think they have made for the Vietnamese border, but I'm confident they will be apprehended. Think of our victory, Comrade, a dissident group which had taken years to create was crushed in less than an hour. This is an impressive achievement which no one can take away from you.'

'Yes, that is particularly sweet. So what of you, Comrade?' he said, turning to Song.

'I'm afraid I have nothing but good news for you,' he said, chancing an ironic smile in response to the President's improving spirits. 'We have been transformed from a regional power into a global force capable of challenging America. The world has not witnessed such rapid change in power alignments since the Soviet Union collapsed under Gorbachev's reign leaving only the Americans to dominate the world stage. China has arrived. Our preparedness to risk nuclear exchange has bought us a seat at the top table. We have changed the world.

'We have won an important victory in that we have the active acquiescence of most South-East Asian nations to our claim over the South China Sea. The West's agreement will follow after a suitable face-saving interval. The way is open for us to move on Taiwan. Japan is a problem, but not an insurmountable one. After all, like America, Japan has commercial interests to protect in China. We should sleep more soundly, not less so.'

Wang sat back, rolling a pencil between his fingers, nodding as Song talked. Then he said, 'But what about the Vietnamese. How did they do it?' as his fist came crashing down on the table.

Tiananmen Square, Beijing

Local time: 0730 Sunday 4 March 2001
GMT: 2330 Saturday 3 March 2001

In Tiananmen Square, dusted with freshly fallen snow, a
soldier raised the national flag. Soon afterwards children
arrived in bright red uniforms each carrying a flag bearing
a portrait of President Wang. A line of kites flew at each
end of the square with the symbol of the Dragonstrike War
printed onto the cloth. Outside the Museum of History
and Development film of the battles and the destruction
was projected onto a large screen. Soldiers, aircrew, and
sailors who had fought lined up squadron by squadron,
battalion by battalion and ship by ship to file through the
Mausoleum of Mao Zedong and pay their respects to the
founder of modern China. They then took their positions,
beginning at the south end of the Square, filling it up line
by line. The JL2 and DF32 intercontinental ballistic missiles
were driven down the Avenue of Heavenly Peace and drew
to a halt as the procession had done less than a month
earlier, facing the Gate of Heavenly Peace. The whole
Square was filled with a mist of sleet and pollution. It was
impossible to make out figures and buildings from one side
to the other, but the hazy, dim atmosphere made the music
and speeches of the Communist leaders even more distinc-
tive. Cheers erupted from swirls of fog. The nation was
told that lost territory in northern Vietnam would be
recovered by the glorious bravery of troops from the
Kunming and Guangzhou war zones; that men from the
East Sea Fleet, the PLA Air Force, Marines, and troops
from the Nanjing war zone would valiantly drive out the
occupying nationalist forces of Taiwan and reunite it with

the motherland; that the governments of Japan, Britain, France, and America had apologized to President Wang for atrocities carried out during colonial times, when China was a weak and corrupt nation; the sovereign rights over the South Sea by the motherland had been acknowledged by all nations. President Wang Feng was a great and glorious leader for the whole of China.

'Never again will China be disgraced and humiliated by foreign powers,' the *People's Daily* said, in a front-page editorial. 'The motherland is now the strongest nation on Earth.'

The Chinese President appeared above the gate of the Forbidden City. He was flanked by the generals who had directed the Dragonstrike War. General Zhao and Jamie Song were there with other members of the Standing Committee of the Politburo; among the international guests were the President of Iran, the Prime Minister of Russia, and the leaders of the Central Asian Republics of Tajikistan, Kyrgyzstan, and Kazakhstan. The Japanese Ambassador found it convenient to be in Tokyo for consultations. In protests reminiscent of the Cold War, Western diplomats boycotted the ceremonies.

The Taiwan Straits

Local time: 0715 Thursday 15 March 2001
GMT: 2315 Wednesday 14 March 2001

The attack came at first light. Twelve Su-27s came in low over the north-east coast of Taiwan; behind them six A-7 light attack bombers. They met no resistance as they made their first pass over Tan-shui, a coastal town at the mouth of the Tan-shui River. The A-7s carried C-802 anti-ship missiles. As they began their first run, sailors aboard ran for cover on board the Taiwanese *Cheng Kung* class frigate *Pan Chao* and the *La Fayette* class frigate *Wu Chang*. But it was too late. Within seconds the missiles had struck the ships, sending superheated shrapnel and exploding ordnance in all directions. Debris burnt all around the waters of the Tan-shui. Thick black smoke billowed into the air; the howls of the injured and dying were finally drowned out by an air raid warning siren. It sounded as the A-7s turned to make their second approach. Their target was a second *La Fayette* class frigate, *Kun Ming*. But the crew had had the vital seconds to react and defend themselves. Through an octuple launcher, they fired a salvo of surface-to-air missiles, destroying three aircraft. At the same time, the Chinese pilots found themselves flying into a blanket of depleted-uranium shells from the American-made close-in Phalanx weapons system on the bow. Firing up to 4,000 shells a minute, it hit two A-7s and blew up their air-to-surface missiles before they were able to hit the frigate.

The Prime Minister's residence, Tokyo

Local time: 0830 Thursday 15 March 2001
GMT: 2330 Wednesday 14 March 2001

There was a knock on the door and Prime Minister Hyashi's Private Secretary entered the room. Hyashi was eating breakfast – fermented soya beans mixed (*natoh*) with strips of raw squid, and rice – and reviewing the morning's press. He looked up. 'Yes?' he said.

'Excuse me, sir, for interrupting you but Defence Minister Ishihara said you would want to see this.'

Hyashi read the two-page document impassively. It described how a Japanese listening post on the Senkaku Islands had intercepted Chinese military communications at 0700 that morning. The Senkaku Islands – which Beijing claimed and called Taioyu-tai Islands – had been upgraded by Japan to a fully staffed and equipped military base in the fortnight following Dragonstrike. The provisioning of the islands had not been completed.

The signals that were intercepted were the orders to PLA Air Force and naval units participating in the invasion of northern Taiwan. Hyashi finished reading and sat in silent thought. He turned to his Private Secretary and told him to convene a meeting of the cabinet's Defence Subcommittee for 0900. 'Also call Ambassador Monroe and tell him that I want to talk to the President after the cabinet meeting. That is all.'

Beijing

The Xinhua News Agency carried a report of the invasion, which it dubbed the 'liberation' of Taiwan. It said the Chinese people had an historic yearning for reunification and called on the Taiwanese military to come over to the Communists' side. It said that those who joined forces with the PLA would retain the rank they held in the Taiwan Army. 'The government of China does not seek retribution, only reunification,' it said. 'All outstanding issues can be settled. Taiwan's people can continue to govern Taiwan. Taiwan's status as a member of international organizations will be preserved. The Central People's government seeks only peace and one China,' Xinhua said.

Xinhua also carried a statement from President Wang Feng. It was a veiled warning to the United States to keep out of China's internal affairs. 'If someone makes a show of force in the Taiwan Straits, that will not be helpful but will make the situation all the more complicated,' he said. Xinhua then warned him how China would respond if US warships entered the 200 kilometre wide passage between Taiwan and the Chinese mainland. 'If someone threatens the use of force against China this – as has been shown by past experience – will not spell any good results.'

The Prime Minister's residence, Tokyo

Local time: 0900 Thursday 15 March 2001
GMT: 2400 Wednesday 14 March 2001

The meeting room in which Hyashi liked to hold some of his Cabinet committee meetings filled with the now familiar faces. Ishihara from the Defence Ministry sat on the Prime Minister's right; on his left, Kimura from the Foreign Ministry. Wada and Naito (Finance and Trade respectively) were next, followed by General Ogawa, Director, Defence Intelligence Headquarters.

'Well, General Ogawa, what is your assessment?' the Prime Minister began.

'From what we can tell so far,' the General began, 'based on telecommunications intercepts and information from an AWACS we sent up soon after the first interception at 0700, the Chinese have launched a two-pronged assault on the north of Taiwan. They have landed at Tan-shui on the north-west tip of the island and at Hsin-chu further south down the coast. Our assessment is that they have over-stretched themselves. Taiwan is well defended and the military possesses the latest, or near to latest, American and European equipment.

'Taiwan has 425,000 active servicemen split between the army (289,000), navy (68,000), and air force (68,000). The cornerstone of its defence, however, is its relationship with America. The US–Taiwan military relationship has remained strong, in spite of attempts by Beijing to drive a wedge between the two. Washington has sold or leased modern weaponry, including frigates, F-16 jet fighters, attack helicopters, early warning aircraft, tank-landing ships, anti-ship missiles, anti-submarine-warfare equipment, and ballistic-missile-defence equipment. According to one source, "most of the armaments are suited for repulsing a sea assault or thwarting a naval blockade". If China is successful in making a beachhead it will face fierce local resistance. Taiwan has more than 300 tanks, of which at least half are located in the north-east. At sea, with 22 destroyers, 11 frigates, and 4 submarines it will be able to put up a stout defence to the Chinese.'

The Prime Minister quietly sucked air through his teeth. Ogawa knew it was time to stop. Hyashi thanked him for his report. Ogawa rose and left the room. Hyashi then turned to Foreign Minister Kimura.

'Kimura-san, why have they done this?' he asked. 'Our navy has completed its first escort of our merchant ships through the South China Sea. Now the Taiwan Straits are effectively closed. That's not a serious problem, I grant you, but what does this action by the Chinese mean for our islands of Senkaku?'

'There are two questions there, Prime Minister. To the first the honest answer is, we do not know. However, we think this attack is based upon a misreading of the politico-military situation in Taiwan. The proximate cause would appear to be some statements made by the leaders of Taiwan's New Party. The New Party was founded in 1994 and is a breakaway faction of the Kuomingtang, or KMT. The New Party has always favoured reunification and has despaired as the KMT has run a line, both domestically and internationally, that seeks an independent identity for Taiwan. The New Party's spokesmen were particularly bellicose on China's behalf during the Dragonstrike conflict. Some even suggested that Taiwan should unify with the mainland to present a united Chinese face to the world. Significantly, at a meeting in Taipei at the height of the conflict – on the twenty-second of February – a number of important generals, including General Yen Chi-tsai, who controls the army around Hsin-chu, were present at a meeting with senior New Party officials. A colonel on General Yen's staff, a Hung Tzu-lin, went to Beijing the next day – the twenty-third of February. We do not know what he did in Beijing but our information is that he visited Zhongnanhai and the Taiwan Affairs Office. Our best guess is that Beijing, which as you can see is well informed about affairs on Taiwan, has acted on the belief that General Yen was an ally and that the Taiwanese military is deeply divided. We further believe that the troops landed at Hsin-chu are no more than a token, symbolic force and are not intended to spearhead a major invasion. As further evidence for this I offer the Xinhua News Agency's initial dispatch. It is notable for its lack of hard-line rhetoric towards the rulers in Taiwan.

'As for our position on the Senkaku Islands, no one – internationally, this – takes China's claim at all seriously. The Chinese call the islands Taioyu-tai and include them on their official maps. There have been skirmishes in the past. A Chinese campaign to regain the islands cannot be ruled out, especially in the face of this latest crisis, based, as it is, on national reunification. We need to be vigilant. Our navy should escort merchant shipping not just out through the South China Sea but also through the waters of the East China Sea where the Senkaku Islands lie.'

Hyashi was still. 'I have been preoccupied over the past week or so with our relations with the United States. We spoke about this, Kimura-san, only two days ago. Every time I see Monroe, the US Ambassador, he is on at me to visit Washington. Perhaps this latest disturbance might prove useful. At times such as these a country like Japan needs friends. I will be placing a call to President Bradlay after this meeting.'

The White House, Washington, DC

President Bradlay had just returned to Washington from a visit to Chicago. There he had reacquainted himself with the city whose terrible riots the previous summer Bradlay had stemmed and, in the process, brought himself a much needed boost in the opinion polls. He toured the Southside ghettos and spoke to civic leaders and community representatives. His Communications Director billed the speech as the most important presidential statement about urban reform since George Bush went to Los Angeles in the wake of the Rodney King riots in 1992 and promised federal aid for the inner cities. Bradlay was with advisers when Martin Weinstein, his National Security Adviser, entered with news of the Chinese attack on Taiwan.

'This time I think they have met their match,' he said as he briefed Bradlay on the situation. He also told the President to expect a call from Prime Minister Hyashi. 'He's ready to come back into the fold,' Weinstein said.

'How should we play this, Marty? I mean, what is Wang up to here? Three weeks ago he tells me on the telephone that he will return the islands to Taiwan that they took, and now he is engaged on a hare-brained adventure against the Taiwanese. Doesn't he know Taiwan has one of the most sophisticated arsenals in Asia? What does he expect us to do? I gave my word to the American people that we were leaving the battlefield with honour. He's made a fool out of me!'

'Mr President, your analysis is, as usual, as perceptive as ever,' said Weinstein. 'But consider this. We think, and our

Japanese friends agree, that Wang launched this attack in the belief that the Taiwanese military would not fight. He has been proved wrong. It is by no means certain that mainland China will prevail. The Taiwanese are well armed, and they hate the Communists. Yes, Wang has gone back on his word to you, but my recommendation is that we stand back – we don't want to get involved directly – but support the Taiwanese with all the military hardware and advice they need.'

Just as Weinstein finished his report the President's secretary entered the room to inform him that the Japanese Prime Minister was on the telephone.

'Nobby, how are you?' Bradlay opened with his customary familiarity. 'I'm always happy to take a call from our friends in Japan, no matter what the hour.'

'You are too kind, Mr President,' Hyashi countered. 'I'm calling, as you know, about the situation in Taiwan . . .'

'Yes, yes . . . I know about that. What's your reading? Can the Chinese pull it off?'

'Unlikely. Our best estimate, Jim, is that the Chinese won't be able to last much more than twenty-four hours. We think that based on faulty intelligence they have overplayed their hand.'

'That's our assessment too, Nobby. However, I think we can take advantage of Beijing's discomfort. I know that Monroe in Tokyo has been on at you to visit Washington. We'd very much like to have you here.'

'I've been giving some thought to our relations as well. There can, of course, be no question of Japan ever again assuming a subordinate position; however, I believe that stability in East Asia can be secured only if the United States and Japan work together. You are absolutely right when you said relations have been allowed to drift. I will be more than happy to come to Washington. It will send a strong signal in this part of the world, and one I know that will be welcomed more widely in South-East Asia ... though not Beijing, of course.'

Bradlay laughed. 'Indeed, Nobby, indeed. Why don't we initiate this new friendship between us with a joint statement condemning the Chinese invasion of Taiwan and tie to it your forthcoming visit to Washington?'

'An excellent idea, Jim.'

The Taiwan Straits

Local time: 1300 Friday 15 March 2001
GMT: 0500 Friday 15 March 2001

The air raid sirens wailed through the deserted streets of
Taipei, the capital of Taiwan. Overhead, the skies appeared
crowded with fighter aircraft engaged in a deadly game of
aerial acrobatics. The mainland Chinese flew Su-27s fitted
with their infra-red and radar-homing air-to-air missiles;
the Taiwanese flew F-16s armed with not only the AIM-9
Sidewinder air-to-air missile but also, having fitted a new
radar, the AIM-7 Sparrow radar-guided missile. The Taiwanese pilots put in more training hours than their
mainland counterpart, but, thanks to Dragonstrike, the
mainland pilots were battle-hardened. The early successes
went to the Su-27s. In an attempt to escape one, the pilot
of an F-16 climbed vertically and, while discharging the
contents of two chaff pods in the hope of confusing the
approaching radar-guided missile, banked sharply right.
Unfortunately he had lost energy and deployed the chaff
too early. The missile relocked and plunged into the F-16.
Pieces of wreckage littered the mountain which provided
the protective fortress for the National Palace Museum, on
the north-east outskirts of Taipei.

But the F-16s had their day. In a dogfight that was
shown on television around the world, the pilot of an F-16
shot down an Su-27. It was a classic one-to-one encounter
and the Su-27, with its larger clutch of missiles, should
have won. But the Taiwanese pilot knew his aircraft. The
dogfight started over the presidential palace in the south-
east part of Taipei. Both aircraft's radar missiles had already
been fired and the infra-red homers were left. The F-16's

problem was how to evade the Su-27 and its deadly arsenal. In a whirling vortex each turned at maximum G and tried to get a firing solution on the other. The human factor proved critical. The Taiwanese pilot was equipped not only with an anti-G suit, but also with partial pressure-breathing which cut in under high G. This reversed his normal breathing process, making him use conscious effort to expel oxygen from his lungs, inhaling simply by opening his mouth, the pressure filling his lungs automatically. He had practised this regularly, because it enabled him to sustain the forces of the high-G manoeuvre better than his enemy, and he steadily caught him up in the turn. He launched an infra-red missile when within the launch envelope, lock-on being signified by the characteristic growl in his head-phones. This missile was decoyed by flares from the Su-27, but then the pilot made the error of reducing his turn in an effort to escape. This enabled the F-16 to fire a salvo of two further missiles just at the time it was in a perfect firing position – in the centre of their engagement envelopes. The first hit home on one engine, exploding the other engine as well when the warhead detonated. The other was slightly behind and detonated in the fireball.

The Taiwanese military might have been caught unawares at the beginning of the mainland Chinese offensive, but by noon of the first day it was clear that the tables had turned decisively in Taipei's favour. 50 kilometres to the south-west, the Chinese expeditionary force of 5,000 men that landed on the coast near Hsin-chu, the country's leading site for the manufacture of semiconductors and computers, had expected to be welcomed as a liberating force by the local garrison, whose commanding general was thought to be a supporter of Beijing. But soon they found out how wrong Chinese intelligence was. They met fierce resistance from the Taiwanese garrison. The fighting was hand-to-hand and the Taiwanese had the better of it, pinning the mainlanders down on the outskirts of the town. The Chinese had badly miscalculated. Unable to land any tanks or any other vehicles of their own, their men had to defend themselves with what they had to hand. By late morning the 5,000 Chinese troops had been reduced by more than half. It was slaughter by another name. Most got lost in unfamiliar terrain. The remaining 2,000 or so troops were disorganized and holed up wherever they could find shelter – including schools, a hospital, and a Buddhist temple. There were reports that some small groups of soldiers had surrendered, but these were vociferously denied by Xinhua in a noon dispatch. Reports of surrender were 'vile lies' propagated the United States and its 'running dog' supporters on Taiwan. But for all Xinhua's bluster even it could not conceal the fact that the campaign had not gone according to plan. In what was seen as a prelude to full-scale retreat, it said China had 'taught the Taiwanese separatists a lesson'. It warned of 'sterner measures', if the leaders of the island state did not respond positively to the Chinese people's yearning for reunification.

The White House lawn, Washington, DC

Local time: 1130 Monday 30 April 2001
GMT: 1630 Monday 30 April 2001

It was a bright, sunny Washington spring morning. The cherry trees along the Potomac River were in full blossom. Prime Minister Noburo Hyashi of Japan had participated in an impromptu *hanami* – or flower-viewing picnic – with Ambassador Katayama before their meeting with President Bradlay. It looked well on television and Hyashi, who had gained some of his media savvy in the weeks leading to his Washington summit with Bradlay, used it to underline the warmth of ties between Japan and America. When a reporter called out: 'What about the bomb?' Hyashi, without batting an eyelid, turned and said: 'Extreme situations demand extreme measures; my country sought to demonstrate the capability rather than the intention to deploy nuclear weapons. We remain opposed to the deployment of nuclear weapons.'

The lecterns were arranged side by side on a small but adequate podium. President Bradlay was in an expansive mood, joking with reporters as he and Prime Minister Hyashi of Japan made their way to the rostrum.

'The defence of the free world is a responsibility the United States has shouldered since the end of the Second World War. And it is a responsibility that this nation, in concert with its allies, has never taken lightly. Recent events in East Asia have focused our minds on the tasks before us of preserving freedom in that great and commercially vibrant part of our world. Prime Minister Hyashi of Japan has been our guest for the past three days. We have met on numerous occasions and have arrived at a common view on the way ahead. I am very pleased to announce that this morning Mr Hyashi and I signed a new agreement for the mutual protection of our territories. This treaty, which I hope will be speedily ratified by the Senate, reflects the concerns of both governments over the increasingly belligerent posture adopted by China. The treaty is an unequivocal warning to anyone in East Asia that the United States and Japan will act swiftly and resolutely to defend our mutual interests when those interests are threatened. We are not alone in these concerns. I've had telephone calls recently from the leaders of many South-East Asian countries expressing their concern about China's aggression. Our fight is not with the Chinese people but with the men who seek to repress them. I am telling you today that we will not stint in our determination to prevail. Thank you.'

The East China Sea

The Japanese destroyer *Kirishima* was on routine patrol, escorting a supertanker and assorted container ships bound for Yokohama past the Senkaku Islands. The calm of the early morning was shattered by a klaxon sounding battle stations. In the operations room the sailor operating the ship's sonar had detected the unmistakable acoustic signature of a Chinese *Kilo* class submarine. The Captain gave orders for the ship to come about and prepare its anti-submarine torpedoes for launch. The *Kilo* had opened its bow doors and appeared to be preparing to launch its torpedoes.

AFTERMATH

China and Japan averted further bloodshed in East Asia with a direct telephone conversation between Jamie Song and his Japanese counterpart. A joint Sino-Japanese force occupied different sectors of the Taioyu-tai Islands – but the situation remained volatile. Offers of UN observers being stationed there were refused by both governments. **The United States and China** made the first steps to mend fences with a large Chinese order for Boeing aircraft. An American warship visited Shanghai. But the two governments entered into a nuclear strategic arrangement of Mutually Assured Destruction reminiscent of the Cold War policy with the Soviet Union. **President Wang** was hailed as the New Helmsman and lauded as a worthy successor to Mao Zedong and Deng Xiao-ping. He allocated the profits from manipulating the international markets to rebuilding and streamlining the Chinese armed forces into a hi-tech modern fighting force with emphasis on missile development and naval power projection. **Jamie Song** resigned from politics and went back to business. He floated his company, New China Computer Inc., on the Shanghai Stock Exchange. Song was a frequent visitor to the US, often to see his friend Overhalt at Boeing, and occasionally President Bradlay. **President Bradlay** was elected for a second term in 2004. He was hailed in many of the opinion polls as one of the great American presidents. He reversed the downsizing of the American armed forces and won fund allocation for ensuring the United States' position as the most powerful country in the world. **The New**

Communist Party was hunted down by the Chinese security forces. Eleven ringleaders were jailed for between 13 and 20 years. Two, who were accused of carrying firearms, were executed with a single bullet in the back of the head. Five members, arrested in **Hong Kong**, were taken straight across the border to China, so they could receive harsher sentences and prison conditions. There were no objections from Hong Kong's legislative council or from the media which by now was controlled by Chinese interests. In the same way, the government in **Taiwan** ruthlessly wiped out any pro-Communist elements in the armed forces and political life. The **New Party** was destroyed. **Vietnam** declared its war with China a victory. In official announcements there was no mention of the French assistance. French companies were awarded contracts to modernize the roads, railways, and port facilities. The anniversary of the second battle of Lang Son was commemorated as a national holiday. **South Korea** ruled the north as a colony until 2003 when official unification was declared. In the interim, South Korean companies invested heavily in **North Korea** and built up the infrastructure. The workforce was disciplined and cheap. By November 2001, all American troops had left the peninsula.

The **Far East** remained a flashpoint for a Pacific war. Each country in the region made sure that next time it would be better prepared.

REFERENCES

8 For too long, Comrades . . . : *Jiefangjun Bao* [Libera-
   tion Army Daily], 30 April 1988. Quoted in John W.
   Garver, 'China's push Through the South China Sea:
   The Interaction of Bureaucratic and National
   Interests', *China Quarterly* (1992), pp. 1013–1024.

15 Like Hong Kong, Taiwan, Macau, and Tibet . . . : this
   is a modified quotation taken from Tang Fuquan,
   'Reunderstanding Our Country's Naval Strategy', *Jiefangjun Bao* [Liberation Army Daily], 15 September
   1989.

18 Down at surface level . . . : John Downing, 'China's
   Maritime Strategy', *Jane's Intelligence Review*, April
   1996, p. 186.

32 Radio Hanoi broadcast: the text of Hanoi's response
   to Dragonstrike is excerpted from a Vietnamese
   Foreign Ministry document detailing Vietnam's claim
   to the Spratly and Paracel islands that was broadcast
   in two parts by Radio Vietnam on 26 April 1988 and
   translated and published by the BBC in its *Summary
   of World Broadcasts*, East Asia section, on 11 May 1988.

38 Bryant's State Department briefing: parts are drawn
   from *Asia Wireless File: State Department Report*,
   Tuesday 19 March 1996, China/Taiwan p. 1.

45 long-range AWACs in the air . . . : due for delivery in
   1998/1999.

51 State Security or MSS . . . : Nicholas Eftimiades,
   Chinese Intelligence Operations, Naval Institute Press,
   1994, p. 27.

55 In California, exports to China keep 216,000 people employed . . . : 1995 figures.

55 There are a number of blue-chip companies . . . : Karl Schoenberger, 'Motorola bets big on China', *Fortune*, 27 May 1996, p. 42.

56 Mr President, I watched . . . : this is a slightly altered version of the quotation attributed to Lloyd Bentsen, former US Treasury Secretary, in Peter Behr, 'US Businesses Waged Year-Long Lobbying Effort On China Trade', *Washington Post*, May 27 1994, Section A, p. 28.

67 No, we don't think so . . . : Bloomberg, 30 May 1996, Bank for International Settlements survey of foreign exchange market.

83 Over the past hundred-odd years . . . : Li Peng to James Baker, November 1991.

89 Matsushita Electric Company: Jetro China Newsletter No. 115, March–April 1995, p. 21.

98 The current configuration of our armed forces . . . : 1992 Pentagon Mobility Requirements Study.

101 This pattern of economic dominance . . . : East Asia Analytic Unit, Australian Department of Foreign Affairs and Trade: *Overseas Chinese Business Networks in Asia*, Canberra 1995, especially pp. 35–89.

112 Then stop thinking about agreeing . . . : some extracts taken from Markov, Sergei: *World Press Review*, October 1995, v. 42 n. 10 p. 17(1) (reprinted from the Moscow *Times*, 28 June 1995).

117 He was not starry-eyed about China . . . : for the experiences outlined see Dori Jones Yang's review of E. E. Bauer's *China Takes Off: Technology Transfer and Modernization*, University of Washington Press, 1986, in *Business Week*, 31 March 1986, issue no. 2939.

127 The piece pointed out . . . : Ann Devroy, 'Politics Of

Invading Haiti Disputed; Past Popularity Gains Were Short, White House Says To GOP Charge', *Washington Post*, 11 September 1994, Section A, p. 10.

128 The overwhelming majority of Americans . . . : ibid.

134 The *New World* was the pride of Shell's fleet . . . : this ship is fictitious but its specifications are based on the supertanker described in 'Hyundai Hands Over Its New Concept VLCC', *Lloyd's List*, 4 May 1994, p. 8.

139 The South China Sea, Local time: 0010 . . . : this chapter is based in part on Paul Richardson, 'Pirates renew reign of terror: Asian sea traffic subjected to more attacks as armed bandits move further south', *Lloyd's List*, 26 February 1994, p. 3, and Kevin Chinnery, 'The nightmare that Indonesia dreaded: the body of a British sea captain murdered by pirates in the South China Sea has been flown home for burial', *Lloyd's List*, 30 December 1992, p. 5.

156 First of all there had been an important change . . . : 'Energy security in North Asia: the opportunity for Russian gas', Investment Report prepared by the research staff of ING Barings, London, December 1995.

157 Nansha's oil reserves . . . : Zheng Hongfan, '"Manly Pride" of Spratly's Troops', *Renmin Ribao* [People's Daily], Beijing, 3 July 1995.

157 Daqing . . . : 'China's Daqing pumped 56mln tonnes of crude in 1995', Reuters, Beijing, 1 January 1996.

158 British Petroleum had made major gas discoveries . . . : Terry Knott, 'Oil set to become Vietnam's rising star', *Lloyd's List*, 22 June 1995, p. 5.

173 the Nye initiative . . . : Tadakazu Kimura, 'Japan–US security accord needs to be redefined', Asahi News Service, 23 June 1995.

173 When I was Defence Minister . . . : Akio Morita and Shintaro Ishihara, *The Japan that can say 'No' – The*

new US–Japan relations card, in a Xeroxed translation by the Japan Society of New York [nd], pp. 14–15.

185   It is unlawful and ludicrous...: quotes and data from John Mintz, 'As Aerospace Firms Land Overseas Contracts, Unions Say US Loses Jobs', *Washington Post*, 26 November 1995, Section A, p. 26.

211   People of China...: Zheng Hongfan and Yin Pinduan: 'I Love You, Nansha', *Renmin Ribao*, 3 July 1995, p. 3.

212   Let me explain why...: 'PRC Stance on Spratly Dispute Explained', Zhongguo Tongxun She News Agency, Hong Kong, 6 August 1995.

213   We have the experience...: quoted in Allen S. Whiting, 'Chinese Nationalism and Foreign Policy after Deng', *China Quarterly*, June 1995, n. 142, p. 305.

229   There was an air of quiet control...: Kosta Tsipis: *Understanding Nuclear Weapons*, Wildwood House, London, 1983, chapters 2, 3, and 4.

256   This left Japan with little choice...: Motita and Ishihara: op. cit., pp. 16–17 with slight modification.

257   Our new position in the world...: ibid., p. 51.

257   Let me explain...: ibid., p. 32 except last sentence.

258   In spite of the legacy...: ibid., pp. 70–71.

307   The ability of America's eyes in the sky...: this account is drawn from Kosta Tsipis, op. cit., ch.11 ('Telemonitoring'). See also Peter Hayes, et al., *American Lake: Nuclear Peril in the Pacific*, Penguin Books Australia, 1986, ch. 11 ('The invisible arsenal').

320   The Ambassador shuffled his feet...: Allen S. Whiting: op. cit., p. 310. The quotation has been modified to include Japan and substitute Wang Feng for Deng Xiaoping.

336   The equipment would have to be sturdy...: for the

physical effects of an EMP see Kosta Tsipis, op. cit., pp. 58–61, 268–270.

339   Eric Wallace, father of two ...: the preparations described here follow British government guidance as published in 'Protect and Survive', HMSO, 1980.

339   Home Office study: *Protective Qualities of Buildings*, Home Office Scientific Advisory Branch, London 1981.

361   During American–Japanese war manoeuvres in the Pacific ...: William L. Chaze and Robert Kaylor, 'Deadly game of hide and seek (nuclear submarines)', *U.S. News & World Report*, 15 June 1987, v. 102 p. 36(6).

376   At the same time, Congress could seek refuge ...: Gavin Esler, 'America's secret of last resort; Top hotel masks nuclear bunker for government; Greenbrier', *Sunday Times* 5 November 1995.

377   The Federal Reserve Board ...: Ted Gup, *Time Magazine*, 9 December, 1991; Ted Gup and James Carney, *Time Magazine*, 10 August, 1992; Steven Emerson, *U.S. News & World Report*, 7 August, 1989.

379   The *Washington Post* estimated ...: M. Anjali Sastry, Joseph J. Romm, and Kosta Tsipis, 'Can the U.S. economy survive a few nuclear weapons? (Small nuclear attack)', *Technology Review*, April 1989, v. 92 n. 3 p. 22(8).

379   Through the years ...: Bernard T. Gallagher, Mount Weather, in Ted Gup and James Carney, 'The doomsday blueprints', *Time Magazine*, 10 August 1992, v. 140 n. 6 p. 32.

380   Those remarks were followed ...: Leo Bourassa and Bud Gallagher, fomer directors at Mount Weather, ibid.

403   If someone makes a show of force ...: the quotation is Li Peng's, cited in Steven Mufson, 'Beijing Warns

US On Naval Display; Two Carrier Groups To Monitor Chinese Maneuvers In Taiwan Strait', *Washington Post*, Beijing, 18 March 1996, Section A, p. 21.

405 According to one source . . . : R. Jeffrey Smith, 'China Plans Maneuvers Off Taiwan; Big Military Exercise Is Meant To Intimidate, US Officials Say', *Washington Post*, 5 February 1996, Section A, p. 1.

INDEX

The entries '[Country], navy' appear after the main country entry and list every named ship, surface vessel, and submarine, and separately named class, by type. The entries for air forces work in the same way.